THE PASSENGER

High over a small town on the Scottish borders, a bomb explodes on an American airliner: an act of international terrorism. There are no survivors. Two years earlier, three old spies play out one last move in their life-long game. What is the connection between these two events, one headline news, the other terrifyingly secret? One man should have been on the plane and among the dead. While he changed his plans, his son flew on. Now investigators are asking questions about his son — was he involved? Was he duped into carrying the bomb? Or did he even get off the plane himself? Drawn to discover the truth, the father enters a murky world of arms deals and illegal back channels — a world dominated by the former CIA spymaster, James Jesus Angleton.

CHRIS PETIT

THE
PASSENGER

Complete and Unabridged

CHARNWOOD
Leicester

First published in Great Britain in 2006 by
Simon & Schuster UK Ltd
London

First Charnwood Edition
published 2007
by arrangement with
Simon & Schuster UK Ltd
London

British Library CIP Data

Petit, Christopher
    The passenger.—Large print ed.—
Charnwood library series
1. Pan Am Flight 103 Bombing Incident, *1988*
—Fiction 2. Suspense fiction 3. Large type books
I. Title
823.9′14 [F]

ISBN 978–1–84617–618–0

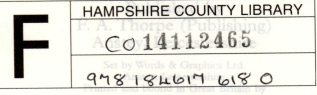

F. A. Thorpe (Publishing)
Anstey, Leicestershire

Set by Words & Graphics Ltd.
Anstey, Leicestershire
Printed and bound in Great Britain by
T. J. International Ltd., Padstow, Cornwall

This book is printed on acid-free paper

For Murray, Robert and Louis
and for the sake of the dead

46.5 Seconds

The plane pushed back from its Heathrow stand just after six in the evening and took off twenty minutes later, an hour behind schedule. The captain was not hopeful of making up the time against head-winds. The forecast was for intermittent rain and showers, with a night visibility of fifteen kilometres. As they reached cruising height the cabin crew served drinks from the trolley. For the first thirty-seven minutes this was just another transatlantic flight, with everyone settling down for the long haul.

Thirty-one thousand feet below, a herd of cows stampeded across a field, the first sign on the ground something was wrong.

* * *

The bang is not even that loud at first, surely not loud enough to rip up the lives of 259 people. The plane does not explode, which would be the kinder death. It falls apart, accompanied by an ear-splitting thunder that people on the ground think is a nuclear bomb; it disintegrates in mid-air and the stewardess who welcomed aboard is sucked into the void, and the cabin lights go out, baggage spills from overhead lockers, so quick there is barely time to scream, and the dozing man wakes to think: this can't be real! Within three seconds the whole of the nose

1

of the plane snaps away, a vast wave of rushing air hits the main cabin and outside the fuselage skin stretches, blisters and petals into starbursts, unzipping along rivet lines, tearing from hole to hole, shedding panels, and a tiny, sane nugget of your whimpering brain is trying to shout: These babies were never meant to fly! And the whole of your life until that moment peels away and you wish you were anyone but you while the plane yaws and lurches, and in all the terror is an absurdity of embarrassment at wondering whether you are allowed to hold on to the stranger next to you. It is a calibrated process, the stages of an air crash — as reconstructions invariably show — and the mind holds many positions as the churning chemical slurry of your body registers all the responses of shock and disbelief, each stage stretched far longer than the split second it takes, no time for an original thought, only the beyond-sad realization of the interrupted narrative of your/my/our lives, and the desperate banality of praying this is the nightmare from which you will wake. Yet in the time it takes to plummet, there is a stage after terror, not of consolation exactly, but of a kind of crazed mental energy that kicks in as fear short-circuits the brain, bringing one last surge of intense concentration and a sense that this final great roller coaster through the dark — the unseen ground waiting to receive — is a universal journey as much as the personal one of your death, my death, the death of the falling man in row twenty-five, the child across the aisle, the infant in her mother's arms, the young woman flying to meet her fiancé and the very tall American who got himself upgraded, and in a moment nothing will matter.

★ ★ ★

At nineteen thousand feet the body of the plane goes into a vertical dive and crashes into the ground at a speed of more than 200 mph, 46.5 seconds after the bomb has detonated. It is December 21 1988.

The Crash

When he heard the news, his first thought was for his son, flying at that moment. The television was on in his room at Heathrow's Post House Hotel when the news flash interrupted the scheduled programme to say a passenger plane had gone down in the Scottish borders. Collard checked his watch and sat down, shaky but relieved. It couldn't be Nick.

Collard's panic returned when the carrier was named. He tried to reason that it could have been a flight to San Francisco, Los Angeles, Denver, Miami, Washington, perhaps not a Heathrow departure at all. Besides, the timing was wrong. He pictured Nick high over the Atlantic, probably asleep.

He thought about the people on the plane that had crashed and felt shamed by his inadequate response, tempered with relief. He regretted parting with Nick on such unsatisfactory terms.

The news flashes became more frequent but didn't confirm the flight number. Collard rang the emergency line, which he found repeatedly engaged. He wondered whether to call Charlotte in New York then decided against alarming her.

Eventually the engaged tone drove him from the room. The empty lift was claustrophobic. People sat in the bar and restaurant as normal, and checked in at reception as though nothing had happened.

He waited under the hotel awning for a shuttle bus to the terminal. The weather was blustery with gusts of thin rain. Night was little more than an electric twilight, the vast illuminations of London staining the sky. He breathed the heady, mildly nauseating airport smells of scorched tyre and aviation fuel, imagining being trapped on a plane as it went into its final dive. Did people cry and scream or sit resigned, alone with their last private thoughts?

To the east, lights flashed on a plane landing, bellying in, made graceless by the drag of gravity.

The terminal hall was silent, as though the news had stopped everyone in their tracks. No one seemed sure how to behave in the face of unfolding disaster. A woman with a blue-rinse perm said in a stage whisper that trembled with morbid anticipation, 'They haven't said yet.'

No one was saying.

The departures boards still rippled, as they had in Frankfurt four hours earlier, and Collard remembered Nick's rueful wave of good-bye in the Heathrow transit corridor as he walked away, dressed uncharacteristically in army-surplus trousers and black military-style anorak with a complicated array of pockets, both picked up on his travels. One unlaced sneaker flapped and his hair stuck up where he had slept on it during the flight from Frankfurt. Collard had been sur-prised by the different Nick that turned up. He'd had an ear pierced and wore a ring. Sensing Collard's disapproval, Nick said it was done to annoy him. Three months was a long time away.

Ahead of any official announcement, people started to name the New York flight, to the anger of a middle-aged man who spoke for Collard when he snapped, 'How can you know? People here have friends and relatives on that flight.'

After the longest time, a senior official arrived, harassed and inconvenienced, and reluctantly announced that Flight 103 to New York had crashed thirty-five minutes after take-off. A delay on the runway prevented its scheduled departure by half an hour.

Someone sounding very distant asked Collard if he was all right. He nodded and walked unsteadily to the other end of the hall where he stood patting his pockets for cigarettes he didn't smoke.

An American voice behind asked, 'Are you with us?'

Collard stared uncomprehendingly as the man asked again. He knew the answer was no. He was not one of them, whoever they were, gathered in small groups around him, carrying hand luggage. They looked official and purposeful, something to do with the crash. Collard had given no thought to what he would do — go home, he supposed, and wait.

He looked at the man and said yes.

★ ★ ★

A maze of corridors took them away from the usual channels. No one spoke to him. No check took place as they left the building; no boarding cards or head count.

They walked across tarmac to the plane, a normal short-haul carrier stripped of civilian markings. Collard heard someone wonder why it wasn't leaving from somewhere less conspicuous like RAF Northolt. Faced with the gangway steps he had to grip the handrail to force himself up into the fuselage.

Getting on the plane was hardest. Collard went to the back and took an aisle seat. The cabin was full but silent, with no pre-takeoff muzak, and only a skeleton crew. He found he was incapable of praying.

A man in front of him said the programme he had been watching when he heard the news was *This Is Your Life*.

★ ★ ★

They landed at Carlisle. Collard stood shivering on the runway, waiting in the queue to board the buses. He had spent the short flight failing to stamp out the images in his head of Nick trapped in the crashing plane.

'Would you look at that?' said a man with a London accent behind him in the queue.

Collard turned round in spite of himself. A luggage trolley stood on the tarmac and a single coffin was being unloaded from the hold.

'What are you supposed to do with that?' the man asked. He was smart, with an Italian suit and casually long hair. He wanted to know what Collard was doing there. Collard mumbled

7

something about technical reasons.

'You're not anti-terrorist, then?'

He shook his head.

'My guess is at least half of them here are. We're from the Met. Are you all right?'

Collard thought he might faint, the pitted tarmac rushing up to meet him at any moment. What would it be like being blown out of the sky at thirty-five thousand feet?

'There are a lot of Yanks here, shitting themselves it's terrorism.'

It took all Collard's concentration to stay upright and get on the coach. With everyone seated, an officer announced that the plane had broken up in the air and landed partly on a town. Survivors were not expected. Because of the scattered wreckage they would have to wait for daylight to do a proper assessment, a task made no easier as it was the winter solstice, the longest night of the year.

Collard hoped for Charlotte's sake she had heard the news as late as possible and he experienced another rush of panic, realizing she would think he had been on the plane with Nick.

The Disaster Zone

Collard walked through the emergency centre, ghosted by the experience, unable to believe it had anything to do with his son. Nick hated fuss. Doors were labelled as rooms were requisitioned. A coffee machine was being installed on the ground floor. People shared the same bewildered, tense look, as though they were about to be tested for an examination they were bound to fail.

He knew he had to call Charlotte, and searched in vain for a phone. Every one was commandeered. In an otherwise empty room, he found a harassed woman on the telephone, saying they needed hundreds more lines. She listed the police, the press, the army, fire brigade, medical services, crash investigators, civil-aviation experts, government observers, the emergency call centre, and a second tier of bereavement counsellors, caterers, accommodation, computer operators, transport coordinators and office workers drafted in to handle extra paperwork.

'I've probably left some out,' she said, catching Collard's eye. She sounded local and sympathetic.

He dug deep into his dwindling reserves, and thought that life would never be the same for that small Scottish town. Already things had changed for ever.

He waited for her to finish and told her he had to call New York. He didn't say why. It would be the first time he admitted Nick's death aloud.

'I need a break anyway,' she said. 'Guard the phone till I get back otherwise someone else will take it.'

He tried dialling Charlotte's number but couldn't get past the code.

'It may be that the lines are overloaded,' the woman said when she came back. She tried the number, dialling fluently, hung up and frowned.

'I've heard people are having trouble getting through to the United States. Someone said American telephone engineers have arrived from their naval base and all calls are being routed through them.' She shrugged at this latest in a long line of inexplicable events. 'You might have a better chance with a public call box.'

★   ★   ★

The first kiosk Collard found across the road from the emergency centre was occupied by a reporter filing his story, with a queue waiting.

Sections of the town were already cordoned off. The public Christmas decorations were still switched on. Collard marched on, head down, breath visible and ragged in the cold air. The reek of aviation fuel was palpable and threatening.

On the outskirts, a fleet of ambulances, blue lights flashing, lay idle and waiting. Collard couldn't persuade himself it was because there were no survivors, just as he couldn't believe that

10

the boy who had laughed at him that afternoon was dead.

The first free phone box turned out to be empty because it had been vandalized. Collard stared at the guts of its receiver hanging out and wondered how he could carry on.

Beyond the town's limits, he found another kiosk, occupied, but with no queue. He waited, watching one coin after another being shovelled in the slot, concentrating on the disappearing money, the biting cold and his waiting.

After twenty minutes, he claimed the kiosk and used his business phone card and listened to the digits hum down the transatlantic line.

The number was busy.

He redialled continuously, wishing Charlotte would clear.

In the end he had to give up the booth to an ambulance man.

The town drew him back against his will. He saw the first television crews arrive, wearing expensive anoraks and Timberland boots. A woman in a window was taking down the lights from her tree. The crackle of a two-way radio bled into the clatter of an approaching helicopter.

No one questioned Collard when he ducked under a crime-scene tape.

The other side was illuminated like a film set. Lights on stands, larger versions of the ones the television crews were setting up, were fed by snaking, thick black cables from a noisy generator truck.

A shoe lay in the road. A miniature bottle of

gin was cradled, unbroken, in a hedge. A woman's cardigan had caught in the bare branches of a tree. An intact aircraft seat snapped off from the rest of its row lay in the road, a tray nearby and a torn in-flight magazine. A suitcase had burst on impact. Collard stared at the strewn belongings as the implications of his escape sunk in for the first time. The case he had checked in at Frankfurt had flown without him and would be lying somewhere.

A parcel in bright decorative wrapping lay intact on a verge. The plane had been full of Christmas gifts, including his for Nick and Charlotte. The reunion with Nick should have been a cause for celebration, but in their last ever meeting he had failed as a father.

The Search

Collard bought walking boots, thick socks and a waterproof, preparing for the worst, knowing what volunteering to bring in bodies would entail, knowing he should be with Nick among the dead.

The shopkeeper said, 'What has the town done to deserve this?'

Outside, tinny megaphone announcements gathered the search parties, their faces tense, like soldiers about to go into battle. Collard hoped he had the strength to handle what he would find. He thought there was still time to try and call Charlotte again before joining the parties as they moved out.

Each of the closest phone boxes had a line of reporters waiting; the press centre was still to be set up. A few streets away, Collard found a kiosk with no queue, in which a brash young man was dictating from a notepad, taking his time.

The search parties started leaving quicker than Collard expected. Frustrated, he rapped on the glass of the booth and was waved away. With a vehemence that shocked him, Collard wished the man had been in the plane to feel the starburst of terror as the dark skies opened beneath him.

The reporter hung up at last, telling Collard not to be long because he needed to make another call.

13

Collard's fingers automatically dialled Charlotte's number. The line connected, but her answerphone was on. He told her to pick up. His voice sounded hollow in the echo of the transatlantic line.

She answered and cried with relief. She thought he had been on the plane. It followed Nick was safe too.

He had to lean against the phone booth as he explained that he had been delayed but Nick had flown on.

Talking to his wife, Collard wondered whether some sixth sense had steered him away from the disaster. And he wondered too about Charlotte's unasked question — in that case, why hadn't he taken proper care of his son?

He listened to Charlotte's soft crying three thousand miles away and recalled the shuffle of the departures board in Frankfurt and thought: All this from that.

★ ★ ★

The search parties had already left by the time he returned, so he walked out of town after them. It was a grey winter morning of the kind that would barely rise beyond twilight. Helicopters droned overhead like mechanical insects.

Charlotte had insisted on coming over. Collard, barely coping, suggested she wait. At the end of the call she said, 'I unfroze him a turkey from Thanksgiving. He always hated turkey but the one year we didn't have it he complained.'

14

Collard passed through an empty stretch of countryside. Even the noise of helicopters disappeared. There were no cars, no searchers. It was like time had rewound. Collard stopped and looked at a saturated field, aware only of being miserably alive.

A passing van stopped with a woman at the wheel. She was from the Salvation Army, on her way to serve hot drinks to the search parties.

'You can help me. The urns are heavy. I can't lift them by myself.'

Collard got in. Her name was Mona.

'Emergency or no emergency, you can't expect people to be out in this weather with nothing to eat or drink.'

In town there wasn't a bun or sandwich to be had.

Mona's efforts reduced the disaster to coping. She showed no curiosity towards Collard, who only hoped she wouldn't start talking about God.

They stopped at the municipal golf course. The pay hut was manned by a policeman. Mona announced they had tea. The policeman tried and failed to summon the searchers on a walkie-talkie.

'There was nothing wrong with it a minute ago,' he said, shaking it.

He couldn't leave his post so it fell to Collard to go and find the searchers.

'They've not got far,' the policeman said. 'They're only over the hill. You can probably shout from the top.'

Collard ran to attack the shock of what he

might see. He was breathless when he reached the brow of the hill. What he saw below him stopped him short. It was devastation beyond comprehension. The nauseous feeling, caused by the stink of aviation fuel that had surrounded him since his arrival, returned. It was not a crash in any recognizable sense, more a long, vast scattering that made him think he was witness to a huge cosmic visitation. The aircraft had shed its contents as it broke up, leaving an enormous trail of debris back to the horizon, marking the path of its fatal journey.

A hundred yards away two figures from the search party crouched, putting a corpse into what looked like a black bin liner. Collard moved towards them. The bag's zip sounded like an impossibly loud tearing when they closed it. As they tried to lift it the weight was too much and the bag ripped. A bare female arm fell out, waxy pale in shocking contrast to the shiny plastic. A bracelet was still on the wrist.

Collard averted his eyes too late, the bare arm flopping out of the bag more shocking than if he had seen the whole body.

The elder, a man of about fifty, said, 'These bags are worse than useless.'

Collard said there was tea at the hut.

The second, a lad of no more than twenty, said, 'We can't leave the body.'

The first man asked, 'Do the cups have lids?' He suggested the lad carry the teas back, so they wouldn't both have to go.

★ ★ ★

It was Collard's first dead body. He was aware of the inadequacy of his reaction: a little dizzy and dry-mouthed but more uncomfortable at the absurdity of offering tea. Perhaps Mona was right. The disaster had to be reduced to what was manageable.

He walked on, following the trail of debris, punctuated by groups of men guarding bodies. A pair of hiking boots, laces tied together, lay on a green. He nearly trod on an intact tube of toothpaste, the brand unknown to him.

The second body he came to was a child.

The searcher marking it spoke with tears in his eyes.

'She can't be more than five or six.'

The man's young companion appeared unhinged.

'She bounced. See where she landed.'

He pointed to an outline like a cartoon in the damp ground.

★ ★ ★

The disaster acquired its first sponsors when two large confectionery firms donated bars of chocolate and sweets for distribution. Collard's worst imaginings were kept at bay by a mechanical repetition of the indefatigable Mona's bidding, driving back to town to fill up the urns and going out again.

By late afternoon even her resolution wavered.

'My belief is severely tested by what we have seen today. I know this is man's doing, but how can God let it happen?'

17

She asked if he was a believer.

'Not at the moment.'

'You should see this place in summer. Beautiful country.'

Collard thought back to Nick leaving school less than six months before, marking the end of a stage and the start of his adult life.

It was almost dark. Tall pines lined both sides of the road. Collard had no idea what he would do about organizing a place to stay. He told Mona to stop. She looked embarrassed, thinking he wanted to relieve himself.

'This is fine. I'll walk back.'

'It's five miles to town. Are you all right? You're very quiet.'

He said the walk would clear his head.

In the last of daylight he entered the wood, finding it blank and inviting, wanting to lose himself. The trees were so close it was impossible to keep direction. But it was less cold. He pushed in deeper. The ground was a bed of needles, dry, inviting him to lie down and rest.

He heard a helicopter. In a few moments it was overhead, low down, not much above the level of the wood, the din of its engine smothering the only other sound, of wind in the treetops. The helicopter had a searchlight. Collard's heart raced. Light splashed through the branches, opening up a channel. The search was slow and methodical.

By the time the helicopter moved away, darkness had fallen.

The woods ended abruptly. Collard stood on the edge of a field, covered in a low mist. He wanted to turn back even as he moved forward, feeling his way, awkward tufts of grass underfoot.

A muffled cough came from close by. Collard froze. His first thought was that it was a patrol connected to the helicopter — but why would search teams be out in the dark with no torches? Something moved with a stealthy shuffle, and he stumbled on blindly. Then he heard the soft trample of hooves and recognized he was among cattle, except they were not keeping their distance the way cows did. They were near enough to touch, their tension palpable. Collard realized they must be in a state of collective shock, after witnessing the enormous fireball and hearing the crash, which a woman in town had said sounded like a huge boiler exploding.

Collard knew the cattle were guiding him to Nick. That was his punishment. His worst fear was that Nick had been so disfigured there would be no way to recognize him.

He trod on something and tripped. As he fell he was certain the animals would stampede and he would die there after all, trampled underfoot to be found next to his son.

Nothing happened. The cattle seemed to be protecting the body. Collard felt sodden material then icy flesh of a lifeless hand, the wrist and a watch. He could just make out a grey blur of face, darker at the bottom. What he thought was a terrible disfigurement was the man's beard.

★ ★ ★

Beyond the field, after a short climb, Collard found a narrow road, above the level of the mist, with the shrouded field and dark mass of wood just visible behind him. He had no idea in which direction to head. He walked on, away from the woods into open country.

The noise of the helicopter returned.

In its approaching searchlight Collard caught sight of a large canvas screen erected in a field, guarded by armed men in unmarked uniforms.

He ducked down as a Land Rover appeared near the screen, its arrival masked by the clatter of the helicopter. Four more armed men jumped out, moving like a well-drilled team.

Several long, narrow crates were winched into the helicopter. Collard knew he shouldn't be a witness to this.

He was hit hard from behind. Someone jumped on his back, knocking the wind out of him. His hair was grabbed and his head pulled up. He saw pointed guns. A blinding light shone in his face and a man shouted at him. He sounded American but with the noise of the helicopter Collard couldn't be sure.

Collard managed to say he had got separated from his search party. He sensed panic behind the men's aggression. Their violence seemed in some way linked to the greater devastation and provoked by it, not by him.

A boot pressed down on his head, shoving his face into the earth, making it hard to breathe. A gun barrel was pushed against his neck.

'Waste the fuck,' someone said.

20

Another laughed. 'No shortage of stiffs around.'

They couldn't go shooting people in fields, Collard prayed. People would hear the shots.

They hauled him to his feet and forced his hands in the air.

'Who are you?' Collard asked.

He was punched without warning in the head, hard enough to make him stagger and leave his ears ringing.

Something was thrown over him and he was frogmarched across the field, stumbling blindly, fearing what they had in mind. He would be put in the helicopter and thrown out. He hadn't cheated death after all. It had come to find him.

The Old Spy's Fate

James Jesus Angleton thought: Only fragments remain; the rest so hard to retrieve. Life makes no more sense now than it did then. However much was forgotten, it was always an old spy's fate to remember.

He remembered long office nights of tough decisions, in the room, at the desk, blinds down, dry reasoning to justify cutting a man loose, followed by bad conscience that soured the whisky. He remembered always being impatient for the next drink, alcohol and nicotine his great mistresses, downing half and rubbing his mouth in the same way he had half a century earlier, after drinking pure spring water on the school run called the Ledder, one clear blue day in the Malvern Hills (not a Yank at Oxford but near enough). ELO's 'Mr Blue Sky' was one of his favourites.

He remembered saying: 'They're setting him up.' He had done the same many times, set a man up.

He remembered a cardinal, a future pope, skittish after three glasses of wine, saying, 'Welcome to the labyrinth.'

He remembered thinking: Once you understand the principles of betrayal and negotiation, there are only certain well-established tracks.

He remembered saying, 'You think Nazir is working for Six,' but could not recall the context.

He remembered being never happier than on solitary fishing trips, drinking beer in a country bar with the juke for company. Legend had him down for a highfalutin dandy, master of ambiguity and reader of poetry, where he saw his real tastes as simple: catalogue clothes, detective stories and Coke. The Brits he knew didn't understand popular culture.

Hindsight let him see what he hadn't then: another old spy searching his room, noting the neat sparse regularity of his personal possessions in contrast to the favoured chaos of the working method — a stage set dressed for effect, lowered Venetians, pools of light, wreaths of smoke, towers of files, and that huge desk.

He remembered splendid hangovers and monitoring signs of his rebelling body, ticking them off, and reacquainting himself with old friends such as Philby, who agreed Washington restaurants were so bad that in his words, 'One is more or less reduced to liquid. Shall we?'

He remembered doing his best thinking drunk, drinking for many reasons apart from the obvious of what the alcohol did: test the boundaries of self-control while loosening some of the constraints. How close had the Great Traitor been to blurting, 'Jimmy, old boy, I'm in a hell of a hole?'

He remembered a lifetime of dead secrets that lay scattered in his head like dried husks of grain. He felt older than Methuselah.

The American

Collard had no idea where he was or who the men questioning him were. The helicopter had landed almost immediately after taking off and he had been taken into a building, with his head still covered, into what was revealed to be a tiny windowless room. At first he was interrogated alone, at length, by a hostile Englishman with dirty fair hair and a flat Essex accent. The man insisted Collard had been spying in the field and wanted to know who he worked for. When Collard tried to explain why he was there he was shouted down.

They were joined by a second man who just watched. Neither his appearance nor manner seemed official. His large bald head was fringed by a monkish tonsure, except at the back where it had grown long and was tied in a pony-tail. Collard finally managed to say that he should have been on the crashed plane and was about to explain about Nick when the second man spoke.

'Let me get this straight. You were booked through to New York. You flew from Frankfurt to London but you changed your mind and didn't take the rest of the flight.'

He was American, his voice soft for such a big man. The gentle, admonitory tone threw Collard. Silence followed. The American's bulk made the space seem smaller. He looked at Collard with hooded, hazel-flecked eyes and said he wanted his personal details.

Collard gave his name. As the American wrote it down his pencil snapped and he swore and walked out of the room, leaving the Englishman to take over.

Collard gave his address and particulars. He couldn't imagine returning to a world of travel, meetings, deals and conferences.

He gave his profession as businessman.

'What kind?'

He said technical equipment and left it at that.

The American returned and sat down. Collard was aware of him listening hard as he told them again how he had got off the flight in London.

'Why?'

'A last-minute business meeting.'

'What happened to your baggage?'

'I checked it in at Frankfurt.'

'Did you change your ticket?'

'I was going to when I heard the news.'

Collard heard the defensiveness creep into his voice.

'You didn't catch the flight but your baggage did.'

The questions were irrelevant and Collard's anger surfaced as he addressed the American.

'I was kidnapped by your men who led me to believe they were going to throw me out of a helicopter. Your friend here thinks I'm a spy. Now you want to make something of the fact that I failed to take my suitcase off the plane.'

'You are an anomaly in the system by your own admission. What baggage did you check in?'

'As I said, a suitcase.'

'Describe it.'

'It's just a regular large suitcase.'

'Colour?'

'Yellow.'

'Make?'

'I don't know.'

'Made of?'

'I don't know.'

'Canvas, leather?'

'It's a hard shell with rounded edges, some man-made fibre.'

The American nodded at the Englishman who produced a photo of a suitcase.

'Like that?' the American asked, leaning forward.

'Like that.'

'It's a Samsonite.'

This was how they trapped people, he thought, with the simplest questions.

'There must be millions like it. Am I being charged with something? Can I know who you are?'

The American put his face so close Collard could smell his breath.

'What were you doing in Frankfurt?'

'Business meetings.'

'Did you buy anything while you were away?'

'A personal organizer for my wife's Christmas present and a Walkman for my son at Heathrow duty free.'

Collard thought of the presents, inadequate and hastily chosen.

'What's the matter?' the American asked.

Collard remained silent.

'Did you pack your own suitcase?'

'Of course I did.'

'Nobody gave you anything to carry for them?'

'Are you saying there was a bomb on the plane and it was in a Samsonite suitcase?'

'Is that what you're saying?'

Collard's temper snapped. 'Terrorists blew up the plane. You know and I know.'

'How do you know terrorists did it?'

'It's what people are saying. I've seen the damage. Only a bomb could have done that.'

'You're a lucky man missing that flight,' the American said, insincerely.

Their questions began to mesmerize him. Whatever they asked contrived to make him sound ambiguous. They returned to the question of what he did.

'What sort of technical equipment?'

'Cameras mostly, for security.'

'Surveillance equipment,' the American said, sounding like he was correcting him.

'Surveillance equipment,' Collard repeated obediently.

'Have you ever been to Northern Ireland?' the Englishman asked.

He had. His company had been contracted to install security systems in barracks because local firms feared reprisals.

'Do you have or have you ever had contact with a member of the Irish Republican Army?'

The Englishman sounded like he was reading from a script. Collard stared at him in disbelief.

'You're wasting your time, whatever you want to prove. Part of my work is for the Ministry of

Defence, for which I have clearance.'

As if on cue, the Englishman stood and up and left.

The American's silence emphasized the force of his presence, a barely contained animal strength. Collard pictured him padding naked through whatever space he inhabited, a Scotch to hand. The observation disconcerted him. He wondered if the man was homosexual.

The American asked, 'What was the purpose of your visit to New York?'

Collard explained his wife was American and had gone to New York two years earlier, once their son was old enough, to complete her doctorate.

The American stared at him with curiosity and strange tenderness.

'Do you call it a marriage?'

Thrown, Collard replied stiffly. 'That's none of your business.'

'You didn't get on that plane. That makes you very much my business.'

Collard asked if they were finished as he had to meet his wife.

'Your wife.' The American sounded dismissive. 'Why is she joining you?'

Collard was overcome at the thought of Nick. The American seemed to anticipate him.

'Tell us about your son.'

'What do you mean?'

'Why are you sweating?'

The Englishman walked back in.

'You bought him a Walkman at the duty free,' the American said.

28

'He'd been away.'

The two men looked at him.

The Englishman asked, 'Why are you holding out on us?'

The American asked gently, 'Where is the boy now?'

'I don't know. Out there,' Collard said, breaking.

Charlotte

Collard saw Charlotte first, looking so lost his heart went out to her. She stood by the information desk, glancing anxiously around the crowded hall. He saw again how much Nick had taken after her. She raised a hand in weary greeting. They kissed awkwardly. Her eyes were red from weeping. She asked if they had found Nick. He shook his head.

He had spent the rest of the night with his mysterious interrogators going over his movements. The fact that he had been on the investigators' plane led to more questioning. They finally released him so he could meet Charlotte and ordered him to stay in the area in case they needed to speak to him again.

The centre was so busy it was hard to talk. Mourners stood around ignored, uncertain and lost, set apart by their grief in the face of such huge organization. Electric green lights from a bank of photocopy machines passed unceasingly back and forth, spewing paper. Ashtrays made from tin lids overflowed. The coffee machine already had a piece of paper stuck on it saying out of order. Everyone looked disconnected, caught up in their own personal drama.

Collard heard Spanish, Italian and German as they moved outside, past more arriving television crews and radio reporters. A van parked outside the centre handed out free hot dogs. The

Christmas decorations had been switched off. The police and military presence was more like wartime than a civil emergency. Everywhere still stank of the crash.

They waited in clumsy silence for a table in a crowded tea room with steamed-up windows. A reporter on the phone in the corridor was saying that children were being kept indoors. Charlotte swayed with her eyes shut. Collard took her arm and asked if she was all right. She nodded, her eyes still closed.

When a table came free she ordered tea and a muffin, saying she had to eat. The café was full of mute search-party members. An elderly bereaved couple sat by the window. Had it not been for classical music in the background the silence would have been unbearable. Charlotte crumbled her muffin. The linoleum was covered with the marks of wet bootprints.

'They are starting to say it was a bomb.'

'What does it matter? Knowing that won't bring Nick back.'

He sensed her stirring resentment, his presence a reminder of her son's absence.

Sentences formed in Collard's head and fell away, every one an insurmountable hurdle, each rehearsal sounding like an excuse.

A local girl took the reporter's place on the phone and said the bodies were being kept at the ice rink.

Charlotte wore red nail varnish, which he didn't associate with her. Her hair was shorter and more styled.

'What are we going to do?' she asked.

Collard suggested they hire a car and look for a place to stay. He knew that was not what she meant.

'I got a car at the airport. At the risk of sounding insensitive, what I most need is a bath.' She added, sounding almost normal, 'The car's some make I've never heard of.'

★ ★ ★

Collard drove despite not being insured because Charlotte asked him to. He felt as self-conscious as a learner. Everything that had previously been automatic required the greatest concentration.

To fill the silence, he talked hesitantly about missing the flight. He had called the office to wish everyone happy Christmas and learned a Belgian named Tresfort who was part of a big deal wanted urgently to reach him. The man's name sounded like something from another life as he said it.

'He was adamant about meeting.'

Charlotte stared out of the car window. He said he had suggested to Nick he stay over too. Charlotte flinched at the mention of Nick and they drove on in silence.

Everything Collard told her was true, but without the crucial details he sounded like a man trying to construct an alibi.

After an exhausting round of rejections, they found the last room at a hotel in the countryside, half an hour from the town. The guests were all there for the disaster, the regular Christmas bookings having cancelled or cut short. The management had hiked its rates. The hotel smelled of overcooked food.

Their cheerless overheated room with its disastrous carpet was primped and genteel. Once they would have laughed at it.

Charlotte had her bath. Collard stared out of the window at the damp lawn, pocked with worm casts, and a circular gravel drive.

Charlotte came out of the bathroom with her hair wet and took a dryer from a drawer. The fluent way her hands played through her hair made everything seem normal for a moment. Collard caught the smell of singed air from the dryer. The noise of the machine made talk impossible. She didn't usually make him nervous. He thought: Grief makes actors of us.

Charlotte slept. Collard got as far as putting his boots on, intending to go out and look for Nick. He stared at the undone laces as Charlotte cried silently in her sleep.

A television quiz show played to the empty residents' lounge. Collard sat down and took none of it in.

★ ★ ★

When he woke it was dark outside, with several people in the room watching the evening news. Collard recognized places he had walked. The reports bore little relation to the seesaw of his emotions. Their way of dealing with something so vast only as a terrible aberration sounded wrong.

They said the crashing plane had taken less

than a minute to hit the ground. Collard counted the seconds on his watch. Three seemed a lifetime, five an eternity.

All their lives were paper houses. His had been blasted away by the repercussions of the bomb as surely as if he had been on the plane.

★ ★ ★

Charlotte's grief contained a level of accusation, as though it was his fault Nick was not with them. It paralysed everything. He said how cheerful Nick had been in Frankfurt, and wondered for whose sake he was lying. Nick became the censored subject between them.

In the town near where they were staying one shop had a loudspeaker blaring 'Jingle Bells'; otherwise the mood was of festivities cancelled. On Christmas Eve they attended a meeting in a school hall and sat on folding chairs with several hundred mourners to whom the rudiments of consideration were shown. A police officer said his job was to reconstruct the crime and arrest those responsible. The other task, equally hard, was to mourn. At that Charlotte wept. When Collard took her hand she shook him away.

★ ★ ★

The hotel bar was taken over by reporters. Collard drank several whiskies, hoping they would help him sleep. Charlotte was upstairs. Nothing he said could comfort her.

34

As the bar grew more crowded, the atmosphere became one of grim circus, led by a dissipated-looking English reporter everyone called Evelyn. He spoke with a pronounced drawl and was accompanied by an attractive young woman. Evelyn held forth, sarcasm oiled with liquor. He complained about being stuck so far out of town.

'No room at the inn. So we're stuck in the bloody stables witnessing the investigation equivalent to a virgin birth.'

Someone asked what he meant.

'Nobody's got a bloody clue, if you ask me. No one has owned up.'

Terrorists were mentioned.

'But which terrorists?'

The man's cynicism was insensitive and misplaced but there was something so wheedling about his voice it was hard not to listen.

'What are we to make of the warning posted before the crash in the American Embassy in Moscow?'

The young woman with him said, 'It was a standard bulletin. There had been rumours for weeks that something was going to happen.'

'Specifically advising staff not to use American carriers during the holiday period because of warnings of bomb attacks.'

Collard turned and looked at Evelyn.

'What are you saying?' he asked.

'Don't think we've had the pleasure,' Evelyn said, ignoring him and turning to his companion, who grimaced and said to Collard, 'Don't mind him.'

35

Evelyn went on. 'There must have been an almighty balls-up. That's all I'm saying. If there was the security to know something was going to happen, why wasn't there the security to stop it?'

Collard thought how easy it had been to get seats. Nick had called him from abroad on the twelfth saying he had swapped his ticket from the eighteenth, the day they had arranged to fly, to the twenty-first. Collard had been annoyed at Nick's thoughtlessness, protesting that he would have to rearrange meetings and might not be able to get another flight, because of the holidays.

Evelyn said, 'The plane was a third empty four days before Christmas when it should have been loaded to the aeronautical equivalent of the gunnels.'

The call with Nick had ended up being less pleasant than Collard would have liked but he was wrong about the flight. His travel agent sounded surprised. 'It's pretty good right now with plenty of space, but it will fill up nearer Christmas with everybody wanting to get home.'

It hadn't.

★   ★   ★

Charlotte walked into the bar. She appeared brittle but had made a careful effort to look smart. She had been unable to sleep, she said, and asked for dry sherry, a drink Collard couldn't remember her having.

A burst of laughter came across the room.

Collard wondered how the reporters could switch off so easily.

Charlotte tasted her sherry and pulled a face.

Someone said a row of passengers had been found sitting upright in a field, with their fingers crossed.

Charlotte looked like every word scratched her. He asked if she wanted to go back upstairs. She shook her head.

Someone else had seen a passenger who had burst on impact.

Charlotte said, 'I suppose these things are better not bottled up.'

Most of the time, she appeared too numb to speak; now she seemed irritated by him. Whatever he said came out sounding wrong. Talk faltered. Charlotte announced she was going out for some air. She had barely touched her drink but appeared unsteady on her feet. Collard wondered if he should follow and make sure she was all right.

Evelyn got up and talked to a man standing behind Collard who said, 'No one was saying who they were, what they were looking for or whose authority they acted on.'

Evelyn said, 'The Yanks are driving the local coppers mad, disregarding all the rules of evidence.'

Collard went to the toilet. When he came back he was surprised to see Charlotte in one of the reception telephone booths.

He slipped back into the bar before she saw him.

Evelyn was saying, 'Someone knew in advance

a body would need to be removed, which means they didn't want that particular body to be part of the investigation, which is pretty rum.'

Collard remembered seeing the coffin unloaded from the investigators' plane. What had the bomb threatened to expose that involved a body being taken from the accident and helicopters hovering over fields at night, accompanied by armed men? And then there were the warnings and the empty seats.

★ ★ ★

Collard's eyes pricked with tiredness. Discarded tea bags lay on a dirty saucer the hotel cleaners had failed to remove. He stared at the vortex made from stirring his and Charlotte's tea. He asked: How do you measure death?

★ ★ ★

On Christmas Day, he and Charlotte built a stone cairn for Nick, to prepare for the next stage, the identification of his body.

★ ★ ★

Decompression. The word banged around his head all Boxing Day, followed by a riptide of panic.

Interrogation

The police came early the next day for Collard at the hotel. Their call woke him. He was surprised because he hadn't given them his hotel, and then dully acknowledged the persistence of his naivety. Charlotte remained asleep. She had taken a pill. Collard dressed in a hurry, fearing the worst.

They were downstairs in the lobby, two uniformed men in fluorescent jackets and peaked caps. They took him out to a marked car. One held the door open for him. Their professional silence increased his worry. He was sure Nick's body had been found. That kind of news would be broken face to face.

They drove him to the ice rink that was acting as a morgue.

The big American and his sour English companion waited at the entrance. Collard found it difficult to stand up.

The American said, 'We need your help with identification. This won't be pleasant.'

'Give me your name,' Collard said, desperate for any delay. 'So at least I know who I'm talking to.'

The American waved his hand. 'Call me Sheehan. A good Irish name. He's Parker.'

Collard stepped into the building, aware of a fall in temperature and an astringent, clinical smell.

The ticket office had been turned into a security desk. Sheehan signed in for Collard. Not knowing had inevitably been turned into a kind of hope that was about to be shattered.

He was led to a changing room lined with lockers where a body covered by a sheet lay on a trolley.

'Is this your son?' Sheehan asked.

The sheet was removed. Collard had a glimpse of a swarthy young man.

'Jesus, they got the wrong one,' Sheehan said, whipping back the sheet. 'Stay there.'

He left Collard with the body.

There were benches in front of the lockers and he was relieved to sit down. He had been surprised as much as shocked by the face he had just seen. It was badly damaged where the bone had been smashed but still seemed familiar. He thought it was perhaps the agitated young man he had noticed in the Frankfurt passport queue.

He looked around at the empty lockers. The place was unimaginable as somewhere people went for amusement.

Sheehan returned, complaining about the incompetence of the bureaucracy and how they couldn't number anything right. He led the way to the main arena. The ice rink was frighteningly still. Collard looked at his feet to avoid the sight of so many shrouded bodies.

The bodies were tagged by number. Sheehan took them down several rows before he found the right one then had to take Collard's arm to steady him. The cold of the ice rink showed their breath, a painful reminder of being alive.

Sheehan drew back the sheet.

The face was unmarked, the eyes shut.

He had been so ready for Nick's face he needed a moment to focus and not burst out laughing in relief. He shook his head.

'Not your son.'

'No.'

Collard looked Sheehan in the eye and realized he knew that already.

'But you recognized the first boy.'

Collard's escape left him giddy. He had been certain it was going to be Nick. Now it wasn't he was willing to talk about anything although he suspected he had been softened up. He said the first boy had been in front of them in the passport queue. He had been travelling alone, a sullen, beefy, young man with a thick neck who seemed nervous.

'Nervous how?'

'He kept glancing around like he was expecting someone. I suppose I thought he was worried about someone who was going to miss the plane.'

'He stood directly in front of you in the line?'

Collard nodded.

'Did your son and Khaled exchange words or looks?'

'Of course not. Khaled?'

'A Lebanese student. He happened to be the only non-American, non-white-European passenger. Why of course not?'

'The boy was a stranger. They didn't know each other. What are you trying to imply?'

Sheehan raised an eyebrow and Collard again

41

had the feeling that showing him Khaled's body had been deliberate.

'What did you make of his nervousness?'

'I told you. Maybe he was meant to fly with someone who was late. Maybe he was just afraid of flying.'

'Did your son remark on that?'

'No. Look, can I leave now?'

'Let's go to the broom cupboard I call my office.'

Collard was uncomfortable walking next to Sheehan. The whole event felt like it had been stage-managed. Outside the ice rink, the streets were deserted, with house curtains permanently drawn as a mark of respect.

Sheehan's office was the room where they had first questioned him, in a Victorian building up several flights of concrete stairs. The corridors were empty, but Collard had the feeling that behind closed doors the building hummed with secret activity.

The taciturn Parker was waiting. He said the passenger boarding lists had come in from Heathrow and he handed several photostat sheets to Sheehan, who waved Collard towards a chair. Parker surprised him by offering coffee. Collard declined.

'Two sugars,' Sheehan said without looking up. He took a long time reading. Collard thought of the two dead young men in the morgue. Perhaps loss of air pressure and the freezing cold shut down the brain quicker than the time it took to fall. Ten, fifteen, twenty seconds?

Sheehan shuffled through the pages, checking.

'Interesting,' he finally said and passed Collard the sheets. 'Your name's on the list but your son's doesn't appear to be.'

'My name is on the list?' He heard the tightness in his voice.

'People who booked and didn't get on the plane are on the list, which doesn't make our job easier. But your son isn't, which is curious.'

Collard read through the list twice. His eye kept being drawn back to his own name. His throat was dry and his hands shook. Nick definitely wasn't among them. Had he changed his mind too and decided not to get on the plane? Then why wasn't he on the list? Had he never intended to get on?

For the first time he dared to hope. He had been convinced it would be Nick in the morgue. Now Sheehan seemed to be saying he might be alive. Collard had held himself together since the crash, but this threatened to unhinge him altogether. It took all his self-control to maintain his composure in front of Sheehan.

Sheehan seemed oblivious to what he had just suggested. 'I have three girls, one around your boy's age. She could just as easily have been on it. There was a whole bunch of students on the plane.'

Collard didn't want to know. All he could think was that, against all the odds, Nick might still be alive.

'Tell me about your son. How long was he away?'

'Since the end of July.' Collard was almost incapable of speech.

43

'Travelling where?'

'He had a rail card for Europe.'

'Where is he now?'

Collard gestured helplessly, shaking his head. He had no idea.

'First you tell me you didn't get on the plane, but your bag did. Now we find out your son wasn't on the plane. Is it something that runs in the family?'

Collard tried to interrupt. Sheehan held up a hand.

'Listen, look at it from my side. I'm asking, did you know? Did he know? You flew up here pretending to be part of the investigation. Maybe you're an embittered crazy and you put the bomb on the plane and came to gloat. Far-fetched? Or you're a time-waster and taking up valuable resources, which makes you as bad in my eyes.'

Collard allowed himself to shout, 'I'm an ordinary man with an ordinary job and an ordinary son.'

Parker returned with the coffees. Sheehan grunted when he tasted his.

'Why can't the English make coffee?'

'It's Scottish coffee, technically,' said Parker with no trace of humour.

Sheehan looked at Collard. 'Was he travelling alone?'

'He left on his own.'

'Would you describe your son as a loner?'

'No, I would not describe my son as a loner,' he said as levelly as he could manage. 'He turned up with a girl in Frankfurt.'

44

Sheehan stared with uncontrolled hostility.

'What is this now? Are you going to sit there and insult our intelligence? Do you think we're idiots? Why the hell didn't you tell us that before?'

'I didn't think it important.'

'I decide what's important. Who was this girl?'

'I don't know. I never met her.'

'So how do you know about her? Did your boy tell you?'

'I heard them in his room.'

'Heard them how?'

'Passing his door.'

'What were they talking about?'

'They weren't talking.'

Parker smirked. Collard knew what he was thinking. He remembered standing in the hotel corridor, transfixed by the sound of the girl's moans.

Sheehan stood up and leaned over Collard.

'Damn it, man! Why didn't you tell us?'

For the first time, Collard felt that Sheehan was confiding in him.

'What's the problem? He had a girl in his room.'

Sheehan sat back down. He looked sober and exhausted. 'It's how they work. They use innocent, gullible young people.'

'You don't know Nick. She was just a girl in his room.'

'Don't be obtuse, Mr Collard. We're talking about nearly three hundred lives destroyed by a bomb.'

'That has nothing to do with my son.'

Sheehan stared at him, challenging.

'Ask the young Irish woman who was persuaded by her Syrian boyfriend to carry a package for him. On that occasion a planeload of passengers was very lucky the Israelis were on the job.'

'Nick is an ordinary middle-class English boy.'

'And she was an ordinary young Irish woman. I'm not talking about your son's character. I'm talking about whether he was used.'

Collard was rattled. He barely knew where Nick had been in three months. They had spoken only four or five times — calling was expensive and lines were hard to get. A postcard from Bucharest had taken over a week to reach him.

'OK,' Sheehan said, 'from the top. You met your son at the airport the day before the flight.'

Collard had booked a room at the Sheraton airport hotel for them to share but Nick insisted on his own, saying he wasn't a child. The underlying accusation was that Collard was too mean to pay for an extra room.

'How did your son seem, generally?'

'He was tired from travelling. We got off on the wrong foot.'

'Just the usual family stuff?' Sheehan was friendly again.

'You could say.'

'Did he mention meeting anyone on his travels?'

'I wouldn't expect him to.'

'You weren't close?'

'It was up to him to tell me if he wanted to.'

46

'Maybe he thought you weren't interested.'

'I suppose the tension was about Nick wanting to be with the girl and not subjecting her to an awkward dinner with his boring father.'

They had eaten in the Sheraton restaurant, the two of them. Nick laughed, saying as he rolled his bread into pellets, 'It's just a crappy airport hotel, Dad.' Afterwards he had gone to Nick's room to ask if he wanted a drink and heard them. The next day he could smell the girl on Nick. He wanted to spoil his secret by saying he knew about her and it didn't matter, but he hadn't because he thought he would end up embarrassing them both.

'Has your son had a lot of sexual experience?'

Collard had no idea. He'd met a couple of London girlfriends. Sheehan wanted to know what they were like. Ordinary middle-class North London girls, was the answer.

'There was nothing extreme about them?'

Collard didn't understand.

'Politically extreme.'

'I know my son, Mr Sheehan.'

'That's as maybe. These are not pleasant speculations. The way it usually works is they use a patsy to carry a gift-wrapped package for delivery at the other end. If anything goes wrong the dupe gets arrested and if the operation is successful the dupe gets the blame. The question is if your son was the dupe how did he know to get off the plane?'

Collard couldn't care less about Sheehan's accusations. He knew Nick would never get involved in anything like that. He wanted to be alone to savour the possibility of Nick being alive.

Sheehan seemed to relent. 'We need to talk to him so we can cross him off the list. Where do you think he is?'

Collard had no answer. Nick was impetuous but would he really run off and not tell anyone or call? He wondered what his pierced ear was meant to indicate.

'Go get your wife, come back here and we can start to find your son.'

School friends. Relatives. Friends of friends. Favoured locations. Old holiday sites. Sheehan ticked them off his fingers.

'I'll find him,' said Collard.

★ ★ ★

Charlotte wasn't at the hotel. Her hire car was gone. Then he saw her letter. His name on the envelope looked considered and ominous. Everything had become so fragile it seemed death could snatch them at any moment, or hand them back on a whim, the crueller the circumstances the better. Collard feared Charlotte would be found dead in the sealed car, with a tube fed in from the exhaust just as he had learned Nick might have been spared.

Instead, Charlotte wrote that she had gone away to be alone for a while, to start to come to terms with losing Nick.

Collard was angry with her for slipping off and unnecessarily extending her grief. He resented too the undercurrent of blame; when it came to that he was quite capable of punishing himself. Once, the mystery of the girl in Nick's room would have been something they would have shared. Now telling her was inconceivable.

He phoned around London to see if anyone had heard from Nick and left a message at Charlotte's number in New York in case he had turned up there. He called the house in London and checked his answerphone in case Nick had left him a message. None of the calls led anywhere, but, for the first time, he truly believed Nick was alive.

The Reporters

Charlotte's whereabouts was less of a mystery. She had been to the Isle of Lewis as a child and often talked of going back. It seemed the obvious choice.

Collard took a bus to the town. The mundane journey was a return to reality. He hired a car from one of the big rental agencies and bought several travel guides before reporting to the incident centre as instructed by Sheehan. The room he was sent to was manned by a young constable hardly older than Nick. It was the first time Collard had seen anyone in the investigation underworked. The constable was only vaguely aware he was supposed to take down all the contacts Collard could provide for his son. He wrote in a jerky hand with a leaky biro that stained his fingers. The smudged ink left Collard fearing for the efficiency of the investigation. At least the young policeman said, 'Is this about the boy who didn't get on the plane?'

★ ★ ★

The rest of the day Collard spent telephoning hotels and boarding houses on Lewis. He tried the Kyle of Lochalsh, where the ferry departed, and drew a blank. He widened his search to other islands, still confident. There weren't many places to stay, and most of them were closed for winter.

★ ★ ★

Evelyn now kept the best table in the bar, from which he would not be budged. His companion seemed to have been adopted as a mascot, a role she played with some self-awareness. Evelyn only ever addressed her as Stack.

Collard was at the bar when Evelyn called him over.

'How does it feel to be alive?'

Collard didn't know how Evelyn knew he had missed the flight, and wasn't sure how trustworthy the man was. Then he decided he was happy to tell his story, of two lucky escapes.

'Two magpies,' Evelyn said with a bark of laughter. 'One for sorrow, two for joy. You and your son are very lucky. Fate is a strange thing. I would be dead now if I hadn't noticed my shoelace was undone. Beirut, 1985 — bent down and a bullet smacked the wall where my head had been. What are the chances? Sit down.'

Collard decided to allow himself the luxury of getting pleasantly drunk with them. Little was demanded of him except to listen. Evelyn played up the image of boozy old hack and raconteur. He chain-smoked Silk Cut, coughed phlegm into a silk handkerchief and got angry if anyone tried to put ice in his whisky. Collard wondered if Stack and Evelyn were an item.

That afternoon he had read his first newspaper since the crash, including an article about how the clothes of the dead were being washed by local women volunteers to get rid of the smell of fuel before their return to the next of kin. It turned out Stack had written the story.

'They're developing all the film in the cameras they find in the hope of identifying the owners and returning the photographs to relatives,' Evelyn said. 'Tomorrow Stack's talking to the copper in charge of gathering the luggage and trying to match it. Aren't you, my dear?'

Collard supposed he should make an effort to retrieve his and Nick's baggage.

'Fucking awful way to die,' Evelyn said. 'Have the tabbies been on to you yet?'

'Tabbies?'

'Tabloids. You'd be right up their street: the man who got off. Don't worry, we shan't tell, shall we, my dear?'

He squeezed Stack's arm.

Collard suspected Evelyn was lonely. Stack looked like she wanted to be taken on her own terms but what those terms were was hard to say.

Evelyn lit up. 'What I can't work out is whether it's all bloody obvious — Allah versus the infidel — or something deeper. What do you think? Are you of the deeper school, chummy?'

Collard realized he was being addressed.

'Everyone's saying it's terrorists from the Middle East.'

'And why would they do something like that?'

'For the usual reasons, I don't know.' Collard had stopped caring.

'And what are the usual reasons?'

'Palestine?'

'You think Palestinians blew up the plane?'

'They have a history of terrorism,' Collard said lamely.

'Do you have anyone else pegged? Iraq, for example?'

'Stop being a cunt, Evelyn,' Stack said and turned to Collard. 'Don't let him bully you. It's only because he hasn't got a clue that he's taking it out on someone else.'

'Bollocks to you, my dear. You don't know what you're talking about and I do. That plane was bombed as a simple act of revenge. Last July the Americans shot down a civil Iranian Airbus. The plane was full of pilgrims on their way to Mecca — there were 290 people on board, almost exactly the number on Flight 103. Syria put the operation together on behalf of Iran and subcontracted it to a terrorist organization called the Freedom Group for the Liberation of Palestine, operating in West Germany.'

'And the reason for Syrian involvement?'

'Strapped for cash.'

Collard had no recollection of the Airbus incident.

'But why would the Americans shoot down a civil airliner?'

'The USS *Vincennes* was patrolling the Arabian Gulf when it picked up a plane flying out of Iranian air-space, which failed to identify itself. After deciding it was a hostile F14 fighter aircraft, the venerable Captain Rogers gave the order to fire two surface-to-air missiles. The Airbus exploded in mid-air, much like Flight 103.'

Collard was struck by the religious angle: the Airbus full of pilgrims; people going home for Christmas.

'But the Americans must have admitted it was a mistake.'

'Like hell they did,' Evelyn snorted. 'They handed out medals all round and refused to apologize, which was in keeping. The *Vincennes* was known as 'Robo-cruiser' in the Gulf. Personally, I would have apologized.'

Stack snorted back. 'You never apologize.'

'If I had just blown a load of innocent Muslims out of the sky I probably would, if only from expediency. The Iranians may have a point.'

Collard protested. 'How can you say that? There's no point, just the opposite.'

'Calm down, calm down. I do not condone cold-blooded retaliation. What I am saying is if the Yanks' diplomatic skills had been more honed they might have saved the lives of those on board Flight 103.'

Collard was surprised by how swiftly things had changed — three days earlier Evelyn had said no one had a clue who bombed the plane. Now, in spite of his apparent inertia, he seemed very well informed. Collard found his theory reassuring. It still sounded very remote and political, and made Sheehan's aggressive, even desperate, questions seem even more absurd.

The Bombeat

Charlotte telephoned, waking Collard from a deep sleep. She sounded distant and was slow to accept that Nick might be alive.

'It's fantastic news,' he said in an effort to inject some enthusiasm into her. 'I'm telling you, I've seen the passenger list and he's not on it.'

'What are you saying?'

She sounded muddled. Collard thought she had been sedating herself.

'What's the matter?'

'Why hasn't he been in touch? You know he would have called.'

Charlotte, pourer of cold water, as always.

They were cut short because she was in a call box and running out of money. He offered to call back but she didn't want to talk. Collard sensed she had been about to tell him something but his news prevented her. He hung up, exasperated, and only then realized he could have refuted her definitively with Sheehan's investigation.

In the breakfast room, Stack was eating alone. She offered him the place opposite her, saying it was too early for Evelyn. She told him not to take offence at Evelyn's rudeness.

Collard wasn't sure if he wanted company after the unpleasantness of Charlotte's call, but he couldn't bring himself to refuse. He remembered Stack was due to see the collected luggage that morning and thought he might ask for a lift so he could retrieve Nick's belongings.

'When's your son joining you?'

'Soon, I hope,' he said and asked about her work.

She told him she had to go to Frankfurt to talk to a contact in the German intelligence services.

'They're saying the bomb was put on the plane in Frankfurt. The Germans had the Palestinian cell under observation. They caught the bomb-maker and at least one of the bombs but another slipped through the net. That was what blew up the plane.'

'They know who made the bomb! Isn't this news?'

'It's too early. They're waiting for forensic evidence. And they're in no hurry — it's not exactly a public-relations triumph that they were watching the cell and still lost the plane.'

Her easy assumptions about what was happening were a long way ahead of him. He wanted to know obvious things such as who organized the cell and whether there was someone you could point a finger at.

Stack offered without prompting, 'I'm chasing a story on an arms dealer. He has his own bank and jet and his hobby is sponsoring terrorists.'

Collard felt depressed about Charlotte's call. Stack's company underlined his lack of anyone to talk to. He wondered if as a reporter she would know how to go about tracing Nick beyond what he had already done.

'How do I go about finding my son?'

'What do you mean?'

'I can't find him.'

56

Stack drove him to the warehouse where the possessions of the dead were stored. Sections of the town remained closed off with traffic rerouted. The town was still in mourning, with almost no one out.

After the relief of being able to air his worries about Nick, Collard decided he was being indiscreet talking to a reporter. He didn't care.

'This American gave me a rough time over Nick. He tried to scare me with stories about innocent people getting used.'

'They're starting to say that about a Lebanese student called Khaled. They think his bag carried the bomb.'

Collard was alarmed by the unexpected mention of Khaled. He thought of the body Sheehan had shown him, and puzzled over how Sheehan was trying to tie Nick in. Thinking of the agitated young man he had seen in the passport queue he wondered if Khaled was naturally nervous or if he'd had some inkling.

★ ★ ★

He was unprepared for the dead's belongings. Row after row of luggage, with tables for personal effects — one for watches and another for jewellery, trays for pens and keys, dozens of cameras, some undamaged. Hard fluorescent lighting made everything look overexposed and defenceless.

The forlorn display took up most of the

warehouse floor. Everything there ought to have ended up in the tired ritual of the baggage carousel. After any flight Collard was struck by the temporary confinement of so many separate lives, prior to going their different ways. The crash was a cruel parody of that process: an intensely concentrated and violent dispersal.

Uniformed police manned a checking centre in a wooden garden shed that was set up in the warehouse and looked brought in for the purpose.

Stack signed in first and turned to give him an encouraging wave. He watched her walk down the aisle studying the luggage. The space looked like a bizarre modern exhibition of the kind that wasted columns of newspaper argument. Collard felt the cold of the concrete floor through his shoes. He gave his name and was unsettled to be told he was expected.

Parker came down, complaining that Collard was early.

'Early for what?'

'Didn't anyone call you?'

'About?'

'Coming in to locate your son's belongings.'

Parker sported a severe new haircut, cropped blond stubble like a cornfield after harvest. His breath smelled of Polo mints as he said, 'You'd be surprised how few people label their bags.'

Parker pointed to the unlabelled luggage and asked Collard to see if either his or his son's was there. Collard sorted through piles of clothes. A pair of black Levi 501s, size 30, could have been Nick's but nothing else told him one way or the other. It dawned on him that he had no idea what Nick's bag looked like, beyond being a rucksack, any more than he could have identified his clothing, other than knowing it consisted of the usual high-street names. He felt ignorant and unobservant. Did he really have so little sense of his son? What he could remember might as easily be in a drawer at home. He actually had no idea. He knew Parker was watching and he felt tested.

Parker was replaced by Sheehan in an aggressive mood. He made Collard look through filing boxes of the victims' photographs, each set separated by an index card. He wanted to know if any were of Nick.

Each snapshot was a moment of private history he was never meant to see. Among them: two middle-aged women tourists, bags over their shoulders, stood self-consciously to attention before the Trevi Fountain; a group of what he supposed were students, to judge by their sweatshirt logos, clambering on a sofa and mugging to camera; a soulful teenage girl whose sultry look must have been for her boyfriend taking the picture; a couple of babies notable for their unselfconscious belligerence. So it went on. Landscapes. Travel shots. A set of mildly risqué pictures of a woman posed topless on a hotel bed.

None of his son.

Sheehan made him go through everything twice. He seemed desperate, urgent and keen to humiliate. Collard applied himself to the pointless task. He suspected Sheehan was taking it out on him because someone higher up was on his back.

Eventually he gave up, saying, 'This is a waste of time. There's nothing here. Can you tell me what sense there is to any of this?'

'There were 259 people on that plane and they're dead. There were others who were supposed to have been on the plane but weren't, you and your son included. Maybe there were people who shouldn't have been on the plane but were. I'm an exasperated man, Mr Collard, and getting shorter-tempered by the minute.'

Sheehan's hostile stare was broken by Parker returning with a list of further luggage and its contents.

'Look at this and tell me if anything is yours or your son's,' Sheehan said.

Collard's resistance was sapped by the display of orphaned belongings, more harrowing than the random devastation outside for having been collected together.

The listed contents of a Samsonite suitcase included a man's suit, grey, and three plain shirts, two white, one blue, long-sleeved, regular button cuffs. They might have been his.

He shrugged, helpless. Everything was so divorced and unconnected.

Sheehan continued to regard him in an unreadable way.

'Where are these bags?' Collard asked.

'With forensics.'

Sheehan studied Collard like a man setting his sights.

'Did you or your son own or travel with a

60

radio-cassette player?'

'Not me. I can't answer for Nick.'

'A Toshiba. Something called a Bombeat.'

Collard looked for signs of irony and found none.

'Bombeat? Is this terrorist humour?'

The unfunny Parker smirked.

On Nick's behalf, Collard denied him owning a Toshiba Bombeat.

'How can you be sure?' Parker asked.

'Nick's pretty cool. Toshiba isn't.'

He laughed in astonishment when Sheehan put it to him that he had broken his journey because he had been warned by his son.

'Well, I can put an end to *that* idea — far from warning me, he was warned himself.'

He enjoyed their bewilderment.

'An old man accosted us at Frankfurt airport.'

Collard had noticed him wandering around the terminal muttering and trying to talk to people.

'What did he look like?'

'Old. Silver hair and tortoiseshell glasses. He wore a long black coat and a homburg, like someone from another age. He could have been a diplomat except his clothes were too threadbare. He seemed confused — I thought he was drunk.'

'Go on.'

'I noticed him talking to Nick in a bookshop across the hall. Soon after that the old man approached me and asked if I was taking the London flight to New York.'

Collard remembered the embarrassment of

61

being singled out. The old man had seemed deranged. Collard recalled the face very clearly: unnaturally pale and finely boned, with fishy eyes, the overall effect austere and forbidding. The man's throat made a strange click when he spoke. The accent wasn't quite anywhere.

The mildly surreal quality of airports had contributed to the strangeness of the episode and the old man seemed to be having trouble deciding what was real.

He had said something in Latin. *Sapiens qui prospicit.* It sounded vaguely familiar but by then Collard had decided the man was either mad or ill.

'Nick and I talked about him and he said the old man had told him the plane from London was going to crash.'

Sheehan's patience was being tested.

'Why didn't you mention this earlier?'

'We didn't believe a word he was saying. He was just some old drunk man.'

'But you changed your flight.'

'Not because of that. A business meeting came up. I had no choice.'

One reason he hadn't mentioned the old man, or even thought of him, was he could not allow himself to believe the man was right. In reality, the warning had left him nervous — that private, suppressed fear shared by everyone in the terminal that the unthinkable might happen — and Nick laughed at that. Collard had let it go, his anxiety curbed by the fear of appearing foolish to his cool young son he felt he hardly knew. He still refused to believe he had altered his plans because of this knowledge.

Now he didn't know what to make of the old man's warning or Nick's reaction, or his own. Had part of him been secretly relieved at the opportunity to change his flight? He had suggested to Nick he stay over too, but Nick wasn't interested in a delay. He gave a strange laugh and said he would take his chances. It seemed almost a point of principle that he flew despite the warning. But whenever Collard caught a glimpse of him in the odd unguarded moment the bravura was absent and he saw instead something he could not identify: yearning, almost, and anxiety, tempered by something much deeper that he thought was sadness and a fear of the future.

He mentioned nothing of these anxieties because for Sheehan it seemed like Nick was a blank page waiting to be filled in.

★   ★   ★

They went back to Sheehan's office. Parker skulked in the background. Collard was given more pictures to look at, taken by security cameras in the Frankfurt terminal on the day of the crash. He saw Nick. He saw himself. He saw them standing behind Khaled in the passport queue.

Each picture had the date and time stamped on it. They were black-and-white images of milky quality.

There was no sign of the old man. It was almost as if he had been airbrushed out.

All Collard could do was repeat what he had seen and what Nick had told him.

'Nick must have taken the old man's warning seriously after all and changed his mind at the last minute.'

Sheehan shook his head.

'His name would be on the passenger list.'

'He was on the flight from Frankfurt. Why wasn't he listed on that?'

'I'll tell you what I think. The Lebanese kid, Khaled, was the patsy. Your boy didn't get on the plane because he gave the Toshiba to Khaled, meaning he knew, and he passed on the warning to you because he didn't quite have the heart to blow up his father. You worked that one out, which is why you made up the story about the old man.'

Sheehan was granting him an ingenuity he didn't possess. Collard pointed at the photographs.

'These are time-lapse pictures. I remember other people there who aren't in these pictures.'

He was thinking of a very tall American and his two companions he had noticed and been curious about. The tall man had reminded him of Gene Hackman and their behaviour alternated between boisterous high-fives and urgent conversation.

'The system's not infallible,' Collard went on. 'The cameras could have missed him. You're the one making up stories about Nick. You've got no proof in any of this.'

'I'll get it. In the meantime I'm happy for you to prove me wrong.' Sheehan laughed

64

unexpectedly. Perhaps he was enjoying the contest.

★ ★ ★

The second time Charlotte called she told him she was in Plockton. She sounded like she resented him looking for her. He remained upbeat, despite making another exhaustive and fruitless round of phone calls in search of Nick. Charlotte didn't want to believe Nick might be alive because the pain of accepting his death precluded any return to hope. She admitted as much, describing her time away as a kind of breakdown. She was no believer in miracles and short of being able to see and touch her son she was unable to nurse what might turn out to be false hope.

He wanted to make her better. But he had no proof to offer, meaning there was little to distinguish his belief from her despair, only a matter of interpretation while the central subject remained elusive.

Their brief telephone exchanges were like thermal drifts, no more than the slightest breeze of disagreement that would not materialize but would have a cumulative effect. Despite his feeling the calls were driven by his anger and frustration they always remained polite, even courteous.

He told her to come back. They had to talk about Nick, however difficult that might be. She told him she would be there for the memorial service.

They ended in stalemate. He nursed his fragile hope, hoping it would be enough for both of them. But sometimes, waiting for her return, when he was about to cross the street or watching the contrails of a transatlantic jet high on its indifferent way out towards the ocean, he became paralysed.

Sapiens Qui Prospicit

'God Almighty!' said Oliver Round. 'We thought you and Nick were dead.'

Oliver Round was Collard's oldest friend. They had not spoken since the crash because Round spent his Christmases in the Caribbean. They had first met aged eight at boarding school in East Sussex and gone on to Malvern together.

'I'm coming up to see you,' Round said after Collard explained. The snap decision was typical. 'Are you sure you're all right?'

'Apart from worrying about Nick.'

Round was Nick's godfather and Collard's overall boss.

'I'm bringing up Joost Tranter. I want him to take over the Belgian deal for you. You've enough on your plate.'

Collard groaned inwardly. Tranter was one of the new competitive breed and a favourite of Round's.

'We'll fly up this afternoon. We've got things to do in Edinburgh.'

Flying up involved a private helicopter, Round's preferred form of travel now he was rich and could write it off as a business expense. They landed on the hotel lawn and sat with Collard in the lounge, which they had to themselves. The reporters were out chasing stories.

It was nothing that couldn't have been done

over the telephone but Round and the unsmiling Tranter were men of meetings. Round's company was purchasing a major Belgian arms concern and Collard's arrangement to provide a new security system was subsidiary to the deal. Collard had been negotiating with a man called Tresfort for whom he had missed the flight. Tresfort turned up in London as arranged and, unable to find Collard, left feeling snubbed.

Joost Tranter said, 'Don't worry about Tresfort. He's in the picture now.'

Tranter had a marked South African accent and clipped his words in a way that was consistent with the rest of his tightness. His dourness was a match for Tresfort's persistence. Collard felt like a convalescent talking business; slow and finding it hard to keep up. Round offered his place in Tuscany.

'Take a break. You need one.'

Round was wearing his old school tie. He set store by such traditions. On Round's advice, Collard had been wearing his on the day of the crash. Round was very keen on a show of British tradition when dealing with Germans, as Collard had been over a huge security installation. It made the Germans jealous because their traditions were up the creek.

Collard still found it hard to connect the sleek entrepreneur sitting opposite him with the plump schoolboy of tiresome enthusiasms who had arrived the term after him. Round, fat and sensitive, was not up to the usual bullying handed out to newcomers and Collard had fought his corner. It left him wondering how much his present position was a favour returned.

His company, Opticon, had struggled until he ran into Round in Threadneedle Street, a chance meeting that resulted in becoming part of Round's Trevayne Group. One of Opticon's first assignments had been the installation of security cameras at an old RAF base bought by Round at a knockdown price. Collard remembered sitting with Round in a pub called the Hatchet on Garlick Hill in the City, giggling over a pint and a bag of crisps, as he wrote down the figures Round told him to for his tender.

★ ★ ★

'Are you all right?' Round asked.

'Sure.'

'Nick'll be all right,' Round said, frowning.

'What's the matter? Have you heard from him?'

'No, not at all.'

Collard knew Round well enough to detect embarrassment.

'What is it?'

'Tell him, Joost.'

'You're being investigated.'

Tranter was the type to relish handing out bad news.

'Investigated! By who?'

'Customs and Excise.'

The company's VAT accounts were all in order. He could see no cause for concern.

'Unfortunately, they're investigating you personally,' Round said.

'What am I supposed to have done?'

'They're not saying yet.'

It sounded as far-fetched as Sheehan and Parker's accusations.

'Ridiculous, I know,' Round said, 'and just ghastly timing. I wanted to warn you that my impression is they're prepared to be perfectly bloody. Are you sure you don't want to go to Tuscany?'

Collard smiled at his friend's attempted humour. After what he had already been through he could hardly be bothered to take the charge seriously. Let them waste their time.

'Why did they come to you?'

'Because they couldn't find you and yours is a subsidiary company.'

'Tell them I can't talk until I've sorted this business with Nick out.'

'Take as long as you like. Joost will cover for you.'

It was a sign of the times that Round now travelled with Tranter. Collard didn't like Tranter with his controlled body language and overconfident air. Round had brought him on to the Opticon board as a consultant. The man cropped up all over the place: one moment attached to a bank; constantly travelling; turning up on this or that board; earning lucrative consultancy fees. Collard wasn't sure if he wanted Tranter covering for him.

He had been staring at Round's school tie, which reminded him of what the old man said at the airport.

'What was the school motto?'

'*Sapiens qui prospicit*. Wise is he that looks ahead. Why on earth do you ask?'

He knew Round would have been bound to remember.

'Someone quoted it to me the other day. I couldn't place it.'

The old man must have recognized his tie. More than that, he must have some connection to the school; how bizarre.

Round left, promising to keep 'those Customs buggers' off his back. Tranter shook hands, looked Collard in the eye, and said, 'Good to see you, sport.'

'Tell Nick to call when he gets back,' Round said with a parting wave.

Collard was grateful to Round for making everything sound normal, like Nick was on holiday or something. Tears pricked his eyes. Their leaving made him realize how lonely he was. Charlotte was gone. Stack was off, following her German leads. Even Evelyn had moved hotels, having found a room nearer town. They had exchanged a few words in the lobby as he checked out. In Charlotte's absence, Collard had been concentrating on getting through the days. In the rational hours of daylight he had no trouble rejecting Sheehan's insinuations. The nights were harder and the reasons why Nick hadn't caught the flight became darker. Days were spent in his room on the phone, trying and failing to locate Nick. He had called the hotel in Frankfurt. He had stayed there enough to be familiar with one of the receptionists, but when he tried to reach her to ask if she remembered seeing Nick with a girl he was told she was away on holiday.

Nights were spent awake.

The news had been returning to normal. There was a lull in the investigation. Forensic evidence was still being collected. The plane had been removed, its parts transported for reassembly in a vast hangar. The dead had been brought in. The television crews had started to drift away. Children had begun to be seen in the streets again. Americans were less in evidence and the town lost its air of being under occupation. The show had moved on. Politicians talked with quiet confidence about the net closing around those responsible.

Collard watched Round's helicopter crank its way up into the sky.

Sapiens qui prospicit, he thought.

Fugue States

Angleton was stuck in Frankfurt airport, sick and almost too dizzy to stand, stumbling on, forcing himself into another tour of the terminal. He was nervous of the departure boards, knowing that any lapse of attention would mean he could miss his flight. Then he couldn't remember where he was or why he was there. To do with a bomb. Or a boy. He got distracted by a man's tie.

That happened. Jesus, it had happened all the time as he got older and the famous Angleton memory went on the sputter. The day that I grow old was a line from a song; he failed to recall the name of the singer, a little guy with a rug whose girlfriend had taken a high dive out of a window. He'd kept up. Some of his best sources had been at the *National Enquirer*.

Angleton's first moment of reckoning had come years earlier, standing at his desk, staring with no idea of what he was doing. He had ignored the warning signs. The start of the boozer's shake, the razor nicks, reveries at red lights, cars hooting behind, and a growing sense he was no longer on top of the beat, the night sweats, the start of absent-mindedness: Now where was I?

Where he was: back in Ryder Street in London, 1943, hanging around like a damned idiot in front of the tea trolley in the hope of an appearance by Graham Greene, the most famous man in the building. There was artificial milk and sweetener because of a sugar shortage. Angleton had admired rather than enjoyed *Brighton Rock*. Author as spy, spy as author, was in his estimation the most glamorous combination.

Greene's cautious oyster eyes checked him over. Angleton, keen to flatter, was daunted. Sourly boyish at forty, Greene worked on an upper-floor in palatial surroundings compared to Angleton's hutch, shared with a secretary with the delightful name of Perdita Doolittle.

'American?' Greene asked.

'Kind of,' said Angleton.

Greene smoked Sweet Aftons. Angleton obliged with a light, cupping his hands to protect the flame. Mrs B, the trolley woman, gave a high-pitched laugh and Angleton knew he was blushing and Greene had seen. Greene grunted thanks and wandered off, mug in hand, before turning to ask, 'What do you mean, kind of?'

Angleton told him he had been born in Idaho, lived in Italy and gone to school in England. Greene lost interest. 'Poor you,' he said, leaving Angleton, who had been hoping for more, crushed.

Greene's verdict on Americans: insufficient geography.

In Memoriam

Charlotte's return was marked by her further withdrawal. Denial took the form of refusing to hope or even to discuss Nick beyond insisting he would have got in touch. Her silence was thrown back at him and his grew in the shadow of Nick's greater silence.

Collard, driven from the room, sat useless in the lounge then in the bar where he was surprised to see Evelyn at his usual table.

'Had a bloody row with the other hotel. Stack's in Germany and I want to go home. They won't let the bereaved view the bodies, did you know? The psychiatrists decided it would be too distressing.'

Collard thought of the bodies he'd seen.

'How will they identify them?'

Evelyn shrugged.

The ice rink had become a building people avoided. An area had been put aside for the body parts they hadn't been able to match up.

'The ones they had to scrape up with a spade they put in special boxes,' Evelyn said. 'The bereaved seemed oddly consoled by the idea of a presentable corpse. My abiding memories of this trip will be the stink of aviation fuel and formalin. The only thing that gets rid of the smell is whisky. Fancy one?'

Collard had nothing else to do.

'I spoke to one man who had privately

managed to beat the embargo on viewing the dead to see his daughter, only to be man-handled out of the rink by the police afterwards.'

Evelyn thought such aggression would become symptomatic of the investigation.

'Once it becomes clear things might drag on for years, hostility will become a feature of the authorities' behaviour.'

'Years!' Collard said. 'You said they know who did it.'

'Knowing's not proving.' Evelyn reached for another cigarette and knocked over his drink. He made no effort to retrieve it, staring at it listlessly. Collard got a cloth from behind the bar and mopped it up.

'Are you all right?'

'Never better.'

'You look out of sorts.'

'Nothing that a pipe of opium and a couple of Manila whores wouldn't cure. The dead will not be answered. That bomb changed everything. It was a defining moment, like the assassination of the archduke in Sarajevo in 1914, or the liberation of Dachau, or the dropping of the atom bomb. The tectonic plates of history shifted, as they did here.'

It would be a symptom of this new age that people and things and witnesses would be paraded before the world, would be told this was how it happened, and guilty men and culpable countries would be served up for its hostile delectation, but truth would be the first victim of the explosion.

'You may think you know the answer, but you don't,' Evelyn said. 'Mark my words.'

★ ★ ★

By the time the Prime Minister and her retinue attended the memorial service the public mask of grief was in place. She listened to the intonations with a grave expression and a cocked ear, reminiscent of the hard of hearing. Her husband had replaced his usual grin. The Prime Minister's immediate circle was all men, clearly in thrall. Before the service, Evelyn had said it was a pretty good turnout in terms of seniority. Collard encountered him outside, almost unrecognizable in a dark suit and tie, his unruly hair slicked down. Stack was back at his side, smart in a black suit. Charlotte hung back, reluctant to be introduced. Collard wanted nothing more than to sit down with the three of them and discuss the absurdity of Sheehan's insinuations.

Charlotte and Collard sat among the mourners. The American Ambassador read of Christ's raising Lazarus from the dead. Collard felt like an impostor. He spent the service alternating between thinking about Nick, wherever he might be, offering clumsy prayers for his safe return, and discomfort at attending what could have been his own memorial service.

The mysterious Americans from the first wave of the investigation were conspicuous by their absence. Given the number of senior officials, there was a heavy security presence: bulky men, awkward in suits, distinguished by their faraway look as they scanned the crowd.

It was a show of solidarity the British were very good at, Evelyn said afterwards.

'Turn up, hijack the show and make sure no one asks tricky questions.'

Charlotte looked away, angered by his levity.

They were standing outside after the service. The mourners were mainly silent. Some wept. Television commentators intoned in their most serious voices. Evelyn lit up a Silk Cut.

At the memorial tea party, senior civil servants and clergy with suitably grave expressions on their plump, well-barbered faces snaffled the sandwiches. Charlotte and Collard talked to the bereaved. Collard sensed anger replacing the initial shock. The airline was being blamed for lack of security and dragging its heels. Collard overheard someone say a farmer had found a suitcase full of drugs. The authorities denied its existence. How long before Sheehan fed Nick into the rumour mill? Collard wondered. How long before Evelyn and Stack turned on him, sniffing for Nick's story?

He went out for some air.

He thought of what Evelyn had said about the dead, no closer to being properly represented, and of the core of secret activity evident from the start, whether purposeful or panic he had no idea. Something had been going on, a separate investigation — or several — that had nothing to do with the official one. Even now Collard fancied he could recognize harder, grimmer expressions on select faces, reflecting more than tragedy; a failure of security perhaps. That was what they were afraid of. Evelyn was right. No one would satisfy the dead or the grief of the bereaved: so many brutally interrupted lives and the cruel agony of their dispersal.

For the dignitaries, turning up was a matter of show, a mild inconvenience, best represented by the Minister of Transport, who had refused to cancel his Caribbean holiday after the crash. The investigation would become about accumulation. Any proper explanation would be lost in the mess. It was happening, in ways he never could have imagined, with Nick.

A Japanese photographer stuck a camera in his face and took his picture. Collard was aware of Sheehan watching then turning and walking away.

Back inside, he found himself steered into a line of mourners being admitted to the Prime Minister's circle. When they shook hands she seemed to look deep into his eyes while intoning, 'Our deepest sympathies are with you on this saddest of days.'

Collard inspected her for insincerity and found none, even when he saw her eyes were blank and glazed and not focused on him at all.

'Prime Minister,' he said, not knowing how he would continue: either by saying the dead were being failed or his son was maligned by mysterious parties as sinister as the perpetrators of the outrage. Before he got the chance he was taken firmly by the arm and moved on.

Collard saw the security men sizing him up. He wondered if he looked dangerous or about to lose control. He had seen panic flicker in the

Prime Minister's eyes. He thought of all the anger that had coursed through him since the crash. It had returned with the Prime Minister's condolences and he understood how the aggrieved might select her as an outlet for their frustrations. To his shame, he had wanted to hit her because he sensed when it came to answers she was as powerless as he.

Separation

At Charlotte's insistence they walked up to the cairn.

She said, 'We need to talk.'

Her tone was the first sign her preoccupation was about more than Nick. Collard knew, in the stretched seconds before she told him, she would be leaving.

Everything made belated sense, from her physical awkwardness to her decision to go off, which he had misread as part of his failure to cope. She was half-gone already. Part of him felt inured, cauterized by the events of the last days. However angry he might feel — which was different from being hurt — he resolved to be reasonable. Part of him wondered, absurdly, how they would spend the rest of the day.

He felt bound to say he didn't see how she could walk out of his life like that.

He asked the usual questions, knowing what the answers would be. Yes, it was serious. No, she hadn't been looking for an affair. He said he didn't want to know about the man or who he was. 'Why are you telling me now?'

She didn't want her mourning to be overshadowed by a lie.

He wanted to yell Sheehan's accusations at her, to show how much more complicated everything was than she believed.

'Would you have told me anyway?'

There was no dignified way to conduct the conversation. Deep down, he had been expecting the worst since she went to New York. More than once he had resisted a pre-emptive strike with an affair of his own. He had resented her independence.

Down the hill he could see the red hire car; otherwise the only other sign of life was a yellow dump truck making its way to the horizon. He couldn't think of anything smart, understanding or vicious to say. He couldn't decide whether Charlotte's decision involved a moral courage or she was hiding behind Nick. The speed at which everything had unravelled alarmed him. He half-expected to see the debris of their marriage strewn across the landscape like the crash.

She said, 'I'm going to walk back.'

He stepped away to avoid kissing her.

'You're wrong about Nick. You'll have to tell him, you know.'

He remained after she had gone. The cairn they had built for Nick seemed pointless. She was wrong. There was no death to commemorate. He kicked the stones to pieces.

The Frame

Charlotte was gone when he got back to the hotel. Collard checked out although it meant paying for an extra night and he had nowhere to stay. The phone in the room rang before he could leave. He thought it would be Charlotte, stepping back, but it was Sheehan ordering him in.

'I'm busy.'

'It's about your son.'

'Have you found him?'

Collard held his breath. Sheehan's answer was negative. He wanted to tell Sheehan to fuck off. He wanted to get away.

Sheehan was waiting in the small interview room they had used before. He lit a panatella, which stank. He insisted on going over Nick's ticket arrangements.

'Who paid for the ticket?'

'I did.'

'Bought it personally or wired the money?'

'There was a pre-paid ticket I bought by credit card over the phone, waiting at the collection desk. Nick would have changed it when he rebooked.'

'Why did he rebook?'

'He said he was going to be late getting to Frankfurt.'

'What was his reason?'

'He didn't say.'

83

'You didn't think to ask?'

'He had already done it. I didn't want to be a bore about it.'

'He just told you he had changed the date. He didn't talk about it first?'

'He called and wanted to know if I could still travel with him.'

'When was that?'

'On the twelfth.'

'None of this seemed odd?'

'What is this about?'

'Did you see him collect the ticket?'

Collard shook his head.

'He cashed it in,' said Sheehan.

Collard's elation returned.

'This is not necessarily good news.' Collard saw then that Sheehan had brought him there to knock him down. 'Your son wasn't listed with the regular passengers because he was travelling as a courier. He was under the name of the company he was delivering for.'

Collard didn't understand.

'Your son cashed in his ticket so he came out ahead and arranged to deliver for the courier company.'

'He could have asked me for the money.' He stopped. 'Don't tell me he was on the plane after all.'

'Not necessarily. How well do you know your son?'

Collard was haunted by the sarcasm of the question.

Did Nick take drugs? Sheehan wanted to know. Collard refused to defend Nick against such a speculative accusation.

Sheehan relented, saying as a parent he knew how painful it was to discuss this sort of thing. But a lot could happen in three months, to someone young and impressionable.

'Of course, he was supposed to have been coming back with you, which would look less suspicious than a backpacking teenager.'

Collard protested. Sheehan ignored him and produced a garish postcard with a 3D picture that alternated between a nude and the Virgin Mary.

Collard slowly turned it over and saw their London address and Nick's name. The message was typed and read: *My dear friend Nick, I am sending you good wishes and hope we will see each other before maybe you get this, your very good friend Khaled.*

The card had been stamped in Cyprus and franked on November 5, 1988.

'How did you get this?'

'From your house. Search warrant.'

It was a sign of how serious Sheehan was. Collard stared at the card and asked, 'Do you know anyone who types postcards?'

'Khaled is at the centre of our investigation.'

Everything until that moment had seemed like something Collard could argue Nick out of. Previously he had not let himself think that Sheehan had a case.

'How did your son finance his trip?'

'He worked weekends in a restaurant and I gave him a hand.'

'Two thousand pounds' worth of hand?'

'I gave him a couple of hundred pounds twice, maybe five hundred altogether.'

Sheehan reached into his pocket and passed Collard a copy of Nick's bank statement.

It showed several deposits, fewer withdrawals because Collard had persuaded Nick to take travellers' cheques. Collard recognized his two payments of two hundred and fifty pounds. Up to August, deposits were small and frequent, reflecting Nick's wages.

In November there had been a big jump, with over two thousand pounds paid in. In the first week of December there was another deposit for the same amount. There was no legitimate source for sums like that in such a short time.

The last deposit was for seventeen hundred pounds made on December 23, two days after the crash.

The same amount had been withdrawn the day Sheehan told Collard that Nick wasn't on the passenger list.

The payments into the account had been drawn against cheques issued by a company named Bar-L Export from an account in Antigua. Nick's withdrawal had been made at the BCCI branch in Sloane Street, meaning he had been in London and perhaps still was, hiding somewhere. Collard's certainty returned.

'What are you accusing him of?'

'The bombers took advantage of dope smugglers. I'm sure you've heard about the suitcase full of heroin they found at the crash site.'

86

'Are you saying my son and Khaled were smuggling drugs?'

'I know how tough this is for you.'

'I thought the drugs business was cash only. Since when did they sign cheques?'

'When they want to launder money so your son can appear on a set of books, paid for some unperformed task.'

Nick had been in London and hadn't got in touch, which meant he hadn't wanted to, which gave credence to Sheehan's theory. Collard found himself not wanting to know. It was the last thing he would have associated Nick with.

Bank statements didn't lie. The latest withdrawal was proof that Nick was alive, not the kind Collard would have liked, but proof nonetheless. If that that was the price of Nick's survival, so be it.

Collard wondered how he'd feel if Nick really had been involved with Khaled and used him as Sheehan insisted, giving the boy the bomb to carry. What if the old man's warning had been Nick's way of getting him off the flight? And who on earth was the old man anyway, given his apparent connection to his former school, of all places?

'This is nonsense. You're just looking to blame Nick. This is all speculation.'

'Prove me wrong.'

He felt Sheehan's power, testing as he went along, improvising like a skilled musician.

Summoning his last reserves, Collard said, 'You are deliberately trying to undermine everything I believe about my son.'

'Mr Collard, you are in denial.'

Something so quick and offhand about Sheehan's response made it seem almost reckless, almost as though he needed Nick to be guilty.

'Did your boy ever mention Quinn?'

'Who's Quinn?'

Sheehan produced a photograph of a busy café somewhere sunny that looked like it had been taken from a car across the street. Nick was sitting at a pavement table. He was wearing dark glasses and a loose shirt, and leaning back in his chair, his expression unreadable. Seated at the same table was an older man, very thin, with a wolfish face and a white crew cut. He didn't look obviously American, though Collard was sure he was. Despite his casual clothes, the man had a hard professional air about him.

'Is that Quinn?'

'Do you recognize him?'

'Of course not. Where was this taken?' Collard was still thrown by the unexpected picture of Nick, looking mysterious and not the boy he remembered.

'Cyprus. Among those dead on the flight were three American secret agents.'

'Was Quinn one of them?'

'He was the fourth member of the team. He didn't fly.'

'Where is he now?'

'That's what I'd like to know.'

'What was he doing talking to Nick?'

'Same answer as the last question. Did your son ever mention anyone called Barry?'

'Barry?'

'Colonel Charles 'Chuck' Barry.'

''Chuck' Barry? No. Was Barry one of the ones on the plane?'

Sheehan didn't answer. Collard thought again of the three men he'd seen at Frankfurt airport, including the tall man.

'I badly need to speak to your boy, Mr Collard. On the one hand, I've got him connected to the main suspect and not getting on the flight. On the other, here he is seen in the company of an American secret agent who was part of the team that was perhaps the reason the plane was bombed.'

'Are you telling me there was a motive when everyone is saying it was a random act of terrorism?'

'Both. Colonel Barry's was an anti-terrorist unit, gathering information on the main suspect for the bombing.'

Collard remembered Stack saying she was trying to track down a Syrian arms dealer.

'Nazir al-Badawi. If anyone was using your son it was almost certainly his people. The question is did they use him to get at Barry and his team?'

'Are the police looking for Nick?'

Sheehan gave an unexpected laugh that bounced round the room.

'I'm sure plenty of people are looking for your boy. The police are the least of his worries. Your son contacts you or you find him call one of these numbers.'

He wrote them on the copy of Nick's bank statement. 'Be sure you stay in touch. Where are you going to be?'

Collard said he was going home to London.

* * *

Before leaving he returned to where he had been that afternoon. There was enough of a moon to see by as he walked up the hill. He wondered where Charlotte and Nick were now. He would prove Sheehan wrong about Nick. Slowly he reassembled the cairn he had destroyed, thinking of everything that had been taken away.

Departures

Angleton awaited his call, checking the departure boards for a flight as yet unscheduled, as much of his life had been.

The CIA in the 1950s had been a dull organization but what opportunities for deviancy! Washington had been a dreary company town on a par with Hollywood when he arrived. He grew familiar with its structures and created his own shadow versions.

The list of the dead in his life: too many he had known about at the time, and too many more he had never heard of. He appreciated the full extent of the wilderness of mirrors; saw himself drunk again, dancing solo to early Presley records (true) at one of those interminable dinner parties that threatened to topple into alcoholic and extramarital disgrace. The wife of a friend had called him a lonely dancer.

The small moves: another pack of Virginia Slims, equalling 21,900 a year at 60 a day, equalling how many million in a lifetime, give or take (cough cough, no regrets)?

Drawly Brits had been his undoing. That shit Greene sending a postcard of Haiti stamped in London: *Did you know CIA doctor Louis J. West who treated Jack Ruby performed LSD experiments on an elephant and was doctor to Aldous Huxley, died 22 November 1963? Poor Aldous, always a literary reputation in eclipse, pushed off the front pages by an Irish-American upstart. Shall we talk about who whacked Jack? Do let's.*

★ ★ ★

Now he could feel nostalgic about all those back-channel deals that had tested the nerves so hard.

O ye seekers of truth, there is no holy grail waiting, just some shat-on pot — oh, that! — amounting to nothing compared to all the confabulations and the juice that went into the stories surrounding it, all those gunmen on grassy knolls. Integral to the theory is the fact it all stops making sense at some point. Shuffle the pack and after the seventh or eighth time none of it adds up, however much it appears to.

He revisited the last crisis of his life before his final illness when he had gone and sat by the river, barely bothering with the fish, and reran old movies in his head: *The Killers* with Lee Marvin, one of the leg-breakers of cinema (terrorizing a blind woman), shot for real in the ass as a young Marine. Marvin's violence in that film reminded Angleton what he had sanctioned and not been witness to. So little he had seen.

★ ★ ★

The departure board did its jig: so many destinations, so many being called. This time his name would come up.

This is good, he thought: the spook's spook

92

back in action, the return of the old pistolero — whose father had ridden into Mexico with General Pershing in pursuit of Pancho Villa (and returned with an eighteen-year-old bride, his mother) — loosest of cannons.

This is really good, he thought, watching the board turn over.

Detour

Collard was stopped by police on the M6, past Charnock Richard service station. When he saw the flashing blue light he thought it was Sheehan wanting him back.

They had clocked him doing 95 mph. Earlier he had noted 105 on the speedometer. He had been driving in the dark at the limit of his skill and concentration, knowing it would take only a tweak of the wheel to send him smashing into the concrete pillar of a bridge.

He stood on the hard shoulder in spitting rain, buffeted by the slipstream of the big trucks, waiting for his breathalyser to show negative. He had heard when the police issued tickets they awarded themselves league points based on snooker scores, which was why more red cars got booked. The hire car was red so he was surprised they let him go with a caution.

He drove on, chastened, relieved to be away but fearful for the future. Either Nick had been involved with the Lebanese student Khaled, as Sheehan suggested, or someone wanted it to appear that way. He found he had to accept that Nick might have got himself caught up in a smuggling operation, for the romance of it, or the danger, or the money, and then fallen under the shadow of the bomb plot. But he had no idea how these things worked or what Nick's role would have been or how drugs got swapped for bombs or why Nick thought he could have got away with it, let alone accept a cheque for the job.

He had spoken to Stack before leaving. Evelyn was resting upstairs and she was worried. He was complaining of headaches and chest pains. They shared a gloomy drink. Stack's German trip had not gone well.

'You follow a trail and it makes sense but it ends. Then there's another trail but you have no idea if it connects. It's like getting lost in the woods.'

As for Khaled, reporters had been talking to the boy's relations. His immediate family were refugees from the civil conflict in Lebanon who like many of their people had resettled around Detroit.

'His father trained as a lawyer but now is part of a monopoly of local families that run the gas stations.'

Collard tried to picture Nick being introduced to Khaled in a bar or a nightclub. They were around the same age. Nick on his travels would have been open to meeting new people.

'Are people still saying Khaled was a drug smuggler who got used by the bombers?' he asked.

'Historically, Khaled's family come from one of the country's leading drug clans. In the 1920s his forefathers struck a deal with the American gangster Lucky Luciano to set up the first Lebanese connection to supply heroin. Today, the family is split between the Westernized pro-American side and fundamentalists involved in the Syrian-controlled heroin trade.'

'Fundamentalists run the heroin trade?' Collard wasn't sure he had heard right.

Stack nodded. 'Syria supports the regime in Iran and sponsors terrorists, including the Palestinians. The drugs are the economic base for that. The poppy crop is grown under army supervision.'

'If the fundamentalists control the drug trade does that mean Khaled was working for them?'

'Maybe indirectly, but I can't see it. He was into fast cars, girls and bodybuilding. 'Like the rest of us,' Evelyn said.'

'So the people who control the drugs were responsible for the bomb.'

'That's the theory.'

'Is your Syrian arms dealer called Nazir?'

Stack looked surprised. 'Yes. You seem up to the minute. He's issuing denials through third parties but in terms of profile he pushes all the buttons.'

Collard wondered what distance separated Nazir from Nick, and how two people from such different backgrounds might conceivably be thrown together.

He wanted to know more but said goodbye instead, wondering how much Stack knew about Nick.

★　★　★

The road emptied after midnight, apart from long-distance haulage. A white Mercedes played tag, overtaking and being overtaken, until it

96

exited north of Birmingham. He tried the radio for company, found nothing and switched it off.

At Birmingham he missed his turn in the tangle of Spaghetti Junction. At school there had been an expression, 'accidentally on purpose', and now he found himself driving in the direction of Malvern, wondering whether it was possible that the old man, who had recognized Collard's tie and been able to quote its motto, had been educated there too.

Collard had nothing to go home to and being the weekend would make it worse. There was his life before December 21, 1988, the black hole of Scotland, and now the certainty that his old life was gone for ever.

At the next service station the forecourt smell of gasoline brought back memories of the crash zone. In the mostly deserted cafeteria he sat under garish strip lights, nursed inadequate coffees and failed to eat a greasy egg while watching the nocturnal drifters, wondering if they didn't all belong with the living dead.

At Worcester South he left the motorway and followed signs to Malvern, seeing again the familiar hills, a giant slumbering hog's back, out of place in the surrounding levels.

Malvern was an old spa, Victorian colonial wealth long gone, large villas wedged into the steep sides of the hills, feats of solid construction from a more expansive age, now a town of too many schools. The Boy's College was neo-Gothic, festooned with gryphons, set round a showpiece cricket ground with an extravagant pavilion reminiscent of the Raj. Buildings once huge now looked small. At what point had he forgotten about the gryphons, once such a permanent feature of those years? Collard had liked his time there — the security of institution, the regulations of a daily timetable — and been happy to identify, with pleasant memories of damp winter afternoons after games, slouched against hot classroom radiators.

An ancient classics master who had gone to school there himself dealt with his enquiry. The man had no memory of having taught him in his first year and Collard in turn had forgotten the master's name. Was it Holly? The name wasn't offered, nor was a handshake, and Collard recalled the paralysing shyness that had reduced Latin classes to a whispered monotone. The man smelled of chalk dust and pipe tobacco, as redolent of the school as corridor floor polish and the thin, bitter stink of damp games clothes in changing rooms.

They sat in a panelled study, untouched in decades. No refreshment was offered.

He explained he wanted to identify an old boy from before the war, an American probably there in the 1930s. He suspected there had been very few Americans in the school. He could remember none in his time.

They started with photographs of chapel prefects from 1930. They reached 1936 when the old master drew his attention to a tall boy standing in the middle of the back row, an American who had been in Number Two House, as had Collard.

It was impossible to tell much from the sepia

98

group portrait of half a dozen young men formally dressed to look older. The prefects weren't named. The most he could say was the tall, handsome youth in the photograph was darker and more romantic than the grey-faced man at the airport.

'Who was he?'

'Angleton. His family lived in Italy. He was below me but I remember he was known as the Yank.'

Is this the moment of revelation? wondered Collard. He was embarrassed he couldn't remember the master's name. Insulated by school life, the man had barely aged. Hair, now white, still fell in a boyish fringe.

He looked at Angleton again, annoyed not to be more certain. The photograph was elaborately produced, typical of its type, with the name of the studio printed at the bottom. Underneath the handlettered 'Prefects 1936' lay a stamped engraving of the school shield, which intruded into the space of the photograph, stopping above young Angleton's head. Beneath the shield on a furled banner was the school motto, the words spoken to him at Frankfurt airport: *Sapiens qui prospicit.*

It was uncanny, this bizarre confirmation of their unlikely connection. Collard accepted the careful placing of the motto above Angleton's head as a sign this was his man. But who was Angleton?

The clock struck and Collard was taken back: in term time the bell would be ringing for the end of the first morning class, with the noise of scraping desks, the swell of chatter after the silence of the lesson, and the sound of feet everywhere. He supposed nothing had changed. The routine would be the same, with all the familiar noises that made up the regulated day. Things probably hadn't sounded any different in 1936 when Angleton had been there.

The past overwhelmed Collard and old habits of deference blunted his curiosity. He half-expected to walk out of the room and find himself eighteen again, his life before him, and mysteriously armed with some piece of arcane knowledge to keep Nick from future harm.

Collard stared at the old school photographs that seemed so of their moment: nameless faces and the expectation of privilege. Somewhere in these albums he would come across a record of his own boyhood progress, marked by images of a younger self who might now be as unrecognizable as the young Angleton. The sun came out and warmed the room slightly. The old master was too timid to end the meeting or show interest in Collard's quest, and Collard felt himself reclaimed by a particular kind of institutional listlessness he hadn't experienced since, paralysing his earlier resolve. He wanted only to stay there, tracing the lives of those forgotten boys. His insignificance was brought home: what did any of it matter?

The master stood up and adopted a pose that Collard had forgotten: head cocked to one side, dry-washing his hands which were clasped in front of his flies in a way that used to make them snigger.

'Do you know what happened to Angleton?'

Collard still couldn't get used to addressing the man as an equal.

'Yes, as a matter of fact. He went on to become quite a famous spy.'

There was a gleam of private amusement in his eye. Collard wondered whether he hadn't been stringing him along from the start. He probably knew exactly who he was after.

Collard experienced the quickening he had been hoping for, fear and excitement.

The old master said, 'He'll be in the Red Book.'

The Red Book gave old boys' details. It had been last updated in 1977, and Collard found James Angleton listed as a third-term entrant for 1933, born 1917, which made him seventy. If anything, the man he had seen looked older. Collard was puzzled by the man's middle name — Jesus — so unlikely for an American. Angleton had been a house prefect, then went to Yale University where he played soccer. In the war he rose to Major in something called OSS and received the US Legion of Merit and French equivalent. Of his main career, it only remarked, cryptically, Chief, Counter-intelligence, 54–74. Distinguished Intelligence Medal. He was also listed as Chairman, Security & Intelligence Fund and the author of *Essays by American Cause*. Married with a son and two daughters. The most useful information was an address: 4814 N 33rd Rd, Arlington, Va 22207.

As Collard wrote down Angleton's address,

the master said, 'Arlington would mean that he was CIA.'

Collard looked up in surprise. The old master was not the fool they had all taken him for. He had watched them with a contempt that more than matched theirs, and he remembered Collard perfectly well, disliked him still and had surrendered this last piece of information only to make that clear.

★ ★ ★

On his way back to the car, Collard ran into another master called Manners, who, after some peering, recognized him. Bald-headed Manners with his high colouring and wire-framed spectacles was exactly as Collard remembered.

He learned from Manners that Angleton had returned to the school as little as three years earlier, on his way to Wales to fish the River Usk at a hotel where Manners was a regular guest.

Manners' description of Angleton matched the man at Frankfurt airport. Collard's lethargy fell away, followed by a sense of something deeper and preordained.

'Is it true he was a spy?'

Manners shook his bald dome with a vigorous swivelling familiar from his lessons. 'We only talked about fishing. He was certainly familiar with Vaughan's poem about fishing on the Usk because he quoted it. I'm sure you know it. *The weir is the world; the salmon, man; and the feather, deceit.*'

Collard thought of Nick and the lure of deceit

102

and wondered if that was Angleton's world.

Manners, always the teacher, said, 'Henry Vaughan, and to give the poem its full title: 'A Latin Sonnet to his Friend Thomas Powell, Doctor of Divinity, of Canref to Accompany the Gift of a Salmon'. The owner of the hotel is a splendid woman named Valerie Traherne. Perhaps she can help you with what you need and do pass on my regards.'

Manners sounded strangely smitten.

★   ★   ★

Collard found the motorway beyond the Severn at Upton and drove for an hour, past Bristol, and crossed over the suspension bridge at Aust.

In Wales a bad rainstorm closed in until he was aware only of the elements and the overheated capsule of the car. When the dual carriageway stopped his progress became erratic, slowed by a succession of towns, traffic and rain that eased briefly to reveal a mountainous, dramatic landscape. He found the turning after Crickhowell where Manners had said. It gave on to a poor road running up the side of a hill through dense woods. Collard followed it for a mile. The rain started again. It fell so hard he had trouble seeing with the wipers grinding away on full. The headlights were little more than a watery diffusion. It was so dark it might as well have been night.

The Gray Ghost Watched

Angleton saw himself: an old man fishing on the Usk on a fine, cool day in March 1986 with high broken cloud and a north-east wind. There had been a short rise at midday and he used a dark olive fly.

His hotel sat handsome on the side of a hill behind him, above the river valley, with splendid views of the kind favoured by eighteenth-century landscape painters.

He dressed for dinner as required. The other diners were elderly and, like him, retired. He was courteous without being forthcoming. Since his arrival he had been drinking again.

He looked like a former professor or a funeral director rather than a man who had a body-count going back forty years, and had dined with criminal masterminds and black-mailed the highest in his land.

After dinner he chuckled his way through a rerun of Hemingway's *The Killers* on TV in which Ronald Reagan, in his last screen role, wore a brown suit and played the heavy until shot by Lee Marvin, his flinch an exact rehearsal of the real thing at the hands of John Hinkley; always the actor, Reagan. Hinkley's shooting had left him aged and confused, for all the autocue bravura of 'Honey, I forgot to duck!'

Angleton went to bed too drunk to read. Light-blue pyjamas, white piping; teeth cleaned more carefully than usual, because drunk; last cigarette. He kept his glasses on until in bed, knowing he looked lost without them. Pointless vanity. He said goodnight to his family aloud.

The Hotel Register

The hotel reminded Collard of a big Italianate country house, once grand, now faded, but still well appointed and reliant on the loyalty of a regular band of ageing guests.

Judging from her brisk landowner's accent and sensible tweed jacket, he was signed in by Valerie Traherne herself, a handsome, fit-looking woman in her fifties wearing boots and jodhpurs that made it easy to see why Manners was affected.

She asked if it was his first time and how long he would stay. A couple of days, Collard said, glad not to face his empty house, full of Nick's things and his absence.

'Take room number one. Nobody else is here at the moment.'

He signed the register, giving his London address.

She handed him a heavy key with a large wooden tag.

He said he was trying to trace an American who had stayed at the hotel three years before.

'We get Americans all the time for the fishing.'

'His name was Angleton.'

She looked doubtful. 'It's an uncommon name and I'm sure I would remember. I know most of our guests.'

'He was here to fish. He came in March three years ago.'

'The season only starts in March. The Americans normally come later.'

He checked into his room. When he came downstairs there was no sign of Valerie Traherne. He took the hotel register, hoping she wouldn't mind, and went and sat in a bar decorated with fishing memorabilia and threatening photographs of the Usk in turbulent flood. The red leather-bound register was so large he had to prop it on his knees.

Collard found no Angleton listed for March 1986. He checked the whole of that year then went through all the March registrations before and after and ended up going through all the names in the book, annoyed at getting excited for nothing.

He replaced the register on the reception desk. In a large drawing room off the hall a fire had been lit. There was a table with a stack of leather volumes whose wide, rectangular shape reminded him of score books for school cricket matches. It was too hilly for cricket. They were the hotel's fishing diaries, recording visitors' catches.

He listened to Valerie Traherne's heels on the parquet as she crossed the hall. She had changed into a skirt and low heels. She asked if supper at seven thirty was all right by him.

'As it's just you, I'll serve it in front of the fire in here rather than have to heat the dining room.'

She was gone as briskly as she had arrived.

Collard turned to the diaries. Under March 1986 he found a sequence of entries in the same spidery, educated hand. The first listed fine, cool weather, with a north-east wind and a short rise between 12.30 and 1.00. A dark olive fly had been used and nothing caught. Each entry was signed J. Troughton. Collard smiled at the pun in the name, thinking the man had had little choice in his hobby.

He got up and walked to the window. Darkness was falling. The rain had stopped and a low mist was rising in the valley. He opened the tall window. He could hear the river in angry race. Had Angleton stood in the room he was now in? Angleton was intimate with the dormitories and classrooms Collard had lived in for five years. Angleton had talked to Nick. Collard experienced the uncanny feeling that he was chasing his own past as much as Angleton.

He went back to the diaries. The weather pattern and time of the rise had continued for several days, with Troughton alternating the dark olive fly with a pheasant tail, without success. Low pressure and a March brown fly had brought a 3lb 6oz trout. After that the catch improved. Troughton's entries covered ten days. He was the only angler. There were no other recordings.

If Manners was right about the date and Angleton had been there to fish then Collard ought to be looking at Angleton's record. Angleton; Troughton. Fishermen.

★　★　★

The empty hotel unsettled him after Scotland. He didn't feel like eating alone and when Valerie

108

Traherne served him he asked on impulse if she wanted to join him.

She looked taken aback then said, 'Why not? There's no point in standing on formality.'

They ate plain food well cooked by her, a beef stew with carrots and fennel. There was no sign of staff. She said she managed by herself between the New Year and the end of February, and kept the place open only because she lived there.

She was a good conversationalist, sticking to generalities of weather, the locality and her dislike of individual packs of butter that most hotels served. She seemed to sense he wanted distracting.

Collard struggled to finish his food, not because he didn't like it. He left his wine untouched.

Valerie Traherne put her knife and fork down. Collard was aware of her studying him.

'It is an hotelier's job to observe and never comment on the guests, so please excuse me if I ask what has happened to you.'

'I don't know,' he said. 'My life was quite ordinary and now it's not.'

He told her from the beginning.

Afterwards she said, 'Come with me. There's something you should see.'

She led the way upstairs to a back landing decorated with hunting trophies, then stopped in front of a small and unspectacular fish in a glass case.

'Not impressive in itself, but its uniqueness depends on rarity not size. It comes from an obscure breed known as the red-eyed trout, found in certain Welsh rivers but never the Usk until this catch, with none caught since. It's a one-off.'

Under the trout an engraved plate named the angler and donor: J. Angleton.

'Troughton was Angleton.'

'Yes.' She laughed. 'I teased him about it later, asking him why he hadn't just called himself Mr Fish.'

'Did he give a reason for not using his real name?'

'I think it gave him a childish pleasure. I also think he was sentimental about the trout. Later on he sent some money to have the original plate changed to Angleton, and he asked me to hang it out of the way and not mention the matter to anyone. And until you came that's what I did. If he was trying to tell you something perhaps he still is and I see no reason to stand in the way. Would you like to see the photograph of the catch?'

What's My Line?

Wales, March 1986: sleepless as always, Angleton flicked through different channels in his head, replayed the last episode of the US edition of *What's My Line?* in 1965, with the popular reporter Dorothy Kilgallen. Kilgallen had interviewed a British cabinet minister in the 1950s, confirming the existence of aliens. She had interviewed Marilyn Monroe the day before she died. Jack Ruby, Lee Harvey Oswald's killer, had given her an exclusive from his prison cell because he was a fan of her show. Monroe, Ruby and Kilgallen (suddenly and unexpected) all dead; Oswald too (with reason).

Angleton knew a lot (knew too much).

He knew the invisible links that connected the political and criminal family trees of sixty years, with show business the go-between. He knew about the brown-bag money ($2 million) that the old Jewish gangster Meyer Lansky delivered to Harry Truman's 1948 election train, Truman's price for supporting the founding of the State of Israel. Lansky was to organized crime what he himself had been to counter-intelligence; two men who shouldn't have been in the same room. He knew about the tax-shelter earnings invested by future CIA chief Allen Dulles in the Third Reich. He knew about Dulles ghosting Nazi and Croatian war criminals out of Europe, many of them future big contributors to Dick Nixon's successful 1968 presidential campaign. He knew about the $30 million distributed from Washington (also by Allen Dulles, on sabbatical from Cromwell & Sullivan) through the Vatican in black (rather than brown) bags, to prevent the 1948 election going to the communists. He knew about the weapons inspectors sent to Israel by President John F. Kennedy in 1963. He knew about Marilyn Monroe's wiretap the year before. The report dated the day before she died noted a conversation between Monroe and Dorothy Kilgallen regarding the Roswell UFO crash of 1947 and Kennedy's politically motivated NASA Apollo moon programme. Hah!

He knew about the pro-forma invoice from an Austrian arms manufacturer, dated March 24, 1984; knew the illegal end-user was Iran when the certificates said otherwise; knew the deal was negotiated between a British mercenary working for the CIA and a Syrian arms dealer with Iranian connections; knew the order placed with Hirtenberger was for $40 million.

Forty mill was a lot of cut.

He bet Slobbery Bill Casey was getting his; Bill, once the helping hand to Croatia's war criminals all those years ago, now head of CIA and cosy with the White House.

Wales would be Bill's comeuppance. Bill Casey not knowing anything of what was going to come down on his dandruffed head. Slobbery Bill left looking an idiot for not knowing. Angleton reflected on the sweetness Casey's humiliation would bring. Angleton, disgraced spy, restored to glory and that messy eater Bill left with a lot of metaphorical egg on his face, the errant pupil taught a lesson by his old master. Angleton would laugh that cartoon laugh he saved for the bathroom mirror: heh heh!

The wilderness of mirrors would become a hall of mirrors, each offering a perfect reflection of a lifetime's career that would finally make sense.

He awaited only the arrival of his guests. They would drink the finest wines Valerie Traherne could provide. The menu would reflect the momentousness of the occasion. A rib of the rarest roast beef. To finish, the most extravagant cheeses and port more delicious for its hint of closure. The boat was coming in and wrongs of a lifetime would be put right. The return of the prodigal son as guest of honour, and Angleton's great, final vindication. The Western world would be rocked to its foundations. Angleton waited for the banquet to be served.

Goodnight, Bill.

The Check-ins

The photograph of the catch was in the drawing room in an album kept for guests who sent souvenirs of their stays.

Collard's first surprise was that it wasn't only Angleton in the picture. The names were listed underneath: Messrs Scobie, Troughton and Furse record a catch.

He was disappointed the photographer had done such a poor job, framing them with too much river in the background and revealing little of their faces, which were further obscured by hats. Angleton was dressed in waders and fishing gear, caught trout in one hand, rod in the other, the top half of his face hidden in the shadow of his tweed fishing hat.

Scobie stood tallest, to Angleton's right. He wore a white raincoat that was out of place in the rural surroundings. A rakishly angled trilby obscured his face.

Furse looked short and tatty, comic by comparison with scraggy beard, flat cap and an old sheepskin coat.

'Mr Furse seems not unfamiliar, if you know what I mean,' said Valerie Traherne, 'and Mr Scobie even more so.'

They looked like men who usually avoided having their picture taken.

Valerie Traherne carefully picked the

photograph loose from its mounts with her nail and asked only that he return it.

★ ★ ★

According to the register, Troughton stayed for ten days in March 1986. The handwriting in the register matched the diary. The address was Angleton's: 4814 N 33rd Rd, Arlington, Va 22207. Collard had missed it the first time.

★ ★ ★

'Were Scobie and Furse with him the whole time?'

'Mr Scobie came and went a couple of times. Mr Furse only came at the end.'

'Were they old friends?'

Valerie Traherne cocked her head. 'Not exactly, though my impression was they had all known each other a long time. For Angleton it was a big event. We do a lot of wedding receptions and he reminded me of a nervous father making preparations for a wedding. Everything had to be just right.'

'What were they celebrating?'

'He never said. Whatever it was made him very excited, although he tried to hide it. Sometimes I would find him sitting alone in here almost hugging himself with glee.'

They were sitting by the fire in the room where they had eaten. Valerie Traherne pointed out Angleton's usual armchair in the far corner.

'Once we were discussing how hard it was to

115

make ends meet running this place and he said not to worry, soon it would be a source of pilgrimage.'

'Why would that be?'

'He didn't say, and I didn't ask. Angleton wasn't one for explaining anything. He hated questions.'

'What was Scobie like?'

'Tall, a dry-Martini man, older than Angleton but still with an eye for the female staff. He seemed awfully familiar. He looked like someone who might have been in those old black-and-white Maigret shows on the BBC.'

She consulted the register. Scobie's address was care of the Travellers' Club in Pall Mall.

'Yes, he travelled. Expensive luggage, at any rate. My impression was he and Angleton disliked each other. Scobie seemed to want to cultivate a sinister aura. He was magnificently offhand and always complained about the smallest things: one night because there was ice in his drink; the next because there wasn't.'

Mr Donald Furse gave his address as Leylands, Crowborough, Sussex. He arrived last and stayed two nights.

'Again, quite a familiar sort, fitted in well,' said Valerie Traherne. 'Very detached, rather chatty and the most English. He stuttered, which always makes me feel protective. He looked at everything askance, like it was a source of huge private amusement. Reminded me of uncles who had spent years in the colonies — fond of his sports pages and smoked a pipe, said he was fed up with Murdoch for ruining *The Times*.'

'Were they all the same age?'

'Thereabouts.'

Collard wondered if he had stumbled across nothing more sinister than an old boys' reunion. He asked Valerie Traherne if that was likely.

'Up to a point, but it all seemed to go terribly wrong.'

'They fell out.'

'No. Something happened before Mr Scobie and Furse turned up that made Angleton very distressed.'

The Worm of Uncertainty

Angleton's Welsh reading included Ambler's *A Coffin for Demetrios*, under its English title, *The Mask of Demitrios*, *The Aleph* by Borges, Greene's *Our Man in Havana*, and *The Daughter of Time* by Josephine Tey, all bought second hand from Priory Books in Malvern. He read thrillers for escapism. None got close to the intense molecular activity involving the Vatican, US intelligence, Nazis and the Israelis circa 1945. He looked in vain for an amoral diagnostician to guide him through the labyrinth; his own role exactly; looked in vain for stories that got deep inside — Ambler came close, with barely a gun in sight — in which men scared themselves silly by the enormity of what they were doing; stories that understood the ambiguity of isolation; that followed the money; that grasped how the black secrets cast their long shadow on men like him. Ambler would have understood Quinn (who didn't bear thinking about). A nice man, Ambler, married to Joan Harrison, who worked with Hitchcock. Angleton and Hitch dined together occasionally in Washington. Hitch was a fan. Angleton had given him the McGuffin for *North by Northwest*. The ideal McGuffin was the perfect zero: the idea that drove everything and explained nothing. Angleton told Hitch that he and Greene had once invented an agent in Rome who didn't exist. 'Perfect,' said Hitchcock.

Quinn was close to the ideal McGuffin except for one thing. He existed and he was close to explaining everything that could not be revealed, the fattest book imaginable.

★ ★ ★

British television seemed to show little other than old movies, including a job lot of Don Siegel. Angleton the film buff was happy to get drunk and smoke and drift off to Tourneur's *Out of the Past*, with Mitchum, an old favourite, or *The Shootist* (more Siegel) with Big John Wayne in the role that Angleton now reluctantly found himself in, strapping on his guns again for the last time, under the waiting shadow of the Big C, Valerie Traherne his unrequited Betty Bacall.

He liked actors. He identified with them and the need to learn lines and deliver those lines as though saying them for the first and only time. His craft similarly involved a great deal of premeditation and the ability to appear spontaneous. They were both in the business of looking convincing while trying not to appear forewarned.

119

Late Arrivals

Angleton himself, in Valerie Traherne's assessment, was educated, secretive, very much an indoors man apart from his fishing, a constant smoker, two bottles of wine a night at least, and often noisy in his room after midnight. She found him charming but thought he was in the grip of deep psychosis.

'When he got drunk he started moving the furniture around. Certainly the room was quite rearranged by the time he left. Yes, and he insisted on the same place in the dining room. He refused to eat until he got the place he wanted, which meant he had to wait to be served until after Colonel and Mrs Danvers-Rigby had finished and they had to be persuaded to give up their usual table for the rest of their stay.'

'What was so special about his place in the dining room?'

'At first I thought he was making a fuss. Some guests do. Then I learned he was very specific about everything and decided he wanted the table with the best view of the room, and being in the corner meant nobody could pass behind him.'

But Angleton's celebratory mood changed when three men arrived before Scobie and Furse. He became a different man.

'Different how?'

'Scared. Very old and beaten.'

'Did they come to threaten him?'

'No, but they were a rough crowd compared to Mr Scobie and Furse. Perfectly well behaved and polite but they looked like men used to dealing with trouble. One, a Mr Hoover, kept to the background. Mysterious man, accent I couldn't place. He turned up first, after I had gone to bed, wanting a room. I wasn't happy about letting him in. I'd already seen him a couple of times lurking in the valley when I was out riding. I told him he should have phoned but then Mr Angleton came down in his dressing gown and said Hoover was with him.

'Events became very bizarre after that. One night there were gunshots in the valley and a flare went up. Another of the men, Mr Beech, blamed the SAS — they're always prowling around the hills on exercise — but I was never altogether convinced. Mr Angleton was on the terrace that night, well after midnight, looking very blown about. He said he'd dropped his spectacles from the balcony. He was in the room you're in.'

'And who was Beech?'

'He turned up the morning after Hoover, before breakfast. Not our usual kind of guest. He reminded me of the soldiers you come across exercising in the hills. In fact, I wondered at the time if he wasn't SAS himself and had driven over from Hereford. Not a big man, very compact and watchful, plain and plain-spoken, fit and tough but not as fit as he once had been. He liked his beer and couldn't say his rs.'

She picked up the register, leaving Collard to puzzle.

'What they were all running around doing I have no idea. I was surprised Beech and Angleton got on so well because they were so different. Despite being American, Mr Angleton was quite aristocratic, and Mr Beech was what Mrs Thatcher might call Essex Man. But he made Mr Angleton laugh where I suspect few did.

'Oh, yes, they all ran up enormous phone bills — Mr Angleton alone spent hundreds of pounds on long-distance calls from his room, not including the ones made from the public call box down by the bridge. He used that so much it became a local talking point.'

The evenings she was on reception, Valerie Traherne had operated the telephone switchboard and placed calls from Angleton's room to Washington DC, Tel Aviv and Majorca.

'It was all terribly glamorous. Usually if we get asked to ring through to Cheltenham it counts as an event. Our guests are not great telephone users.'

'And the third man who came?'

'Another American. At first I thought he had the same name as that American singer Chuck Berry but it turned out it was Chuck Barry.'

Collard felt like he was standing on a high, precarious ledge looking down into the past in Frankfurt, watching the very tall man named by Sheehan as one of the three secret agents who died in the explosion.

He saw Barry. He saw Nick off in the

122

bookshop talking to Angleton. Angleton and Barry knew each other; the evidence was in front of his eyes, in the register. Yet Angleton had warned Nick not to get on the plane, and let Barry die.

Valerie Traherne's description matched the man he had seen.

It's My Party
(and I'll cry if I want to)

Angleton usually got on with Brits. He enjoyed their prevarication, often mistaken for procrastination, and their self-deprecation, behind which bulged tumescent egos. But God, they could be bad dressers and most had dandruff and halitosis, with an absence of dentistry that made their teeth like something found at a road accident. His dreariest meetings reduced him to his silent mantra: *Compared to you stuffed shirts, I'm as loose as a goose.* (It was an Elvis thing.)

In London he had drunk Bloody Marys, when? He supposed in '85 or '86. Two down, three to go would see him comfortable; downriver, Gravesend and the start of *Heart of Darkness*, waiting for the tide to turn, looking back at the Old City. He was with Beech, who couldn't pwonounce his *rs*. When they got drunk together, whenever they met, he made Beech repeat, 'I'm a wuff diamond,' until they were incapable with laughter. He remembered it was to Beech he had said, 'They're setting up Nazir.'

But Beech should not have been in Wales, or Hoover or Barry. Uninvited guests, all. Catastrophe was too mild a word: set up for the espionage equivalent of the come shot in a porno flick, he had been fucked by Slobbery Bill Casey.

124

Worse he had been fucked by Bill Casey's incompetence. Lesson number one: keep your back channels open. Lesson number two: make whatever sacrifices are necessary, within reason, to keep them open. He had patiently explained all this to the operationally green Casey in the privacy of his conservatory. Casey the flatterer: 'They've given me CIA. I'm just a businessman. Give me the master class, Jim.'

If anyone wanted to ruin his appetite in Wales, and give the sourest taste to the savour, they would have kidnapped Quinn. Which is exactly what happened. It was so perfect, so appropriate that Angleton sometimes wondered in his darkest nights if he wasn't the operation's secret author himself: under the list in his head titled 'My Greatest Fears' the idea of Quinn in enforced conversation with the wrong people was top or thereabouts, along with 'My Role in the Assassination of JFK'. That was how high he rated Quinn. Quinn was wet work. Quinn knew where all the bodies were buried. What Quinn knew could get them all sent to jail for a long long time.

Now Casey had sacrificed Quinn, because he didn't know a castle from a pawn. Quinn in the hands of trained interrogators, Quinn a hostage, Quinn with electrodes attached to his nuts, Quinn spilling the beans: the thought could not even begin to be entertained. If Quinn sang, the whole fucking hymnbook would have to be rewritten. Wales was a bust. Hoover had called late — one of those once-in-a-blue-moon nights when Angleton was in the land of nod dreaming

125

pleasant dreams — with the news that Quinn had been snatched from his Beirut apartment and was in the hands of the swarthy ones, who had extracted a 400-page confession from the last man they talked to. That time Casey had been on the telephone every day to Angleton in tears asking what he could do. Bill drooled so much — fact — that his phones had to be swabbed out several times a day, hence Slobbery.

'Do exactly what I tell you,' Angleton answered, holding the receiver from his ear to lessen the doggy noises emanating from Bill. And he did. It took everything both of them had to keep the confession off the table that time.

And now Bill Casey was too embarrassed to take his calls, knowing Angleton would chew his balls off for letting them get Quinn.

Angleton hadn't even known Quinn was in Beirut.

Hoover said he was calling from a phone box down the hill. It turned out Hoover had been watching him all along. The meter on Angleton's paranoid graph went way off the scale.

Down By the River

Nick was in Collard's room, relaxed and laughing. Collard noted how real everything looked as he dreamed. The girl was there too, a tantalizing presence, unseen or glimpsed on the balcony. Collard woke up standing in the middle of the bathroom calling Nick's name.

After breakfast he walked down to the river. The peace was shattered by the roar of a fighter jet flying so low it hugged the side of the valley. A split second later it was gone, leaving him shaken and foolish on the ground. He had thrown himself down, thinking he was hearing the first crack of the disintegrating airliner 35,000 feet above.

Downstream he found the wooden hut Valerie Traherne mentioned. Apparently Angleton had called it his den. It stood above one of the fishing beats. Angleton had asked for an introduction to local anglers. As they were notoriously hard to impress, she was later surprised to learn they considered him a world-class fly fisherman whose observance and guile reading the river were second to none.

The hut was a simple affair with a tiny veranda and windows either side of the door, which was unlocked. The interior was about eight foot by eight, with an old wicker chair, a bench along the back wall and a shelf with a dozen paperbacks.

Collard picked up a battered Graham Greene.

The sun came out and warmed the hut. He dozed off in the wicker chair and jerked awake, filled with inexplicable dread. It turned out to be only Valerie Traherne's dogs barking. He stepped out onto the veranda, thinking it would appear rude to be found lurking. It was the first time he had seen her that morning. Breakfast had been self-service, with coffee and tea in Thermos jugs and egg and bacon on a hotplate.

She pointed to the dogs. 'This one's Lizzie and the other one's Trumper. They're Irish setters. What are you reading?'

'*Our Man in Havana*. Spies. It seems appropriate.'

'I think that was one of Mr Angleton's.'

He thought she was humouring him. Seeing his look, she explained guests were encouraged to donate books they were finished with to the hotel library.

'The dull ones I take down to the charity shop. Mr Angleton donated a healthy stack. I was rather interested in what he had been reading. I thought it might help explain what he had been up to.'

'Did it?'

'Never had time to find out. I don't know whether there are others of his still up at the house. If I find any I'll put them aside.'

★   ★   ★

That afternoon she came in with more books. Collard was in the drawing room. He was still the only guest.

128

'These, from what I remember, were Mr Angleton's donation. There's an Eric Ambler and Josephine Tey. I know the Borges was his because he introduced me to him. Explained he was blind. A bit highbrow for the tastes of a simple hotelier — a lot of it didn't seem to get anywhere. My first husband was Argentinian so I'm probably prejudiced.'

Collard wondered if she'd had a crush on Angleton. It seemed improper to enquire after the whereabouts of the present Mr Traherne. He sensed her loneliness and regretted he had nothing he could offer her in such a romantic, isolated setting.

She held up a copy of *Reader's Digest*. 'I haven't the faintest idea what he was doing with this but it was definitely his because I remember thinking he was the last person you'd associate with *Reader's Digest*. Quite amazing what doesn't get thrown out. This ended up in one of the loos.'

There was only one article in the *Reader's Digest* of possible interest to Angleton — it was about Middle East drugs and arms deals. The eerie relevance gave Collard the same vertigo as the Barry connection. He had the strongest impression Angleton lay close to the centre of the mystery, a feeling triggered by the name that leapt out from the page: Nazir.

He read the article twice. Nazir was cited as a new breed of businessman who operated with diplomatic protection and ran legitimate import-export companies in Vienna, Madrid, Beirut, Damascus and — Collard took note

— Frankfurt. Through Syria he was able to trade with Eastern Bloc countries. There was also business with France, Spain, Portugal and England. Nazir was young, smart and personable and moved in international circles. But the companies were a front for smuggling drugs and arms whose profits financed terror.

It left Nick looking a very tiny and vulnerable figure, with his direct link to Angleton, and indirect ones to Barry and perhaps, via Khaled, to Nazir. It left Angleton with a lot of questions to answer with his connections to all the emerging protagonists, living, dead and missing.

★ ★ ★

Collard spent his last evening with the fishing diaries, which went back to 1933. It was therapeutic to read something so impersonal and unthreatening, except to the fish. Like Angleton's entries, they contained descriptions of weather, conditions and flies used. Valerie Traherne joined him briefly to say it was a Sunday supper, cold meats and help yourself. It was her bridge evening.

'I'm sorry I have to go out. I enjoyed our talk last night. Are you going in the morning?'

'I have to get back. It would be nice to stay. It's very peaceful here.'

'You look a lot less tired than when you arrived. Are those the fishing diaries?'

'Yes.'

'Angleton made his own flies. I watched him once, incredibly fiddly and meticulous, perfect

130

occupation for him. He told me they called him Mother at the office, or the Gray Ghost, which was the name of one of his favourite flies.'

★ ★ ★

Collard stayed up, hoping Valerie Traherne would come back before he went upstairs. He fell asleep in front of the fire and woke up to find it had gone out. Five minutes after he had gone to bed he heard her return. She paused in front of his door. He waited for the knock, waited for him to call out her name, listened to her departing footsteps.

Snow fell in the night. It froze and Collard woke to find the valley blanketed and trees covered in ice.

When he went to settle his bill Valerie Traherne warned him the way down to the main road hadn't been gritted and suggested he stay until the snow melted. Thinking she wasn't serious, he held out his credit card.

'Mr Angleton paid in cash, I remember. A great wedge. Odd that.'

An awkward silence fell as he watched her swipe his card through the machine and realized she meant him to stay.

Collard was getting in the car when she ran out after him. She was flushed and embarrassed.

'I forgot to give you this.' It was an old hardback book with the jacket missing. 'It wasn't Mr Angleton's. It was here already but I remember him reading it because of what it was about. More spies. Kim Philby.'

131

Beatlemania

Angleton remembered that trinity of events, his *annus horribilis*, 1963. Philby, the Great Traitor, gone in the New Year, disappeared from Beirut to surface in Moscow; John Fitzgerald Kennedy gone in November in Dallas, to be followed by the American invasion of those lovable mop tops, the Fab Four, the show-business equivalent of a nuclear strike. How do you find America? Turn left at Greenland.

Millions of screaming girls stifled the noise of the shots that snuffed Kennedy (three, four, five? Quinn knew who), a lot less loud for the wall of sound that followed. Jack became myth (making the facts irrelevant).

Dark days: Philby gone; Angleton smarting; Jack whacked. Jack an embarrassment in death as in life. The revelation came to him late one whisky-sodden night. He discussed it with Allen Dulles, still hurting from getting fired by Kennedy after the Bay of Pigs. 'Jesus,' said Dulles. 'How did you come up with that?' 'It's called lateral thinking.' 'Lateral collateral, I like it.'

They were there within two months of Dallas. In less than a year Jack was history. He was a shrine. (Please God, don't let Quinn blab about that particular skeleton in that particular cupboard.) Of course the joke was Angleton had been plotting the Irish upstart's downfall

— they all had — when he kissed the bullet (from the front). Jack had stated that he wanted the CIA smashed into a thousand pieces and was meant to go down in a sex scandal leaked to the French press via Mossad. The funniest story Angleton had heard was the Vatican had got wind and didn't want the Jews smearing their Catholic President (Number Two RC in the world), realized the gig was up, given Jack's questing prick, so had him taken care of (Mafia gunmen, easy). He hoped Quinn didn't repeat the story and give them all red faces in the Vatican. Like any story, it wasn't true but it could be made to look true, or maybe it was, could he be expected to remember? Fabrication was the cement of truth. When it came to deviance those Vatican boys could teach them all a lesson, knowing the devil as well as they did.

Despite his conservative ways, Angleton had always enjoyed popular culture, Western double bills and bad late-night television, his companion after everyone had gone to bed. He liked Artie Shaw and cheap pop: Roger Miller's 'King of the Road', two and a half minutes of pure nonsense; 'England Swings' was another matter, best forgotten.

So when asked in Washington how to defuse the crisis of the Kennedy shooting in 1963, he said: *First, do not publicly blame the Russians. Second, no mention of a coup d'état. Third, send me on a secret mission to Britain.* Grave Brits in pinstriped shirts wanted to know what they could do to help. *Gentlemen, why don't you send us your Fab Four?* Incomprehension. *Your lovable mop tops.* Incomprehension. *She loves you, yeah yeah waaab!* The penny drops. *Send the Beatles on an American invasion!*

The Return

Collard regularly checked the London answer-phone; listening to his voice saying no one was there, please leave a message, followed by a series of clicks and whirrs, during which he held his breath, hoping to hear Nick. On the morning he left Wales, the machine failed to respond and the telephone just rang. He supposed the tape could have been full. He didn't dare hope it might be Nick back home who had turned it off.

Collard also placed a reluctant call to his bank on Haverstock Hill and arranged to see the manager that afternoon. He was hopeful he could persuade the man not to hide behind the usual restrictions of confidentiality and discuss Nick's account on the grounds that he was still Collard's parental responsibility.

★ ★ ★

Collard drove towards the grey city, past Heathrow where he had last seen Nick. Jams at Earls Court and on the Westway added an hour to his journey. London was cold and meaning-less, an ugly conglomeration that had outlived its use, defined only by what didn't work, which was everything. The failing transport system was one reason Charlotte had been happy to leave.

He paused outside the darkened house he refused to call home any more. His anger at

135

Sheehan returned when he saw what they had done to his front door, smashed down with a sledgehammer and crudely bolted with a heavy padlock, leaving him with no way to get in.

He drove the half-mile up the hill to the police station and was made to kick his heels for an hour before being told by a policewoman in plain clothes, 'There was a warrant to search your house. Access was gained by force when no one answered. The door was repaired. I need proof you live there before I can hand over the key.'

'Do I have grounds for complaint?'

'You will have to take that up with Special Branch.'

'I'm surprised Special Branch was considerate enough to think of leaving the key.'

She gave a wan smile. 'So am I.'

He let himself into the cold, dark house. The heating was off. When he went to turn it on he saw how offensive the police had been in their carelessness. One of their dogs had been allowed to take a shit on the stone floor in the kitchen. Collard stared at the desiccated remains. The downstairs toilet had been pissed in and not flushed, a cigarette butt staining the water a foul brown.

The answerphone had been switched off. The tape of messages had been removed. That detail made him realize how thorough and petty these people were. They must have returned to the house more than once, as recently as the day before, because the machine had been working until then.

136

At least the phone hadn't been disconnected. He wondered if they had put a tap on the line, in case Nick did call.

He dialled the code for West Germany then Frankfurt and spoke to the desk at the airport hotel. The receptionist he wanted to speak to had checked them in on the night of the twentieth, professing to remember Collard from previous trips and making a fuss over Nick.

She was back from her holiday now and after reminding understood who he was.

'Yes, I remember you were with your son.'

'It's my son I'm phoning about.' He was aware people might be listening in. 'Can you remember seeing him with anyone else in the hotel, a girl perhaps?'

'Not at the desk, no, I don't think so.'

She sounded polite but mystified.

Collard tried to come up with a question to prompt her memory. He stood there, bereft, wanting to turn the clock back.

'A girl,' she repeated. 'Let me think. I thought about him afterwards because it was the day of the crash and some of our guests would have been on that flight. I know he was in the lobby in the morning because he saw me and waved. That's right. They were standing by the plants.'

Collard seized on the word 'they'.

'They were having an argument because I remember I was surprised when your son stopped and smiled at me.'

'An argument?'

'He was upset about something.'

'Was this with the girl?'

137

'No, it was with a man.'

A man. Pressed for details, she said she could see Nick from her desk but his companion was mostly hidden behind the foyer's potted plants. Collard urged her to remember. She confidently discounted his description of Angleton. All she would say was that she thought Nick was with a middle-aged man. Collard wondered if it might even have been him she was describing. At the end of the call she excused herself sweetly, saying, 'I only had eyes for your son.'

★ ★ ★

Collard looked around the unwelcoming hall. Before Christmas he had left a perfectly ordinary house he had given little thought to, except to wonder occasionally about its market value. Now it had been violated and abandoned. He no longer wanted to sleep in the bedroom once shared with Charlotte. He had been turned into a stranger in his own home. The palpable air of evacuation made the atmosphere all the more oppressive. At the bottom of the stairs he experienced trepidation unknown since childhood: the fear of going up and finding the familiar had become unrecognizable.

Nick's room looked like a bomb had hit it: drawers upturned, cupboards emptied and nothing put back, callousness apparent everywhere. It was like an extension of the crash, more shocking for being in his home. Collard had never felt more lonely or punished. He had been spared being on the plane for what? So anything

138

he cared about could be smashed or taken from him.

He tidied away, aware of being close to prying, knowing the police would have got there first. Collard found painful reminders of Nick's interrupted life everywhere: a half-used tube of toothpaste on his basin; clothes not taken; cassette cases of tapes Nick had been playing before going away. There was no sign of the tapes; removed, presumably, by the investigators.

* * *

He walked up the hill for his appointment at the bank. The manager was straightforward, polite and not to be moved. Collard emphasized his concern as a parent and got nowhere.

They sat in a panelled room that smelt of cigarette smoke. The manager was coming up to retirement age. With his severely brushed hair and military moustache, he radiated discretion. They weren't so different from spies, Collard thought: money and secrecy. The bank's rules and regulations were there to be followed and not open to interpretation. The only way Nick's account could be accessed was by official investigation; Collard would first have to take up the matter with the police.

'I'm not unsympathetic,' said the manager, standing to show the interview was over. It had taken less than five minutes. 'But there are no short cuts I can offer.'

They shook hands. The manager looked shifty and Collard realized there was another reason for the man's caution. He would have been approached by Customs and Excise wanting to access his own accounts for its investigation.

★ ★ ★

Collard was struggling with the padlock on the front door when the telephone rang. He cursed, sure he wouldn't reach it, positive it was Nick. He got the door open and grabbed the receiver, expecting to be cut off.

'Nick, is that you?'

'Nick? No, this is Oliver. You're back.' It was Round. Collard had walked back from the bank depressed at being reminded about the Customs and Excise investigation, and now Round would be calling to talk it over. But it turned out to be Nick whom Round wanted to talk about.

'Have you heard from him?'

'No. What about you?'

'No. Nothing.'

Round had always been a diligent godfather, generous with summer holidays when Collard had been hard up, inviting Nick to villas and farms, waving aside any contribution.

'I don't quite know how to put this, but I've been told there's a file on Nick. Erm, to do with this . . . '

Round's sentences tailed away when he was embarrassed. At the age of eight it had happened all the time; hardly at all now.

'Have you seen this file, whatever it is?'

'Not as such. Nigel Churton told me about it. He recognized the name and asked if it was your

140

boy, didn't know I was his godfather.'

Collard knew Churton's name without being able to place it. He turned out to be the man in charge of the government investigation into the disaster.

'Are you part of the team?' Collard asked.

Round gave a deprecating laugh. 'No, absolutely not. I've known Nigel for yonks. I'm seeing him for a late breakfast tomorrow. I'm sure he won't mind if you came along. It would be a good idea to put our heads together over Nick. Fortnum's tomorrow at ten.'

'Where do you think Nick is?'

'He'll turn up in that charming way of his. Probably got himself in a scrape that otherwise would have gone unnoticed and has ended up under the microscope. This bloody bomb caught everyone on the hop. No stone unturned and all that.'

Round sounded casually optimistic. Why not use his old friend's connections, Collard thought. That was how the system worked: families and connections.

★ ★ ★

Unable to face the house, Collard walked up the hill and checked into what Charlotte had called the Love Motel, where several acquaintances had conducted daytime affairs. The functional 1960s building was out of keeping with the stucco of the area and was already running to seed. He was given a room at the front overlooking the petrol station.

141

He arranged Angleton's books in a pile on the bedside table. Then he went to the mini-bar fridge, took a whisky out and, reminded by the tiny bottle of the unbroken miniature from the crash, burst into tears.

Under normal circumstances it wouldn't have been out of the question to glance out of the window and see Nick slouching home from one of the cafés his friends frequented up the hill.

Collard looked around the room. His single occupancy depressed him. He felt like a man hiding, someone who had done something wrong.

Sleep refused to come. Whenever he closed his eyes he was in the disintegrating fuselage.

At one, he gave up and read about Kim Philby instead.

The book Valerie Traherne had given him covered Philby's career as a spy up to his defection to Moscow in 1963. After the horrors of Collard's imagination, Philby's story of espionage and betrayal was familiar, even comforting. He had followed the scandal as a boy, as a result of having started to read newspapers the year before, for the salacious details of the Profumo-Keeler affair, a mysterious and enticing world of pimps, prostitutes, orgies, swimming-pool frolics and drug parties. Sex was only murkily understood at his school. He remembered Round had once announced, 'I'm going to marry a blonde and screw her every night.' He hadn't succeeded in the first, and given his workload Collard doubted if he had managed the second. He still couldn't

142

decide how the plump schoolboy with his tiresome enthusiasms had transformed into such a sleek entrepreneur.

The Philby book was old, well written and well read, with pencil markings in the text. The first was an exclamation mark next to Philby drinking fifty-two brandies with Guy Burgess while on a binge at the Moda Yacht Club in Istanbul.

Three exclamation marks had been inserted next to Philby's claim that Burgess was an uncontrollable drunk. Burgess's homosexuality was noted with a triple underlining. Burgess had caused an international scandal by defecting to Moscow a dozen years ahead of Philby; against Philby's claim that the Americans had discovered Burgess's sun-lamp could be used as a radio transmitter was written the word 'balls!'.

It was the first and only note, in the same spidery scrawl as Angleton's hand in the register and fishing diaries.

Angleton had several entries. His name was underlined in one instance. 'Angleton's doubts about Philby, formed in the last phase of the war, hardened into suspicion.' A large question mark had been written in the margin, followed by several smaller exclamations.

Angleton emerged as a senior spy with a career dating back to 1943 when he was part of an American elite permitted top-security clearance into the British wartime spy system, with access to its most closely guarded secret, the penetration of coded German intelligence. Angleton had served his apprenticeship under Philby at what was jokingly known as the Ryder Street School for Spies. Other staff included Graham Greene, already established as the author of *Brighton Rock*.

Values had changed since then and Philby had changed them. The old Roman virtues of duty and patriotism betrayed by Philby were replaced by hedonism and self-serving, both characteristic of Collard's more indifferent generation. Did Angleton, that deranged old man stumbling around Frankfurt airport, still subscribe to those Roman virtues? Collard had seen none of the glamorous demeanour of the spymaster in the book. What to make of a colleague of Graham Greene and Philby singling out his teenage son to warn him of imminent disaster?

Collard looked out of the window. The remnants of the Welsh snow had reached London. What fell barely settled before it melted. He hadn't thought to look who had written the book. When he saw he was very surprised.

Limited Omniscience

Angleton saw what he hadn't then, that he and Philby were out of Henry James or Edith Wharton or Ford Madox Ford — an essay in cultural pretension, a comedy of manners, a post-Victorian hangover uncomfortably positioned in the modern world. They became like one of those contrived minuets found in highly developed, decadent court societies, which simultaneously managed to be a game of Russian roulette.

The line, as far as he could decide, was from secrecy to corruption to greed. Or maybe it was a circle.

There were elements of ghost story too, of men haunted by their fathers, also curiously ghostly.

Angleton's job was Angleton's invention, a work of strange genius, quite unrepeatable: thousands of meaningless files and years of futile speculation, the only real penetration the salacious bugging of Washington, starting back when everything was expansive and life was Byzantine, with a sense of fun and future. The fun to be had from blackmailing that old hypocrite and homo-hater J. Edgar Hoover, dirty snapshots of him sucking boyfriend Clyde's dick exchanged for dropping his opposition to the founding of the new central intelligence service. The fun of working with that old Jewish gangster

Lansky, whose technical boys had grabbed the Hoover snaps. The fun of being 'No Knock' Angleton, walking in on Allen Dulles to show him Hoover with a mouthful of Clyde, and explaining proudly, 'It's called a fish-eye lens.' Lansky, also in possession of the evidence, was genial. 'Jim, deep down I think you are another Mexican bandit.'

★　★　★

After they had got rid of Angleton in 1974 no one could figure out how anything worked. It had all been in his head.

★　★　★

The fun, above all, of famous long and boozy dry-Martini lunches: the Kim and Jim show, grand post-war reunion, Kim's stutter brightening the booths of dull Washington restaurants.

Luncheon indiscreet.

On sitting down at Harvey's, an English-style chophouse, Angleton said, 'I am on to you and your KGB friends.'

'Hahahahah!' went Kim, covering so fast Angleton missed the flash of panic, being concerned with ordering the drinks. Both men laughed easily. That night Kim's hand shook violently as he lifted his glass.

They turned into family men with long-suffering wives, embarked on the slow suicide of drinking and smoking which was considered a permissible existence in an age of extraordinary sexual tension (amended by that revolting homo Guy Burgess to: 'Not extraordinary, *atomic* sexual tension!').

The music changed from jazz to rock to pop, from detachment to Johnnie Ray, the Nabob of Sob. Angleton was barely aware of the fault lines. On the surface he lived a tranquil suburban existence, dressed the part in Brooks Brothers suits, with fob watch, New & Lingwood shirts and homburg. Only Kim's house, with Burgess lurking in the basement, and a pack of unruly children, was feral, a ramshackle Bohemian place with an unkempt garden running down to woods.

★   ★   ★

Angleton was back in Rome in a room and so drunk he could feel the fillings in his teeth and his swollen liver. Philby was in tears. He had flown in smashed and unannounced from Istanbul and spent the next three days entirely in Angleton's company, sozzled, on a marathon booze-up. A woman was Angleton's first guess; in fact, a dropped defector, picked up by the Russians.

'The most appalling balls-up! The Embassy phone was tapped.'

Philby did his best spaniel's eyes. 'Good dog, Kim. Have another.'

Whenever in later life Angleton heard the song from *The Jungle Book*, 'I wanna be like you-hoo-hoo', he was reminded of that lost weekend. His children played it on the

147

radiogram all the time. Every listening replete with ironies.

★ ★ ★

Their first meeting: Philby the teacher, Angleton the student, Ryder Street, 1943. Some dozed in the soporific atmosphere of the lecture hall, Angleton shutting his eyes only to concentrate. Philby threw a stick of chalk at him, in its near-silent whistle a memory of old classroom humiliations.

'It seems Mr Angleton can spy with his eyes shut. Perhaps he would care to remind us of the four ways of penetrating a foreign service, other than by signals intelligence.'

'Doubling captured agents. Stealing foreign documents. Exploiting enemy representatives in neutral countries. An agent in place.'

'And what is the advantage of an agent in place?'

Philby stepped from the lectern and climbed the gangway between the tiered benches until he was standing over Angleton.

'The value of an agent in place is as a source of validation. Validation, more than signals intelligence, is the essence of counter-espionage. An agent in place is the surest way of controlling information.'

In the light of Philby's betrayal, Angleton often re-examined that moment for some giveaway missed — the tiniest chink of the traitor at work — but found only Philby's Cheshire Cat grin.

Full English

Collard arrived late at Fortnum and Mason. He had run down Piccadilly and was sweating as he entered that hushed temple for the purveyance of fine foods where no one looked like they ever hurried. There had been a delay on the Northern Line.

Oliver Round and Nigel Churton were waiting in a discreet corner of the restaurant, as English as their surroundings. Churton was a dapper, pampered man in his late fifties, with rigorously smoothed hair and close-shaved cheeks smelling of Lentheric. Gold-rimmed spectacles showed off eyes of the palest blue. His manner and dress were typical of the offhand confidence shown by men secure in the English establishment. The pink shirt hinted at a flamboyance denied by his sober pinstripe; Jermyn Street and Savile Row.

Collard knew Round thought nothing of paying £70 for a bespoke shirt from Turnbull & Asser. He felt very off-the-peg.

Churton resisted the blandishments of the menu and stuck to coffee and dry toast. Collard didn't want to be stuck eating while trying to talk nor did he want to be seen to be copying. He compromised with the Continental breakfast.

Churton, fully in charge, asked Round, who without hesitation said, 'Full English.'

'Good for you,' said Churton, leaving Collard

thinking his choice was seen as a disappointment. 'Oliver tells me your firm's doing well. It doesn't take a clairvoyant to predict that security will be a huge market. The real test is how we handle the second phase.'

Collard couldn't decide if he was being vetted or invited in. He wondered if Churton knew about the Customs and Excise investigation and supposed he probably didn't care, provided he came with Round's endorsement. It was how these people worked, vaguely and by inference, on the assumption that you understood their language. Success depended on fitting in with like-minded men, privately educated and dedicated to repeating the experience for their children. Some irreverence was permitted. Round complained the school fees for his brood cost so much he couldn't afford to replace his car or his wife. His wife's Volvo estate had a sticker on the rear window proclaiming: I'M BACKING BRITAIN. It had been Round's previously and he now drove a brand-new black Jaguar.

Breakfast arrived, choreographed by Churton. 'Excellent! Look at that. The English is over there. The Continental is my friend here and I'm the boring one with the toast. Thank you.'

The elderly waitress blushed from his attention.

Round lanced his yolk and smeared it over his toast. Bits of the white were still slimy. Collard stuffed croissant in his mouth to quell a spasm of nausea. Churton turned out to be of the school that left business until after eating. Round mentioned his Caribbean holiday and talked easily of trips where Nick had been with them. Collard was grateful for this tacit reassurance.

When they were done Churton lit a cigarette. He blew out smoke and said, 'I know you are concerned for your son. We are too. Oliver has spoken to me but I would like to hear your views directly.'

Collard had to be succinct; men like Churton weren't for rambling to.

'I have been questioned by an American official who has a sinister interpretation of Nick's not being on the flight. He made a lot of unpleasant inferences and if the papers get hold of the story they will crucify him. It's not the sort of thing someone that age easily recovers from.'

Collard privately worried he had told Evelyn and Stack too much already.

'The press writes what it's told,' Churton remarked bluntly. 'What kind of unpleasant inferences?'

Churton made Collard's phrase sound disingenuous.

'Nick knew the Lebanese student Khaled. Everyone says Khaled was used. I want to know whether Nick was involved and to find him.'

Churton thoughtfully stubbed out his expensive cigarette, half-smoked.

'How badly do you want to find your son?'

'Very badly.'

'What if the result doesn't have a happy ending?'

'My concern is every father's, whatever.'

151

'Of course.' Round added, 'That your child is safe and not in harm's way.'

'I've seen your son's file,' said Churton. 'It doesn't make pretty reading. There are a lot of bad connections.'

'Where is this file from?'

'German security, initially. They passed it on to the Americans, who share with us. Before we go on you should look at this.'

He produced a photograph from his briefcase. Collard thought it was going to be the one Sheehan had showed him, of Nick in a Cyprus café with Quinn, the agent in Barry's team who hadn't been on the flight.

It wasn't. It was a black-and-white surveillance picture of a busy city intersection, from a high angle, with time code at the bottom. The location was foreign. Traffic waited for the people crossing the street.

Nick was among the pedestrians, under-dressed compared to the others and hunched against the cold. Collard searched for the girl but there was no one by Nick's side or close enough to be her.

He hoped the picture was further proof Nick was alive. He looked at the time code. It was dated the 16th, five days before the crash.

'Where was this taken?'

'Frankfurt,' said Churton.

'Nick didn't arrive until the twentieth.'

'Where did he come from?'

'I don't know exactly. I presumed he came up from somewhere south.'

'Nick can be pretty vague,' Round added

lightly. 'Doesn't march to the same beat as the rest.'

Collard shook his head, mystified.

Round said gently, 'You should prepare yourself for the worst. Nick may not be alive.'

'He wasn't on the plane.'

Collard didn't know what else to say.

'I'm not saying he was. Given the kind of people he seems to have been hooked up with . . . '

It wasn't necessary to finish.

Churton said, 'Of course, we hope he is.'

Collard stared helplessly, until he eventually managed to ask, 'Is there anything you can do to help me?'

Churton considered. 'Not in any official sense,' he finally said. 'We don't think your son had anything to do with the bombing.'

'That must be a relief for you,' Round said to Collard, who was irritated by his friend telling him what to think.

Churton pointed to the photograph. 'This in itself is not a reason for grave concern, apart from, possibly, this man here.'

The man was walking behind Nick. He was short and compact, with a shaved head, and appeared watchful where Nick looked lost in a world of his own.

Churton said, 'This is what we have to go on. We have no idea if Nick and this man had met or were about to meet.'

'Who is he?'

'His name is Beech. He calls himself Sandy Beech.'

Round laughed and said, 'Honestly!'

Collard had trouble focusing. The man in the picture matched the description given by Valerie Traherne. First Angleton then Barry and now Beech — they had all been in Wales and then Frankfurt.

Round said, 'Unpleasant-looking thug.'

Churton agreed. 'He calls himself a soldier of fortune, which is a euphemism for smuggling, training terrorists and gun-running. Dangerous customer. We locked up his brother last year for illegal arms dealing.'

Collard was about to mention Angleton then checked. Churton was not the type to volunteer information and Collard thought it wise to do the same. He suspected Churton was a man of ulterior motives.

'Why was German security watching Nick?'

'Through his association with the boy Khaled, who was under surveillance.'

'Which means they knew something was going to happen.'

'German intelligence was getting reports there would be an attack on an airline in the Christmas period.'

'What do the Germans have on Nick?'

'Just the link with Khaled.'

'Do they know where Nick was staying and what he was doing in that period around the sixteenth?'

Collard was thinking about the girl, of whom there had been no mention yet. He saw Churton thought his question naive.

'We're talking about a huge security operation,

154

covering several cities. Your son was noted as a low-level subject for possible further investigation. Alarm bells rang when he turned up in the same picture as Beech, but from what we've been able to find out the Germans had neither time nor resources to follow it up.'

Collard stared at the photograph, fearful of what it might tell him.

'Were they watching Beech too?'

'Yes. As an associate of the man we most want to talk to.'

Round said, 'Of course, it could have been chance that they were crossing the street at the same time.'

'That doesn't explain what Nick was doing in Frankfurt four days before he said he would be there.'

Churton asked, 'Do you recognize anyone else in the picture?'

There were maybe thirty other people in the photograph, half of them crossing the street. Churton pointed to a tall dark man in the background, wearing what looked like an expensive overcoat. Nick was in the foreground; Beech on the other side, in the middle; and now this thoughtful, mysterious figure behind them. Although there was nothing obvious to connect them, the position of all three suggested the man in the overcoat could have just been speaking to either Nick or Beech, or both.

He guessed before Churton told him that this man was Nazir al-Badawi.

Nazir had a Mediterranean complexion that made him stand out from the pasty Germans surrounding him. He looked around forty, prosperous and at ease, not the kind of man to bear a grudge and not at all the fanatic of Angleton's *Reader's Digest* article or Collard's imagination.

Churton said, 'Beech and Nazir go back. They ran contraband around the Middle East in the 1970s then Beech graduated to training Irish terrorists in Libya, at Nazir's instigation. I'm telling you so you know what you're getting into.'

Collard sensed they were moving closer to Churton's real motive. He looked at Round and wondered if he knew; probably not. It was Churton's show.

'You said you want to find your son,' Churton said smoothly.

'Yes.'

'It's not at all orthodox but it might be quite useful for you to talk to this man.'

Collard was astonished until he saw how serious Churton was.

'Why on earth should Nazir talk to me?'

'As a way of talking to us. Nazir is the man we most want to talk to, but as a suspect he isn't going to surrender himself voluntarily, and besides, he has a Syrian diplomatic passport. Nazir claims he is innocent of any involvement in the bombing and is keen to put his case, given the right circumstances.'

'And you want me to act as your go-between.'

Collard was surprised to hear himself say it. He couldn't see that it had much to do with Nick.

Churton read his mind.

'Innocent or not, Nazir knows what happened. He has an extensive network of contacts. Not much goes on that he doesn't know about. If anyone is able to find your son he is.'

'Why should he care or choose to help?'

'With your permission, let's be a little economical with the truth and say Nick is my godson rather than Oliver's. Nazir will cooperate as a way of showing he has nothing to hide and if the senior investigator of the British government says he bloody well wants to find out what happened to his godson, Nazir will jump. His world relies on favours.'

The bill came and Churton paid with a crisp new twenty-pound note.

By way of parting he said, 'It may take a couple of days to organize. Nazir can do something useful, helping you find your boy, while we keep an eye on him prior to reeling him in.'

Collard took that to mean the man was guilty.

Churton shook hands. 'Appreciate it.'

Amazons of the Bidet

In the weeks before Angleton left London for Rome, Philby indulged him in ferocious drinking sessions in the Red Lion, a pub off Jermyn Street crowded with uniforms and thick with smoke.

Philby spoke in an urgent, hoarse monotone, undercutting the hubbub, stammer variable as a faulty radio signal. He had only Angleton's best interests at heart, he said, a remark that sounded like it came from his seduction manual. He proposed a private line of communication when Angleton was in Rome to be used only by them. 'Strictly between us, till you're up and running.'

It wasn't necessary to point out how hopeless American security was compared to the British.

Angleton, dizzy from matching Philby's drinking speed, was flattered to have this private connection, knowing he had only Philby's word that what passed between them would remain in confidence. He would have to judge how naive Philby thought he might be.

Afterwards Angleton defined the moment in terms of himself as the trout wondering whether to rise to the bait.

'Always bear in mind the Vatican,' Philby said.

Angleton had no idea what he meant or why Philby showed him a tattered second-hand copy of a book picked up in a Rome market, *Amazons of the Bidet*, a well-known pornographic novel from before the war. Its author, Virgilio

Scattolini, had given up pornography after a religious conversion and worked as a film critic for a Vatican newspaper until his literary past came to light and he was fired.

'Greene's going to come along tomorrow,' Philby said. 'We're going have some fun with Signor Scattolini.'

* * *

Standing in the Red Lion again, this time with Greene, Philby told Angleton that Greene knew of an operation being run in Lisbon by an agent code-named Garbo, who with the help of a good map, a Blue Guide and a couple of standard military reference books had fooled the Germans into believing his detailed reports on Britain's defences were the work of a national spy network.

'Made the whole thing up from thousands of miles away,' declared Greene. 'And the Germans bought it hook, line and sinker. Bugger me!'

He told Philby it could work up into a good story.

Philby said to Angleton, 'If an idea's worth using once it's worth using again.'

* * *

Out of the Garbo ring in Lisbon, an old copy of *Amazons of the Bidet* and Angleton's impending posting to Rome grew the Amazon affair, which returned to haunt him three decades later, after his own career had ended in ignominy and disgrace, when he was forced to crawl to George

159

Bush, then CIA Chief, because a Vatican historian was about to request the Scattolini files through the Freedom of Information Act.

Bush had wanted a favour in return. They met in some bit of fakery he called a club where the air of expectant hush was as phoney as everything else. Bush, for all his old money, had pulled off the astonishing trick of appearing nouveau riche. He sat legs crossed, showing skin as white as a plucked chicken's, wearing tan shoes with black socks, which earned a silent tsk! tsk! from the sartorially correct Angleton. Bush was awkward around waiters. With drinks on doilies — they drank Coke — he relaxed. Angleton was required to explain while Bush listened with dutiful bug-eyed politeness. Angleton knew he was being indulged. The oil business, in which Bush had grown up, was not known for its naivety.

Angleton levelled, more or less, and Bush let him back into the library archives for three nights, armed with a black Pentel, to delete anything compromising, which amounted to whole documents.

When he was done there was nothing left for any researcher to make sense of, no hint of deception.

Scattolini had been Angleton's first intelligence trick, the losing of his virginity, the template for everything that followed. It proved durable, was revived in many forms and outlasted Angleton. Without it Bill Casey would never have got in as deep as he did. Without it Flight 103 might never have happened.

Coincidence of Geography

Leaving Churton and Round at Fortnum's, Collard made a pilgrimage to a street only a couple of minutes away in Mayfair. Ryder Street was a small backwater, tucked behind Jermyn Street, where forty-five years earlier the young Angleton occupied a small cubby-hole of an office on the first floor of number eleven. Collard wondered at the coincidence of geography that had led him to meet Churton in Angleton's old stamping ground. The area remained the heartland of the establishment, with all a gentleman's needs available within a square mile of where he stood: tailor, club, office, restaurant, pied-à-terre, call girls. It would have been more remarkable had Churton elected anywhere else to meet.

★   ★   ★

Collard's company office was the polar opposite to Mayfair, on an industrial estate, marked by its impermanence, on the edge of the city, at the bottom of the A1, near the new orbital link, which made it well placed for getting around and little else. He parked to the side of the building, nervous at the thought of facing the staff on the ground-floor open-plan office. He didn't want to talk about his escape. His mortality was something he had so far failed to confront.

161

He took the back fire stairs, which led directly to his corridor. The familiar water cooler still stood next to the photocopy machine. He took a deep breath and walked into his secretary's room to find it empty. Lotte's desk was clear and her diary was shut.

Collard broke into a sweat of panic. His discomfort increased on finding Joost Tranter at home in his office, feet up on his desk, telephone cradled to his ear. Tranter interrupted the call to say, 'Talk of the devil. I'm just on with Ollie Round. Catch you in a minute.'

Collard went off to make coffee, suspecting his irritation had showed.

When Collard returned, Tranter was gathering his papers. If he was put out at having to move he gave no sign.

'Where's Lotte?' Collard asked.

'Sick with flu. Several of the staff caught it. It's a forty-eight-hour thing.'

'Where are we on the Belgian deal?'

'It's good, man. It's good. We're nearly there. Look, there are a lot of calls I need to make. We can catch up later.'

Tranter spoke with focused, monotonous intensity. He had done motivation courses and led his life to fixed goals. 'I'm in Mike Kidder's room,' he added. 'He's out all day.'

Collard felt usurped. He could picture Tranter going through his desk. He told himself the man wasn't important and he was projecting his larger anxieties on to him.

Churton had made the most extraordinary offer. Collard thought Round had been well

162

intentioned but naive in putting them together. While Round was genuinely fond of Nick, Churton would be pursuing his own agenda, searching for any angle, however improbable, that led to Nazir.

There was the further question of how much Churton knew. The Americans were apparently sharing everything with the British, which meant Churton should have access to Sheehan's reports, yet he had not mentioned Nick's mystery female companion. Instinct told Collard to keep that lead to himself.

He sat down at his desk and wrote for a long time, aware of it getting dark outside as he struggled to organize his thoughts, piecing together what he had, trying to keep Nick in the forefront of his mind. He crossed out and refined until he had reduced the matter to its essence.

Wales and Frankfurt were converging in a way that left Collard frightened by what he might have stumbled across. Angleton and Beech both seemed to know Nick. Angleton had knowledge of the crash, and yet had let Barry die in it. Perhaps killing Barry was the purpose of the crash. Perhaps Barry and his team had discovered something (Collard remembered the urgent whispers and the high-fives) that they shouldn't have. Quinn was a part of that team. Quinn also knew Nick. Did Nick know what Barry had died to protect? The thought terrified Collard. Was it something to do with Nazir, the constant presence on the periphery? What if instead of finding Nick, Nazir wanted to kill him? And how did Beech fit in?

★ ★ ★

The dead end he kept returning to was Nick and the impossibility of fathoming how men described as 'spymaster' and 'soldier of fortune' related to a boy whose school reports he had been reading until six months earlier, marking him diligent, helpful, conscientious and hardworking.

Collard knew he was bound to accept Churton's offer for Nick's sake. In doing so he would be inexorably drawn into a world beyond his understanding. He wondered how Nick had felt on being enticed into whatever they had involved him in. Had he realized he was being used or had the recklessness of youth left him keen to join up?

Collard had nothing on Quinn, except what Sheehan had told him. But he had the addresses copied from the hotel register before leaving Wales.

Hoover's was in West Berlin. No Hoover was listed there in the international directory.

Scobie's was care of the Travellers' Club, which Collard called and was told it had no Scobie among its members.

Furse was equally unrevealing: none in Crowborough; even had the number been ex-directory the operator would have said.

At least Beech's number was listed under the same Bury St Edmunds address. When Collard rang he was told the line was disconnected. Another dead end.

There were a lot of Barrys in the Maryland

164

phone book, a couple of Charleses, none matching the address Collard had. He supposed some might be relatives but the task of phoning round seemed a pointless long shot at this stage.

He made progress at last, with a phone listing for Angleton, under the Arlington address, which Collard considered extraordinary; spies in the phone book! The thought of being able to telephone Angleton direct seemed like being able to call another planet.

Clumsy fingers twice caused him to redial as he wondered how to introduce himself. His anxiety was groundless. No one answered.

He was about to give up for the day then remembered the telephone company had a directory unavailable to the public that listed numbers by address. He knew Joost Tranter had good connections in telecommunications and picked up the phone and spoke to him, making a point of sounding casual. Tranter showed no curiosity. Less than two minutes later Collard had the Crowborough number.

'There you go, sport,' Tranter said.

A woman answered and Collard asked if anyone called Furse lived there.

'Are you selling something?' she asked, suspicious.

Collard wondered why the English always sounded affronted if they thought you were trying to sell them something.

The call was unproductive. The woman had lived there for the last ten years and before that her mother since the late 1950s. He could hear Radio Four in the background and what sounded like *The Archers*. It was past seven o'clock already. He hadn't realized the time and was surprised Joost Tranter was working so late.

Collard gave it one last go and asked if he had the right address. The woman reluctantly confirmed it was. He said he had been given exactly that one for someone called Donald Furse.

'Never heard of him. Is this one of those calls about Kim Philby?' she asked sharply.

Thrown by the mention of Philby, Collard lamely repeated that he only wanted to speak to Furse.

'I told you I have never heard of him. Aileen Philby, however, was a Furse.'

'Aileen Philby?'

'Yes. She was Philby's wife until she died.'

Collard was more bewildered. He was aware of the woman's impatience.

'Do your research next time. My mother bought this house off her mother after Aileen died. Philby née Furse. Never heard of Donald, so stop wasting my time.'

She hung up, sounding pleased by her outburst. Collard supposed Furse could have been Aileen Philby's brother. He tried Angleton again, without success.

He had no inclination to go home. His nearest lead was Beech, disconnected but still little more than an hour's drive away, up the motorway and across country.

The Chinaman

Greene told Angleton he liked sniffing cunt on his fingers and always fucked women until they were dry. Angleton sensed that Greene's insistence on the forensic quality to his sexual questing was his way of saying he considered Angleton a novice. A wife was hidden away in the country, along with a couple of children; there was a mistress in a London mews and frequent visits to Piccadilly tarts. Greene was alert to the distinctions of paid and unpaid sex, what he called the duty-free advantages of the financial transaction. Angleton was jealous of the grubby ease with which Greene and Philby inserted their way into women's lives. At the end of one drunken evening a woman had asked with amused exasperation, 'Well, do you want to or don't you?' To which he had thought: If it were that simple.

Philby, Angleton and Greene were in the Red Lion as usual to talk about Angleton's imminent posting to Rome. Rome was a 'sellers' market', according to Philby. Since the Germans had pulled out the city had become an intelligence bazaar and Scattolini a main provider.

'Information commands incredibly high prices and in the excitement sources often remained unchecked.'

An unchecked source was a dangerous source and American intelligence was lazy and

167

susceptible. Part of Angleton's Rome brief would be to check internal security.

Angleton had lost count of how much they had drunk — God alone knew how many pints of watery English ale and at least five Scotches. Philby and Greene showed no signs of flagging.

Greene said to Philby, 'I think you should make Jim a present of Scattolini when he takes over the X-2 desk.'

'What a good idea,' Philby replied, managing a good impression of a man hearing an idea for the first time. Angleton never really saw what was coming.

Philby ordered another round. His excitement showed in the enthusiasm he displayed firing up his pipe.

Scattolini would approach American intelligence offering the exclusive sale of secret documents — in reality false but convincing material purporting to come from the heart of the Vatican.

'What a cherry that would be,' Greene said. 'Vatican security is traditionally as tight as a virgin's crack.'

Scattolini would make his approach to the Americans before Angleton's arrival in Rome, giving the deception time to bed in. The whole thing would be as fictional as Garbo's intelligence to the Germans.

A hopelessly pretty Wren, known in the office as 'the piece of furniture', showed off her exquisite profile to double advantage in the join of two wall mirrors while men played court.

'Pay attention, Angleton,' said Philby and they

168

laughed. 'Seriously now, we're going to bowl the OSS a Chinaman.' He looked at Angleton. 'Do you know what a Chinaman is?'

'It's a left-handed googly.'

Greene looked irritated. 'I thought Yanks weren't supposed to know about cricket.'

Philby asked, 'All right, Mr Know-It-All. What's a googly?'

Angleton had to shout to be heard above the noise of the bar. A googly was an off-break delivery, he said, disguised by sleight of hand to resemble a leg-break action, thereby deceiving the batsman as to which way the ball would turn.

Greene was disgruntled by such showing off. Philby, keen cricket fan, used the sporting example to illustrate the business of espionage.

'You offer the other fellow three deliveries. He gets one chance to read the googly, one to play it and the third you give him a real leg-break, which he misreads for a googly, and he doesn't know where he is, if you get my drift.'

Scattolini's approach would test the thoroughness of American inhouse investigative and security measures. In that respect it was a legitimate deception.

Philby said, 'They're meant to run any espionage contact past our respective departments for checking, but they won't because they'll be jealous of guarding what they believe is an exclusive top-level source.'

'I bet you anything you like they won't spot it,' said Greene. 'That's how hopeless they are.'

'Are you all right with this, Jim?' asked Philby,

drawing contentedly on his pipe. 'It's going to be your show.'

Said the spider to the fly, thought Angleton, knowing he would need all the help he could get, however loaded. The X-2 department he was going to head was small and unproven and deemed unimportant by fellow American intelligence officers, who were nevertheless jealous of its high-level access to British intelligence.

Greene, doing a good job of pretending they were chums, said, 'And Jim at some point will 'expose' Signor Scattolini for a fake and reveal the dire state of OSS security.'

Greene gave him an oblique look that Angleton took to mean that he should be grateful for what he was being handed on a plate. Angleton made his gratitude plain — 'This calls for another drink!' — and kept his own counsel. Philby and Greene disliked and mistrusted the Americans and, for all his Anglo ways, Angleton was one. In the practised hands of Philby and Greene it was quite likely he was being set up as part of a larger deception and, unless he was very careful, would be enticed by them into spying on his fellow-countrymen.

At the same time, the set-up was irresistible: knowing everything by running the agent his rivals in US intelligence believed was their man.

Playing God.

In the Angle

Collard left the A1 at the Royston turning and took the A505. The country flattened as he moved into East Anglia.

On the outskirts of Bury he bought a local map at a late-night garage. He located Beech's place in a cul-de-sac on a new executive estate, beyond the old barracks. Collard drove through the estate. The houses, of traditional appearance, typified the lack of imagination that had gone into the recent building boom. Cars were parked inside their attached double garages or on the cobbled aprons outside, giving the place an American air.

As there were no cars standing in the street Collard thought it prudent to park outside the estate. He walked back through the deserted enclave. Most houses had lights on. Televisions flickered behind drawn curtains. Beech's by contrast was dark and looked unoccupied.

The door at the side of the garage was open and led to the garden, which gave on to woods. He tried the back door. It was locked. He checked for burglar alarms. There weren't any, not even dummy ones. It would be a safe, secure area where people didn't necessarily lock up.

The back-door key was in the second place he looked, under a milk-bottle holder.

He didn't know what he was doing going in other than risking arrest and scaring himself by

171

prowling around in the dark. But he wanted to breathe the same atmosphere as Beech. And something more. Finding Nick meant stepping across a personal threshold. Beech's abandoned house represented that. Collard was not one of life's risk-takers; at the same time only his risk would retrieve Nick. It was a test of nerve for the meeting with Nazir: he pictured a dusty road and bumpy ride to a remote desert destination and escorts of masked, armed men with their safety catches off, and the distinct possibility of not being alive for the return journey.

Collard stepped into the dark house.

★ ★ ★

Downstairs the furniture had gone, apart from a large television on a broken stand. The glow from the street lamps outside showed the marks in the carpet where the furniture had been.

Upstairs the main bedroom with shower en suite was empty. In the second bedroom, a bunk bed had been left, with kids' posters on the walls and the ceiling decorated to look like the night sky. The bathroom linen basket hadn't been emptied nor had the medicine cabinet. Someone travelled. There were malaria pills.

The third bedroom was used as an office, again with signs of hasty departure. Most of a filing cabinet had been cleared out, apart from old domestic bills. The desk drawer contained stationery. A single sheet of paper lay dropped under the desk.

Collard took it over to the window where he

made out a proforma invoice to Beech from an Austrian firm, dated March 1984: 140,000 rounds of howitzer ammunition M107, filled with TNT, complete with fuze PDM557, percussion primer M82 and charge MMA2 @ $285 per shell.

The amounts seemed sinister and meaningless. The whole order was for cannon shells. Collard was staggered by the size of it: forty million dollars.

The lights of an approaching car made him pull back and wait for it to pass. Instead of carrying along the crescent a black Range Rover turned into the cul-de-sac and pulled up outside Beech's garage. Four men got out, dressed in the same dark clothing worn by the men who had roughed him up in Scotland before throwing him into the helicopter.

★ ★ ★

The men said little as they moved about the house. They kept lights off. Collard heard nothing apart from the occasional movement.

It was too dark to see in the loft. There had been no time to retrieve the ladder or close the hatch, which was an open invitation. Balanced precariously on all fours, the beams cutting hard into his knees, he swiped blindly with his hand, feeling for something to hide behind. The loft appeared to be empty. He crawled across the beams, testing each one to make sure it didn't creak, trying to put distance between himself and the hatch. He located the water tank and groped

173

his way behind it and was caught poised between two beams when a man started to climb the loft ladder. Torchlight splashed over the roof above him.

Collard froze. The water tank gurgled.

Someone laughed downstairs. Grumbling voices, wanting to leave, complained of wasting time. The man on the ladder said the loft was empty. One of the men on the landing farted, long and loud, followed by stifled laughter and swearing.

Collard waited until he was sure they were gone. When he finally dared to move he brushed against what felt like a small empty shoebox. He took it with him and felt his way back to the hatch.

Before leaving he checked the front of the house from upstairs. The Range Rover was still parked on the apron with the men inside. He could see two of them talking and smoking. His heart still thumping, he let himself out of the kitchen and left by the garden, shinning over the fence. A footpath fifty yards into the woods brought him out near his car.

He drove back through the estate. The Range Rover was gone but he came up behind as it waited to turn on to the main road.

The road was busy at first. Traffic dwindled as they moved into unlit countryside and soon there was nothing between the two vehicles. Collard dropped back, keeping his distance. Following was easy on the straight open road. He wasn't sure what he was doing but he felt safe enough in the protection of his car.

The Range Rover turned off without signalling. Collard let it go. He pulled up in a lay-by.

The shoebox he had taken from Beech's loft contained a dozen snapshots of unpopulated foreign views, azure skies, blue seas, desert landscapes, remote bars. Not holiday photographs, Collard thought; assignments. Only one picture showed anyone: two men in sweat-stained desert fatigues, arms loosely around each other, sub-machine-guns casually toted, as they did thumbs-up for the camera and grinned like monkeys.

The print was small, the colour faded. The stiffness of the paper and its curly border suggested a certain age. One of the men was Beech. Collard didn't know the other.

He took out the other photograph from his wallet of Angleton and his mysterious friends on the bank of the Usk. He looked at Furse with his unlikely beard. Furse stammered, he remembered, and Beech had trouble with his *rs*.

Collard placed the two photographs back in his wallet. He suspected the second was as germane to his investigation as the first: the old spy in mufti and the souvenir of battle. Beech and his companion were bleached from over-exposure, making the background hard to read, but, unless he was mistaken, there were bodies at the foot of a wall, looking like they had just been lined up and shot.

Telephone Line

Collard didn't know why he didn't go home, instead of taking the single-track road the Range Rover had gone down, or why he kept thinking of Furse. Furse had reminded Valerie Traherne of someone who had spent years away in the colonies. Furse had given a fictitious address previously belonging to Philby's wife.

Valerie Traherne believed Angleton, Scobie and Furse had known each other a long time. If Angleton had checked into her hotel under a false name then Furse might have too.

Thinking it through, Collard was tempted to draw an impossible conclusion, a historical bombshell that made nonsense of everything before.

He drove on, dazed by the enormity of his hypothesis. Could he have stumbled across some bizarre secret endgame to the Cold War? Had it been one of the first signs of the big change now apparent everywhere in East Europe? The Soviet front had thawed to such an extent that Oliver Round was extending business feelers into Moscow. Collard wondered if he wasn't becoming one of those crackpot theorists who read everything as conspiracy.

The bright moon led him on. He couldn't remember when he had last seen a house. He wanted to go back but found nowhere to turn.

Philby stammered. Evelyn's book said he did.

Collard was still surprised that Evelyn had written the Philby book; he wondered if the old reporter had any inkling of events in Wales.

He drove on until the road divided and he took the fork that he hoped would take him back to the main road. Instead he ended up in a darkened farmyard where the parked Range Rover stood. Collard switched off his lights, turned and drove carefully away.

He left by moonlight. The network of lanes was more complicated than he remembered and when he turned on his lights again he wasn't sure where he was. He came to a divide in the road he didn't recognize and ended up on a dirt track in a landscape of marsh and reed, which, instead of leading back to the road, took him into an open arena surrounded by a chain-link fence. Collard stopped the car and wound down his window. The stench of rotting garbage carried on the breeze. His headlights lit up a telephone box, solitary and incongruous. He got out. To his surprise, the phone worked; too remote for vandals. He used his card. Valerie Traherne answered straight away. She sounded very cool.

'Do you know how late it is?'

'I know. What I'm going to say makes no sense but tell me what you think.'

She gave a cautious laugh that had nothing to do with amusement.

'Is it remotely possible Donald Furse was Kim Philby?'

She laughed again, incredulously. 'The man was the biggest traitor to his country. Why

177

should he come back or why should the British or Russians let him?'

'Yes, you're quite right, but what if, somehow, it was him?'

Spies were always up to the most extraordinary business. He had enough sense of that from Churton wanting to set up an unofficial meeting with Nazir, a terrorist who for some reason had a line to the British government.

'One thing Philby couldn't change was his stammer.'

'A lot of men of that generation stammered. It doesn't make Furse into Philby.'

'Would you say there was a resemblance?'

'It's too late for this conversation.'

From her reticence, Collard wondered if she hadn't been in on the whole thing too.

'Look,' she said carefully, 'I'm worried you've had a terrible shock with everything you told me about you and your son. I think you should talk to a doctor.'

'It's not that bad.'

'You're putting me in a difficult position. I think you must seek medical help.'

'Medical help?' He knew he was under pressure, but it wasn't clinical.

She sighed. 'For some reason you have become fixated on Angleton. I told you I thought he was in the grip of psychosis.'

She trailed off. Collard sensed something had happened to make her change her mind about him. From the start of the call she had sounded not hostile exactly, more disappointed in him.

'Help me, please. I'm lost here.'

178

'All right,' she said eventually. 'I wasn't going to tell you. A man spoke to me about you. He knew all about you.'

'An American? Was his name Sheehan?'

'He didn't give his name but he was an American.'

'What did he look like?'

'We spoke on the telephone.'

'Was his voice high-pitched, a little sinister?'

'Will you listen, please. His voice has nothing to do with it. It was what he said.'

Collard could not work out how Sheehan had traced him to Wales.

'Was he the one who said I was mad?'

'He was politer than that. He said you had built a house of cards. Everything you told me was based on the fact that the man you saw on the day of the crash was Angleton.'

'Yes. There was the motto, the school. The man was your guest in Wales.'

'It couldn't have been Angleton you saw that day. Angleton's dead.'

★ ★ ★

Collard stared at the receiver after Valerie Traherne had hung up, refusing to believe she was right. If she was then he had been chasing phantoms.

Reeds shone bone-white in the moonlight and rippled in the wind. On the horizon a moving vehicle lit the night sky. Collard saw he had left his own headlights on.

Collard carefully dialled the Arlington number

179

and listened to the connection being made down the overseas line.

This time his call was answered. A woman said hello. She sounded bright and elderly. Collard pictured parquet flooring, simple, elegant furniture.

He asked to speak to James Angleton.

'You can't. He's not here.'

'When will he be back?'

'He won't be back.'

Collard stared hard at the night. The lights from the moving vehicle were brighter.

'Is there a number where I can reach him?'

'Not as far as I know,' the woman said drily. 'Jim passed on.'

Valerie Traherne might still be wrong, if Angleton had just died.

'I'm sorry. I saw him only just before Christmas.'

'Who are you?'

The woman's voice was sharper.

'He recognized me because I was wearing his old school tie.'

'This Christmas past?'

'Yes.'

'I am afraid you are very much mistaken, young man. Jim's been dead nearly two years. He died in 1987.'

'He quoted the school motto.'

'What school was that?'

'Malvern, in England.'

'Certainly Jim was there but it wasn't Jim you talked to, not last month.' Her voice was not without amusement. 'Jim would have been intrigued by your story. It's the kind of thing that appealed to him.'

'It was the day of the big airline crash.'

'Oh, I see. Either you have a sick mind or this is a joke in very poor taste.'

'Honestly, it's not. I've just come from the hotel in Wales where he stayed in 1986. One of the men who died in the air crash was there with him. Colonel Barry, Chuck Barry, nearly the same as the singer — '

'Jim never went to Wales.'

'Not officially, of course.' He floundered. 'He was there for a secret meeting with Kim Philby.'

'Now you are being ridiculous,' she said and put down the phone.

★ ★ ★

Collard walked out of the phone box, back to the car, determined not to be undone. A peripheral movement made him look up.

He couldn't understand what the man was doing there or where he had come from.

It was Sheehan's sidekick, Parker.

Parker stopped, equally surprised. The Range Rover was parked down the road behind him, its lights off. Parker's blow caught him on the temple and stars danced before Collard's eyes and he thought stupidly, as he slipped into unconsciousness, that it was not just a figure of speech.

★ ★ ★

Collard came to in what smelled like a chicken coop. His hands were bound in front of him and his head throbbed. Two men waited for him. They had removed his shoes and socks, and now hauled him to his feet and blindfolded him. The wire binding him cut into his wrists. The men had to support him as they moved outside across sharp, open ground. Collard felt ploughed earth underfoot, the ridges making it hard to balance.

After several minutes they stopped and told him not to move. He heard the men walk away. When he was sure they were gone he removed his blindfold. He was standing in the middle of the field and Parker was walking towards him. Collard saw the gun in the man's right hand. Running was out of the question in bare feet.

He ran anyway, stumbling painfully, unbalanced by his tied hands and the ridged field, his breath hoarse in his throat. He kept tripping and falling and hauling himself on, a pathetic spectacle for Parker's amusement. The last time he fell too awkwardly to get up and lay helplessly on his back like an insect waiting to be squashed. Parker leaned down and placed the barrel of the pistol against Collard's forehead and asked why he had been following them.

Collard denied it. Parker cocked the pistol. Collard lay staring at the black dome of the night, less afraid than angry that he could do nothing for Nick now. He had taken stupid risks, telling himself it was for Nick's sake, only to end up getting shot.

Parker gave a grunt of cruel satisfaction as he

knelt down and grabbed a fistful of Collard's hair, yanking his head back and jamming the pistol under his jaw.

'Who are you working for?'

Collard squeezed his eyes shut and waited for the bullet to tear through his throat, up into his brain. Instead Parker offered him a last chance to talk.

'Or it's lights out.'

Collard sensed a glimmer in the blackness of his head. When he put it into words he wondered why he hadn't thought of it before.

'I'm working for Nigel Churton,' he said slowly. 'Who are you working for?'

'Fuck,' said Parker, and for a moment Collard thought he would pull the trigger anyway.

* * *

He hobbled uncomfortably back over the broken field while Parker said nothing. Collard sensed the man was sulking. At least he had agreed to untie him which made walking a little less difficult. The moon was lost behind clouds making it harder to see.

Parker led him to a darkened outbuilding and locked Collard in, telling him to wait.

Collard felt more foolish than anything; an amateur among professionals.

Parker clearly thought so too when he returned with Collard's shoes and told him he could go. He escorted Collard to the car and gave him the keys. Collard got in and saw the shoe box and invoice were gone.

Parker grabbed his door as Collard tried to close it and he again thought Parker wasn't going to let him go after all.

'Go home,' Parker said. 'You are way out of your depth.'

Dead Man Dreaming

Angleton had a map in his head.

He was a ghost in his own afterlife — though strictly there was no after and no life, only the state of in-death. As a posthumous spook, a faulty receiver as in life: the only thing he had learned was you kept making mistakes.

He dreamed even in death, of a future television programme in which a wife warned her mobster husband, 'None of it lasts.' True.

Fly fishing: the names of flies always reminded him of those innocuous sounding companies that operated out of towns near Langley, fronts for Company sub-contractions.

He missed movies. Double bills of Westerns had been his favourite. The Jimmy Stewart films with Anthony Mann the director, preferred to that sentimental old bullying drunk Ford. Raoul Walsh, another eyepatch man. *Terror in a Texas Town*, the name of its director long forgotten. He could see blind Borges sitting in the back of darkened cinemas of Buenos Aires playing his beloved Westerns, picturing their terrain from the dialogue and soundtrack.

He recalled Francis Ford Coppola's turkey, *Apocalypse Now*, saved by Duvall, an actor he made a point of watching, and his line, 'Charlie don't surf!', which echoed his own refrain, 'Jews don't have oil.'

He saw Philby's father, St John, Arabist and

maverick adventurer, around 1922 or 3 standing next to Allen Dulles, young lawyer and future 'spymaster', as the newspapers would like to call him, in the dirt of the Middle East. (Oh, that old Mesopotamian Rag! So elegant, so swellegant!) They carved up the twentieth century between them, as effectively as anyone had; oil its necrophiliac lifeblood, America's addiction.

Look to the fathers; but no one did.

Those Spooky Boys

Lotte was back in the office, armed with a double box of Kleenex. She fussed over Collard. Facing the staff hadn't been as bad as he feared. They were as keen to avoid the subject of the crash as he was. Only Lotte had examined him closely for signs of distress. He in turn thought something was worrying her. She waved his concern aside.

'I could have done with another day in bed, that's all.'

She was dressed disastrously as usual, with a grey cardigan over a bright pink tracksuit, and her hair was rinsed an even more startling blue than Collard remembered.

After Parker's warning of the previous night, he had decided that turning up for work as normal was the best prescription. Otherwise he would be left stranded on his high ledge looking down at his tiny life.

'How is everything?' he asked Lotte, who jumped like she had been caught doing something wrong. She snatched a handful of tissues and blew her nose.

Her phone rang.

'For you. A Ms Stack.' She pulled a face. To her women were Miss or Mrs.

Collard took the call in his office.

'Evelyn's been in hospital,' was the first thing Stack said. 'Heart attack. He's home now.'

'My God.'

All the usual ambushes were still in place. The larger disaster did nothing to stop those. Evelyn was only fifty-eight. He seemed older, with the wear and tear of booze and nicotine. The plummy old-school mannerisms and toff's drawl were from another generation.

Stack said, 'Have you time to meet later? There's something I need to talk about.'

'We can talk now if you like.'

'I'd rather not on the phone.'

He wondered if she thought his telephone was tapped.

She turned out to live less than a mile from him, between Chalk Farm and Kentish Town; another coincidence of geography, he thought, as he suggested his hotel bar. She said eight o'clock was fine.

Collard hung up, curious, and rang Evelyn who sounded falsely cheerful. 'Ticker's good as new. Can start all over again.'

He failed to disguise the fear in his voice.

'What can you tell me about Kim Philby and James Angleton?'

'Dear boy, what do you want to know? I wrote the book.'

★   ★   ★

Evelyn lived off West End Lane, again not far from Collard, who wondered if he would be visiting if Evelyn had been stuck in South London. His voice sounded frail on the outdoor buzzer. Frayed carpet slippers added to the

188

impression of battered convalescence. He looked little more than skin and bones.

The flat took up the first floor of a large stucco house. The fixtures hadn't been replaced in several decades nor, Collard noticed as he passed through a dark corridor, had the place been decorated or tidied. Housekeeping was clearly an alien concept, heroically so.

Evelyn led the way down into a high kitchen. He hadn't graduated to an electric kettle and lit the gas ring.

The view was of bare gardens and trees. The room was big enough to take a large table in the centre where Evelyn worked, on a battered portable typewriter. A gas fire made the room too hot. Evelyn, looking glum, said he felt the cold more than usual at the moment. Collard wondered how many people had ever come into the flat. Evelyn's socializing would have been done in the bars and lobbies of the world's hotels.

Evelyn laced Collard's tea with a splash of whisky, but left his own.

Collard explained everything that had happened from the impossible sighting of the man he believed was Angleton to Beech's disappearance. Evelyn fiddled with a packet of cigarettes as he listened, taking one out, putting it in his mouth and replacing it unlit, then repeating the action.

'Bravo,' he said when Collard was done. 'Never mind that the initial sighting which prompted your investigation defies rational explanation unless you were the recipient of a psychic visitation. Do you believe something like that happened?'

'No.'

'Me neither. Pity.'

Evelyn phoned his paper and asked for Obituaries. He flirted with someone that sounded like an old flame.

'Angleton, James Jesus, died 1987. Fax it over, there's a love. And send Philby while you're about it. Initials H.A.R. making his full initials HARP which is what he's playing now, if he's lucky.' He looked at Collard. 'Because of his initials his code-name for himself was Angel. Did you know that?'

Collard didn't even know that Philby was dead. He skipped obituaries but that would have been news. He must have been away.

'Two dead spooks,' Evelyn went on. 'Spook, as in spy, becomes spook, as in spirit or ghost. The question is what kind of spook did you see? Certainly not a black man.'

He was laughing at his joke as the phone rang.

'That'll be the fax. Save my legs, would you? It's in the study, second door on the right.'

Evelyn's study consisted of an old partner's desk, faded Oriental rug and thousands of books and newspapers, stacked floor to ceiling, some on shelves, some in towers. Every available surface was covered, including the desk and the floor. Nothing had been thrown out or dusted in years. Collard sneezed. He located the fax by its hum, hidden under more papers.

It was Angleton's obituary: a photo portrait

190

came through upside down showing him still young.

Back in the kitchen, Evelyn asked, 'Is that your man?'

Collard looked at the picture the right way up, a younger version of what he remembered, skin stretched like a mask, the eyes with the same mirthless humour, suggesting the hollow laugh of a man who, in ceasing to find life a joke, had stumbled across the biggest one of all.

'Here's a coincidence,' Evelyn said. 'Angleton and Philby died on exactly the same day, a year apart. Angleton kicked the bucket on 11 May, 1987 and Philby in 1988. Uncanny! Spooky even!'

Evelyn giggled and after a moment said he had thought his heart attack would kill him, too. It was like being grabbed by iron claws.

Evelyn had been a reporter in Beirut, arriving there at the end of 1963, just after Philby's defection. 'He used the lobby of the Hotel Normandie as his unofficial office. He had an arrangement to collect his mail there.'

'Where was Angleton?'

'Still in Washington, head of CIA counter-intelligence. A story went round Beirut that Angleton was gunning for Philby. My impression was Angleton once had a crush on Philby. Nothing homo, but Philby was everything Angleton wanted to be. It had made the betrayal all the harder. Philby had committed the unforgivable sin. The story in Beirut was Angleton was using a former spook to tail Philby and was close to bringing him in.'

'But Philby slipped the net before Angleton could close it.'

'Tipped off by British intelligence, according to some sources.'

'Does that make sense?'

'Presumably it preferred Russia had him to America.'

Collard took the photograph of Angleton from his wallet. Evelyn examined it for a long time.

'Not the most specific picture I've seen. It might be Jim Angleton. The same with Mr Furse; could be Philby. Let's take Angleton as given, but I've not heard a squeak about Philby wanting to leave Moscow.

'The tall gent in the white mac, however, is no more Scobie than I am. I'll bet anything the third man in the picture is none other than the author of *The Third Man*.'

'Graham Greene!'

'Scobie was Greene's character in *The Heart of the Matter*. Angleton, Greene and Philby all knew each other in the war and Greene met Philby in Moscow in 1987, the first recorded meeting since his defection. Perhaps this photograph shows that there had been previous unrecorded ones.'

'Why would they meet in Wales?'

'Maybe Philby wanted to come back and got Greene to play go-between. You could ask Greene but you'd not get anything. He'd want the story for himself.'

Collard showed Evelyn the photograph of Beech.

Evelyn grunted. 'His brother went down for

192

gun-running, squealing all the way that he had been fitted up, that he was a secret agent on a government assignment who'd been shafted.'

'Was he?'

'They all say that, standard defence. As for Sandy Beech, I suspect I know him as 'Mr Nero'. He tried to sell me the 'truth' behind his brother's arrest. The name certainly came in quotation marks, and I guessed the same would go for the truth. Only spoke on the phone.'

'Valerie Traherne said he had trouble pronouncing his rs.'

'That's your man. Story never got anywhere because 'Mr Newo', while making startling allegations, could not marshal his facts and after several calls broke contact.'

'Why would Sandy Beech end up with Angleton in Wales?'

'Not impossible. Beech wrote a book once, one of those 'as-told-to' jobs, in which he claimed MI6 blackmailed him into becoming an agent and sold him out to the IRA to protect an agent in place. He escaped to the United States where he surfaced as a freelance for the CIA. Angleton got sacked in 1974 — he was barking by then and completely paranoid but the fundamentalists in the agency continued to feed him scraps. He could have linked up with Beech that way.'

Evelyn, tiring of his ritual with the unlit cigarette, lit up and immediately stubbed it out.

'Test of willpower, old boy. Angleton never got over Philby. Anything to do with Angleton begins and ends with Philby.'

The demons Evelyn had been keeping at bay returned. He slumped back, his fingers exploring around his heart. He waved his other hand ineffectually.

'Be careful for yourself and your son. The wilderness of mirrors, Angleton called it. Keep Nazir in your sights — he's the likeliest answer. Don't get distracted by the Kim and Jim show or you will end up totally lost.'

The Two Lieutenant Angletons

Angleton saw himself again as a young man in Rome. Behind his back they called him the Cadaver and the Poet. He would later state that William Empson's *Seven Types of Ambiguity* was sufficient preparation for a life in counter-espionage. In Rome he vomited too much, blaming the food and the water, anything other than his nerves. Before the war, Ezra Pound, commuting between wife in Rapallo and Venetian mistress, broke his journey to discuss economics with Angleton's father, Hugh, who had leased the Italian concession of an American business nicknamed the Cash, a hard-sell company that sold cash registers and advocated clean living as a requisite for commercial success and whose training manual was devoted to the psychology of the aggressive pitch. Angleton recalled Pound's amusement at his father's description of company sales methods likened to Mexican banditry.

A solitary light in the window of an otherwise dark street: Lieutenant Angleton's office, 2.30 a.m. He was familiar with Fitzgerald's 'Sleeping and Waking' and Hemingway's 'Now I Lay Me', referred to by Fitzgerald in *The Crack-Up*: 'In the real dark night of the soul it is always three o'clock in the morning, day after day.'

Rome was about the invention of his legend:

195

eccentricity combined with dandified ruthlessness, a marriage of poetry, his mother's Mexican
guile and his father's hard business head. It was
a rehearsal for the bigger act with Central
Intelligence, the one-on-one style, fuck with the
bureaucracy, the taste for vest- or hip-pocket
operations, run with minimum consultation or
authorization, bypassing all established channels,
passim: from the Cold War through to Watergate,
keeping the world safe — for and from what?

He kept files on everyone, including himself.

Marked for his eyes only, he wrote his
schizophrenic reports on ANGLETON LT. J.J.
with objective suspicion.

LT. ANGLETON is a bright and talented
young man but the wide effectiveness of his
Italian method seems too good to be true,
even for someone of his ambition and
efficiency. It makes LT. ANGLETON
— whose natural methodology is one of
reaction — curiously active. He may be a
natural operator but given the poor record
of US intelligence in Italy, his achievement
is so remarkable that one is bound to ask
— as LT. ANGLETON would if called
upon to examine this file — what is really
going on? The question is who runs LT.
ANGLETON?

Was it a manifestation of his early paranoia
that he kept a file on himself, written in the
objective third person? Who indeed had run
Angleton? It was not an answer he could provide

and scarcely a day passed when he did not reflect on the ambiguity of his relationship with Philby. His worst paranoia had him wondering if he was run unwittingly, not through mind control or any of what the Brits would call 'barmy' CIA experiments, but because someone like Philby had known him well enough to second- and triple-guess him every time. Angleton, who had always cherished the illusion he was a closed text, had in fact been an open book.

At the same time, because it was one of the basic lessons of counter-intelligence that any given event was open to every possible interpretation, he believed *any or all* of the following had happened: Philby had come to him, his old protégé, as the Burgess and Maclean scandal broke in 1951 and confessed that he worked for the Russians as a result of youthful indiscretion but had seen the error of his ways. Fearing he might one day have to cross to the other side, he offered himself to be run by Angleton in the ultimate hip-pocket operation, exactly the kind of deep penetration they had dreamed of in Ryder Street. With Philby's defection in 1963, Angleton had his spy in the Kremlin while everyone else thought Angleton had gone potty on the job, almost destroying the CIA in the 1960s looking for communist moles. His aggressive behaviour appeared to make nonsense of this scenario, *unless of course* it had been to distract anyone from finding out about his prize jewel.

Equally he believed the opposite. The theory emerged at the end of Angleton's mole hunts that all his furious activity was a charade to prevent anyone from realizing that he, Angleton, was the mole, and Philby had turned him for the Russians. Alternately, Philby had really messed up Angleton's head by *pretending* to be his man in the Kremlin, the better to destroy him. Even if any or all of these theories were true, Philby, unable to remember or pretending he was unable, would only give his vaguest smile and say, 'What's that, old boy?'

The Polaroid

It was raining hard when Collard returned home
and he got soaked in the short distance between
his car and the front door. He was struggling
with the padlock when someone came up behind
him. He turned to see Sheehan.

'I brought your son's things back.'

Sheehan held up Nick's rucksack. Collard
didn't know what to say other than make a weary
crack to ask if Sheehan was in the habit of
appearing out of nowhere, like his unpleasant
friend.

'Hey, come on,' Sheehan said. 'You've me to
thank that Parker didn't kill you. Aren't you
going to invite me in?'

Collard reluctantly held open the door and let
the American step inside.

'How did you know I was in Wales?' Collard
asked as he took them to the living room.

'We put a tracker on your car. Actually, two
— the first one fell off. Remember the police on
the motorway?'

Sheehan offered Nick's rucksack. Collard took
it.

'No hard feelings,' Sheehan said. 'You have a
very powerful protector now in Nigel Churton. I
still can't decide if you have been a spook all
along. I take two sugars, by the way.'

'There isn't any milk.'

Sheehan shrugged and said, 'I found the girl.'

He appeared more at ease in the room than Collard, who was slow to see what he meant.

'The girl. The girl in your son's room. *Capiche?*'

The patronizing tone took the edge off Collard's excitement.

'Who is she?'

Collard wondered why Sheehan was really there. He was uncomfortable with the man being in his house.

'Her name is Fatima Bey. She lives in Frankfurt. She comes from the Lebanon and met Nick on holiday. She's twenty-three, with a kid of four. The grandparents looked after Junior while she was away. She's a German translator and speaks lousy English.'

Sheehan raised his hands like someone who had successfully performed a complicated trick.

'Do you want to meet her?'

It was too much to take in.

'How did you trace her?'

'There was nothing to trace. She came up in the monitoring of incoming calls to the incident centre. I didn't find out till later because they have a fucking computer they don't know how to use. Your son's name produced one call from her, the week after Christmas, asking if he had been on the plane.'

'What did they tell her?'

'No confirmation of boarding.'

Collard thought of Sheehan talking to Valerie Traherne and Parker's hair-trigger aggression, yet here was Sheehan acting like they were friends.

'What do you think about Nick now?'

'I worry how he got the money.'

'Do you still suspect him?'

Sheehan shook his head. 'The investigation has moved on. He's your business now.'

How straight Sheehan was being, Collard couldn't tell.

'I just wanted to tell you about the girl,' Sheehan went on pleasantly. 'I've got kids. I know what it's like. I hope you'd do the same for me if you were in my position. I gave you a rough time. We were under pressure to get a result.'

'Do you have it?'

'Any day now.'

'Nazir?'

Sheehan shrugged off the question. 'From what I hear Customs and Excise want to send you to prison.'

Collard was disturbed. For the first time he wondered if Sheehan was working for Churton. Or vice-versa.

'What business is that of yours?'

'None. All I'm saying is you should put your house in order. See the girl, come back home and wait for Nick to turn up.'

'What if I am a spook, as you suggest.'

'You're not a very good one. Parker's right; way out of your league.'

'Why do you think Nick hasn't been in touch?'

'Because he caused you a lot of trouble and is ashamed what you might think. Call Fatima Bey. I'll give you her number. Arrange to meet. Like I said, her English isn't terrific. Maybe Nick has

201

been in touch with her.'

Sheehan sounded sincere enough when he added, 'I hope you get lucky. Tell me how you get on. You have my numbers.'

'Why did you tell Valerie Traherne I was mad?'

Sheehan laughed. 'Well, how did you feel when you learned you'd been speaking to a dead man?'

'I didn't know he was dead at the time.'

'And now? Don't you wonder at yourself?'

Collard had no answer to that. Sheehan laughed again.

'Angleton pulled off all kinds of strokes but, as far as I know, not resurrection.'

'Unless he never died.'

Sheehan was quick to shake his head. 'Faked his death? Why would he bother? Anyway, that's beside the point now you've got Churton. Be careful you don't get left out in the cold. It can get very draughty. Call me.'

Collard watched Sheehan from the window getting in his car, and decided the real purpose of his visit was to say he knew about Churton and far from trying to discourage Collard, he was keen for him go in deeper. Maybe Collard was Sheehan's way to Nazir too.

★ ★ ★

He opened Nick's rucksack. The clothes smelled of detergent. He remembered Stack's story about them being laundered by volunteers to get rid of the stink of fuel. He had thought little about it at the time. Now he sat dazed by such a

202

simple act of charity.

No diary or notebook, but that didn't surprise him. Any personal possessions would have been in Nick's hand luggage and the police would have retained anything suggestive. A well-thumbed European guide had the tops of pages folded, marking, Collard supposed, places Nick had been — Vienna, Prague, Budapest, Bucharest. He could not think of a single reason to go to Bucharest. Nick seemed to have got as far south as Istanbul, then crossed to Athens and Cyprus before making his way north to Austria and then Frankfurt. Collard had no idea he had been so adventurous. It made his efforts at that age — working on a campsite outside Bordeaux — puny by comparison.

He recognized an old black jersey as one of the few things of his Nick had agreed to inherit. He put it on without thinking. It was loose and warm.

He was ashamed how unfamiliar Nick's belongings were. Even the rucksack he couldn't swear to. He wondered if it was in fact his.

He laid everything out. The more he looked the less certain he became. He began to think things had been tampered with. Was the route suggested by the turned-down pages in the guide really the one taken or had it been made to look like that? What else did Sheehan have in mind?

He rang Fatima Bey's number. A woman answered, dutifully repeating the number, and confirmed she was Fatima Bey. Her English was worse than his German, which made the most basic exchange a struggle. Collard wondered how she and Nick had coped. She said she had been expecting his call. Even that involved a to and fro before they understood each other. He asked if she had heard from Nick.

From what he understood, Nick had called her, the week before, promising to come soon.

The telephone made any real communication impossible. Collard needed to see her face to face, to read her gestures and make more sense of what she said.

'You spoke to him?' he repeated. '*Sprechen sie mit Nick?*'

That changed everything.

He told her he would come to Germany as soon as he could. In the meantime, if Nick called she was to tell him not to worry. Everything would be taken care of. He wasn't sure how much she had understood. The fact that she had spoken to Nick was all he cared about.

He wandered back into the living room and refolded Nick's clothes. The qualified hope and uncertainty of the past weeks had left him estranged from his feelings. He was disappointed by his lack of elation. It would come, slowly.

Nick had taken only casual stuff — T-shirts, jeans and trainers, and several checked work shirts. As Collard folded the last shirt, he became aware of something in one of the breast pockets. He undid the button, lifted the flap and felt inside.

It was a Polaroid.

The image had survived its laundering with distress. Enough remained to make out the silhouette of a naked girl in front of a bright window that emphasized her slim figure and sharp outline of her breast. The face, not in profile, remained obscure.

Despite its intimacy, the picture gave no clues. An unselfconscious naked girl in a sunny foreign room; a souvenir of a night spent together. It looked like Nick had taken it from the bed.

Holding the Polaroid to the light Collard saw the indentation of writing on the white strip at the bottom. The ink had been washed away. He used greaseproof paper from the kitchen to make a trace of what was written: *I'm the one and don't you forget it!*

Collard's misgivings about the guidebook returned: was the Polaroid a real or false clue? That simple sentence was beyond the fractured English of the woman he had just spoken to. Perhaps she and Nick had written it together. Or maybe he wasn't looking at Fatima Bey at all.

He added the Polaroid to the other photographs, laying them out side by side. Angleton, Greene and perhaps Philby standing on the bank of the River Usk in the spring of 1986; Beech and another man in the desert, date unknown; and a Polaroid taken by his son sometime in late 1988 of a naked girl in a room.

If he could work out the story of each photograph he would understand why everything had happened.

The Polaroid was his only souvenir of Nick's time away. It left him feeling very vulnerable.

He was carefully placing the photographs back in his wallet when the doorbell rang.

His hopes of finding Nick on the doorstep

were dashed. It was Oliver Round, a surprise in itself as he rarely came north.

'I was driving past and saw the lights were on. I need a minute.'

'Come in.'

'I won't. I'm late as it is. On my way up to Hampstead.'

They stood under the porch. It was still raining. Round looked tense and Collard wondered at him calling on the off chance.

'I'm here to give you a bollocking. You can't go charging around breaking into houses and saying you're working for Nigel Churton.'

'A man was threatening to blow my brains out.' Collard's temper was close to snapping. 'What the fuck was I supposed to say?'

'Don't go where you're not told. Beech is the subject of a highly sensitive investigation. It's big boys' rules and if you go fannying in you'll end up in trouble.'

He wasn't used to Round ordering him about. Although Round was technically his boss, their relationship had always been equable.

'I'm concerned for Nick. You were the ones who brought up Sandy Beech.'

'How did you know where he lived?'

'Off a reporter,' he lied. 'Beech's brother's trial was in the papers.'

'Stop playing the amateur sleuth. Churton is not impressed.'

'Meaning you've gone down in his estimation?' Collard could not resist the dig.

'I know the pressure you are under and I am doing my best to help.'

206

Collard relented and apologized.

Round said, 'It must be hell not knowing. A wonderful boy like Nick. I suppose these bloody people don't care who they use.'

Collard wondered what exactly Round's interest was in the affair. Ambition, probably; sucking up to Churton to gain leverage. Still, it was useful to have friends in Round's position.

'There has been a development on the Nazir front,' Round said. 'A party's being held tomorrow night in Frankfurt. You need to be there.'

A party was the last place he could imagine himself, or Nazir.

'And Nazir will be there?' he asked, incredulous, surprised it was that easy.

'He uses a German playboy as his go-between. Call my secretary when you get to Frankfurt tomorrow and she'll give you the details.'

Collard frowned at the casualness of the arrangement. 'Is this how these things usually work?'

'I'm only the messenger. Churton's people said they'll send someone to watch your back.'

Round looked at his watch, pantomiming his lateness.

'Are you all right? Joost Tranter thought you seemed distracted.'

'Only because I found him sitting in my office.'

'You don't have to do this, you know, go to Frankfurt. I can tell Churton you don't feel up to it.'

'It's just meeting a man at a party.'

207

Round laughed and said, 'As am I and should have done half an hour ago. Best of luck. I'm sure this will help you find Nick.'

Round left, turning his collar up against the rain. Given the timing, Collard wondered if he had known about Sheehan's visit.

★　★　★

He locked up the house and went up the hill to the hotel for his meeting with Stack. He was late. She was even later.

Her lack of punctuality was starting to irritate him when she hurried in. Her arrival caused a stir as men turned to look. It was not a dignified entrance. She clutched several plastic bags, including a couple from the local Europa supermarket, which suggested she was carrying her supper. The bar waiter was more attentive than he had been to Collard. She asked for a gin and tonic and apologized to Collard, who decided he was pleased she was there after all.

'I saw Evelyn this afternoon.'

'I know. He told me about the man you met at Frankfurt.'

Sensing his annoyance at Evelyn's breach of confidence, she was quick to reassure.

'Don't worry. He only told me because he's not well enough to work so we're pooling sources. What do you think happened?'

Collard repeated what he had decided. 'I should have been on that flight — I suppose I fantasized the episode.'

That didn't really answer the question, except

208

as a way of externalizing whatever deep impulse had prevented him from flying. There was the guilt too.

'But that doesn't explain the other connections,' he went on. 'Angleton led me to Wales and Barry — and Barry *was* on the flight.'

Collard looked at her and didn't want to be alone, with all this talk of death. He pushed the thought aside.

'Are you sure the man you saw at Frankfurt was Colonel Barry?'

It was obvious what she meant. With the sighting of Angleton discredited, Collard became a less reliable witness.

'Are you about to tell me I am wrong about him too?'

'The passenger list shows Barry flying direct from Cyprus to Heathrow on the morning of the twenty-first, connecting with Flight 103. According to the record, he never went through Frankfurt.'

According to the record. However much he doubted himself, Collard was sure it was Barry he had seen. Perhaps the record was about others now wanting to make it look like Barry had never been in Frankfurt.

Collard couldn't tell if Stack was sympathetic or sceptical.

'What are you doing tomorrow? Can you take a day off?'

He stalled, not knowing what to say.

'Come with me to Frankfurt. I've got a date with my contact in German intelligence. We're going to speak with a Customs man who was on security the day of the crash.'

Collard wondered at her keenness to include him and whether she was the one being sent by Churton to watch him.

'All right,' he said.

'There's another reason to do with your son.'

Collard recoiled at the unexpected mention of Nick.

'What exactly are you being told about him?'

'Are we talking off the record?'

Stack looked hurt. 'Of course.'

'That he's mixed up in something, drugs at the very least. They're saying there's a connection to Khaled.'

'That's what I'm hearing. I'm getting fed a lead that Khaled was often in the company of an English boy.'

'Are you going to print any of this?'

He could see Nick's pictures all over the papers, a deliberately bad one, like that they had used of Khaled, contriving to make him appear stupid, sinister and furtive.

'It's not a reliable source.' She touched his arm. 'I'm sure it will turn out to be nothing.'

Collard wasn't so sure.

Limited Omniscience

No flights were called. Departures was a campsite. Bad weather all over, the worst in his head. Whenever Angleton's thoughts turned to what might have happened on December 21 he found the way blocked, whole memory terrains cut off by adverse conditions, to be replaced by unbidden, cranked-out stuff over which he had no control: the flickers of a dying man, except he was already dead.

Washington blizzards, thermometer falling: the winter of 1950/51, he guessed, and what would be a mixed year, good for him, bad for Philby. Greene would publish *The End of the Affair*, prompting Angleton to snigger, 'Which one?' Icicles hung from gutters: Cold War weather, hard sunlight and snow whitening everything. Half-blinded by winter sun, Angleton imagined the nuclear flash; it was only a matter of time. Galoshes worn to protect his shoes, frosty exhalations as he cleared the path to the house, breathing from the exertion, the harsh drag of spade metal on tarmac, the postman getting through, hand raised in greeting like he was some fucking hero.

Then he was out on the river night fishing with Cord Meyer, taking a canoe out into the open still water for the big cannibal-trout. They cast a short line with a fake mouse. There was a huge smash when the trout took the mouse and

211

it was another twenty minutes before the fish was on the boat.

He told his daughter, 'You enter the life of the trout, and you try and see the world he lives in, in terms of his world, but you're fooling him. You give the *illusion* of a real fly, with the colouring of your hackle and wings and the feathers you put on, and it floats down the river, and you give it a little twitch, and the trout really believes it is a fly — and that's when you strike.'

And which was I, thought Angleton, the feather or the trout?

Movies with snowfall he always liked, for the white. Bob Mitchum (again) in Wild Bill Wellman's *Track of the Cat*, Mitch in a plaid jacket, fighting a bitch of a mountain. And *McCabe and Mrs Miller*, not for the foreground but for the carpentry of the town they built for the set and the dead sound of a land under snow, and 'The Gambler's Song': waiting for a card so high and wild he would never have to deal another. You bet. Story of my life, thought Angleton, who hoped he was bound some place like the one in *McCabe*, sometimes plodding (the sound of fresh snow packing underfoot like no other), sometimes skating free. In life he had not appreciated death's variable offensive, how close it had been to attack: it could have happened any time. He saw road accidents missed by seconds, imminent river drownings from slipping while wading, at least two KGB plots that could have gone either way, and so on and so on, including nights when he could have died from the amount of alcohol ingested, and

212

even now he missed cigarettes.

All flights delayed. He had no idea how long anything took any more. Clocks made no sense. 46.5 seconds was a lifetime. It was a fucking eternity. No one warned you that afterwards involved constant enfeeblement. Once in an effort to board a flight (and what an effort) without a card, he was told for everyone to hear: 'This man is too sick to fly.'

On the loudspeakers the cancellations were repeated in three languages. He heard a small boy say, 'That's good because no planes can crash.' Angleton couldn't tell about people, whether they were regular Joes or waiting, in quotes, like him. There seemed to be no Masonic code of recognition. It was pretty solitary. He hadn't found anyone to talk to.

Then, without warning, clear reception, all the way back to the days of rock and roll. He was the Lonely Dancer again, doing those weird, solitary fandango steps to a thin Elvis; imagine, a thin Elvis. Among those in the house, Toni and Ben Bradlee, Cord Meyer, prematurely white, and his wife Mary who would cause them big grief later on, getting murdered on a Washington tow-path, forcing Angleton to houseclean in person ahead of the cops because Mary's diary was flagrant about her affair with Jack Kennedy (also deceased): Jack the jack-rabbit man, on and off in jig time and Mary taking it upon her to slow him down, except he was too busy chasing his date with destiny. Mary Meyer — another MM, he'd never noticed that before; how inobservant could a man be! — had needed a lot of watching

with her free-spirited, artistic ways, dropping
LSD with that old charlatan Tim Leary, then
'turning on' the fucking President. Jesus, what
would Moscow have made of that?

'Hi, Mary,' he'd said as she came through the
door to watch him dance. There was a Navajo
rug on the wall behind her head and she looked
just perfect. Men wanted to fall in love with
Mary. He too, except his solitary vocation
required him to be the unrequited type.

'Is it a blue moon?' she asked, taking her cue
from the song.

'It's always a blue moon,' he said, laughing.
'What are you drinking?'

He couldn't recall why he had been so happy.
It was one of the few occasions when he had
been able to say he was at the time. Happy.
Wherever he was now, the concept was alien. He
knew what it meant and knew it was important
but he could no longer describe it.

He wanted to ask Mary who'd really killed her
but she faded too fast.

There were a lot of parties in Washington,
mostly innocent, Pick-a-Stick, after-dinner
games, entertainment at home because people
had kids. In charades he'd done *Ace in the Hole*
and *The Lemon Drop Kid*, a Bob Hope picture
through which he had sat stony-faced.

His days bled into each other, the start of his
retreat into that cold place in his head. He could
be charming but there was always something
withheld. Guilty phone calls home when there
was nothing to feel guilty about except
domophobia: he was not a domestic animal, but

214

he was functional, he managed a passable imitation, rinsing and drying the dishes, not that the family ever ate together. Mental snapshots included him mowing the grass, in May to judge from the blossom — how domestic could you get? — using an old Atco diesel mower bought second-hand off the British Embassy. Sitting in the car in the shuttered garage, listening to the engine settle, a small moment of respite between the divisions of his life. The sound of leather sole scraping on garage concrete; he had always liked his shoes, what he called Oxfords and the British called brogues. Guy Burgess wore suede. Burgess in his jackets with double vents. Graham Greene years earlier, droll in the Red Lion — or was it the Duke of York? — saying not apropos of Burgess: 'Never trust a man with double vents.' And the questions always asked of Angleton after Burgess and Philby were gone: Did you know? Did you suspect? Did you guess?

Never the important one: Did you care?

Nazir's Trail

It was difficult going back to Frankfurt, difficult flying again, after Collard's overexposure to the crash, and strange to think of spending the day in the company of an attractive woman he barely knew. Their only association was through the disaster, which made them kind of intimates already. In spite of his slurry of anxiety as the plane taxied down the runway, he marvelled at the wonder of flight as the big lump of metal dragged itself off the ground and up into the air.

While Stack worked, he read a selection of papers that, in the context of flying, made uncomfortable reading. The articles all shaped a Middle East terrorist plot to explain what had happened to Flight 103, with reference to previous atrocities — the *Achille Lauro*, the massacre of passengers at Vienna airport, back to Carlos the Jackal and the plane hijackings of the 1970s. Several pointed out the attack of Flight 103 represented a major strategic shift, with the demolition of a United States civil carrier. One of the more considered articles wrote of a new age of threat, with increased security an inevitable consequence. An unpalatable irony of the affair was that it would be good for Collard's business.

What was not questioned was the whereabouts of a missing English youth whose bag went on

216

the plane when he did not, but how long before it was? Collard wondered whether the press was muzzled as Churton had hinted. Again he questioned the motive of the apparently sympathetic young woman next to him.

He put the papers aside.

'How did it work?'

'How did what work?'

'The Frankfurt Connection. Nazir used the profits from arms and drugs to fund terror. How does it work?'

'Nazir smuggled drugs on regular flights from Frankfurt using baggage handlers infiltrated into the system. A lot are foreign, many of them Turks.'

Collard associated drug smuggling with light aircraft and remote airstrips or high-speed boats — it was disturbing to think of huge quantities of narcotics being moved around in exactly the same way as people's personal belongings.

'How did the regular runs work?'

He was thinking of Nick more than Khaled.

'A suitcase gets checked in as normal. That's swapped in the baggage-handling process for an identical one, containing the drugs, which is collected the other end at arrivals in the usual way.'

'What happens to the original case?'

'What do you mean?'

'Why not check in the drugs at the airline counter? Who's to know?'

'They say it was done by a swap.'

'It doesn't strike me as the most reliable way to smuggle drugs when you have to walk it past

217

US Customs. How do you beat the random search?'

'Through sheer weight of numbers, I suppose. Thousands of people pass through airports every day so the odds must be in your favour.'

Collard brooded on the problem for the rest of the flight. There was something not right about the Khaled story. He couldn't see what but was afraid it would affect Nick.

'Two things,' Collard said as they were told to fasten their seat belts for landing. 'Why should Nazir blow up his own connection?'

'It's a good question. I don't know the answer.'

'And why the swap?'

'What do you mean?'

'Normally a bag gets swapped for the drugs. Now people are saying the drugs were swapped for the bomb. But if it's a matter of getting a bomb on the plane why not just feed it into the baggage system? Why the complication of a swap? That's what I don't understand.'

'I don't know. I only know what they're saying.' Stack sounded defensive.

Collard wondered where that left the case of heroin found at the crash site. Was it Khaled's — which meant the bomb hadn't been a swap — or part of another consignment, maybe even to do with Nick?

★ ★ ★

They were to meet Stack's contact at the airport viewing terrace. This was reached by a broad rooftop walkway between office blocks whose windows revealed an array of functional, repeating rooms. The scale of the airport was more apparent than in the terminal: office after office; rooftops housing miles of complex ducting; blocks five or six storeys high housing thousands of workers. It was a small city, dedicated to processing people. As many as ten thousand could work there, in addition to thousands of passengers passing through every day. However good security was there was always a way round.

Nearer the terrace they walked past glass arrivals corridors in which they could see passengers disembarking, who looked to Collard as though they were part of a strange posthumous process.

They stepped out of the shelter of the buildings into a brisk wind. The universal airport smells of aviation fuel and scorched tyre dumped Collard right back in the crash zone.

A man waited for them by the railings. Stack introduced him as Schäfer. He was leonine-looking with long hair and a pleasant, puzzled expression, and scruffily dressed. Stack explained that he had been part of the original anti-terrorist operation.

Schäfer spoke fast American-style English, learned, he told them, from the American Forces Network. Stack spoke good German and they switched between languages for Collard's bene-fit. As a policeman Schäfer struck him as the opposite of Parker: thoughtful and intelligent and not in the job for the power and the bullying.

219

★ ★ ★

A cold January morning was not a popular time for visiting the terrace and they had it to themselves. Spread out below lay a vast arena in which hundreds of planes took off and landed in an unceasing flow. At that time of day they came in every minute, lined up and waiting.

Stack and Schäfer talked in German while Collard watched a jumbo jet being towed to the gate below them. The empty expanse of airport made the activity around the plane seem toy-like. A catering truck arrived to remove the food containers. The holds fore and aft were opened and the huge steel luggage containers were craned down to flatbed trucks then transferred to floats pulled by buggies, which trundled a quarter-mile across tarmac into the belly of the arrivals building.

At some point on the day of the 21st the journey had been made in reverse, with a bomb.

Collard said to Schäfer, 'It looks terrifyingly easy to put a bomb on a plane. Where's the security?'

'The emphasis is on schedules. Real security means delays, which cut into profits. Tens of thousands of passengers and items pass through here every day.'

Watching the industrious scurry back and forth from his privileged angle, Collard knew getting the bomb on the plane would have been the easiest part of the process. But the placing of the bag needed to be precise. If the bomb was shielded by other bags, it wouldn't have had the force to blow a hole in the container and damage the fuselage, causing the plane to break up. It was one thing feeding a bag into the system, quite another to make sure it was positioned.

By definition someone airside had to be involved.

★ ★ ★

They returned to the terminal. The place was so big staff rode bicycles down the corridors. Collard thought: Anyone could be doing anything.

Schäfer went off to buy cigarettes and Collard showed Stack where he had seen Angleton and Barry. The casino-like riffle of the departures boards shuffled through their destinations. With as many as six planes leaving at once, the sound was constant.

'Angleton was there,' he said, pointing, the distance closer than he remembered. 'The shop where I saw him talking to Nick is over there.' Schäfer was walking in the shop's direction. 'Barry was where those seats are, though he came forward a couple of times to look at the board and I wondered what he did. I'm positive it was him.'

Stack cocked her head. 'Why?'

Collard realized she didn't know about Wales. 'I spoke to someone who knew him.'

He made a poor liar and knew she could tell.

When Schäfer returned Collard excused himself, saying he had to make some calls. They agreed to meet outside the Sheraton.

He took the walkway to the hotel and called Round's office from reception. The secretary gave him a time and address for that evening. The name of the man he was to meet was Patrick Bauer. Collard hung up, realizing he had brought nothing to wear for the party, not even a suit.

His receptionist was on the desk. He reminded her who he was and she confirmed that the photograph of Nick he showed her was the boy she remembered. It did nothing to prompt her memory about the man Nick had been with.

He asked to make a reservation for that night in the room Nick had stayed in. The young woman had to look up the room number. It was technically booked, she said, but as the guest hadn't checked in she arranged for Collard to have it.

*　*　*

Schäfer was waiting outside the Sheraton in an old Mercedes 200, the colour of rust. Collard had to clear empty cartons, old bottles and newspapers yellowed with age off the back seat.

Stack sat in the front and put on dark glasses against the low winter sun that came out as they drove the fast link road over the river into a city more modern than anything in England, with its American-style towers and sleek highways, all rebuilt after the city was bombed flat in the war. The result looked neither American nor European, more like a city in Esperanto.

'I'll show you what I know,' Schäfer said. 'This

afternoon we will talk to a Customs man at the airport. First I can take you where they now say the bomb was made.'

' 'Say' the bomb was made?' Collard asked.

Schäfer shrugged and drove them to Neuss, an hour away on the autobahn. He spoke German to Stack, who translated.

'He says they conducted an extensive surveillance operation last autumn into a plot to bomb an airliner which led to many arrests.'

At first Schäfer's unit had been watching an apartment in Frankfurt on an intelligence tip-off. A man had flown in from Damascus on a false British passport and paid cash for the rental. He contacted another Palestinian, also travelling on a false passport. The second man had only one leg and gave the purpose of his visit as medical treatment.

Stack turned round and asked, 'How would you feel if Nick turned out to be implicated?'

Collard thought the question tactless. He sensed she was fishing for her story.

'I can't accept he was involved willingly.'

His sour look upset her. He thought she was about to cry.

'I hate this job sometimes. Get this. Get that. Find out how they feel losing a loved one. How they really feel. I don't have children. I can't imagine.'

'Everything else is conditional. Children aren't.'

He turned away and stared out of the window, aware of a hard anger. He had gone to Scotland to mourn and left with a broken marriage

223

and not knowing whether his son was dead or alive.

He wanted to hold someone accountable for his life being ruined. His anger took the form of cold fantasies in which he took his revenge on those responsible, and enjoyed watching their faces as he pulled the trigger. He knew it was childish. On the flight he had tried to imagine the moment of detonation and everything blowing apart; Stack sitting close enough for him to smell her skin.

★ ★ ★

Neuss, part of the seamless conurbation of Düsseldorf, was raw-edged and little loved. Collard saw traditional German bakers and cake shops alongside Turkish food stores, travel bureaux advertising cheap flights to the Middle East and a store selling electrical goods whose brand names he did not recognize. No one looked pleased to be out.

Schäfer drove them to a street off the centre, and pulled up and pointed to a grocery store with a broad orange awning.

'We had the shop under surveillance because the Palestinian with the one leg had stayed at the owner's apartment.'

The store struck Collard as an unlikely companion to terror, with its open trading and modest, respectable shoppers. The goods on display included a huge cardboard container holding more white cabbage than he had ever seen.

'The man drove here the morning we arrested him. We picked him up after he made a call from the phone booth there.'

The phone was further down the street. Past it were a main road and a gantry with directions to the autobahn.

'In the boot of the car we found a Toshiba radio-cassette player, which had been converted into a bomb designed to explode at altitude.'

Collard said, 'They were looking for a Toshiba in Scotland.'

'The bomb-maker was in the car too. We found a telephone number on him for his terrorist headquarters in Damascus.'

It seemed incredible that all the scars and damage of the crash funnelled into this forlorn street. Collard could only marvel at the expertise involved in tracking such a haphazard trail.

'If it was all so neat and easy at the time, how did the disaster happen?'

Schäfer said, 'That's the big question.'

Collard decided he could learn from Schäfer, who seemed to question the investigation in the way he was learning to.

He looked out of the car window and thought: Why this street, why this town, why this country? Why Nick? What quality made someone single him out? Was there something about him that made him easy to exploit, perhaps even expendable. Or were there other characteristics Collard had chosen to ignore: opportunism, ruthlessness and calculation?

It left him questioning his own role. He hadn't been the best father, too absent, physically and

225

emotionally. Had he cared in a precise enough way?

'Tell me about the bomb-maker,' he asked Schäfer.

'His name is Marwan Qudsi. He was a TV repair man living in Amman. He flew in from Jordan with his wife. The man with one leg picked them up from the airport and drove them to the storeowner's apartment where they stayed.'

Collard thought it hardly credible someone with such expertise should work at something so mundane.

Stack said she needed to make a call from the phone in the street. Collard and Schäfer bought 7-Ups from the store. Schäfer said the owner had sold up after Marwan's arrest.

The shop had the same dry-goods smell as cut-price shops the world over, the universal chilled trench displaying cheap cuts of meat, and cigarettes behind the till. They sold brands like Kent, which he hadn't seen for years.

Collard waited by the car with Schäfer, sipping his drink. The simple act of leaning against the bonnet reminded him how little respite there had been.

'How did your unit feel about the arrests?'

'They were punching the air.'

'Not you?'

Schäfer shrugged. 'The police in this country are very security-conscious.'

'What do you mean?'

'We had twenty-four-hour monitoring of sixteen targets in six cities. The size of the exercise seemed more important than the result. We were ordered to go in too early.'

'When was that?'

'At the end of October.'

'And nearly two months later one of the bombs made by Marwan found its way onto the plane.'

Schäfer shook a Gauloise out of its packet.

'That's what they want you to believe.'

They were joined by Stack, and Schäfer said, 'I can show you the apartment where the bombs were made.'

They drove under the autobahn and turned off the main road, over a railway line and into an area of housing blocks fringed by an industrial estate.

They pulled into a large residential car park in front of a five-storey building with balconies. The fourth-floor apartment had a rolled-up awning that matched the orange canopy of the grocery store. Collard thought it the last place anyone would think to look. It was hiding in plain sight.

For a moment he believed he could will the explosion into reverse, like a film rewinding, so the plane reassembled, and the damage became recoverable, letting those on board fly on unharmed.

Schäfer showed them a surveillance picture taken with a telephoto lens of two men talking in front of the same block. He drew their attention to the one on the left. Tubby was the only word that came to Collard's mind, not one he had consciously applied to anyone in years.

'Marwan Qudsi, the bomb-maker.'

'If he is under arrest why hasn't he been charged? Why haven't the others been named?'

Schäfer smiled at some private joke. 'We watched Marwan for a long time and so little went on we thought we had the wrong man. Day after day we had to listen to the store owner's young son practise on his electric keyboard while Marwan sat around and his wife did housework. When we questioned the intelligence we were told Marwan had blown up a Swissair jet in 1970 and an Austrian jet on the same day, both from Frankfurt, and in 1972 he was the main suspect in the bombing of an El Al plane flying out of Rome.'

Collard looked at him again: a swarthy, benign-looking man with a moustache and thinning black hair, a picture of indolence.

'Soon after that, two deliveries were made to the apartment: one by the man with one leg and, the following night, by another man in a Peugeot 205 with Paris plates.'

Schäfer showed them a second surveillance photograph, a *fuzzy* picture of the Peugeot's driver about to enter the building. The last time Collard had seen him he had been wearing a long dark overcoat in the surveillance image shown him by Churton.

'That's Nazir,' said Stack.

'I still don't get it,' said Collard. 'Why wasn't all this dealt with after the crash, with all this evidence?'

'My question too,' said Schäfer. 'But there are two things to understand.'

He spoke to Stack in German; she translated.

228

'The usual arrangement with the Palestinians was they were left alone so long as they didn't carry out operations in West Germany.'

'There's a deal with these people?' asked Collard, astounded. He had presumed terrorism was so far outside the law it was beyond negotiation.

Schäfer said, 'I don't know about deals. I'm not a politician.'

He spoke in German again.

Stack said, 'For his department the Palestinians were never a problem, so he was surprised by the size and scale of the operation, especially as the Palestinians had never previously done anything to jeopardize their position.'

Schäfer spoke again and Stack translated. 'He says he doesn't understand what the Palestinians thought they were doing. He knows from talking to anti-terrorist units in other countries that the Palestinians are smart, they are careful and they are capable of working in secret, where this operation was wide open from the start.'

Collard asked, 'But if it was so easy to follow these people before their arrest why — if the same people were responsible for the bomb — did nobody stop them?'

'You tell me,' Schäfer said. 'When Marwan's arrest warrant needed an extension the judge refused. We had to let him go.'

'You caught Marwan red-handed and they released him on a technicality?'

'We lost others the same way.'

Collard turned to Stack. 'Why isn't this news?'

'The investigators have vetoed any naming of

suspects until after arrest.'

'You mean re-arrest.'

Stack's admission suggested the press was controlled as Churton had said. Collard drew some comfort. With Churton's protection at least Nick's story was safe.

'Where's Marwan now?'

'Back in Jordan as far as anyone knows.'

'Repairing TVs!' Collard looked at them. 'It's incredible. Is it incompetence?'

Schäfer said, 'That's what they want it look like, making out we fucked up.'

'Wasn't there a big scandal when Marwan was released?'

Schäfer put his finger to his lips.

'They kept it very quiet.'

'And you're saying there's a big gap between arresting Marwan and one his bombs being put on the plane.'

Schäfer nodded. Since the anti-terrorist unit made the arrests their intelligence had gone cold. Whatever had happened between then and the bombing was a black hole.

The Waiting Room

After the war Angleton had used Corsican muscle to control the docks to stop them from going over to Italian communists; the same in Marseille. The untold price in the equation was the establishing of the French Connection, which made the more or less sanctioned supply and distribution of drugs a central invisible fault line of the Cold War. Ditto the Frankfurt Connection, which was an extension of the same deal, with a different set of players. In the long sleepless nights Angleton regretted the decadence and degeneracy he had inadvertently caused: youth rioting in the streets, smoking pot and shooting up, and still dressing up like they were in the nursery.

He suspected Philby's guiding hand behind Nazir: was that so out of the question? Everyone wanted a piece of Nazir. Nazir swam in Bill Casey's back channels as sleek as a salmon. Nazir had become indispensable, working the Iranian end of Casey's channel while Sandy Beech took care of the other end, which Casey had looped through the Brits in order to create space and distance from the doves in Congress. The Brits coveted Nazir too. Angleton knew all this and it got him nowhere nearer to understanding the events of December 21. What Barry had known had died with him. Angleton, a hapless Poirot, was confident that Nazir had done it but had no wind-up speech. What he couldn't see was who had ordered Nazir. Someone had, because Nazir was an enabler not an instigator. They would have to get rid of Nazir of course because he knew too much.

Angleton predicted that would play out the way he had set it up all those years ago: subcontract to Mossad; no questions asked. If he were Churton he would be thinking of Collard, stumbling around lost and in search of his son, the perfect patsy.

Airside

Schäfer said the German Customs officer they were to meet had been part of airside security on the day of the crash, but he wasn't optimistic. 'No one is saying very much. Everyone is too busy covering his ass. We can only ask.'

They parked in a multi-storey at the airport and went from the terminal into an area marked Crew Only. An official in a glass booth checked their names against a list and issued temporary passes. Schäfer then led them away from familiar airport corridors into a scuffed warren where nothing was signposted and there was no evidence of security. Twice they crossed a grubby underground road system. The grilles and gantries reminded Collard of a submarine. He had a sense of being in the guts of something enormous and complex.

At the centre of the lair they found Schäfer's Customs man, Becker, alone in front of a bank of monitors in a room not much bigger than a cupboard, the screens showing smeared images of anonymous corridors and baggage areas.

Becker looked like he had been exiled to the equivalent of a remote colonial posting. Wherever the central monitoring area was, this wasn't it. Collard wondered if his banishment was a result of the security investigation since the crash.

Becker was a weary, ageing man with thinning

hair and pouches under his eyes, and sounded nervous as he and Schäfer spoke in low, fast German.

Schäfer turned to Stack and Collard. 'He says he is under orders not to talk to anyone but he will show you the baggage system.'

The monitors displayed a complex array of conveyor belts arranged on different levels, like something that might have been constructed for an amusement park. The sorting system was computerized and the most advanced of its kind.

'Bags at check-in are placed in tagged plastic containers and sensors direct them to the right baggage cart,' Schäfer said. 'There are nearly a hundred kilometres of conveyor belts.'

'That's an awful lot of baggage,' Stack said.

'And a big job for security. Twelve thousand pieces an hour, up to one hundred thousand a day.'

'And the margin of error?'

'One or two cases every thousand, but there's a double-check at the end.'

Watching the luggage trundle along, Collard understood the point of the Frankfurt Connection for Nazir. Its automated system made it less prone to human intervention and the security cameras could do only so much. There were always blind spots.

He asked, 'How long are the tapes kept before they are wiped?'

Becker was reluctant to answer.

Collard said to Schäfer, 'Tell him I'm looking for my son. I am worried he was used in whatever went on. He was seen with a man who

234

is an American agent. I'm not trying to get Mr Becker into trouble, but they were using kids to smuggle drugs through this airport. Does Mr Becker have children?'

Becker stared at the ground. Collard thought he wouldn't say anything, but eventually he asked for a description of the man seen with Nick.

Collard described the white crew cut, thin face, the predator's look, knowing he was probably being indiscreet mentioning Quinn in front of Stack.

Becker said in slow English, 'I have two children. The answer to your question about the tapes is they are wiped after twenty-four hours. But in the case of an incident they are kept longer.'

He anticipated Collard's next question. 'The tapes from the twenty-first were removed. No one knows where they are. Some persons say they have been wiped.'

'Through inefficiency or because they contained something compromising?'

'I said too much already. Talk to the Americans.'

'The Americans?'

Becker explained in German to Schäfer, who said, 'The Americans have been calling the shots since the crash and everyone else has been cut out of the picture.'

'Who are these Americans?'

Schäfer again translated. 'He doesn't know if they are airline security or government investigators. The point is they say our security is to

235

blame and we lost the tapes.'

The Americans were operating the way they had in Scotland, overriding the local authorities. Collard presumed Barry's operation, whatever that had entailed, was behind all the panic.

Collard was sure they were close to something. Schäfer knew it too but was unable to persuade Becker. They stood there looking at each other, sensing the importance of the moment, then Becker turned away.

They trooped off, disconsolate.

Schäfer said, 'Becker is coming up for his pension. He said his superiors have threatened to take it away.'

Collard was sure Becker had recognized his description of Quinn. He could leave now or he could go back. It was a decisive moment.

Becker was in front of the surveillance monitors. He seemed unsurprised by Collard's return.

'I only need to know if you have seen the man Quinn who was with my son.'

'He was here on the day of the crash.'

★ ★ ★

Collard returned to where he had left Schäfer and Stack, mystified and waiting.

'There's a Scottish handler we need to speak to.'

Schäfer led them to the conveyor belts and they followed them to a dispatch point where several handlers were standing idle between arrivals.

It took another twenty minutes to locate the Scotsman sitting alone in a scruffy staff canteen. His sleeves were rolled up and both arms were decorated with tattoos. He had the watchful look of a man who'd had training — Collard guessed the army.

He seemed amused by their appearance. 'Who are you guys? At least you don't look like cops.'

Collard showed him the photograph of Nick and explained he had been missing since the crash.

'Four Americans were here that day and the one that didn't get on the plane knows Nick.'

'Who told you about me?'

'A German Customs officer spoke to you because the Americans were looking for a baggage handler who understood English. Their leader was very tall, wearing jeans and a short suede windcheater, with untidy hair, going bald at the front. He had a moustache.'

'He said it was a security check.'

Collard couldn't resist a triumphant look in Stack's direction. Barry *had* been in Frankfurt.

Stack was quick to sense the Scotsman might talk more easily to her and asked what had brought him to Frankfurt.

'My wife's Turkish.'

His name was McCullough and he was from Renfrew. He had a personal interest in the disaster because he had cousins in the town where the plane had crashed.

Stack asked, 'Has anyone else asked about the Americans?'

'A strange thing that, but no. I spoke to

237

management and was referred to the airline but nobody got back to me.'

'What did you make of that?'

'They don't pay me enough to make anything of it.'

The sentence hung in the air.

'Two hundred marks,' Stack said.

'Call it three and I'll tell you whatever you want to know.' McCullough gave a wry smile. 'Time is money and I haven't got long.'

Stack surprised Collard by producing the cash out of her bag.

'Two hundred,' she said, 'and the rest if you make me think you're worth it.'

'Try me.'

'Tell me.'

McCullough had taken the Americans onto the tarmac and they helped load several items directly into a luggage container as it was about to go into the hold of the London flight.

'They loaded items onto the plane?' Collard asked slowly. 'What kind of items?'

'Regular luggage.'

'Including a Samsonite suitcase?'

'Including a Samsonite suitcase.'

Collard wondered how reliable McCullough was beyond repeating everything.

'Does this kind of thing go on a lot? Bypassing the system and personally loading stuff on planes?'

'Not to me personally, but you hear stories.'

'What kind of stories?'

'American security was often present airside. Frankfurt is part of the American Zone so it's

238

their show. There were stories about Americans turning up and supervising their own loading.'

Schäfer said, 'It's an obvious point that is easily forgotten. West Germany is technically under military occupation and Frankfurt is under American control. We are still under its supervision from the war.'

'So there was nothing particularly unusual about the behaviour of the men on the day?' Collard asked.

'They knew what they were doing and acted like they had the right to be there.'

'Who did you think they were?'

'I thought some kind of military police.' He laughed. 'When I was in the army I had my share of military police. The only unusual thing was they also took items off.'

'Took items *off*?' Stack repeated.

'Two identical suitcases from the luggage container.'

'Removed?' Collard asked, thinking McCullough's habit of repeating everything was catching.

'As in they were looking for something.'

'Were they also Samsonite cases?'

'They looked at all the Samsonites.'

Including his, Collard presumed; it would have been in the container.

'Were they looking for something specific?'

'It seemed so. They took away the two cases that were the same colour.'

'Then what?'

'The tall guy asked for a private room. One of them went inside with the bags for maybe fifteen minutes.'

McCullough's description of the man in the room matched Quinn.

Thinking of the mixture of celebration and urgency shown by the three men in the terminal, Collard asked how they had behaved.

'They were very excited. Like they had found what they wanted.'

'What did they do with the two cases?'

'Put them back in the luggage container.'

'Did they position them in any way?' Collard asked.

'No. They just chucked them back in.'

'Can you remember what other items they loaded?'

'A medium-tan leather grip and a larger black canvas holdall.'

'No rucksack?' Collard asked.

The answer was negative. Whatever had gone on it seemed not to have involved anything belonging to Nick.

McCullough looked at his wrist to signal their money was running out.

Stack asked, 'Did any of the men say anything?'

McCullough answered sarcastically. 'They didn't say they were looking for a bomb, if that's what you mean. At the end the tall man smiled and said, 'Job done.' '

* * *

They took the lift from the car park directly up into the Sheraton. Collard left Schäfer and Stack in the café and went up to his room. He didn't

240

feel much like sharing his thoughts about Nick and Quinn or telling Stack about Fatima Bey, let alone that evening's party.

He let himself into the room. It was the oddest sensation trying to picture Nick there with the girl.

The window was high up, overlooking the runway. A plane took off, the thrust of its engine reduced to a whisper by layers of toughened glass.

Nick, Quinn, Beech; all their whereabouts unknown. At least he had been right about Barry. The likeliest explanation he could think of was that Barry had been acting on a tip-off and had either missed the bomb or been betrayed. This would explain the American panic afterwards, especially if they needed to cover up Barry's error.

Collard looked around. The room had twin beds. He imagined Nick's disappointment.

As he picked up the phone to call Fatima Bey there was a knock on the door. Assuming it was the maid come to turn down the beds, he opened the door to find Stack.

'Later,' he told her. 'I need to be alone.'

Stack nodded and burst into tears.

Collard had bottled up his own emotions for so long he didn't know what to do. She stood, rigid to attention, tears streaming down her face. He took her awkwardly in his arms, aware it was his first physical contact with anyone since Charlotte's brief kiss of welcome in Scotland. He sat her on the bed and fetched a tissue from the bathroom. She dried her eyes and blew her nose.

241

'What is it?'

'I'm sorry,' she said with a weak smile. 'Not very professional.'

She rummaged in her bag and produced a photograph.

'It's about this.'

It was of Nick — another surveillance picture like the one shown by Churton. This time the location was a busy pedestrian shopping area, with Christmas decorations and a sea of shoppers. There was a time code. Khaled was closest to the camera, alone, with Nick several yards behind. The flat perspective made them look closer than they would have been. As with the Beech picture, there was nothing to connect them. At the same time any inference could be drawn.

Collard lost his temper. He didn't know what else to do. He accused Stack of using him to chase her story on Nick.

'Don't look at me like that. It's not like that.'

'Where did you get this?'

'It was sent anonymously.'

'Is that equivocation or professional integrity?'

The picture again looked real enough. At the same time he wondered why they didn't just *show* Nick talking to Nazir or Beech or Khaled, like the one Nick and Quinn in the Cyprus café.

That had been taken with a regular camera, Collard remembered, with no time code on the print.

Becker's airport monitors and the surveillance pictures of Marwan and Nazir had identical

242

formatting and the same style time code, meaning German Customs and anti-terrorist teams shared the same technical provider. Collard knew from experience it was a small field.

The format and time code of the images of Nick with Beech and Nazir, now this one with Khaled, were quite different, when — if their provenance was German intelligence — they should have been the same. The inference was plain. German intelligence was not the source, which meant Churton had been misled and Stack was probably being used.

He thrust the picture back at Stack. It now looked as though someone was actively promoting Nick as part of the plot.

'What's this about?'

'I was told to follow it up and see if there was a story.'

'Told by who?'

'By my editor.'

'How did he know about the picture?'

'It was sent to him. He assigned me. He knew you had been in Scotland and asked if we had met.'

'I'm starting to wonder who doesn't know about me.'

'I know,' Stack said with a wan smile.

'And is there a story, in your professional opinion? Let me put it another way. Was stringing me along part of that?'

'Please, I don't want to fight. I didn't know what to make of the picture. There's been no other mention of Nick in the whole of this investigation. But it's my job to follow these things up.'

He didn't know whether he believed her. He thought of Nick and the girl in the same room and wondered whether there had been tension between them.

'I wanted to help,' Stack said. 'I thought bringing you with me was a way of protecting you. I hoped we would find a lead to Nick. I wanted to talk about all this on the plane and put it off. That's my story. You're quite within your rights to shout at me.'

He walked out of the room instead.

Just Like a Ballerina

Collard took a taxi to Fatima Bey, along the ring road past the Botanical Gardens. When he had called her from the lobby of the Sheraton she said it was a good time to come because her child was being looked after for the evening.

Staring at the numbers of the taxi meter ticking over, his thoughts returned to Khaled. Disposable, a lowly drug runner, a small cog, but photographs were in circulation, rumours too, trying to show he was a terrorist. If someone wanted Khaled to appear involved that meant it was not a random act of terror but premeditated. That frightened Collard because he was growing more certain that Nick had been framed in a similar way. That was the feeling he'd had looking at the security pictures, realizing Nick was in them because someone wanted him there.

Collard stared out at the lights of the traffic and wondered if he would ever feel connected to the world again.

After passing a sports stadium, his taxi turned by a large cemetery. Fatima Bey lived near an autobahn on an estate of medium-rise apartment blocks. The estate was deserted, its tidiness superficial — on a dark winter's evening there was nothing to hang around for. In succession, Collard passed a crushed syringe, a used condom and a bright yellow stool of shit. He wondered if Nick had stayed there.

Fatima Bey lived on the third floor. He rang her bell and told himself to stop thinking of her as a girl. She was twenty-three, a mother.

She was waiting for him in the open door of her apartment. Her embrace surprised him, so tight it was like she was trying to transmit some desperate message. Collard smelled soap and nerves.

Fatima Bey turned out to be more Slav than Mediterranean, with dark, almond eyes. She was attractive rather than beautiful and very tentative. Collard couldn't tell if she was the subject of Nick's Polaroid; it was too silhouetted. She excused her English and mimed for him to take off his shoes. He felt self-conscious in socks. The aroma of coffee filled the small apartment. She showed him into the living room. Collard watched the traffic on the autobahn and thought of Nick and the young woman who was preparing coffee in the kitchen. In a hundred years there would be nothing to remember, no trace of any of them apart from a few official records stating the bare facts of their lives.

The apartment's furnishings were cheap and modern. Everything was tidy. There were no toys out. Framed photographs of Fatima Bey and her child stood on a storage unit. They were marked by a sense of enforced brightness and formality that made Collard think of religion. His first impression was of someone fundamentally sad. Several pictures showed an older couple under the same cypress tree.

Then there was Nick.

Not framed. A snapshot as Collard had never

246

seen him: hair longer than in Frankfurt, laughing the spontaneous laugh of someone happy with the moment.

The coffee came with evaporated milk and expensive chocolate biscuits that looked bought for the occasion. The effort she had gone to made him want to cry. Their faltering attempts at conversation were full of shrugs and uncomfortable smiles. Fatima Bey covered her embarrassment by speaking too softly. Even leaning forward, Collard found it hard to hear.

She sat next to him to show her pictures of Nick she had pasted in an album. Many were of him with groups in bars, the flash turning everyone's eyes red. They were typical snapshots of any travelling eighteen-year-old. Other photographs showed Mediterranean views and shots of Nick sightseeing or in budget-hotel rooms.

Collard was reminded of the photographs Sheehan had made him go through at the crash site. As evidence of destroyed lives they had been almost too much. Collard looked at the images of his lost son, so much more relaxed than he remembered. Sheehan had asked how well he knew Nick. Sitting in that strange apartment, he wondered if he had known him at all.

He was conscious of Fatima Bey next to him, fragile and in need of protection. He supposed Nick had felt that way too. He wanted to put his arm around her, suspecting she was the kind of person who was bound to end up hurt. Her vulnerability invited it.

Between them they laboriously patched together an account of her meeting Nick on her

247

first holiday since the birth of her child. Her mother's small win on the lottery had paid for her to visit Athens to stay with an old friend. She met Nick sightseeing at the Acropolis. She couldn't remember the word Nick had used for what happened between them. When her English faltered she reverted to German and he got the gist with the help of a basic dictionary.

'Clicked,' Collard eventually said. Her whole expression changed and her face radiated tenderness. Collard saw then how Nick could have fallen in love with her.

They had gone to Cyprus, where Nick had a promise of good money. She didn't know what kind of work. When her holiday was over and she had to return to Germany, Nick promised to visit. For their rendezvous on that last night at the Sheraton she had arranged for her child to be looked after.

'He asked me to marry him.'

Collard wondered whether he had misunderstood.

'What did you tell him?'

She had told him he was too young and needed to do his studies. Then Collard wondered if she had misunderstood Nick.

He asked if Nick had seen anyone else in Frankfurt. He mentioned the man at the Sheraton. Her sad look told him he was asking the wrong questions. He probably was. He just couldn't see Nick's proposal. Sensing his scepticism, she excused herself and ran to the kitchen.

He found her sitting crouched, head in hands.

She looked up and repeated a sentence in German and wept inconsolably. Collard thought she had said: I was certain he was dead.

In very approximate German he asked if she had heard from Nick. She nodded, half-hysterical. A torrent of German followed. Her lyrical lament took him as much by surprise as her sudden breakdown. He understood its meaning through her transparency of expression. She had mourned for Nick, believing him dead, until he telephoned. He would not say where he was but wanted to see her. He didn't know when. Every day she waited, hoping.

Collard asked if she thought Nick was in trouble. He showed her the word in the dictionary. She shrank from it and said she had been concerned since the last days in Cyprus when Nick had grown distant and secretive. She described finding him in a café with an American. Nick said the American was just a tourist he had run into but she was sure they knew each other.

Quinn.

She nodded at his description and agreed the man was very thin and looked like a ghost.

Collard wrote a note and left it for Nick, telling him to come home, however bad things were, or at least make contact.

He repeated himself several times, saying, 'Make sure he gets this.'

There were tears in her eyes again and he left uncertain how much either of them had understood.

The Abyss

The party was high in one of the big new super-towers, in an exclusive space with commanding views of the nocturnal city. Collard kept his overcoat on to give his appearance a semblance of formality. Otherwise he would be in jersey and jeans at a black-tie affair. There was no sign of anyone resembling Nazir.

The party was a world away from the locations he had visited that day and not what he expected, which was a low-key affair reminiscent of dull embassy drinks parties, rather than a brash, noisy gathering with a heaving crowd getting drunk on complimentary champagne. Quite how he was meant to find Patrick Bauer in the squash he wasn't sure.

Collard pushed into the crowd, trying to imagine what Bauer looked like. People shouted to be heard. Most guests struck poses. A clique of elderly, immaculate patricians displayed an ease of manner that came from a lifetime of ordering people around. Otherwise a lot of winter suntans dressed with too much gold shouted wealth, no taste or class. Younger men tended to be bland and good-looking; the women more angular and interesting, feral even, in haute couture post-punk.

Collard stood in the middle of the room, wondering how much more he could take, when a voice in his ear said, 'It takes the

250

Germans to make punk dreary.'

Collard turned to find Stack grinning at him, champagne in hand. She looked reckless and drunk.

'What the hell are you doing here?' he asked, not pleased.

'My question to you exactly.'

He took her by the arm and drew her aside.

'Why are you following me?'

'Let go. That hurts.'

He hadn't realized he had been gripping so hard.

'I'm not following you. I'm following a lead on Nazir.'

'Through a man called Patrick Bauer?'

'How do you know?'

It crossed his mind again that she knew exactly why he was there because she had been sent to watch him.

'Do we have a conflict of interests?' she asked.

He couldn't stop her chasing her story. On the other hand, her presence as a journalist would hamper his chances.

'I'll give you the story if you go along with me. Whatever you do, do not let on that you are a reporter.'

'What story will you give me?'

He saw the gleam of ambition. It didn't matter, really. He had already told Evelyn most of what he knew and she would get it off him anyway. Before he could answer a woman joined them and asked if he was Collard.

She was the only other casually dressed person at the party, in a pressed white linen shirt, faded jeans and American boots. Even Stack had changed into a black suit.

The woman said her name was Marisa. She knew he was there to meet Patrick Bauer. She spoke English with confidence and graced Stack with an enquiring look.

'My wife,' Collard said.

Drunk or not, Stack was willing to go along with the charade, shook hands with Marisa and said, 'Interesting party.'

It was being given for a private screening of the next big Hollywood movie, she told them. Her ironic manner left them in no doubt what she thought of the film. 'A lot of the people here have tax-shelter money in the picture.'

Stack held her champagne glass in her left hand, the absence of any wedding ring very visible. Collard offered to get her another drink. Stack smirked and said she was old enough to fetch her own.

Marisa chatted inconsequentially, telling him she had started out as an actress in Italian Westerns and English vampire pictures, then moved on to a degree in history of art and now did interior design.

Stack returned with more champagne. Marisa went off to search for Patrick Bauer. Stack accused him of flirting.

'I was being polite.'

'Interior design! If that's what you call choosing rich people's wallpaper.'

Collard wondered how long before they could get out. He thought of Nick with these people and wanted to scream the party to a standstill.

He asked Stack what had got into her.

'They remind me of my father.'

'Meaning he's German or disgustingly rich?'

They were interrupted by Marisa's return with a young man in evening dress who announced himself with what Collard swore was the faintest click of his heels. Patrick Bauer wore patent-leather pumps and was sustained by a frightening absence of humour. He declared a fortune that stemmed from investment in the early films of Steven Spielberg.

A tanned, fit-looking man in his late thirties joined them, necessitating further introductions. His name was Bobby. He had once reached the quarter-finals at Wimbledon and now sold tennis to the Saudis. Bobby shared the same radar as Bauer: a constant sweep of the room that dismissed anyone not of immediate interest. Bobby made eyes at Stack while feigning indifference. He looked like he was cruel in bed and didn't care who knew.

'What was the film you saw?' Stack asked Bauer.

'*The Abyss.*'

'By the man who made *Terminator*? I hear it's no good.'

Bauer looked pained.

'Are we meeting Nazir?' Stack asked recklessly.

Collard wasn't sure what he made of her commandeering the show but found he didn't care.

Bauer said, 'Let me give him a call.'

He produced a portable phone and waited for it to be admired. It was small for a start instead of the size of a brick, the prototype for the next generation, he explained, proud of his toy.

Collard was glad it still had technical hitches. Unable to get a signal in the room, Bauer excused himself, leaving them to more deadly small talk. Marisa said the house she was decorating was an original design by a young architect from Damascus who had studied in Germany. She showed no interest in their business.

Bobby went off and returned, sniffing ostentatiously, to concentrate on Stack. He told her tennis was a mental game. Collard asked if Marisa knew Nazir. The effect was like he had livened up a dull conversation. Marisa's version came as a surprise: Nazir, like Bauer, had made a fortune in tax-shelter investment and was now an investor and philanthropist. Looking at the room, Collard thought Nazir didn't stint when it came to fraternizing with the enemy.

Bobby had his hands on Stack, the better to show how to improve her serve, with a snap of the wrist.

On such moments evenings turned, thought Collard as Marisa told him the young architect from Damascus was sponsored by Nazir. The house had won prizes.

'He is attracted by talent.'

Collard wanted to announce loud enough for everyone to hear that Nazir blew up planes for a living and how did that strike her as an act of philanthropy.

Stack disentangled herself from Bobby. Bauer returned, fed up. Collard was pleased, thinking

254

his phone hadn't worked.

Bauer said, 'If you give me the number where you are staying Nazir will contact you.'

Stack said, 'We're at the Sheraton.'

★ ★ ★

They took a taxi back to the hotel. Out of politeness Collard suggested a drink in the bar. Stack had yet to get a room and he left her at the desk.

The bar was full of international businessmen.

Stack joined him and said, 'It looks like you're putting me up.'

He thought she was joking but the hotel was full. A flight had been cancelled. There was also a big trade fair. Collard offered her his room, saying the desk could find him another hotel and a taxi.

'You've an extra bed. It wouldn't do much for our cover if it turned out we were staying in different hotels. We'll manage for one night.'

She gave him an ironic look and he couldn't say if she was amused or embarrassed. Everyone at the party had been playing games and now it seemed they were too. He was too tense to feel comfortable about sharing.

He let her go up first while he had another drink and contemplated spending the night with a woman he hardly knew in the same room Nick had shared with someone he hadn't known at all. He couldn't put it any better than that; tiredness made his thinking clumsy.

She was asleep when he got upstairs. He got

255

into the other bed and listened to her breathing, thinking how accustomed he had grown to nights alone. There was a vanity to dispossession as there was vanity to everything.

The telephone rang in the middle of the night. Stack answered before Collard was fully awake.

'Oh, Bobby,' she said.

The fluorescent numerals of a digital alarm on the bedside table showed 2.30. Bobby was downstairs. Stack tapped her nose to say that Bobby was on a cocaine rush.

'You don't have to come upstairs to tell me.'

He droned on.

'No, Bobby, I'm not coming downstairs. Tell me what we need to know then say goodnight like a good boy.'

After he had finished she hung up with a groan and said, 'The car's at eight in the morning.'

He lay awake, listening to her sleep, then fell into a series of ragged, alien dreams, an endless European road movie following mysterious patterns of migration in which he was fleeing oppression or financial deprivation for locations like the ones they had visited that day, where he was consigned to dreary, demeaning jobs and subjected to the lumpen humour of the natives. He was aware of suspense, without being able to locate it, his moves determined by others. In one part of the dream he drove across Europe to exchange a left-hand-drive automobile for a right-hand one. In another he imported clothes from Malta and in another he was an educated man reduced to running video rentals from the back of a van, in the hope the video boom would turn into the next gold rush.

Côte d'Azur

Nazir's car arrived promptly at eight for Collard and Stack and drove them to the smart Nord-West section, near the Botanical Gardens and embassies. Zeppellinallee began unpromisingly as a four-lane highway before turning into an exclusive residential street offering prestigious real estate five minutes from the centre of town.

Their destination was the house designed by Nazir's protégé architect. The board outside announced in German and English a luxury development of six apartments, an expensive-looking modification of the Bauhaus style, with pitched roof and glass penthouse.

Collard expected an armed minder to frisk them, but Marisa answered with the benefit of her artificially white smile. They stood in the marbled hall while she explained about the house at sufficient length for him to think she had mistaken them for buyers.

'Would you like me to show you around? The penthouse has its own lift.'

She told them that Nazir had personally supervised the details of the development. Everything was understated and in the best of taste. The units were all in the process of being sold, she said, and Nazir used the penthouse when he was in town. Collard imagined him waiting upstairs, the mastermind in his tasteful lair, prepared to be charming, frank and

258

endlessly deflecting. He was certain the opulence of the party was part of the man's ploy. A setting more distant from the devastation of Scotland was harder to imagine.

Marisa took so long showing them around that Collard decided Nazir was giving them the runaround. Decorators were already in despite the earliness of the hour and it being Sunday. Marisa spoke sharply to one, criticizing his work in a language Collard didn't recognize, Turkish perhaps. Collard wondered if the young man had trouble shaving such a prominent Adam's apple. He hung his head while Marisa pointed to his mistakes.

A phone rang, trimly and discreetly — even it sounded expensive — and Marisa answered and handed the receiver to Collard. It was Patrick Bauer.

Twenty minutes later a black Mercedes collected them and drove them to the airport away from the main terminals to an area used by private aircraft.

Nazir had flown to Nice on impulse early that morning with Bobby and Patrick Bauer to play tennis at Bauer's villa. They had taken his Lear jet leaving Stack and Collard to follow in Bauer's plane.

Bauer had sounded offhand, like he took his luxuries for granted, leaving Collard to consider the absurdity of chauffeured limousines and a private plane taking them to Nice for the day. He felt compromised by Nazir's insistence on bouncing them around Europe. He had no wish to be beholden.

Before hanging up, Bauer had pointedly told him that it was all right to bring his wife.

★ ★ ★

The South of France was sunny and springlike. Stack had said little on the flight other than to admit she was nervous. Collard spent the time looking out of the window at the ground below, making a conscious effort not to think of the crash. It was a clear day. He tried not to dwell on the casual way in which Churton had insinuated him into whatever play he had in mind. He hoped they would be safe.

Their new driver looked more like a bodyguard. He took them west along the coast. White hotels and bright holiday apartments made Frankfurt look like a hard financial town.

Stack wore dark glasses, which made her enigmatic. She sat next to the driver, saying nothing. Collard's nerves were stretched tight. He knew that Parker had been right, that he was out of his depth.

Bauer's villa was twenty minutes from the airport, situated between the road and the sea, protected by iron gates, a high fence and security cameras. The size of the grounds was not apparent from the entrance.

A manservant in a white jacket collected them and took them through the house. The hall smelled of expensive polish. The living room was furnished in a conservative English manner with floral prints and nineteenth-century maritime paintings. As they stepped onto a terrace Collard

260

heard the thwack of tennis balls. The view belonged to a very wealthy man. The grounds fell away to the sea, with a swimming pool built into the rocks. It had been emptied for the winter. To the right were guesthouses.

Nazir was as usual conspicuous by his absence.

The manservant took them to a terrace on a mezzanine level. It was unseasonably warm. A breeze moved the tops of the pines and the sun burned. Cushioned wooden chairs reminded Collard of his colonial childhood. The noise of tennis balls was louder. They were being hit with aggression and venom, accompanied by feet sliding on a clay surface.

The manservant brought bread, coffee and scrambled eggs, which came without asking. They hadn't eaten the previous day and Collard's hunger got the better of him.

Collard was positioned looking back at the house. A French window was partly open and inside a man walked up and down like he was on the phone. He was dressed in yellow slacks and a cream top that made him look like a Riviera playboy.

'I think we've just had our first sighting of Nazir.'

Stack got up and stood admiring the view then turned and looked back up the path, arching her back like she was stiff. Nazir made his entrance, moving lightly on the balls of his feet as he came down the path. He sat down without shaking hands. It was a performance of studied informality.

261

He was the man in Schäfer's surveillance shot and the picture shown him by Churton. Collard was surprised the word likeable came to mind. Nazir had none of Bauer's unpleasant front. He appeared open and agreeable, with the candid eyes of a man who didn't look like he condoned or ordered mass murder.

'I must apologize for the inconvenience of dragging you down here. Are you being properly looked after?' His Oxford English was quaint for being perfect. 'It's not my taste, this business with butlers. Patrick is very German in his admiration of the English.'

The manservant appeared on cue to remove their plates.

Nazir's easy laugh showed no signs of being dutiful. Still smiling, he turned to Collard.

'Forgive my asking, but may I see your passport.'

Collard didn't mind. He was more worried about Stack's.

Nazir flipped the passport open and checked the photograph against Collard.

'Thank you,' he said, handing it back. He asked for Stack's. Collard watched her bowed head as she fiddled in her bag, stalling, caught out before they had started. Stack's passport would state her profession.

Nazir sat back looking relaxed and amused.

Stack at last produced her passport and said, 'I can explain.'

Nazir held out his hand. His expression didn't change as he turned the pages. He checked her picture and handed it back.

'Interesting,' he said, turning to Collard. 'I understand Nigel Churton is godfather to your son.'

Nazir appeared well briefed. Collard was curious to know how Churton had communicated this information.

'He says you can help me find him.'

'I don't think I have met your son.'

Collard sensed he was being played with.

'You were in the same photograph as Nick and Sandy Beech.'

'I doubt it somehow.'

'It was taken in Frankfurt last December 16.'

'I would have to ask my secretary where I was that day. I know Sandy, but your son, I don't think so.'

Collard showed him a photo of Nick. Nazir shook his head and said he had a good memory for faces. Collard glanced at Stack, who was still smarting.

'Tell me what you know about me,' Nazir said equably.

Collard thought there was no point in standing on ceremony.

'You pump drugs through Frankfurt airport and used that connection to blow up the plane, maybe with the help of your old friend Sandy Beech, who once trained terrorists sponsored by you. You financed the Palestinian cell that made the bomb.'

Nazir stared back, his expression veiled. The moment passed and he relaxed, opening his hands to show he had nothing to hide.

'Do I look like a fanatic?'

'Your name comes up a lot,' Collard said. 'Fanatic or not. You may even have had a personal motive. Three American agents died in the explosion. One theory is they had enough evidence to bring you down. The fourth agent, who didn't die, is a man named Quinn, who was in contact with my son. I'm here because I doubt if there is anyone in a better position to tell me what my son was involved in. Perhaps Quinn worked for you too.'

'A rogue agent? I congratulate you on your candour. And where do you think your son fits in this?'

'I believe he was used by your organization to smuggle drugs. He should have been on that flight but changed his mind at the last minute.'

Nazir interrupted. 'Permit me to be cynical for a moment. Times are too good for me to indulge in mass destruction. I don't deal in drugs. You assume I am involved in things that have nothing to do with me — drugs and blowing up that plane. I am an arms dealer. I trade in weapons, very successfully. It's not the most ethical world — then neither is most business. It gives us something in common. We are both in the business of security.' He regarded Collard levelly. 'You are going to tell me you don't go around blowing up aeroplanes, but I dare say your business has already benefited from the disaster in terms of increased orders. Soon these cameras you sell will be everywhere.'

Nazir produced a packet of menthol Kools and asked Stack's permission to smoke. He tapped his cigarette on the back of his hand and lit it with a gold Dunhill. Seeing Collard watching, he threw the lighter to him.

'It's a fake from Hong Kong.'

Collard was uncomfortable handling something so recently touched by him. He threw it back.

'As for your son, we need to find out whether he changed his mind about getting on that flight because he knew what was going to happen or whether there is a perfectly innocent explanation.'

'He was warned by an old man at Frankfurt airport.'

Nazir sat up. 'Really? How do you know?'

'We discussed it. I was with him on the day and saw the man. I should have been on that flight too but had to rearrange my schedule.'

'You must feel very lucky.'

'I would feel luckier if I knew where Nick was.'

'What do you think happened?'

'I believe he took the old man's warning to heart, not about the plane, but because he realized the danger of what he was involved in. Scared he might get arrested in New York, he ran away at the last minute. After the crash he was too scared to surface.'

'Fascinating. I would like to help but I have already told you I don't deal in drugs.'

'I thought arms and drugs were the same in your world.'

'No. Your Mrs Thatcher and her son provided arms to the Saudis but you would not to accuse them of dealing in drugs.'

Collard listened to Bauer and Bobby knocking

hell out a tennis ball. Nazir puzzled him. He was in control yet seemed to want Collard to give him the benefit of the doubt.

Nazir flicked the ash off his cigarette. 'Do you play tennis, Mr Collard?'

'Badly and not often.'

'I'm sure you do yourself a disservice. I had nothing to do with this,' Nazir said like he was still talking about tennis, 'but it suits people to blame me. For them to say I bombed the plane makes it easier to discredit what I might say.'

'Which people are you talking about?'

Rather than answer, he turned to Stack. 'I know your father, by the way.' He sat back and enjoyed her surprise. 'That's why I let you stay.'

Stack blushed at being caught out a second time.

'I don't get on with my father,' she mumbled, her day in ruins. Collard felt protective of her.

Nazir said, 'She writes under her mother's name.'

Stack's father was an international multimillionaire tycoon with far-sighted visions for global media, including satellite technology.

'I have investments in this technology. You don't need to be clairvoyant to see it is the future.'

In less time than it took the plane to crash, Collard thought, Nazir had turned everything on its head, demonstrating how within seemingly random and far-flung events a tight set of connections operated, putting Stack, to all intents an outsider, one move away from the principal suspect. Collard felt as he had in

266

Neuss. What had made perfect sense on one level, on another made none at all; he felt the same about Nazir.

'Who was responsible for the plot if you weren't?'

'The same people trying to discredit me, perhaps even kill me.'

'Who are they?'

'Before we get on to that, let's discuss the so-called Palestinian cell I'm supposed to have financed. It had a very good reason for not carrying out attacks in West Germany.'

'We've heard they were left alone so long as they didn't select German targets.'

'Exactly. It wasn't in Palestinian interests to conduct military operations in West Germany. Do you know the reason behind this rather unusual act of laissez-faire?'

Neither did. Nazir went on, like he was holding an Oxford tutorial.

'Trade.'

'Trade?' Collard echoed.

'Terrorism is governed by laws of business like anything else. When the Ayatollahs rid Iran of its American puppet, the Shah, the United States imposed embargos on the new regime. Since then West Germany has become a major exporter to Iran and terrorists have avoided West German targets in exchange for that commercial investment.'

'Perhaps political or ideological reasons overrode those considerations in this case.'

Nazir looked around for an ashtray for his cigarette. Finding none he casually flicked his butt on the terrace where Collard watched it smoulder.

'No,' Nazir said. 'That Palestinian cell was a fabrication from top to bottom.'

'A fabrication?'

'An exercise to discredit. A sting. Disinformation. Whatever you like to call it.'

'Are you telling us it had nothing to do with Flight 103?'

Nazir sat up sharply. 'No. That's not what I am saying.'

'Then what are you saying?'

'I will put it in the form of a question you need to ask.' Nazir smiled. 'Who provided the initial intelligence on the Palestinian cell to the Germans? Who told them to watch these people?'

'Who did?'

Nazir casually brushed away a fly. 'The Israelis were the sole providers of intelligence to the Germans.'

'The Israelis!' Stack interrupted. 'Aren't you bound to say that, given your background?'

'The question is not worthy of you. I am not dragging you into the murky waters of anti-Semitic propaganda. I am reporting a fact. It is a trick the Israelis have pulled before.'

'What trick is that?' Stack asked.

'Israeli agents foil a big terrorist plot at the last minute, ensuring dramatic headlines: bomb found on plane. The Palestinians get blamed and the papers go to town on what monsters these terrible people are.'

Collard said, 'That's a very big fabrication.'

268

'Not really.'

'How does it work?'

'Completely for real. It only takes one or two people on the inside. Real terrorists are recruited and real bombs get made and real anti-terrorist units set up real surveillance and real Israeli agents break it all up. Except it's invented, a simulation.'

The theory mirrored Schäfer's misgivings about the operation.

'Was that why the bomb-maker was released?' Collard asked. 'Because he really worked for the Israelis?'

'He was a Jordanian agent hired by the Israelis.'

'The plot should have been exposed on the day rather than weeks before. The Israelis didn't get their grandstand finale.'

'Because someone deliberately spiked the operation by getting the Germans to move in too soon.'

Stack added, 'That means someone else knew besides the Israelis.'

'That's right. Now imagine what was supposed to have happened.'

'The plot would have progressed and been thwarted and the plane would not have blown up.'

'Exactly, and I would probably have been shot resisting arrest then they could say what they liked in terms of my being a terrorist mastermind — drugs, guns, private depravities. They would be free to paint a picture of me as a Westernized decadent, thus damaging me in the eyes of the suffering Palestinians.'

Meeting Nazir felt like an extension of Collard's dream of the previous night about lines crossed, boundaries blurring. Truth and plausibility became confused and willingness to believe depended on the persuasiveness of the teller. There was a narcotic element to Nazir's information, with levels of initiation and the flattery of being invited to look into Pandora's box. In his version Nick receded again, became an enigma, a loose end.

High above, against the blue sky, a bird drifted lazily.

Nazir said, 'The Israelis work with dupes, innocent parties drawn into the plot. This means someone is arrested unwittingly trying to put a bomb on the plane, disguised as a wrapped present, which they have been asked to carry, a not unreasonable request at Christmastime. After the operation is done, a suspect can be pointed to, someone for the newspapers to get their teeth into.'

The butler returned with fresh lemon juice. Collard remembered Valerie Traherne's story about Angleton changing the layout of his room and thought Nazir had similarly managed to rearrange the furniture in his head.

'Your son, perhaps,' Nazir said quietly, snapping Nick back into focus. 'Maybe he was the intended dupe. Imagine the headlines. A nice English boy caught up in a bomb plot. What copy that would make. It would shake Middle England to its foundations. I could be made out to be even more monstrous, preying on innocent

270

young English boys.'

'Are you suggesting that my son was meant to be arrested at Frankfurt with the bomb in his bag? What about Khaled?'

'Perhaps they meant to implicate Nick and Khaled in a drug-smuggling operation. It's not out of the question. It is how these people work. Don't you see? If you set up and control the outcome you can walk it back however you want. The purpose is to discredit, in this case the Palestinians. The Israelis wanted them out of Germany.'

'What went wrong on the day?' Collard asked.

'Like I said, these operations are real up to the last minute, with real bombs and real passengers. They probably come down to one person making a telephone call.'

'Or not making a call?'

Nazir opened his hand in acknowledgement.

'Why wasn't Nick arrested on the day, or Khaled either, come to that?'

'We can only suppose someone cancelled the operation believing its security was compromised.'

'Not realizing someone else would carry out the plot for real.'

'That sounds right.'

'What do you think happened?'

'In the first instance, someone persisted with the Israeli plan the Germans had spoiled.'

'Why did the Germans spoil the plan?'

Nazir shrugged. 'I can only repeat, another party infiltrated what was left of the original operation and put the bomb on the plane. These things work under deep cover and those on the ground have limited contact and understanding of what they are doing. The difference between an operation being a controlled exercise and turning horribly real is about this much.'

Nazir held up his thumb and forefinger to reveal the tiniest gap. He turned to Stack. 'Is this the kind of story you might write?'

'If I can verify it,' Stack said carefully.

'Of course,' Nazir said lightly. 'Don't just take my word.'

'You still haven't said who you think is responsible.'

Nazir snapped his lighter again. 'Someone's putting a frame around me, like they say in the movies. Identify those responsible then I can't be blamed. That's what I want you to find out.'

Stack produced the surveillance shot taken outside the Neuss apartment where the bomb was made and asked Nazir if he was the man in the picture.

He leaned forward and made a show of studying it.

'It's a likeness but not good enough to stand up. I am six foot one. Measure this man's height against the door frame, you will find he is no more than five foot nine. What did the Germans tell you, that I hired a car in my own name in Paris and personally drove the bomb components to Neuss? Even if I had been involved would I really have done that? Why? For the thrill of it?'

Stack said, 'You say you're not involved in drugs yet it's a matter of public record you were tried in England and deported for dealing in them.'

Collard looked at her in surprise. He hadn't known. Neither of them had fully revealed their hand.

'I was held in prison so long without trial the judge had no choice but to let me go. He deported me to save face because I refused to work for British intelligence. British intelligence had trumped up the charges in the first place.'

The man had an answer to everything.

'Nigel Churton asked if I could take any message back,' Collard said.

'Good old Nigel? Of course.' Nazir could have been discussing a friend in common. 'Nigel and I have had our differences. But as I know the Middle East I sometimes advise him on local matters.'

For the first time, there seemed an element of the fantasist to Nazir, who appeared keen to prove he was in with everyone: the man supposed to have blown up a civil airliner was now telling them he had acted as a security consultant to the man in charge of the British government's investigation into that bombing.

Nazir went on lightly. 'Tell Nigel about the Israeli operation. Tell him I think he knew all about it right up to the end, except for when it went bang. Ask him if he is ruthless enough to permit his godson to be exposed to that cosy little false plot.'

'That is out of the question,' Collard said, losing his temper.

'Be careful,' Nazir shot back, his ruthlessness

273

evident for the first time. 'You are my guest.'

Collard stared out at the flat sea. Nazir's ridiculous hypothesis upset him less than the realization that there were still deeper and unsuspected levels of Nick's past to uncover.

Nazir leaned forward to drive home his advantage.

'Listen to me very carefully. There's always a personal angle to these things. Nigel's knowledge of the fake bomb plot would be compromising in itself. Nigel stands to be embarrassed but he's conveniently in charge and in a position to find out what went wrong. I don't know the answers to his questions but I know enough to cause great damage if he doesn't lie down quietly. With respect, tell him not to send an amateur next time.'

A train went past in the distance. Real life sounded a long way off. Stack looked subdued. Perhaps like him, she was dizzy from so much speculation.

Nazir switched back to being charming. 'Let me see what I can find out about your boy. I know Khaled's family. Leave your numbers. Yours too,' he said to Stack. 'I was fond of Khaled. For his memory as much as my own innocence I want to know who was responsible. I can pay for information.'

The offer hung awkwardly, unanswered. Nazir wrote their numbers in a leather notebook, and gave them one to memorize in return, saying a message could be left any time and he would answer within twenty-four hours.

He was gone in a hurry, saying Bauer would

274

arrange their return journey.

Bauer was in no mood to do so. He and Bobby were not conditioned by the same diplomatic parameters, being possessive, unpleasant, unwilling to take no for an answer and keen to retain them as a captive audience, particularly Stack. Bauer refused to have his driver take them to the airport, saying they would all go back in the morning, and offered them separate guest suites. Collard resigned himself to a disagreeable evening. Stack said she was going to take a bath. Bauer pointed out Collard's room from the terrace and made no offer to take him down or let his manservant.

Collard was contemplating being a semi-prisoner in luxurious surroundings when there was a tapping on a back window. It was Stack.

They left, avoiding the paths, climbing through the shrubbery. Collard wondered if anyone would try and stop them. He remembered the high security and hoped the system controlled entry only. He was right. The pedestrian gate next to the main entrance had no code and opened to the press of a button.

L'Age d'Or

Nazir's act was pretty good, Angleton thought, for a worried man. He was correct to fear the Israelis, and by extension the Americans, but he underestimated the role of his Syrian protectors. And the English were naive in their persistence that Nazir had been exclusively theirs, flying him in and out of London — technically illegal as he was banned following his arrest for drugs — to attend and advise in anti-terrorist conferences. Angleton had to laugh: Nazir and anti-terrorist conferences! That was how crazy the world had become.

Angleton's sightings of Nazir reminded him of old movies by Buñuel, particularly *L'Age d'Or*. Ancient radio dials he thought of too, showing all the old European stations: Hilversum, Luxembourg, AFN, the Light Programme and the BBC World Service.

According to Nazir, those crafty Israelis were still pulling a stunt taken from the Angleton book of methodology. He was the one who had shown them how.

He had worked so well with the Israelis to a point where some in the Agency had accused him of being their paid-up agent. The Israelis were professional, alert, super-paranoid hawks. Angleton took care: there was nothing sleepy about them; none of that mañana shit. They were real gunslingers. It was hard not to get pissed off sometimes; they were so in your face.

It figured they would set up a false Palestinian cell and feed intelligence to the Krauts to bring them into line and stop the Palestinians using the place as a haven because Bonn was trade-pally with Tehran. Good thinking.

The moves all went back to that pub in Mayfair, 1943, to the birth of Amazon and the blinding realization that fiction lay at the heart of counter-intelligence. Greene already made up stories for a living and so, Angleton realized, five pints down, could they. The stiletto of fiction.

The other object lesson: get someone else to do the dirty work wherever possible, learned later and in his case the hard way, at the hands of those slinky cardinals.

Angleton's greatest unnoticed triumph was sealed as Philby departed Washington in 1951, if not in disgrace then under a large cloud. During their last drink together, a low-key affair, Philby said with his usual air of mischief, 'People are saying you're devastated by the likelihood of my betrayal.'

'Too busy,' replied Angleton cheerfully.

'No time for regret?'

'Quite right. Time for another?'

'Always time for another. We had fun, didn't we?'

'I'll have to file a report on you.'

'Of course. What'll you say?'

'That Guy Burgess was your lodger and the Russians would never risk the security compromise of letting two spies share the same house.'

That night, after leaving Philby, Angleton

delivered a top-secret arrangement for Mossad to extend full service to the CIA, including the subcontracting of awkward jobs that the Agency wanted to dissociate itself from.

★ ★ ★

Angleton's broodings on Nazir produced a strong sense of déjà vu. Every way he looked at it, he was sure it connected back to Amazon and Rome at the end of the war.

Someone had closed down the Palestinian channel but kept it running, as Angleton had with Amazon, pretending it was gone when it wasn't. What had started as a vanity project run smoothly to his command ended in gut-wrenching spasms that reduced him to shaking cold sweats and clutching the toilet bowl like it was flotsam from the wreckage.

At the time the impressionable young Lieutenant Angleton had been distracted by the cloak and dagger of it all, by the splendour of the dark maze of the Vatican, the silky insinuations of ecclesiastical minds, the muted swish of cardinals' robes and sense of effortless ritual and power designed to humiliate (no humility there): godlessness the enemy with communism poised to sweep the Holy Church aside in central Europe, reaching as far west as Germany, with, God forbid, France and Italy in jeopardy, resulting in a besieged Vatican or, the unthinkable, a Papacy in exile.

Cardinal Montini, future Pope, at their first meeting: 'It is our business to be informed.

278

Rome is, with due deference, our city. We know its ways and those of our more wayward children.'

The Vatican took its job seriously, smuggling Angleton in and out of secret meetings in a laundry van, leaving him to wonder who was really running Amazon. He was not naive enough to believe he was, despite Philby's reassurance it was his show. At the second meeting the cardinal suggested Angleton use the Amazon traffic to insert information the cardinal wished to have passed on in secret to Washington.

'We would tell you what to include, broadly speaking. Then, even as a fake, it would, so to speak, have our imprimatur and be less of a fake than Amazon's real fakes.'

The cardinal permitted himself a smile and said the matter was between them.

After Amazon's exposure, as planned and to the enhancement of Angleton, the cardinal offered a toast to the operation's successful conclusion, which Angleton saw as no conclusion, merely the shutting of one door. From what he had thought was in his control, he found himself in the uncomfortable position of not having a fucking clue what was going on. He could hear Philby's hollow laughter, welcoming him to the big boy's game.

★ ★ ★

Angleton wondered if the cardinal was now assigned to the same worldly limbo as he was or

279

was snug in a heavenly Vatican annexe, safe from the travails of transit. Sometimes Angleton knew he was in Frankfurt. Other times he seemed to be stuck somewhere else, caught up in the same endless loop, far from omniscient and wanting to tell Collard he would never really find out what he wanted. There would be no single moment of revelation or understanding, just a gradual acceptance, which would also be a depression, of how events probably unfolded. Angleton looked back at the Amazon operation in terms of its bare necessities, devoid of emotion or involvement, as scratching in the dust; what he needed to do was detach enough to find the similar pattern behind the destruction of Flight 103.

Conscious of his failure at Frankfurt, he was at pains to attach a chronology to what had happened. He recognized all the old patterns of shift and blame. He could read the muddied trail of an operational cover-up like he was an Indian scout. He was the acknowledged master of the same: the Elvis of cover-ups. He saw something of the ghost of Lee Harvey Oswald in the way they had set up Khaled, maybe even the other boy. Poor Lee, a nice bright young man undeserving of what history had in mind. Angleton had always enjoyed that process of set up, creating a fiction, sometimes with the subject's connivance, and watching how the two slid together.

He had missed Khaled on the day, despite searching hard. Recognizing Collard as a product of the same venerable institution that had educated him was of no earthly or heavenly use under the circumstances (the curse of the old school tie). Now he was left with the hopeless task of trying to will Collard into being his agent, the elected representative of his ghost; he who had been fundamentally sceptical about all those mind-control psy-ops experiments that had obsessed the CIA. Collard was all he could find; a man bereft, redeemed only by the prospect of getting Stack in the sack. The joke kept Angleton going. That was another surprise, that there were still jokes, albeit only bad ones, which was pretty much the case everywhere.

Customs

A message at the Sheraton desk told Collard to call Oliver Round urgently. Stack had one from Schäfer, saying he had something important for her and where he could be found that evening.

Round had left several numbers. Collard noted the sevens scored in the Continental way. The desk staff warned him against driving into town because of a bad smash on the airport road causing long delays. Images of the traffic jams were on TV when he switched it on in the room. He thought of Nazir's fake lighter, the needless unpleasantness of his stupid, rich friends and the pointlessness of all their lives in the face of disaster.

He and Stack had got a commercial flight back from Nice to Frankfurt, after hitching a ride to the airport. The episode seemed typical of Nazir's final unreliability.

Stack had said he must think she was just a rich girl playing around. Collard reassured her that wasn't the case while privately thinking that she was closer to Nazir's world than to his. He doubted if she would spend the rest of her life reporting.

His impression of the day was that it had been stage-managed from top to bottom. Nazir had told them only what he wanted, no more, and his purpose was to deliver a veiled threat to Churton. Collard wondered if the meeting really was anything to do with the plot rather than the fallout surrounding it. All these feints and secret appointments were another way of saying business as usual; whatever that was.

It left him more fearful for Nick's safety, given how casually people were used and discarded in these extraordinary fabrications. His guilt or innocence was no longer the point. It was about what Nick knew. Perhaps it wasn't even about that; it was about what others thought he knew.

★　★　★

They were in Nick's old room at the Sheraton, ill at ease and acutely aware of each other.

Stack said the last thing she felt like doing was going out again. With the highway blocked she would have to get the train. He could see she wanted him to take control, which he was reluctant to do beyond making a half-hearted offer to go with her. She shook her head and said she was fine. She still seemed embarrassed by Nazir's revelation about her father. Collard suspected she worked very hard keeping it secret. He doubted if her colleagues at work knew, not even Evelyn.

As she left the room Collard caught sight of his reflection in the mirror, warning him against doing anything impulsive. He was aware of a shared desperation. What their sleeping arrangement was for that night he had no idea. It seemed rude to tell her to get her own room. He had seen the way Bobby looked at her.

He was about to take a bath before calling

283

Round when the phone rang. It was his tame receptionist downstairs saying she had something for him. Collard took the lift, wondering what it was. Ute, her name was, he remembered; she had a tag on her uniform to say so. He tried to imagine her life, restricted to her desk and the thousands of faces that passed each day, and always the obligation to be polite.

With it being the start of her shift, Ute's smile was still fresh.

'I was thinking about our conversations and I have found this for you.'

She handed over a large brown envelope. Collard opened it, puzzled. It was a blurred photograph of the hotel lobby taken by a security camera, with Nick talking to a man immediately recognizable as Quinn. The time on the photograph read 10.36 on the morning of the crash.

Quinn and Nick in a Cyprus café several weeks before the crash was quite a different proposition from Quinn with Nick together in Frankfurt on the day. It put Nick right back in that tight mystery surrounding the explosion.

'Where did you get this?'

'I was in the staff restaurant with one of the security people. Because the hotel is part of the airport he told me they kept the material from the day of the crash as a precaution. It took ten minutes to find the right picture. I made a photograph from it.'

Collard was touched by this unexpected act of generosity. He was curious to know if anyone else had shown interest in the hotel footage from that day. Ute knew the answer. Her friend in security had told her no one had, even though it had been offered to the German police, airline investigators and the airport authority.

He wondered if Nick had appeared elsewhere on the tape and whether it would show Fatima Bey.

'Is there any way I can see the rest of the tapes?'

Ute seemed reluctant faced with this new request.

'I have pestered you enough but it is a matter of my son's life.'

'I thought he was killed in the crash.'

'So did I but now I'm not sure.'

She looked surprised as she picked up the phone. She spoke to the security desk. Her friend wasn't on duty until the following morning.

'I will talk to him tomorrow.'

Collard, aware of a guest waiting impatiently for them to finish, thanked her.

'You're welcome,' she said formally. 'Have a good evening.'

★ ★ ★

Collard returned to the room and forgot about his bath. He tried Round's home first as it was Sunday. Round's wife answered, sounding fed up, and fetched him.

'I hear the meeting with Nazir went well.'

This casual detonation shook Collard. Round was being mysterious and teasing but the remark

285

only served to leave him feeling marginalized and expendable.

If it wasn't Stack reporting back, it meant Churton had a spy, or, more likely, another route to Nazir. Collard remembered his first sight of the man, on the phone. Who had he been talking to then? In any configuration of Nazir, Stack, Churton and himself, he was the odd one out.

'If you know already what was the point of sending me?'

'More as a favour to you. We're sure Nazir's people know about Nick.'

'Nazir says it's you I should be asking about Nick.'

'Me?'

'As one of Churton's people.'

'I am not. I am merely trying to act in your best interests.'

'You said 'we' just now, referring to Churton.'

'You're being paranoid. Anyway, that's not the reason I'm calling.'

'I'm calling you.'

Collard was spoiling for a fight. Round knew him well enough to recognize that and think little of it.

'This is serious. When are you coming back?'

'Tomorrow, unless Churton has more assignations in mind. Isn't it rather pathetic, having to use someone like me?'

'Forget about that. This is far more serious. The shit has hit the fan with Customs and Excise. There's a warrant out for your arrest.'

Collard laughed in disbelief. He couldn't

286

imagine what he was supposed to have done.

'You'll be arrested when you come back into the country. Do you have any idea what you're mixed up in?'

'Don't leave me to guess. Just tell me.'

'Illegal trading.'

His first reaction was Nazir's: that someone was putting a frame round him. If it wasn't so desperate it would be funny. He had apparently gone from being an unofficial go-between for a senior government official to a common criminal in one move, without the faintest idea how.

Round took his silence as an indication of his compromise.

'You can be frank with me. Nothing has been going on, has it, I should know about?'

'You tell me. You know more than I do.'

'I'm sorry. Yes, of course. Are you sitting down? Customs say from 1986 you consistently broke trade embargoes by dealing with Iraq and concealed the transactions with false documentation.'

'This is so far-fetched it's not even ridiculous. Don't they know the bulk of my business is domestic? I flog security to supermarkets, for God's sake. Why would someone have it in for me? It doesn't make sense any other way.'

'I'm sure it's nothing sinister. Try not to worry. I've spoken to our best lawyer and we'll pick up the tab for any legal bills.'

'They could cost hundreds of thousands.'

'I'm going to fight this. In the meantime you will have to go through the rather undignified

287

process of being taken off the plane at Heathrow in handcuffs by Churton's people, so be sure to let me know what flight you are on. That way we can avoid Customs.'

'What happens after that?'

'A council of war. Our lawyers will get on the case.'

★ ★ ★

Round's call brought back memories of Sheehan's determination to corral Nick into his investigation and make the facts fit. Collard imagined being interrogated by dreary men and women who believed it was human nature to cheat.

When Stack returned he was in bed, with the light out, trying to sleep. He kept his eyes shut, listening to her undress and clean her teeth. She got into her bed. They lay there a long time, aware of the other pretending to sleep. Perhaps five minutes passed, perhaps half an hour. He had the impression of drifting off a couple of times. The atmosphere remained tense. His thoughts were starting to turn to dreams when Stack spoke.

'It was Schäfer in that smashed-up car on the way from the airport.'

She had waited in the bar where Schäfer was supposed to be. A man had tried to pick her up. Mention of Schäfer was enough to cause his retreat. Schäfer was a local there. The man said he was surprised by Schäfer's absence. It was unlike him to pass up a drink with such a

288

desirable companion.

Her table had a view of the street and she watched police cars draw up outside a block of flats, followed by a TV crew. She hadn't made the connection until what she had seen being filmed turned up as a report on the television in the bar.

'I'm drunk. They made me toast Schäfer. I'm scared too.'

He got into her bed. He wanted to say something but she put her hand over his mouth and soon lost herself in a space of her own, leaving him to wonder if it was her escape from the blackness of the crash. Their bodies met in a rough collision of desire, fear and desperation. Sex and death were inextricable. Collard let her exorcize Charlotte, in awe of the energy she released in him while thinking that without Schäfer's death they would not be doing this. He drove into her harder, to obliterate the guilty memory of standing outside the room they were in, listening to the girl's moans of abandon as she came to climax.

They were woken by an early call from Stack's editor summoning her back to London for immediate conference. Collard watched her frown, aware of her odour on his body.

He wondered whether to go with her then decided the indignity of being escorted off the plane was something he would prefer to face alone.

She dressed in a hurry and put on lipstick, leaning into the mirror.

'Yardley's Reckless Red,' she said, taking the

289

excess away with a perfect imprint of her lips on a tissue, which she left as a souvenir.

'See you back in London,' she said and was gone.

The Frame

Collard got up slowly, showered and went down late for the buffet breakfast. The other guests had already eaten and the dining room was nearly empty. What had happened with Stack — their raw emotional and physical rashness with no regard of the consequences — left him even more confused.

Confronted with the trays of waiting food he had no appetite and went back upstairs, lay down and tried to work his way inside his son's head. Nick had been in Frankfurt at least five days but did not see Fatima Bey, except on the last night when he asked her to marry him. The following morning he had been seen with Quinn in the lobby.

It was like trying to cup water in his hands. Details made sense individually but nothing added up. Was the proposal to Fatima Bey an act of desperation because Nick suspected he was in much more trouble than he realized? Was she part of the plot? Collard was fairly certain she wasn't the girl in the Polaroid. Nick was attractive. There could have been other girls.

He got up and watched planes take off and land. It was a stormy morning. The glass of the window was cold against his forehead. Outside was freezing. He remembered standing under the awning of the Heathrow hotel after hearing news of the crash and feeling very isolated. Now he

291

was aware of a stirring of deep resistance stemming from the realization he was truly alone. There was only his private resolve.

He checked out. There was a note from Ute the receptionist leaving the name and number of her friend in security. The man who came down was younger than Collard expected, fresh-faced and in his twenties, with a cow-lick of fair hair. He told Collard about the decision to keep the security tapes from the day of the crash and how nobody had shown any interest except him and an American who had turned up that morning and taken them away.

'Did you make him sign for them?'

The man nodded. Collard asked to look at the name on the release form. He was expecting Sheehan's signature, but what he saw brought him up short. The tapes had been signed for by Angleton's mysterious cohort in Wales, Hoover.

Of all those from Wales, Hoover was the one about whom he had been able to find out the least: an address in West Berlin; an American originally from Belgium; Valerie Traherne's description of him as mysterious, the apparent bearer of bad news, changing Angleton's early excitement to panic. Hoover's company name on the release form told him nothing. He wondered if Hoover was still in the hotel and had been watching him all along. He had never thought to look over his shoulder.

★ ★ ★

Collard flew home through a thunderstorm. The cabin crew went through the safety exercises, following the announcement that 'in the unlikely event of an emergency . . . ', then spent the flight with their seat belts on. The plane creaked and rattled like an old three-master when it hit turbulence, lurched and then dropped through an air pocket. Collard waited for the first sound of tearing metal and looked for signs of panic in the other passengers. The majority were businessmen working or reading financial newspapers. An overhead baggage locker sprang open. A coat flew out, like a large bat. Someone screamed. Had the dying on Flight 103 been able to see their breath as they plummeted through the freezing night or had the air been ripped from their lungs by the velocity of their descent? What was the stress factor on a human body pitched from such a height? Collard doubted if all the panic in his life amounted to a fraction of what they had endured.

As they rode out the storm he wondered what lay ahead. He hadn't called Churton's people to tell them of his arrival: from a desire to be bloody-minded; because he wanted to see if they would track him; because he refused to be beholden to Churton's lot any more than Nazir's. He wanted to know what would happen if he walked in the front door, past Passport Control and through the Customs' green channel. He was not even particularly nervous. He had every faith in the inefficiency of large organizations. No one came for him on the plane. His passport inspection was far more cursory than Nazir's and no Customs men stopped him.

★ ★ ★

He took the Underground from the airport and changed to the Northern Line at Leicester Square. He was going to go home then lost his nerve when he realized Churton's people probably had the house under observation.

He returned to the hotel instead, after loitering outside to make sure no one was waiting. Everything looked normal and he told himself he was being paranoid. He checked at the desk. No one had asked for him, only a message from Stack saying she had been trying to reach him and asking him to call back as it was urgent.

She wasn't at her desk when he rang and had to be fetched. She sounded impersonal and efficient and said she would return his call immediately, leaving him to wonder what was going on. Her voice contained no trace of the previous night's intimacy. He had no idea where they stood.

'Sorry,' she said and explained she wanted to use a line in a private conference room.

He thought she was going to tell him their night together was a mistake.

'I have a mole in the MoD and your name is coming up.'

'Oh yes,' he said, not bothering to sound surprised. At least she had the decency to sound embarrassed. He had been expecting something like this since his talk with Round. He wondered if Stack wasn't the real go-between for Churton and Nazir.

'I've been shown documentation that you sold security systems to airfields, military bases and prisons in Iraq.'

'It's a fake.'

'Did you mention our meeting with Nazir to anyone?'

Collard was too surprised to answer.

'Have the two of you had previous dealings?'

'Don't be ridiculous.'

'I'm being told you already had a connection to him, that you provided the covering paperwork for several large arms deals, creating false end-user certificates.'

'It must have been obvious to you I had never met him.'

'I'm told you used Sandy Beech and his brother to handle those orders.'

'Not true. Beech works for Nazir.'

'And you broke into Beech's house to retrieve compromising documents.'

That stopped him. He thought: they can twist it any way they want.

'All right. I did that. I was following a lead on Nick given by Nigel Churton.'

He wondered if she would pick up on Churton's name. One thing was becoming clear. Whatever was going on with the smears against him, it had to be intelligence-related.

'I'd never heard of Nazir until a week ago. Your mole is lying.'

'He may not be. He could be passing it on in good faith.'

'In that case someone is trying to discredit me. You must be able to see that.'

He wanted to add: after last night. He felt threatened and destabilized by the suspicion in her voice.

'Have you been investigating me all along?'

'Of course not. I've been trying to help.'

'Tell me again why you were at that party.'

'For the same reason you were. I had a lead on Nazir.'

'Who gave it to you?'

She wouldn't say.

'All right,' he conceded. He supposed a reporter had a right to protect her source. 'What about last night? Was that trying to help?'

She retreated further into silence.

'Or was it a desperation measure?'

Silence.

'Did I have a sign round my neck saying 'damaged goods; fuck as required'?'

'You know it wasn't like that.'

'Count yourself lucky. The rest just got to fuck my head.'

'I wanted you.'

'As part of whatever game is going on? I have no idea what any of this is about except the refusal of anyone to be straight with me, and you're up there with Nazir and Churton.'

They all had something they were trying to protect, for which they were prepared to sacrifice everyone else.

'You're wrong. Believe me. I can't say any more.'

She sounded sincere but his suspicion tainted everything.

'I'm sorry. I didn't mean to make it personal.'

Collard suspected she, like him, was floundering.

Before she rang off, she said, 'What I wanted to say is be careful. Someone trying to tie you in with Nazir might be because this whole thing is even more connected than anyone realizes.'

'Are you saying I'm being framed as a direct result of the crash?'

She would not say any more and quickly rang off. Collard noted his hand was steady as he hung up. Despite that, he knew his life was in free fall.

★ ★ ★

Like father, like son: they were both being used and positioned to make them look guilty. The meeting with Nazir left him compromised and precarious.

He called Round persistently and was told he was unavailable. He left messages but his call was not returned.

Everything was being fed back through the crash — the present, the past. He couldn't imagine a future. The crash underscored everything and affected it retrospectively. Accusations of his illegal trading with Iraq seemed, incredibly, to be part of it, putting him in a similar position to Nazir, without the resources to fight back. But that sounded too melodramatic. In his case there was nothing to frame.

297

He was an ordinary businessman.

Driven out by frustration, he took the car and headed south through Chalk Farm and Camden Town, pushing it up to seventy on the elevated section of the Westway, for a burst of speed in a congested city. Rooftops skimmed by. At the roundabout he took the spur to Shepherd's Bush and drove across to Hammersmith to the motorway link and out towards the airport where it had all begun the moment he heard the news.

Everything before was prelude, ignorance.

It was getting dark by the time he reached the airport. The inner perimeter road took him past the cargo areas and the aircraft hangars. A barrier was down and he had to wait as a jumbo jet was towed in.

The vast belly of its hold was hugely apparent at ground level and Collard thought, *Anything could have been on that plane*. He had always believed the holds of planes were filled with the passenger baggage that was disgorged onto the carousels in arrivals halls. Now he saw them as massive storage containers capable of holding any kind of mysterious or threatening object. God only knew what the total cubic capacity of this space was across all the airliners taking off and landing every day: thousands of mysterious black holes of which the passengers sitting above remained oblivious. In the security of the cabin with its calculated distractions he had never given a second's thought to what lay beneath. The process of all air travel was conditioned by trivia: the welcome aboard, the muzak, the dreary magazines, drinks and peanuts, menu

298

selection, movies. He had presumed it had all been carefully thought out to allay passenger nerves and break up the tedium of spending too long in a cramped space. But what if it was also calculated to stop people asking what else was on board?

Passengers were just decoration.

A few light flakes of snow fell on Collard's windscreen, the lit sky a dirty yellow.

He had been a passenger in his job too, sitting in the cabin, unaware of what was going on below. He wondered if the illegal transactions had in fact taken place or been fabricated to tie him in with Nazir. He thought the latter. Round was ambitious but he wasn't criminal. Tranter he was less sure about, but if something untoward had been going on Collard was sure he would have heard rumours. His colleagues were decent people and he wasn't so out of touch.

His ignorance led him to wonder whether a cover-up had been necessary after the crash because they *hadn't* known what was on the plane and everyone — including Sheehan, Churton and Nazir — was scared of what they *didn't* know.

★ ★ ★

Collard drove back into the city past the flashing Lucozade sign, once the only landmark in a dreary stretch now modernized with glass towers like children's building sets, their remedial designs and primary colours symbols of a new England, simplified, bright and unattractive.

299

He got held up on the Cromwell Road, blocked solid in both directions because a juggernaut had broken down turning across a major intersection. The night was full of hooting and angry, miserable people trapped in their cars.

The Achilles Heel

The line that haunted Angleton most was Guy Burgess's sneer, 'You are not as clever as you pretend.'

Intellectual inferiority was his Achilles heel, nights undone by a fear that cleverness was not enough. The maze of contradictions in search of interpretation. The clutter left by lesser minds, failure of analysis. The worm of hopelessness (the gut companion to uncertainty): what hope of penetration? Really, in the end?

The stiletto of fiction. That was what he looked to insert into any operation, by way of information and disinformation. The lie must embrace the truth. 'Wild lies, gentlemen, are of no use to us. Rectal thermometers would not be able to detect the heat being given off by a well-placed lie.'

Angleton saw what Collard could not; how could he? Collard was nowhere near to uncovering Quinn. Quinn was the McGuffin. Quinn was also the axis around which everything turned. Quinn would wait (and have to wait).

Collard had yet to learn it was always personal, however big. Bomb plots, like anything, came down to the same motives of opportunity, fear and greed. The trigger was always human.

Collard was in the zone but not yet central. He knew nothing about Operation Ghost, or who had taken the photograph of Beech in the desert (a big clue), or why the CIA agent also in the picture had been tortured to death in Lebanon two years before they abducted Quinn.

The fiasco of Quinn's kidnap had taken the shine off Wales, the supposed final triumph of his career: Philby in the bag. Instead Angleton had been left to tidy up Slobbery Bill Casey's mess.

In Angleton's day spooks were well-turned-out men, a civilized demeanour and properly cut suit reminders of the higher principles required for nefarious work. They understood ambiguity. Casey was too literal. Casey dressed badly. Casey mumbled. Casey broke things. The last time they met, in Angleton's conservatory, Casey knocked over a prize orchid without apology, payback for the tedium of too much close analysis and Angleton's insistence on metaphorical readings. Angleton screeched, 'Do you know how long that fucking thing took to grow?' Casey thought you could plant an operation and reap the benefits. Casey's favourite film was *Rambo*. Casey enjoyed pitching *Rambo*-type scenarios to a President with the attention span of a gnat. Casey played golf (unforgivable), to a poor handicap (more unforgivable). Casey blundered. He was all can-do and kick-ass. Casey failed to understand intelligence, let alone its counterpart. Casey lacked what they used to call application in school. Casey was a problem-solver. Casey didn't give a fuck about Angleton's wilderness of mirrors.

The Favour

Round lived in Vauxhall, across the river, in a huge white stucco house bought at the end of the 1970s for a fraction of its present value. Money had been lavished on it in a way that made Collard's efforts look pathetic. The expensive handcrafted kitchen probably cost more than his entire refurbishment budget for the last fifteen years. Every detail from reinstated moulding to keyhole covers had been thought about. Each time Collard visited he was amazed how anyone had found the time, let alone the money, for such a vast and useless project — useless in that Round's wife was responsible for the constant renovation and none of it alleviated her obvious misery.

Round came to the door with his mouth full.

'Where the hell have you been?'

His crossness made Collard unexpectedly flippant.

'I decided to make my own way back and here I am. We need to talk.'

'We've got guests, a small dinner party.'

'I can wait.'

Decorum prevailed. Round resorted to being the immaculate host and invited Collard to come and join them for coffee and a glass of wine. Collard knew Round didn't like surprises.

The small dinner party consisted of eighteen guests. Collard was put down the wrong end of

303

the table between an attractive woman and a man in Armani. Irritated by his intrusion, they barely acknowledged his introduction and carried on with their witty, lascivious flirtation. Michael Heseltine was up the other end, a sign how much Round had moved up. The party was a very calculated affair, which Collard's arrival in an old jersey and jeans went some way to upsetting. Round's guests were affluent and successful without a moment's doubt between them, the top end of the table taking its cue from the guest of honour, murmuring appreciation at whatever bon mots he chose to drop. Heseltine looked pleased, his leonine mane immaculately coiffed, unmatched by any other man at the table, or woman.

Collard had once aspired to such mutual endorsement of like-minded people, having done his share of dinner parties where he made the right noises listening to dull wives rattle off the names of their children and the various private institutions they attended, or discussed Tuscan holidays and second homes, and been tactfully silent as they moved on to their class prejudices and racial anxieties. Now he had an overwhelming desire to see them put in their place, Heseltine too, and the pathetic illusions of their lives exposed.

He left the room and went to watch television in Round's study. It was as overappointed as the rest of the house, with glass-fronted bookshelves, an extravagant marble fireplace and a television hidden in a cabinet. The News at Ten was coming to an end. Collard heard someone

304

behind him and turned expecting Round. It was Heseltine. He looked at the television, his vague charm at its most apparent, and asked if anything was going on. For a moment Collard was on the verge of asking him what he knew about the bomb plot. The moment passed and Heseltine gave a general smile and said goodbye.

Round found him watching a repeat of *The Sweeney*.

'Are you all right?'

'Sit down. I need to talk.'

'Brandy?'

'No, thanks.'

'Mind if I do?'

'Go ahead.'

For the moment, they were as comfortable as old tennis partners knocking up. Round left the room for as long as it took to get his drink.

'I should have called first,' said Collard when he returned, temporarily paralysed by the deadly politeness of the house.

Round waved the matter aside and turned down the sound on the television with a remote control.

'Charlotte and I have split up.'

It was the first time he had told anyone.

Round obliged by appearing correctly shocked. Collard felt bad bringing it up, cultivating Round's sympathy, to soften him up.

Round fidgeted and sighed. 'What a bloody awful business. Charlotte will come round. You need to be together at a time like this.'

He stood toying awkwardly with the remote.

'Useful gadgets these, when you can find

305

them. The kids are always losing them. I called Customs this morning and spoke to someone called Farrell and pointed out the unlikelihood — '

'I hope you put it stronger than that.'

Round winced. 'Of course. I pulled rank and told him to call off his dogs for the moment.'

'Really?'

Round looked smug. 'In the interests of national security. Now you know why you weren't stopped at Heathrow.'

'Thanks a million.'

'You don't have to be so sour about it. I did you a big favour. You have fucked up with Churton, not coming in as you were told.'

'Nazir said something interesting about Churton.'

'Oh yes.'

Collard detected nervousness in Round's offhand answer.

'He said I should ask Churton if he was ruthless enough to expose Nick to an intelligence operation.'

Round took several moments to absorb the implications.

'The man's talking through his hat.'

'Actually, he was rather plausible. Not at all what I had been led to expect.'

'Don't be disingenuous. Nigel had never heard of Nick.'

'Yes he had, and he also knew of me. He recognized the name and asked you if he was my son.'

Round looked momentarily aghast.

'Did he? I don't remember. Come on, this can't be right. Think about what you're saying. You can't take the word of an international criminal.'

'An international criminal with connections to British intelligence.'

'I'm sorry. Now we're in the world of Walter Mitty.'

'British intelligence once tried to blackmail Nazir into becoming its agent. Nazir implied Churton is senior intelligence. The inference is, Churton was the officer who tried to recruit Nazir, who seems to have ended up working for him anyway, as a consultant on matters of terrorism.'

'No way! The man's a terrorist and murderer.'

'We live in an age of consultants.'

'Not funny.'

'Why did Churton send me to meet Nazir?'

'You know perfectly well.'

'Churton hasn't got an ounce of altruism in his body.'

'Not fair.'

'I think I was there to cover for the real go-between. I also believe Churton had an ulterior reason for putting me together with Nazir, which is not a million miles away from this mess with Customs. It certainly wasn't so we could have a chat about Nick.'

Round stood up, the pulsing vein in his temple a sign of anger.

'I'd take a long look in the mirror if I were you. You are fouling up. You broke into Beech's house then dropped Churton's name to get out of trouble and now you're hell bent on slandering the man. These are serious people. You don't flout the rules with them. God, you're a mess. No wonder Heseltine asked who that déclassé man was who wandered into the party. Go ahead and fuck up if you want but don't fuck it up for me.'

Round's wife interrupted to say goodnight. She didn't loiter and left without any show of affection. Collard wondered how much she had heard.

'You were saying?'

The distraction broke the tension. Round laughed.

'Takes a lot to lose my temper.'

'You have a very depressed wife.'

'She's a walking medicine cabinet.'

'You were going to marry a blonde and screw her every night.'

Round gave a bleak smile.

Collard said, 'I know I'm a mess.'

Round sat down and leaned forward. 'I want to find Nick too. What you're telling me sounds just too fantastic.'

'I agree. It's like stepping through the looking glass. Nazir said there was an intelligence plot to discredit the Palestinians and bring him down. Israeli agents were meant to find a bomb on a plane. To give it an extra kick for the headlines, a nice young English boy was going to be used and arrested as the bomb-carrier, to show how unscrupulous these terrorists are.'

'Does this have anything to do with what really happened?'

'According to Nazir, someone penetrated the operation and the bomb got put on the plane and the rescue operation never took place. He says it wasn't him.'

'He's bound to say that. I don't believe life is that complicated. There are people in this world who are evil and fanatics and they put the bomb on the plane. Nazir is a skilled dissembler and he has led you up the garden path.'

'Maybe, but that still doesn't answer why Churton sent me.'

Round sighed. 'Go on.'

'I even wonder if this is about Nick at all.'

'If it isn't, then who the hell is it?'

'I think Churton's using me as a link in his plot to destroy Nazir and he doesn't care if I go down too.'

'Nigel will laugh his head off when he hears that. Dear heart, you are one of us. You're cracking under the pressure.'

'It's not funny.'

Round composed his features into an expression of mock seriousness.

'There's an interesting word Nazir and Churton both used. Clairvoyant. Churton was talking about security and Nazir of satellite technology. They were saying the same thing: that these were the future, almost as if they had sat down and discussed it. Another thing happened while I was with Nazir. I got landed with a companion. Reporter, daughter of a multimillionaire media tycoon.'

'Which one?'

Collard named him. 'He owns most of the

papers she doesn't write for.'

'You're not suggesting she was there because of who her father was.'

'Churton's probably sucking up to Daddy, who is keen to take a distant, fatherly interest in her career. As it happened, Nazir knows her father too — is an investor in his business, in fact.'

'Pure coincidence.'

'No such thing. Terrorist or not, Nazir's profits oil a lot of legitimate business with no questions asked.'

Round attempted to laugh the matter away. 'If Churton topples Nazir she's in pole position for a scoop.'

'And if he doesn't, it's business as usual.'

'God knows, you've been through enough but you're letting it turn you cynical. You never used to be like this. There are still values left. Those responsible for the bomb will be hunted down and brought to account.'

'If we'd had this discussion two months ago I would have agreed.'

Round looked at his watch. 'I'd better be getting to bed if the wife's going to get her screw tonight.'

Collard ignored the joke.

'What do you think is really going on?'

'I'm as baffled as you are.'

'You can do better than that. I'm in a can of worms. Get me out of it. Call Churton.'

'If you're here for a shoulder to cry on, fine. If you're asking me to make your peace with Churton, no can do. Churton's not interested.

310

He made a point of calling me to say so.'

'What about the meeting with Nazir?'

'He knows all he needs to know.'

'From the reporter that tagged along?'

'Stop going on about the bloody woman. You sound obsessed by her. You wrote yourself out of the picture by not doing as you were told. What the hell did you think you were playing at?'

Collard said nothing, surprised by Round's vehemence.

'Thanks to you, I'm in trouble too. Nigel's not taking my calls. I'm PNG.'

'PNG?'

'Persona non grata. He blames me for introducing you. He has you down as a loose cannon. Not enough of a team player. Bear that in mind when he drops you in the shit from a great height, which he seems to be doing to me as we speak. So thanks a million in return.'

'I'm sorry, I had no idea.'

'Remind me not to stick my neck out for you next time.'

'It's not Nazir I want to talk to him about. It's about me. Whatever this thing is I am being accused of is intelligence-related. I want to know what Churton has to say.'

'What do you mean?'

'I met Nazir on his say-so. I am now being accused by the reporter who was at that meeting of a long-standing association with Nazir that involves illegal arms deals. If Churton *doesn't* know about this then he should. Call him.'

'Oh, bloody hell. I can't.'

'Have you heard of this sort of thing going on,

what I'm being accused of?'

Round shook his head. 'Never. There are export checks and regulations. We're talking about the government, for God's sake, not some tinpot dictatorship.'

'It must be obvious I haven't done anything. Call Churton. As a last favour.'

Round sighed. 'Oh, all right. As a last favour.'

He knew the man's private number off by heart. He shook his head at Collard after asking for Churton, said, 'I see,' a couple of times and apologized for calling so late.

'Woke his bloody wife,' he said, putting down the receiver.

The TV was still on in the background: aggressive cops laying down the law.

Collard left Round his hotel number.

The phone in his room was ringing as he opened the door. It was Round to say he had spoken to Churton. Collard could hear *The Sweeney* ending in the background.

'Not interested.'

'Is that all he said?'

'Categorically not interested. Sorry.'

Collard wondered if Round had spoken to Churton at all.

The Heath Extension

The phone rang while Collard slept and he struggled to the surface hoping it was Stack. The room was dark. He had no idea of the time. A man with a patrician voice asked for him.

Nigel Churton.

★   ★   ★

Churton sat downstairs in the hotel lobby with a red setter on a leash. He wore a Barbour and a flat tweed cap and behaved like it was entirely normal for him to be there with his dog not much after six in the morning. He asked Collard if he had a car. Collard nodded.

'You know where the heath extension is.'

It was the less-used part of the heath, near the Garden Suburb.

'Meet me at the far end in ten minutes.' Churton flicked the dog's leash. 'Come, boy.'

Collard drove up to Hampstead, wiping condensation off the windscreen. He had forgotten his coat. It still wasn't properly light. He wondered if the dog was part of Churton's daily routine. Traffic was already building up down the hill, in advance of the rush hour. He passed Whitestone Pond, glassy in the still air, and took the road down towards Golders Green, turning opposite the park, all landmarks from Nick's childhood.

313

He wondered why Churton had changed his mind. He must have talked to Round after all, to have got the hotel number. Perhaps Round was being cut out as he feared. It left Collard feeling very exposed.

Churton was on the heath in the lifting gloom. The day was raw and Collard shivered as he walked over to Churton, who was exercising mastery over his dog. A pause followed as they observed the dog's retrieval. The dropped stick was wet with saliva.

Collard blew into his hands and stuffed them in his pockets. No one else was on the heath.

'I hear you took a reporter with you to Nazir. Foolish and unwise to involve the fourth estate.'

'I thought she worked for you.'

Churton grunted. 'I understand Nazir told you to ask me about your son because I used him in a sting operation.'

'Did she tell you that or did Oliver Round?'

Churton turned on him with barely suppressed fury.

'How close to the flame do you want to stand?'

'I'll walk into the fire if I have to.'

'Then don't question me and listen. Nick acted as Nazir's informant and we know that from Nazir.'

He stared hard at Collard, forcing him to hold his eye.

'Nazir was our agent.'

Collard felt he was back on his high ledge.

In his voice of authority, Churton gave Collard his most succinct summary of events yet. It pained him to admit that Nazir had fooled them into believing his loyalties lay with the British. Nazir had double-crossed them but they were now in a position to get him.

'Nazir bombed that plane. Don't be in two minds about that. However, we have persuaded him we believe this not to be the case and he has agreed to a meeting. Our representative will collect him from somewhere of his choosing and escort him to a place of ours. He asked for you to be that representative.'

'Me?'

'He said he didn't want any professionals. Send the amateur, is what he said. Take that meeting.'

Collard had been groping his way around in the hope of some illumination. He remembered Evelyn's warning about the impossibility of definitive truth. So far, everything was shades of grey. He said as much to Churton.

'Not at the centre. Nazir is guilty and we know he did it.' Churton gave Collard his chilliest gaze. 'That's why you must take the meeting, so we can arrest him then and there and let the law take its course.'

He suggested they walk while Collard thought the matter over.

'Nazir was in control from the start. The Israelis provided the Germans with intelligence on the original Palestinian cell. What the Israelis didn't know was that Nazir was the real source of that intelligence. He was working for us, essentially setting up and betraying his own people. In a dirty business you don't succeed by

315

keeping your hands clean. In a way you are right, nothing is black and white. I'm sorry you had to get dragged into this.'

The smile was unexpectedly sympathetic.

'Nazir's right. I'm not a professional. I am out of my depth.'

'We've got a safe pair of hands. We won't drop you.'

'Does Nazir trust you enough to come?'

'We have passed on a vital piece of information which gives him every reason to. What that is I can't say. However, I can tell you what happened so you're perfectly clear.'

Churton stopped and looked at Collard, who knew they were moving closer to the heart of things.

'The Americans ran a half-arsed undercover drug-smuggling operation from Frankfurt that was meant to compromise Nazir's. German and American airport security were told to leave certain flights immune. The attraction of the American operation to Nazir is obvious — if he doubled up and used the same flights as the Americans it meant his couriers stood no chance of getting caught.

'Like Nazir the Americans used kids as couriers. Nick was recruited by a man called Quinn as part of the American operation.'

Collard's body pricked with cold sweat despite the temperature. Churton filled in the gaps as he saw fit and Collard clung on, knowing men like Churton had a highly selective sense of what constituted shared knowledge. 'Of course' was a favourite expression for its implied mutual

316

understanding. However partial Churton's account, Collard was persuaded.

'How did Nazir know that Nick had been recruited by Quinn?'

'Through his network of informers. The American operation in Cyprus was not secure. Nazir met Nick personally and convinced him he was a British intelligence agent. Perhaps he charmed him, perhaps frightened him, for the one piece of information he needed, which was the date and flight of Nick's run for the Americans.'

Collard had a flash of Nazir relaxed, smoking and playing with his fake lighter and understood how Nick would have been dazzled by the man's confidence and charm; the perfect English accent and manners, the romantic spin given to the intrigue. Nazir was everything Collard was not.

Collard said, 'The bomb got through because it was a day when security had been ordered not to interfere.'

'Nick was doing his run for the Americans; Nazir's courier was the boy Khaled; Nazir switched Khaled's consignment with the bomb.'

'And what was Nazir's reason?'

'The Syrians suspected he was working for us and put pressure on him to prove he was theirs.'

In his languid way, Churton was as plausible as Nazir. He said it amused Nazir to play with people because he remained at heart a street fighter.

'What happened to Nick? Why didn't he get on the plane?'

'I've no idea. Why didn't you?'

'By complete chance.'

'Maybe he lost his nerve and followed your example.'

They walked up the heath in silence, following the dog, which was after a scent.

'There'll be other atrocities unless we stop Nazir. He's in too deep with the Syrians now to climb back out. That attack is the start of something. I'm asking if you will be the bait.'

Collard hesitated.

'Nazir murdered those people on that plane as surely as you and I are standing here. We have a very small window of opportunity to nail him. He would have murdered your son and he would have murdered you too without a second's thought. You can refuse but for the sake of the dead I am sure you won't.'

'All right. I'll do as you ask.'

'Excellent. In return we'll find your son. Intelligence services and police forces from around the world are at my disposal. They'll locate him in a matter of days. Trust me on this. I'm bringing someone in you know to rehearse the meeting. He's waiting at your hotel.'

'You must have been confident I would agree.'

'One way or another.'

Churton sounded vaguely sinister. Collard believed his version but that didn't make him any more inclined to trust. He felt as he had at their first meeting, unable to tell whether he was being admitted to the inner sanctum or about to be fed to the lions.

He suspected the whole affair came down to

less than a dozen people, all more or less in the know but with only one or two fully apprised, leaving the rest scrabbling to find out what really happened. The answer lay not in the safe houses of Neuss or Frankfurt or in Beirut or Nicosia but in the grand offices of men like Churton, who airily said as they parted he would see if he could make 'the other thing go away', leaving Collard with the distinct impression that Churton had been behind it all along.

The Cathedral of Malign Intent

Angleton interpreted the crash as a seismic shift, heralding vast, unimaginable change — the moment when the dying body of the Cold War could be laid out on the table for autopsy. Buchan had predicted it in *Greenmantle* at the start of the century. The old trouble spots would quickly erupt as communism slid away to reveal the blood feuds waiting. Angleton saw this with posthumous clarity, driven by the logical illogic of any dream, made more urgent by the tenuous belief that if he cracked the mystery he would be allowed to proceed.

★ ★ ★

Sandy Beech had been blackmailed by the Brits in the 1970s into setting up Nazir, both of them bagged by Nigel Churton, then of MI6, now heading up HMG's investigation into Flight 103, on the old principle of giving the job to the man who knew what needed tidying.

The whole thing had been a racket, of course, as Nazir knew. Persona non grata one day; returned to the fold the next. When Slobbery Bill had routed his arms-to-Iran channel through London, Churton took care of the British end and was forced to swallow his pride when Sandy

320

Beech — the man he had double-crossed — turned up in London as Casey's agent, resurrecting his old smuggling chum Nazir to take care of business at the other end! Churton strangled his vowels more than usual when forced to say, 'No hard feelings. Let's bury the hatchet.'

Why not when the war between Iran and Iraq was a long rolling bonanza? Fuck trade embargos! They all queued to get in on the act; even the Israelis shovelled arms through the back door to their arch-enemy Iran.

★ ★ ★

Angleton wanted to bodysnatch Collard — much as Churton's people had hijacked him and were in the process of rewriting the wretched man's past (and pretty spiffily too). He would have taken Collard up the A1 to Coldingham, arriving at first light. Coldingham was an old RAF airbase stuck in featureless countryside near Grantham, announced by a barbed-wire perimeter fence and a guardhouse with security barriers. It had been bought up cheap by Oliver Round ostensibly as a storage depot. Angleton understood its function perfectly.

Collard could have talked his way in. Opticon had been asked to cost an upgrade to the original security system, which he had previously supplied. Angleton saw the smudged black-and-white images of Coldingham's CCTV security system, rotating screens showing nothing happening, frames so empty of movement they

321

could have been photographs. He was struck by the mysterious vastness. Storage bunkers had been added with its acquisition.

Had Collard gained access to those grassed-over humps that covered the new bunkers he would have stood overwhelmed by the secret arsenal of hardware, carefully stored in bay after bay, with enough gleaming cannon shells and short-range missiles to destroy a city. The bays might have reminded him of an enormous library of weapons.

The alien space with its lethal contents was a manifestation of the size of the mystery they faced. The racked calibrations, the precise technology, the inhuman neatness and the destruction it could cause, twinned with the mess and devastation of the crash zone, emotional and physical.

The storage bunkers were no library, Angleton decided, more a cathedral of malign intent.

Import–Export

Joost Tranter looked casual waiting for Collard in the hotel lobby.

'Hello, sport,' he said. Collard almost laughed. They went and sat in Tranter's car, a new 7-series BMW with a set of golf clubs on the back seat. Tranter said he was thinking of hitting a few at the range later. Collard had no idea where Tranter lived or his personal circumstances.

'Are you up to this?'

His tone made clear he didn't think Collard was.

'Ask Churton.'

'It's me who has to make sure you don't go soft on us.'

Tranter stared unblinking, provoking Collard. He produced a manila folder and took out a document.

'So we understand what is at stake.'

It was a sworn statement by Collard's secretary Lotte saying she had organized Collard's travel arrangements to attend the Baghdad Arms Exhibition in 1987 to cultivate Iraqi sales contacts met previously in London. When she had questioned the legality, Collard boasted the system was foolproof and told her to do as ordered because everything was authorized.

'We both know this is a pack of lies. I can

prove it by picking up the phone and speaking to Lotte. My diary would prove I wasn't there.'

'She's gone on a cruise.' Tranter grinned amiably. 'First prize in a competition. You wouldn't begrudge her that?'

The statement continued, claiming he had involved Lotte in a series of phantom transactions that used the company as a shell for invisible orders. The actual contracts did not appear on company books but all official documentation and export papers named the company as the provider, with false end-user certificates stating legitimate destinations such as Jordan, Saudi Arabia and Cyprus rather than Iraq.

Lotte's statement said that Collard had blackmailed her with a 'gift' of £10,000 to pay off her husband's chronic gambling debts.

Collard stared at the paper, guilty that he had known so little about her personal problems. He supposed that part was true.

Tranter passed over another sheet. Collard read that he had been cultivated by the Iraqi procurement agency in Stratford Place. Names of contacts were listed. The document's summary portrayed him as a fantasist whose head had been turned by the prospect of illegal profits. These were held in several accounts at the BCCI bank and in the Bahamas. He had manipulated people by claiming he was working for the secret services.

It was laughable and pathetic, and terrifying.

Tranter said, 'Call it my insurance that you don't mess up the meeting.'

324

'Call it blackmail.'

'Take a swing at me.'

'So you can demonstrate your superior physical skills.'

'You're looking at five to seven years. In fact, we'll make sure you get a judge who gives you the full seven.'

'Go fuck your veldskoen.'

Tranter was too well controlled to react.

'Take the meeting, don't mess up and this disappears.'

Collard, speechless, was incapable of arguing.

Tranter said, 'I'm not going to appeal to your patriotic nature or any of that bullshit because I know it's personal. If you want to find out what happened to your son, catching Nazir is the way.'

Collard wondered how much of Tranter's irritating, sanctimonious South African accent he could take.

Tranter looked at his watch, an expensive, sporty thing that probably kept time in perpetuity.

'Now we go back to your place and call Nazir.'

Tranter drove the short distance to the house without asking directions, leaving Collard with the uncomfortable impression he had been there before. He made no comment about the heavy padlock on the front door. In the hall, the light on the answerphone blinked.

Tranter asked, 'Where's the bog?'

Collard pointed down the hall and played the one message. It was Nick's voice, very distant and distraught and hard to make out, the message over almost as soon as it had begun.

325

Tranter used the toilet without bothering to shut the door. Collard thought of the police dog shit. He rewound the tape, aware of the cistern filling and Tranter padding around, checking rooms.

Collard replayed the message, straining to hear Nick.

What he said was, 'I love you very, very much.'

Nothing else. Tranter strolled into the hall, hands in pockets. Collard was full of shock at the sound of Nick's voice. He resented Tranter's spoiling presence.

'Do we get a cup of tea?'

'No milk.'

'No problem, sport.'

★ ★ ★

Collard set the trap for Nazir, calling the number he was given. He spoke to an answerphone with no message and recited as instructed: 'I have good news from Artemis which must be delivered in person.'

Afterwards, he asked, 'Who the hell is Artemis?'

'It's the old open sesame. There's every chance Nazir will name the Tropical House in the Botanical Gardens in Frankfurt for the meeting.'

'How do you know?'

Tranter looked slick. 'It's like a card trick. The person the trick is being played on always believes he has a choice.'

Collard supposed they had watched Nazir

long enough to know his moves. Perhaps he felt the cold.

Tranter said, 'The Tropical House has two buildings connected by a gangway. Enter by the main south entrance but leave by the gangway that takes you to the north exit. Keep walking away from the main gate across the gardens and go out by one of the far exits. Take a taxi back to the airport. Check the information desk for any message in the name of George Howden. If there is none, wait. We'll book your flight when we know the time of the meeting. A prepaid ticket will be waiting at the airline desk.'

Tranter whistled flatly while he waited for Collard's call to be returned. He seemed used to waiting. He made no effort to pass the time with small talk. He got on Collard's nerves.

'Do you know an American called Sheehan?' Collard asked after an hour.

'Who's that, sport?'

Tranter shook his head at the description. His expression gave nothing away.

Collard wanted only to play Nick's message. It was what he had despaired of getting: proof heard with his own ears. He was desperate to know more. Nick had sounded so distressed and lost.

After another hour he asked, 'What if Nazir doesn't call?'

Tranter laughed for the first time. 'Then it's the slammer for you.' He pronounced it 'slimmer'.

'Are you a spy?'

327

'Import-export, 'old sport'.'

'Like James Bond.'

'Not like James Bond.'

'How long have you been involved with Six'

'Don't be naive.'

Tranter went back to whistling. His taciturn presence made Collard want to brain the man.

At last the phone rang.

A woman's voice coolly confirmed Collard's appointment for 3.30 the following afternoon. She spoke English with a slight accent and asked if he knew the Tropical House in the Botanical Gardens in Frankfurt:

Collard thought whatever choice Nazir had, he had made the wrong one.

She gave precise instructions of where to meet in the Tropical House.

'Please be on time,' she said and rang off.

'Well?' Tranter asked.

'You were right.'

Tranter looked smug and produced a tourist map of the gardens.

'Show me where exactly.'

'In that alcove there is a bench.'

Collard pointed to the wrong alcove, thinking any extra time on the day might be vital. He was increasingly concerned that the trap was for him as much as Nazir.

'I need to make a call,' Tranter said.

He dialled and spoke without preliminaries. He hung up a minute later and told Collard his airline and time of flight.

'Terminal One. Economy.'

'One way or return?'

'You're a very funny fellow. Well, that's it. Good luck.'

Tranter insisted on shaking hands. Collard wondered whose plan he was ultimately part of. He was sure it didn't end with Churton.

'There you go, sport. I'm going to hit a few golf balls. Make sure to get a good night's sleep, and, don't forget, mum's the word.'

'What, no safe house, no minders?'

Tranter ignored the sarcasm.

'You're on your own now, chum. You know what you have to do. I've gone over the terms and conditions and explained the small print. Go and do your job and we tear up the contract. We'll give you back seven years.'

Tranter gave a tight grin to let him know what he had just said passed for a joke in his book.

★　★　★

Finally rid of the man, Collard played Nick's message over. As upset as Nick sounded, Collard hoped the call had been prompted by contacting Fatima Bey and learning of his message.

Fatima Bey's number rang unanswered. Collard supposed she was out collecting her child.

He watched the day cave in. A headache came on while he waited, willing Nick to call again. He didn't turn on any lights in case he was being watched. Fatima Bey's number rang unanswered until long after any child's normal bedtime.

He walked up the hill stopping off at the Europa supermarket for aspirin. The bright light

329

hurt his eyes. He thought he was hallucinating when he saw Stack looking lost in one of the aisles, an empty shopping basket in her hand. He would have avoided her but she looked up and saw him.

They held an awkward conversation that left everything unsaid. She asked how he was and he answered that he was fine apart from a headache. She gestured at the empty basket and said she could not decide what to buy for supper. They talked of eating together, as though they were a normal couple who had run into each other, then made gentle excuses. He still desired her and wished they had met under different circumstances, at another time. When he had first seen her standing in the aisle, beset with indecision, he was sure her heart was in the right place, and his suspicions were wrong. He wanted nothing more than to trust her, realizing that was impossible. He walked with her while she selected a few items and they stood together at the checkout. He wondered if she knew yet about Tranter's material. When it came to paying she was short of five pence, which he gave her.

They stood awkwardly in the street, pretending they weren't saying goodbye. Stack said she had to go and left quickly. Once she paused as if she wanted to turn back, then she walked on faster.

The Tropical House

Collard ignored Tranter's instructions and caught the first Lufthansa plane from Heathrow, leaving from a different terminal than his appointed flight. Passport Control waved him through. He had spent a restless night, failing to reach anyone on the phone, including Lotte and Round, and he fell asleep in the departure lounge. Evelyn had been home but drinking and incoherent. Every avenue Collard's confused thoughts went down led him back to Round: Round had proposed Collard bring his company in under his umbrella and introduced him to Tranter, then at the Midland Bank, promoting an aggressive lending policy for exports, as a result of which Collard was forced to set up a subsidiary company to expand into foreign sales, against his wishes but overruled by Round, who brought in Tranter as a consultant.

Collard jerked awake in time for the last call on his flight. He collapsed again on the plane and his anxieties surfaced in fretful dreams until he found himself being shaken awake by a stewardess and told to fasten his seat belt for landing. He stared out of the window at the cold ground rising up.

Fatima Bey's number still rang unanswered. He had plenty of time to check her apartment, so he caught an airport bus into the city then a taxi whose driver looked about nineteen and

331

played a tape of Pink Floyd's 'Set the Controls for the Heart of the Sun'. It left Collard wondering what he had done to be so punished. Pink Floyd was followed by Jethro Tull. Collard prayed for the journey to end. His directions got them there after a few wrong turnings.

The driver said in English, 'Have a nice day.'

He called Fatima Bey from a call box. Her phone rang. He was certain she was not picking up. He walked past the same dog shit, several days older. He rang her outside bell. No one answered. He waited around for someone to leave or enter. Ten minutes later he held the door for a harassed mother with unruly children and let himself in. He took the lift and rang the bell to Fatima Bey's apartment. There was no letterbox to look through. The floor had three other apartments. He got no response from any of them, and guessed their occupants were at work, though he felt like he was being watched through one of the spyholes.

He hung around the back stairwell, checking Fatima Bey's flat at intervals.

On one occasion he found two youths loitering shiftily on the stairs. They swore loudly at him and for a moment he thought they would attack him. He shouted back in English, glad of the release, until they retreated, grumbling.

There was no sign of Fatima Bey. The hours crawled by. Collard looked at his watch. It was past two o'clock. He stared at the dial trying to work out the reason for his wild panic. He realized he had forgotten about the hour's time difference and not put his watch forward. There was less than half an hour to get to the Tropical House.

He tried the apartment for the last time, expecting the usual lack of response, and heard instead the sound of approaching footsteps on the wooden floor. Something was already wrong. Whoever was answering the door wore heels. Collard remembered the rigmarole of being made to remove his shoes. Fatima Bey had worn thick woollen house socks.

The door opened. He supposed the woman with the bemused expression was Fatima Bey's flatmate. She spoke no English and was clearly German with her pale face and flaxen hair. The pierced lips and ears and elaborate braiding made her an unlikely companion to Fatima Bey.

The desperation he associated with dreams inhibited his efforts to communicate. The name Fatima Bey meant nothing to the woman. Collard decided he must have made a stupid error, like muddling the floor or the apartment.

She kept the security chain on, which prevented him from seeing in. In very broken German he managed to say something that approximated to his having been there only days before.

His desperation must have been evident because she undid the chain and held the door open for him to see.

The place was the same. Missing were any of Fatima Bey's personal effects, as though she were another phantom presence. Collard wondered if there was a parallel world to which he had been given bizarre access since the day of the crash.

He left in a daze. Failure to find a taxi further delayed him until he flagged one down with ten minutes to spare, nervous of all the things he had refused to consider.

Nazir might also be using him as a lure. Nor could he discount the possibility Churton and Tranter wanted him to be arrested with Nazir as further evidence of his involvement in that shadowy underworld. He could see the front-page denouncements in the press. How naive he had been. He had seen Nick distorted out of recognition by Sheehan and Tranter was in the process of rewriting his own past. Innocent people confessed to crimes they didn't commit; Lotte for example. He saw how embracing the lie might be the easier alternative.

He reached the Botanical Gardens with four minutes to spare. A problem not foreseen was finding enough German money for the taxi fare. He shoved a note into the driver's hand and didn't wait for change. A group of twenty or so teenage school children delayed him at the entrance, their supervisor in protracted negotiation at the pay booth. A girl with a face like a young vixen gave him the finger as he pushed past. He glared, knowing he was wrong to draw attention.

Down to his last marks, he had barely enough for admission. He could not believe he had not checked. The most elementary organizational skills had deserted him.

The garden was arranged in strict geometric

paths connecting the different plant houses. Passing the big, ornate nineteenth-century Palm House he seemed to be a solitary person in an empty park. The fact that somebody was bound to be watching made him as self-conscious as a bad actor.

He walked into the Tropical House two minutes late. It was as Tranter had described: two modern clusters of glass, consisting of different interconnected spaces, joined by an enclosed elevated gangway. After the sterility of the outside, he found himself in an exotic state of chaos with an abundance of lush vegetation growing to thirty feet. The hot clamminess was like having flu; the heavy silence reminiscent of days spent ill in bed. Nazir had chosen well. The immediate sensation after a few steps in any direction was of uncertainty and disorientation.

Nazir was not at the appointed spot. Collard waited then searched the other rooms. The cruel contortions of the desert cacti added to the unsettling effect. His ability to think became threatened. It was like being the victim of a perceptual trick whereby a contained space became limitless. His first sign of human life was an elderly couple who smiled warily, like survivors of a catastrophe.

He stumbled on, through muggy rooms, eerily muffled, except for the loud drip of condensation. An occasional figure loomed out of the greenery, none Nazir. He remembered Nazir's habit of sending intermediaries and started to look out for Bauer or Marisa, the interior designer, or Bobby, the tennis player.

He returned to the original spot, marked by a bench in an alcove surrounded by a thick curtain of greenery.

A man waited, standing with his hands in the pockets of his raincoat.

It had always been a source of anxiety to Collard that he would fail to recognize someone, even Charlotte. He experienced the same sensation looking at Nazir. It was the uncharacteristic expression of puzzlement, as though he was trying to work something out.

Nazir had failed to anticipate the trap, far deadlier than Collard had allowed: the perfect ambush. Collard knew then that neither of them was meant to walk out alive. Churton's talk of letting justice take its course was a smokescreen. Collard was the intended victim too, and men with firearms were hidden, waiting to kill. He didn't know whether to turn and run, shout a warning to Nazir or stand frozen, hoping everyone else would too.

Through steamed-up windows he saw the blurred group of teenage children about to enter the building. Any moment they would be among them. The door opened bringing with it a gust of noisy chatter, under which he heard a discreet noise like a polite cough in a public space.

Nazir was taking his hands out of his coat pockets. He rocked gently then fell back into the plants which closed around him, leaving Collard with the memory of a neat hole in the man's forehead, a look of silent surprise and a fine spray of blood as the back of the skull blew away.

An altercation broke out among the children

gathered by the door. Collard thought they must have seen but they were being brattish. The blood on the leaves washed away under the steady drip of water.

Collard tensed for the second shot, waiting for it to drill into his brain. The alcove where Nazir had stood gave no sign of his having been there.

Nothing happened. Collard left the way he had been told by Tranter, away from the main entrance. Then he turned back in case he walked into his own ambush and went the other way.

Seconds passed in an eternity: crash time, he thought as he pushed through the crowd of children, careful not to hurry. The girl who had given him the finger stared at him with the same perplexed look he had seen on the face of Nazir.

The New World Order

Collard waited for the after-effect. No shock kicked in and no one came after him. He shivered in the vulnerable open of the park gardens after the sweat of the Tropical House. The only other person out was an old woman bent by age that made her look like she was inspecting the arse of her waddling Pekinese. Collard was rebellious at the thought of how much his escape would upset Tranter and Churton. Now they would come at him twice as hard.

He followed signs to the main railway station, listening out for the sound of police sirens that never materialized. A bureau de change gave him marks and he bought a ticket to the airport. He ignored Tranter's instructions to check the information desk. He wasn't supposed to be alive anyway. Survival left him light-headed. He celebrated with a drink. He told himself he was behaving normally. He traded the return half of his ticket for a flight from Köln to Gatwick, went back to the main station and took the next train, using up most of his marks. He concentrated only on the most immediate physical details and actions, refusing to ask why someone wanted him dead.

No one stopped him leaving Köln and nobody waited for him at Immigration in Gatwick.

He tried to use his credit card to draw sterling

338

from an ATM in the arrivals hall but it was rejected. He must have exceeded his limit. His ordinary bank account would be in credit because his salary went into it so he used his debit card to request £50. It too was rejected.

Every other machine at the airport refused him, whatever cards he tried. He attempted cashing a cheque at a bureau de change, which confirmed the bar on his name. The teller gave him a pitying look as she tore it up.

Someone didn't want him to access his money.

He hadn't been meant to come back. Now he had, a block had been put on all his accounts.

They wanted to turn him into a non-person.

He had ten pounds and some change, plus some marks, which he converted, giving him just under twenty pounds.

It was enough to get him to Heathrow, where he retrieved his car from short-term parking with a cheque. The attendant took his card details and left it at that.

The petrol gauge showed under half a tank. Collard watched the car-park barrier rise and thought how only yesterday they were going to drop him in prison for seven years, where he would have probably ended up writing mad letters to left-wing politicians accusing the government of conspiracy. Now they would simply remove him as effectively as they had Nazir. Whatever borrowed time he had would run out with the little money he had.

A car hooted him from behind.

His death would be backdated; that's what they would do. They would turn him into a victim of 103 after all.

He drove out of the airport.

The symmetry was perfect: he would end up where he should have been all along. There would be no announcement: his name lost and buried among the list of the dead. So many fictions masquerading as fact.

He drove into town, envious of how secure other drivers looked, even the miserable ones.

He used a phone box in England's Lane and called Round's home. The answerphone was on. He didn't leave a message. He tried and failed to track down Stack. He thought of asking Evelyn to lend him money and reached him at home but Evelyn was reluctant to see him, saying he knew about his affair with Stack.

'It's ancient history.'

Evelyn was protective of Stack. Collard took that to mean he was jealous.

'This isn't about her.'

'I suppose you had better come over.'

Evelyn was wildly drunk when he answered the door. He raised his fist and shook with anger as he tried to punch Collard, only to fall against him and end up on the floor. Collard had to help him to his feet. Evelyn gathered what was left of his dignity and weaved his way stiffly towards the kitchen. By the time he sat down at the table he seemed to have forgotten the altercation.

Collard asked if he knew where Stack was.

'Gone abroad,' Evelyn said airily.

'Where?'

'Malta.'

'What's she doing there?'

'Following a lead.'

'What's the point? Nazir's dead. He was shot in front of my eyes and I'm probably not meant to be alive either.'

Evelyn looked at him in slurred disbelief.

'They're trying to make out I was involved in Nazir's arms deals and now my credit cards have been stopped and I can't use my bank account.'

Evelyn slowly shook his head. 'I might be the only person you can trust. You'd better tell me what happened.'

Collard did and sensed Evelyn was surprised by none of it.

'Do you know Stack is a tame hack for the spooks?'

Again Evelyn shook his head. 'No, she's not. What are you going to do?'

'I need money so I can disappear.'

Evelyn's hand trembled. He looked in pain. More than that, he appeared in anguish.

'There's something we need to talk about first.'

Collard waited expectantly.

'Take me out and I'll lend you whatever one of those bloody machines will give me. You can drop me off in town. I'm in a mood to return to old haunts.'

They took Collard's car. Evelyn remained silent and morose. Collard feared he was about to endure a forlorn declaration of the man's feelings for Stack. Evelyn massaged his leg, which had developed a habit of going dead on him. A coughing fit racked his body, pitching him forward in his seat.

'Is it about Stack?'

'It concerns her indirectly. It's about Churton.' Evelyn was breathless. 'I've known him a long time.'

'Have you been informing on me all along?'

It seemed so obvious Collard felt only embarrassment.

He wondered what had prompted the admission: yet another secret that drew the strands tighter.

Evelyn wheezed. His breathing sounded like an old saw. He was such a wreck Collard found it hard not to sympathize.

'There's no sign of financial benefit. You live like a student.'

'It was never the money. It turned into a pretty shoddy business, but it wasn't always. I was a patriot, even an idealist. In today's jargon that would translate into all the wrong words: racist, imperialist, bigot, misogynist.'

Evelyn coughed again until his face went purple and Collard waited for his heart to explode. The fit subsided, leaving him gasping.

'Why are you telling me this?'

'Not for your forgiveness,' Evelyn said with some of his old panache. 'I'm not sentimental about many things but I am about Stack. I don't like you because of you and her but I'm trying to keep that out of it. You'll get your comeuppance.'

Sooner than you realize, thought Collard.

'When I got sick Stack took over from me for Churton, on my recommendation.'

Collard waited for a red light. He turned up towards the cricket ground and the park,

342

wondering if that was what Stack fucking him had really been about.

'Isn't there anyone who isn't in this?'

'Spare me your anger. Stack's a mole in a way I wasn't.'

Collard thought Evelyn was straying into make-believe, disguising the grubby transaction with fantasy.

'Moles are blind.'

'Suit yourself, but it's true. I was the cynical, boozy foreign correspondent who turned into a cliché. Stack's different. Stack's gold. For years I wrote what they told me, all lies, fixes and backstabbing. I did for Scargill in the miner's strike: all made-up balls. The Guildford bombers, a complete fit-up. Did anyone care?'

'What did that achieve?'

'Nothing, probably. It's all a front to stop people asking the right questions or, rather, the wrong questions. I confessed to Stack after my heart attack. *Mea culpa*. She said she wanted to take my place.'

'As your mole?'

'Exactly that.'

Having done Churton's bidding for years, Evelyn now planned to bite the hand that had fed him. Stack represented his younger, more optimistic self and she had hardened his resolve to smash the rotten system.

'No more secrets,' he said, a wild gleam in his eye. 'Secrets are the cancer of the body politic. It's what the British do. Secrecy and smut. Oh yes, and irony. Stack's a woman. That's important. We're hunters now. We'll show up that

343

bitch Maggie for what she is, drive a stake through her heart, and that shit Churton too. They turn to dust afterwards.'

He was quite mad, Collard thought, almost admirably so. Evelyn giggled.

'Don't believe a word of what I say. In a world of secrecy there is no trust. Perhaps I can't even depend on Stack. She might be working to her own order, using me, and I won't find out until it's too late. But I'll still prove them wrong.'

He seemed to be in the grip of psychosis, like Valerie Traherne's description of Angleton.

'Wait and see. It will be about a whole New World Order. It's the end of an era. The ice pack isn't holding and those nuclear submarines gliding in the deep are dinosaurs. The future will be no fun.'

Collard drove on through the park over to Baker Street and into Mayfair. In the capsule of the car he felt like a time traveller lost in space.

Evelyn said, 'Look around you: signs of the boom everywhere. Boom means explosion too. It's how planes go when they blow up.'

'Is there a connection?'

'Between boom and boom?' Evelyn looked droll. 'I ask myself every night when I say my prayers whether the whole thing isn't about money. The root of all evil, old boy. Ideology, politics, fanaticism weren't responsible for that explosion. It was money.'

They stopped at a Barclays cash machine. Collard stayed in the car. Evelyn became timid when faced with the mechanical rigmarole. Even for someone who was drunk he took a long time working out how to get his cash. He came back with thirty pounds, saying it was all the machine would cough up.

'Thanks. I'll pay you back when I can.'

'Take it. Feel free. It's only money. Won't get you very far.'

'Where do you want to go?'

'Anywhere. I don't mind. Just drive a bit.'

They drove on. There was evidence everywhere of the changing face of Britain, transformed in the last decade to become flatter, harder and more primary. Collard had provided the security systems for the huge new temples to spending, the giant American-style supermarkets and the vast retail outlets. The scale of everything had changed: enormous space was needed to display the bulk buying that fuelled the spending. Over-slick presenters on television declared the British had changed from a nation of shopkeepers into one of shoppers. The blunt fact was the country had become more American, which in some ways he didn't mind after the dreariness of growing up in the 1950s.

'There is a price,' he heard Evelyn's tired voice saying. 'What created and drove that boom was the indiscriminate sale of weapons. Remember Thatcher is a grocer's daughter. She ran the arms business like it was the corner store: profit not scruples. Government, banks, business, the intelligence services all knew and all did it, gleefully, and it all links up from the retail counter to counterterrorism. Iran. Iraq. You name it.'

Collard drove down Piccadilly past Fortnum's,

345

where Churton had first casually mentioned Nazir.

'If you want to know what Flight 103 was really about it's what you see all around you and what really paid for it,' Evelyn said. 'We're all implicated. The boom was created by those illegal arms sales and your business is nothing more than an extension of that: you contribute to the state's security, which will only increase. The cynical view would be it doesn't matter a hoot who put the bomb on board because the whole point was to find something bigger and more tragic and more headline-grabbing than the shit that was about to hit the fan.'

'What shit?'

Evelyn gave a wheezy laugh. 'You should know. You're in it.'

'Arms to Iraq?'

'Or Iran. Once the war between Iran and Iraq was done, the show was over. Questions were bound to be asked. The Yanks got stuck with Iran-Contra and we would have had the same, without the convenient distraction of that explosion. Good timing for a man like Churton, who would have stood to be exposed. Now they can lose all that under the carpet while searching for terrorists. Oh, there'll be a bit of a stink but everything will be arranged to make it look like a few small fry, probably innocents like you, farted out of order. That's what Stack and I are going to expose — the real stink.'

Evelyn faltered like he couldn't remember a word he had been saying. He fiddled with his cigarettes.

'Take me home. It's past a boy's bedtime.'

'I thought you wanted to go into town.'

'Fuck the old haunts.'

Collard thought of Round with his full diary, social and professional, the two rarely distinguishable.

Evelyn said, 'That strange, sinister noise you've been hearing is the shuffle of closing ranks. They're dumping you to save themselves. That's how it goes. It's an age-old story and the only surprising thing is that anyone is surprised when it happens.'

As they turned into Evelyn's road he said with gloomy relish, 'They will probably kill me for my heretic thought. They'd be doing me a favour. The body's fucked as it is and my mind hasn't been right since they put me on medication. Of course the doctors all work for Churton and their pills mess with my head, as you can probably tell.'

Collard stopped outside the flat. Evelyn seized Collard's arm with bony fingers that gripped with surprising strength.

'They'll find me dead, of course. I'll be consigned to a bizarre and lonely death everyone will say was an accident. But you'll know it wasn't and don't worry; I'll find a way to keep in touch.'

The earlier bravura was gone, replaced by a frightened, trembling man. Collard watched, in awful fascination, as a solitary tear made its way down Evelyn's cheek. He sniffed and searched his pockets for a handkerchief, gave up and produced a crumpled notebook. Collard watched him flick through a mess of notes and scribbling. Evelyn tore out a page, folded it and handed it to Collard.

'You'll make sense of it.'

Collard glanced at the jottings of a madman. He put the page away.

'Don't let anyone hurt Stack. It doesn't matter what they do to me but make sure she isn't harmed.'

Evelyn stumbled out of the car. Collard drove away, watching in his rear-view mirror as Evelyn fumbled for his keys and dropped them.

Collard drove back the way they had come, down to Knightsbridge and the river where the old money lived. The marble façades of the last ten years were to be found further east, towards the City.

Evelyn's fractured confession seemed in keeping with the opacity of everything: editions of the truth, liberal sprinklings of fear and fantasy. Evelyn's paranoia had consumed him as Collard watched. He wondered if it was catching, like a virus.

Traffic flowed. Lights were kind. More and more of the capital was illuminated, whole buildings lit up in useless display, saying Britain had money to burn. In Knightsbridge two minor celebrities were leaving Mr Chow's. Pubs had been made over, turned from gloomy parodies of the Victorian parlour into bright cocktail bars for the new female clientele. Smart couples drifted past in foreign cars, staring ahead, not speaking. Once or twice the throb of a loud stereo invaded his sealed space. Signs of sexual availability were everywhere, in body language, on advertisement hoardings, in the gaggle of well-dressed drunken young women he stopped for at a pedestrian crossing; and deep in the cracks of the city, new breeding grounds for sexually transmitted diseases. He had taken no precautions with Stack, hadn't discussed contraception. He had never used a condom in his life. The women he had known had all been on the pill. The first articles advocating condoms as a preventative against new fatal sexual diseases had surprised him. Now papers ran panic stories about bad blood in transfusions, giving the disease a vampire dimension. Collard thought of Evelyn's ramblings: virtually a city of the undead, run by bloodsuckers; of financial and sexual rapaciousness; of Evelyn's jealousy of his penetration of Stack and now Stack's secret penetration, under Evelyn's control, of the rotten order. Once he had been an ordinary man with dull expectations and ambitions. Since cheating death, he belonged somewhere else. Scarcely a minute passed when he didn't remind himself of those last vital seconds, stretched to infinity.

He drove past the houses of government and over the river to Vauxhall. The swirl of black water added to the sense of symbolic crossing.

Round's car wasn't outside his house. Collard remembered the fancy black Jaguar so smooth and silent it seemed to operate independent of Round's uncertain control, the view through the expensive windscreen like in a film.

Collard waited, wondering how to confront Round. Perhaps he would force him to collect more money from cash machines. There would be a certain poetic justice. Round was with the Midland, the listening bank in its advertisements; more like the spooks' bank, given Tranter's involvement.

It was a quarter to two when Collard gave up. Round hadn't come home.

He had nowhere to go. He was tired. He had no plan left. He decided to go and sit in the shell of his home and wait for whoever came.

Damaged Fathers

Collard parked down the street and sat watching his house. Apart from lights still on in a couple of neighbours' windows, everywhere was dark. The street was empty. No one was out. He remembered Evelyn's book on Philby, pointing out how the defection of Burgess and Maclean had been possible because of the English weekend. Collard supposed he wasn't worth a night-surveillance team. He wouldn't be going far on his funds and it would be only a matter of time before they picked him up, if he didn't turn himself in first. He was nearly beaten. There was nothing more he could do for Nick if he was on the run.

He drove round the block a couple of times past the house, to double check, parked some streets away and walked back, seeing no one. He let himself in. The heating was off and the place was very cold. He kept the lights off. The answerphone was blank. What had been depressing him since hearing Nick's brief message was the realization that Nick was never coming back. The message was a farewell. Collard was sure of it. Nick was gone. He could search all he liked and he wouldn't find him. People vanished all the time, walked out of their lives and never went back. Charlotte had done the same, in her own way. Thinking of their life together, Collard thought there wasn't much for

Nick to miss beyond the security, which he probably saw as more constraint than comfort.

However much Nazir and Churton had exploited his paternal fears, he preferred to believe Nick had extricated himself, coming to his senses at the last minute, not trusting the situation. Nick would get work in bars or waiting tables, joining that drifting migrant population that followed the sun in search of an endless summer.

Collard went upstairs, where it was even colder. He had no desire to sleep in his matrimonial bed so he went to the spare room on the same floor as Nick's and wrapped himself in a couple of duvets.

Sleep wouldn't come. He had trouble believing Nazir was dead, that he would have trusted him enough to come. He questioned his own position too. As sure as he was that they had meant to shoot him too, they hadn't. He was still alive. There had been no second shot. But Tranter's seven-year threat remained.

He drifted off and came to, suddenly; sure someone was in the house. He strained his ears, hearing nothing. He decided he had imagined it.

It was dark outside but later than he thought, nearly six. He was about to get up when the stairs creaked. A door opened and closed.

It wasn't the police. They would have battered their way in. Collard was paralysed between thinking it was Nick returning home and someone come to shoot him. He heard footsteps on the wood floor of the upstairs reception room, followed by the sound of someone climbing the stairs. Collard didn't know whether to hide or stay where he was and brazen it out. He took the precaution of standing behind the door.

The footsteps passed by; a man's tread, on the heavy side. Collard heard the door to Nick's room open. He couldn't make any sense of it and even less of what he heard next, harsh, uncontrollable sobs of despair as a man wept.

Collard threw open the door. Sheehan was sitting on Nick's bed and looked up startled. Collard blinked in surprise, unsure what to make of the tears.

'My daughter's dead.'

Collard didn't know what to do other than ask, 'How did it happen?'

Sheehan waved the question aside. He fumbled inside his coat for his wallet from which he produced a photograph of three girls.

'Lara's the one on the left.'

Collard saw an attractive girl, about eighteen, with the winning smile of superior American dentistry.

'She's my youngest. The others are married now, to soldiers.'

Collard handed the photograph back. Sheehan kissed the picture before putting it away.

'What are you doing here?' Collard asked, worried about the man's state.

'I wanted to see your boy's room.'

'Why?'

'Because I think I should have been more forgiving.'

'Of what?'

'It doesn't matter. She's dead. Did you love your boy?'

'Of course.'

'You're bound to say that. I mean really love him. That would be an exception. Most people put up with their kids at best or actively hate them. I loved my girl more than anything.'

Sheehan scared and embarrassed Collard and he wondered how to get rid of him. Sheehan rambling on about his daughter —

Then worked it out and realized and saw Sheehan could tell. Collard sat down, dazed.

Nothing more than the tiniest gesture, the tilt of her head in Sheehan's photograph, had given it away.

The trapdoor he had been standing on for so long released.

The silhouetted girl in the Polaroid held her head in just the same way as the girl in Sheehan's photograph.

The girl in Nick's Polaroid was Sheehan's daughter.

Everything followed from that. It had been her, not Fatima Bey, in Nick's room that last night.

Collard remembered their first interrogation when he had given his name and Sheehan broke his pencil and stormed out. This must have been provoked by the shock of recognizing Collard's name. Sheehan had known Nick *before* the disaster. Who hadn't had a hand in Nick's fate? Collard wondered.

'Start by telling me what Nick was doing on that flight.'

354

Sheehan looked at him with pleading eyes.

'I put him there — but I didn't know what was going to happen.'

'What do you mean, put him there?'

'Quinn, the man in the café with Nick, he was drugs enforcement. Quinn ran an undercover smuggling operation for the DEA through Frankfurt airport.'

'Using the same route as Nazir's.'

'You know. Quinn took Nick on.'

'At your suggestion.'

'I'm not proud of it. I was angry. I let personal feelings interfere. Your boy was fucking my daughter. The values she had been raised to respect meant nothing to him.'

'Her values aren't necessarily yours.'

'You liberal hypocrite. He infected her.'

'Because he was, as you put it, fucking her and you didn't like it, you decided to do what?'

'He was going to get arrested in New York for transporting heroin into the United States.'

'You were going to have Nick sent to prison? Aren't we getting a little Old Testament here?'

'He was going to get a nasty shock then be released. That's all.'

'Nick was coming home. The world is full of eighteen-year-olds falling in love and having to separate.'

'She was running away with him.'

'No, she wasn't — I was travelling with him, remember? She wasn't on the flight from Frankfurt.'

'She got an earlier flight to London. I guess she knew she could pick up your flight there, because there was space.'

'Was her name on the passenger list?'

'Yes. But so was yours — the list included names of those who were late and missed the flight. Passenger lists are temporary, approximate things not infallible or careful documents. The list means nothing.'

'How do you know she's dead?'

'When I heard the news, I believed she was on that plane — ' Sheehan choked. 'I flew to Scotland certain she was, and then you turned up. It became the thinnest of lifelines to ask what if they hadn't got on the plane, what if they were out there somewhere. So I made you believe, in the hope they were alive and you would find them.'

Sheehan stood up and picked up the lamp by Nick's bed like he wanted to smash it. His grief seemed to have turned into a barely contained rage. Collard was afraid the man was about to do something dangerous.

'Nick left a message only the day before yesterday. We can go down and listen to it.'

He thought Sheehan would be safer away from Nick's room. Sheehan put the lamp down.

'They're gone. They were on the plane. Plenty of bodies are still missing. They'll be lying hidden in the thick forests or a lake. They would have fallen together. It seems obvious now. They had no reason not to be on the plane.'

'Come downstairs. I'll play you the message.'

'You don't get it, do you?'

The old meanness was back in Sheehan's voice. Collard realized why the man was there.

356

Just as Sheehan had once built up his hope, he now intended to shatter it, infecting him with his despair. Collard didn't want to listen. Churton could be walking his dog on the heath. Finding a way to confront Churton was more important than Sheehan destroying the little he had left.

Sheehan balled his fist. Collard flinched, thinking he was about to be hit. Sheehan punched the wall instead, making a hole in the plasterboard.

'They're dead, that's all that matters.'

He watched the thin trickle of plaster dust running down the wall.

'It isn't hard to mess around with someone's bank account and that wasn't Nick speaking to you. It was a message to my daughter. I spliced it off and sent it on to you.'

'Why?'

'To keep you going. Maybe you would find them if I couldn't. I was in denial, Mr Collard, as you are now.'

'What made you change your mind? They could be still alive.'

Sheehan shook his head. 'Time. There has been nothing. We would have found them by now. They would have left some trace. There would have been a sign.'

'Who is Fatima Bey?'

'Oh, Jesus. OK, I feel bad about her. She's an actress who hasn't worked in years. There's little call for ethnic roles in Germany. She was happy to fuck me for the part. Nick had nothing to do with her.'

The man's cynicism took Collard's breath away.

'Did you know that plane would get blown up?'

'I swear on my daughter's head I didn't.'

'What does this come down to?'

'It comes down to Nazir. He sold us the wrong information about the plot.'

'But he was organizing the plot!'

'I know. I was the one dealing with him.'

'You were Nazir's American control?'

'Control's the wrong word. It was more like a working relationship. Nazir was in the business of selling intelligence.'

'And Nazir bombed that plane.'

'Correct.'

'At the same time as selling out the plot.'

Sheehan nodded.

'But you said you didn't know it was going to happen.'

'He led us to believe it was going to be the day after. The twenty-second.'

Collard thought: So many lives on board, so many stories being acted out. People running away, people thinking of leaving people, people plotting to cheat on loved ones, people worrying about money, people fretful of undiagnosed illness, balanced against all the hope travelling on that flight, the anticipation, the prayers, the new job, the love and renewal and reunion symbolized by the holiday season, all those invisible threads snapped and irretrievable.

'I would not have put your son on a plane knowing it was going to get blown up. To be

358

blunt, it would have given my daughter too much to mourn.'

'Why did you believe Nazir when he said the twenty-second?'

'Because a senior American official was flying that day. Nazir's intelligence was correct. He identified the official despite his name and travel plans being kept secret. Nazir said the plane was going to get blown up because of the propaganda value of killing that official. We believed him and were ready to move on the twenty-second.'

'What official?'

'Richard M. Nixon. Former President of the United States. But Nazir double-crossed us. He'd intended all along for it to be the twenty-first.'

Police sirens sounded in the distance. Collard worried they were for him, that Sheehan had organized them because he and Churton had been in it together from the start.

The sirens grew louder. Collard left Sheehan staring downcast at the floor and returned to the room he had slept in, opened the window and looked down the street, calculating if he had time to get out before the sirens reached the house. It was a cold, sunny morning. A bright flash from a window opposite caught his eye and was gone immediately; the sun briefly reflecting off something. The sirens continued on up the hill, a reminder that he was probably chancing his luck staying there. There might still be time to find Churton on the heath.

Collard was going to leave Sheehan to make his own way out when something stopped him.

He stood on the landing trying to decide what Sheehan was up to. He opened the door. Sheehan was standing with his back to him. The sound of splashing first made him think Sheehan had turned on the basin tap. Then he saw. Sheehan was urinating on Nick's belongings that had been thrown in a heap on the floor.

Sheehan said, over his shoulder, 'Don't do anything stupid or I'll shoot you.'

He moved round, pissing all the while, until he faced Collard, cock in one hand, pistol in the other. The tight grin did nothing to mask his angry contempt. Collard stared at Nick's sodden belongings. Sheehan's piss steamed in the cold. He wanted to kill Sheehan.

'I've been saving this up for a long time. Your boy was scum.' Sheehan leered and started to laugh. 'That's better.'

Collard was already gone, running downstairs and out of the house. The last thing he heard as he fled was a shot and he didn't stop until he reached his car.

Voluptuous Ambiguity

Angleton thought Sheehan was losing the plot. He was off on some crazy Hitchcock riff, not just making up stories, but actually hiring actors.

Angleton thought of Hitch's *Foreign Correspondent*, where they shot a man's double on the steps in the rain, which allowed for a high-angle shot of a disturbance of umbrellas as the shooter forced his escape through the crowd.

Collard had been a trigger pull from oblivion in the Tropical House. The bullet meant for him had jammed in the gun. It happened more often than people thought.

If Angleton had been writing Nazir's script, he would have made Nazir blackmail Churton into letting him restage the old Harry Lime trick of a false death and convenient disappearance — bloody Graham Greene again!

An alternative scenario would be Churton subcontracting the job to Mossad, keen for the publicity of Nazir's scalp, which Nazir would then anticipate by taking the precaution of sending an unsuspecting doppelgänger to take his bullet, leaving Nigel Churton shitting his paisley silk shorts about the coming home to roost of those secret arms deals with Iran and the prospect of forensic evidence turning up bomb parts with Made in Britain stamped all over them; Happy Christmas, Love Iran.

Angleton appreciated the Shakespearean scale

of it all: a bizarre combination of the political and star-crossed with the two young lovers and their fathers as surrogates. He remembered a detail from the day: a public announcement from airport information; Sheehan trying to reach his daughter. A second announcement had coincided with Nick becoming agitated. Oh, the ironies.

Angleton thought of Goethe: 'And so they all, each in his own way, reflecting or unreflecting, go on with their daily lives; everything seems to take its accustomed course, for indeed, even in these desperate situations where everything hangs in the balance, one goes on living as though nothing were wrong.'

The issues were: who did Sheehan and Nazir ultimately work for; and had Nazir deceived Sheehan from the outset or had he too believed it would be the twenty-second, leaving another party to pre-empt matters?

The possible involvement of unknown third parties had been the bugbear of Angleton's career. His private recurring fear was he had been run all along without realizing, piggybacked by invisible third parties. Spy as bug. Spy as alien body.

He contemplated Milgram's six degrees of separation and how many moves it would take to connect the man sitting in seat 20C to the stranger in 44F. Angleton was waiting for the resurrection of a broken-down old Nazi-hunter whom he previously believed had been nullified into harmlessness.

Justified Paranoia

Collard was too late for Churton on the heath. There was no sign of him walking his dog, only joggers and regular walkers. Collard was still in shock at the revelation of Nick and Sheehan's daughter. Sheehan's eyes had been devoid of any light. The man was so unpredictable that the shot Collard heard could have been him putting a bullet through his head.

He found a bench, sat down and got out Evelyn's hieroglyphics: tantalizing clues without the benefit of coherence, a series of phrases waiting to be organized by thought and turned into sentences: loan rate@0.5%!!!; 'DEFD'; NC chair IMS 74–84; ECGD@85%; 'For agric use'!; TDG=TGM engineering>TI Machine Tools; TI Grp NC dep ch: MATRIX.

At the bottom of the page was scrawled: 'Ask where NSO money goes: ECGD. Abracadabra!'

He knew Evelyn's shorthand was a cryptic summary of his own framing. NC was Churton, who had chaired something called IMS and was deputy chair of the TI Group. Matrix meant nothing. Collard knew about the DEFD and the ECGD because Joost Tranter had been part of it. It was obvious now that Tranter was the interface between banking and the intelligence services. Round had pushed Collard's company to expand into the overseas market, bringing in his own people, including Tranter, who represented the

363

Defence Equipment Finance Department, a banking arm specializing in favourable loans for export business, which in turn had close links to a new government set-up, the Export Credit Guarantee Department, which existed to insure up to ninety per cent of the value of any export risk. Collard, who was concentrating on the fledgling domestic market, had paid insufficient attention, and had anyway been mollified by Tranter's offer of an extended overdraft on the company's domestic business.

★   ★   ★

He used a call box on the edge of the heath. Round's office said he was on holiday. Round's phone at home was on answer. Collard slept in the car and woke with a stiff neck. On another grey morning he hung around the wet heath, waiting for Churton until he remembered it was Saturday. Churton, in the manner of his class, would be out of town for the weekend.

Turning up at Round's house seemed too dangerous if the police were actively looking for him. But Round's wife was a creature of habit, and if she was in town the weekly shop in Sainsbury's at Nine Elms would be part of her Saturday routine.

Collard crossed the river at Blackfriars and parked where he could see the entrance to the store. He bought several newspapers to pass the time.

He was on the inside pages of most of the tabloids and featured in the *Daily Telegraph* and

The Times, named as wanted by the police for questioning in connection with the shooting of a Syrian businessman in Frankfurt. There was no picture. The information read like it had been recycled from a formal statement. There was a reference to a business disagreement. Even Tranter would have laughed at the neatness of Collard being framed for murder.

Shoppers hurried against the damp, pushing crabwise trolleys, piled so high they looked like looters. Collard couldn't remember when he had last done anything so ordinary.

He came to Stack's paper last. Her story shocked him more than the one about him. It came out of nowhere. Her reason for being in Malta was forensic evidence that connected the suitcase containing the bomb with clothes traceable to a store on the island. The bomb had set off on its journey not from Frankfurt but Malta.

It was clear someone was feeding Stack generously. Her report was authoritative, right on the inside, an exclusive, and the first clear indication of a change of direction in the official investigation.

Her article rewrote all previous theories: speculation about the Frankfurt Connection, Nazir, Nick, penetrated terrorist cells, Barry's airside activities, which day the bomb was supposed to go on the plane, switched bags and all the rest counted for nothing because of Stack's latest contention.

Collard was at a loss to understand this extraordinary volte-face. Perhaps Stack would tell him the bomb being put on in Malta didn't preclude Nazir's involvement and nothing had significantly changed, but it didn't read like that, more like the start of a whole new investigation.

The car park had filled up. It was mid-morning and the supermarket was at its busiest. At last he spotted Round's wife, alone, collecting a trolley.

He contrived a meeting among the vegetables, hoping she hadn't read the papers. He doubted it. She wasn't the type to contemplate anything as dirty as newsprint. He needn't have worried. She was vague and tranquillized and seemed to recognize him only from some strange self-imposed distance.

'Where's Ollie?'

Her blank look told him how estranged she had become. It took her a while to recollect Round was taking out one of their children from a boarding school in Wiltshire, near where they kept a second home. Collard had driven Nick to stay down there, in a house tucked under a hill with views across a valley.

He left Round's wife lost in the aisle and returned to the car. He didn't know what to make of Stack's story. It made no sense to put a bomb on a plane in Malta to blow up one leaving London; why via Frankfurt? More logical to send it direct to London and even that seemed an awfully long way round.

Perhaps Stack could explain.

Every new version was like shuffling a pack of cards. The elements were recognizable and the same, the variety infinite. The only indisputable

366

facts were the plane had left Heathrow and never landed and 46.5 seconds was the time it had taken to fall to earth. Collard stared at his watch.

★ ★ ★

Round's place was near the two Donhead villages between Salisbury and Shaftesbury, deep in countryside fed by single-track lanes in which Collard got lost. The winter countryside was a saturated brown and at its least inviting. He eventually found the right village, parked and trudged back through the empty landscape. The light was falling when he took up a position in the trees on the hill behind the house. The child came outside and used a garden swing for ten minutes. Collard made out a television on in the room to the left of the front door. The rapid one-two of a shotgun firing in the distance startled him. It was a miserable afternoon.

Round came up behind him, and would have caught Collard had he not stopped to fire twice more at a fleeing bird. He was twenty yards away in the gloom, gun to shoulder, the shots echoing and the bird's panicked flapping still audible. Collard threw himself to the ground and rolled down the hill to a rhododendron bush big enough to hide in.

Round passed within a few yards. He was preposterously dressed in plus fours and a Norfolk jacket. Unaware of being watched, he looked more like the timid schoolboy Collard remembered. Round would be nervous of the gun and squeamish about shooting but felt

367

obliged to masquerade as the country gent.

Round took the child back after tea, leaving the house without bothering to turn off lights or lock up. Collard walked in, found the shotgun and a cartridge belt of shells, broke the barrel, loaded it and put the safety catch on. He had hardly picked up a gun in his life. It was heavier than expected, also easier and he was surprised how right it felt.

Round returned forty-five minutes later. Collard waited behind the front door and whacked him hard in the midriff with the gun stock. Round jack-knifed and scrabbled on the floor, fighting for breath.

He flinched when he saw who it was, put his hands up and begged Collard not to shoot.

Collard ordered him up. They sat at opposite ends of the big farmhouse kitchen table with the gun on the table, pointed at Round, too far away for him to snatch it.

'They've already pinned Nazir's murder on me. Is there any reason why they shouldn't add yours to the list?'

Round shook his head, uncomprehending.

'I had no idea. Honestly.'

Round insisted he hadn't known about any plot to kill Nazir. 'The last thing I knew Churton was refusing to speak to you.'

'It's in the papers saying I'm wanted for questioning in connection with the shooting.'

Round hadn't seen the papers. He had been taking his brat out for the day. He gave a weak smile, trying to make a joke of it.

The patina of wealth and a life of expensive

food and fine wines usually gave Round a pampered sheen. His shirt collars were cut soft on the neck. Facing Collard, he looked like a man in collapse.

'Are you taking the brat out tomorrow?'

Round thought better of lying and shook his head.

'So it's just us?'

Round nodded.

'In your own words.'

Round tried to exploit what was left of their familiarity, insisting he had been used by Churton and Tranter. He looked up with a strange smirk, believing he could work his way off the hook.

Collard got up and swiped the butt of the gun against Round's head. The force knocked Round out of his chair and when his face smashed into the flagstone floor his mouth bled. Collard watched the bubbles of blood and saliva form and burst as Round wept and he felt nothing.

Collard hauled him up and put him back on the chair. One of Round's teeth lay on the floor. Collard picked it up and placed it on the table.

'I thought you had died in the crash, so it didn't matter.'

'You saw a way of using that to get out of trouble. With me dead you could make up what you liked about me. You were up to your neck in those arms deals.'

Round nodded, so full of self-pity that Collard wanted to hit him again.

'There was going to be an inquiry and I wasn't sufficiently protected. They were already starting to go for me before the crash, saying I was going to be investigated for buying shares as a result of an inside tip-off. That was the start.'

'Did you?'

'Of course I bloody did!' he snapped in an attempt at his old self. 'We all did. Do you know how expensive it is running the whole show?'

By that he meant three properties, heavily mortgaged, two cars, home help, private education, memberships of several gentleman's clubs, the Hurlingham, a stable, two foreign holidays a year and all the other accoutrements of the successful middle classes. Without extraordinary wealth it was hard to meet all the bills without cutting what Round called the odd corner. This was done by insider dealing and an accountant who specialized in off-shore investment.

'It's never enough.'

'What happened when you learned I was still alive?'

'I told Tranter. He came back later and said he had found a way to take care of it.'

'So you shifted the responsibility on to Tranter?'

'It was a nightmare. I was desperate and you were supposed to be dead.'

Tranter had run with Round's idea but enlarged the frame to dump all the British government's dubious dealings with Nazir onto Collard and pass it off as rogue private enterprise.

Evelyn's equations were, as Round confirmed, evidence and Churton's fingerprints were all over it. Churton had set up the Defence Equipment Finance Department for Tranter to run in 1982. Prior to that, International Military Services, a wholly government-owned company started in the 1970s to assist Royal Ordnance, had been chaired by Churton.

'What did it do?'

'One of its main functions was to arm the Shah of Iran.'

'Which would have been perfectly legal then.'

'And after the revolution when the Ayatollahs set up a series of secret arms deals with the United States it made sense for the Yanks to use us as a front. Churton already had the contacts.'

'Including Sandy Beech and Nazir.'

Round nodded.

'Then there's no such thing as an independent arms dealer.'

'No.'

'When you took me to meet Joost Tranter that first time, what was that really about?'

'We needed a company we could route orders through to the Middle East. With what was being offered we would have been foolish not to. It was a licence to print money and it was all authorized on a nod and a wink. We used Opticon and you were too busy with the domestic market to notice or care.'

Round gingerly fingered where his tooth had gone and said he couldn't face prison. It would kill him. He stared at his tooth lying on the table.

'I always was the pompous ass because I knew it got up people's noses and they underestimated me. We never much liked each other from the start, did we?'

'I'm not interested. Tell me about Churton.'

'Any Iraq-related contracts went through Jordan, which was friendly and fronted the deal, and Churton sought to establish a country credit rather than a deal-by-deal credit. The idea was the bank set up a secret credit for Iraq of £275 million. Iraq was supposed to pay Jordan and Jordan pay us. If the Iraqis didn't cough up, the deal was guaranteed by the ECGD. It was fool-proof.'

'And Iraq never paid, of course, and probably never intended to.'

'No. It never paid Jordan as the trade was never supposed to have taken place. Anyway, Iraq wasn't short of alternative offers.'

'Did Churton negotiate with the Jordanians?'

'He was behind it.'

'For £275 million?' Collard was still staggered by the size.

'It was agreed in Amman in 1985.'

'By Churton?'

'Not personally. It was the Prime Minister's son.'

After that both men sat in stunned silence: Round for admitting what he knew; Collard thinking about the recklessness of people who believed themselves exempt.

★ ★ ★

Collard forced Round to drink enough whisky to dull his reflexes. Then he made him write a full

372

confession of everything he knew and told him to copy the finished document, which ran to several pages, twice more.

The documents would guarantee his safety and silence and, in exchange, Round would get him out of the country with £75,000 cash to disappear.

Round protested he couldn't do it — Collard overestimated his powers and it was the weekend and he had no way of getting that kind of money at short notice.

'You arranged for all those arms to be smuggled out. This is no different.'

'How do I know you won't make trouble from abroad?'

'I only want to vanish and start again. The past is no longer of interest. In fact, be my guest. Say what you like about me once I'm gone. Blame me for all those things you were going to anyway and save your neck, on the condition we draw a line under this and Churton's people let me be.'

He watched Round calculating, testing the strength of the lifeline.

'All right,' he finally said. 'You have a deal.'

It took an hour to track down Joost Tranter. Collard listened carefully for any sign of duplicity and detected none. Round told Tranter that Collard had enough on all of them to make the situation non-negotiable.

Collard said, 'I want Churton to deliver the money in person.'

Round sighed. 'Don't rub everyone's noses in it.'

When Tranter next called they spoke for a long

time. There had been trouble finding a pilot because of the weekend.

Collard realized how vulnerable his position was. Tranter knew where they were and Round's confession was still retrievable.

When Round hung up he said they needed to go outside so he could fetch a road map from the car.

Collard covered Round while he fetched the map. Round found the page for East Anglia and pointed to a long, straight road in the Fens.

'There's a private airfield. Someone will fly you out after dark tomorrow evening. You will be taken to the Low Countries. After that you're on your own.'

Collard stared at the map and tried to picture getting on the plane and leaving everything behind.

Round swallowed more whisky, saying his mouth hurt where his tooth was missing.

'I'm sorry we're in this mess.'

Collard had nothing to say to that. 'Get me some envelopes and stamps.'

'I'm not sure there are any stamps.'

Undone by the lack of a postage stamp, Collard thought. He was so tired he was having trouble thinking straight. He grew more concerned that the protracted negotiations had been Tranter stalling so he could organize a response.

Round came up with a sheet of stamps and envelopes. Collard made him lie on the floor while he wrote notes to Evelyn, Valerie Traherne and his solicitor, asking them to open the

374

enclosed sealed envelope in the event of his death.

He wondered if they shouldn't get out immediately but Round was too drunk to drive and Collard didn't trust himself not to fall asleep at the wheel. He had the gun and if men came through the door he would manage a couple of shots first.

Round drank until he passed out at the kitchen table. Collard looked at the envelopes, wondering what kind of guarantee they would provide. His eyes closed and his head snapped back as he forced himself awake. It was three o'clock. Another seventeen hours and he would be gone. He got up and stuck his head under the kitchen tap and drank a pint of water. He turned out the kitchen lights as a precaution and sat in the dark and knew Sheehan was right. Nick was probably dead.

Round woke with a groan and said he was going to be sick. He threw up in the sink until nothing more came up and he was dry retching.

Collard watched, indifferent, calculating how long it would take Round to sober up enough to drive; perhaps three hours, meaning they could leave at first light. He would take Round with him for insurance, all the way to the airfield, posting the letters along the way, stopping to pick up the money from Churton. It was foolish to involve Churton but he wanted to see the man humiliated, for Nick's sake as much as his own.

He ordered Round to make coffee and forced him to drink several mugs. Round became more lucid. Collard sensed the darkness outside beginning to lift.

Round talked, trying to establish complicity at Churton's expense, saying Churton wasn't what he pretended to be. All those upperclass mannerisms had been acquired not bred. A Rhodesian background had allowed him to fabricate his entry in *Who's Who*, naming an elite school not attended.

Tiredness clawed at Collard's eyes. He clung to the conversation in an effort to stay awake.

'Why bother?'

He couldn't see the point. It wasn't as though class was the barrier it once had been. The old establishment had been elbowed aside in the charge led by Margaret Thatcher.

'We laughed at her at first but not for long. She understood incentive and a blind eye were needed to get the country back on its feet. She fancied herself another Good Queen Bess with her loyal courtiers, building a new empire of money with her financial pirates and buccaneers like Churton who assumed the demeanour of the old guard, the better to stab it in the back.'

Round droned on. Collard switched off. He was back in Wales watching the river from Angleton's old fishing hut. The winter rains had turned it fast and full. He remembered however much he tried to concentrate on one spot the rapid movement of water distracted his eye.

Collard came to on the floor. The side of his head felt like it was on fire. Round was standing over him, aiming the shotgun at him and making strange inarticulate noises in his throat, like he was trying to communicate but couldn't. He was wild eyed and transformed. He had vomited again, this time down his front, and pissed his plus fours. For all his derangement, he looked pathetic and funny. There was very little Collard was sure of any more but he was certain Round didn't have it in him to shoot anyone.

He was wrong.

Round fell to his knees, turning the barrel, jamming it hard in his mouth, swallowing a last breath that turned into a shrill keening as he fired both barrels.

In the moment of explosion, Collard saw his friend's eye stare through him into the black infinity of beyond, then the eye and the whole head vaporized, transformed into blood, shattered bone and brain matter that splattered over Round's expensively rag-rolled kitchen ceiling.

The torso toppled forward onto Collard. His ears rang as he contemplated the unrecognizable remains of what little was left of Round's head.

Payoff

Round's body lay on the floor in a pool of congealing blood. Pages of scrawled notes that made it clear he had meant to shoot himself lay on the kitchen table. They gave the reason and, when he read them, Collard, who believed he had grown inured, found he was still affected by the breathtaking callousness of it all.

No one would have heard the shot. The nearest house was miles away. Tranter would tidy up when he found out what happened and by then Collard would be gone. There was nothing left to stay for.

He abandoned his car and took Round's Jaguar. There was no traffic so early on a Sunday morning. Numbness and exhaustion were in danger of sending him to sleep so he stopped in a quiet road and climbed in the back which was so spacious it was nearly possible to lie down. He fell into a deep and dreamless sleep, from which he woke hours later, still exhausted, and continued his journey, concentrating on nothing but driving, stopping only to post the letters in the Euston Road.

The Hampstead Heath extension was busy on a Sunday afternoon. Games of football were being played, watched by well-dressed families bundled up in colourful anoraks and winter coats. It was a bright, still afternoon with a clear blue sky. Collard had used a call box to telephone Churton, who was waiting at home as arranged, to say he was ten minutes away. He spotted him in his flat cap and Barbour, watching one of the games, attaché case in hand and dog sitting by his side.

Churton betrayed no emotion, apart from a working jaw muscle. Seeing him, Collard knew how hollow his small triumph was. Churton was not the sort to admit defeat.

They stood in silence watching the football.

Collard said, 'TDG was Iraq's Technology and Development Group, with representatives in London, and close links to Saddam Hussein's brother-in-law, who was chief of Iraq's secret service. Joost Tranter was an invisible assistor in establishing TDG then helped the Iraqis buy machine-tool companies to develop an indigenous arms industry. In 1987, TDG purchased one such company from the TI Group. You were group deputy chairman and arranged the sale.'

Churton stared into the distance. Collard saw where he had cut himself shaving that morning.

'Tranter was active in setting up a missile factory near Baghdad and helped Iraq pursue the development of nuclear capability.'

Collard was met with an arrogant silence, interspersed with the occasional look of contempt that said that Churton was driven by patriotic duty and a stoicism Collard could not begin to understand. Thanks to Round, Collard knew it was an act, a gutter toughness dressed up as something else.

Churton looked at his watch and said, 'You haven't got long.'

'Who paid for all of it, in the end? All the reneged deals and credit guarantees?'

'You weren't born yesterday.'

'The taxpayer.'

The shortfall had to come from somewhere, diverted from existing funds. The clue was in Evelyn's final comment: 'Ask where NSO money goes: ECGD. Abracadabra!'

The Export Credit Guarantee Department had underwritten all those dubious arms deals, paying out government money to cover any withheld payment. The answer lay in Britain's recent oil bonanza, whose profits had been raided by the ECGD for compensation. Round had told Collard that NSO in Evelyn's equation stood for North Sea oil.

'Pretty dry old stuff, this political dynamite,' Churton said.

'I know about the share trading in the week before Flight 103.'

It was Round's last confession.

Churton turned slowly and asked, 'What are you talking about?'

The real crime behind Flight 103, as Round saw it, was that those, like him, who had known something was going to happen — if not the day — had done nothing and instead speculated on the stock market.

'In the week before the attack there was an unusually high volume of trading in sectors such as air transport and insurance. Shares in British Airways changed hands at about three times the normal level. There was also exceptional and unexpected speculation in the futures market.'

380

Churton's watery blue eyes were hostile. 'Are you accusing me?'

'I'm telling you what I know. Anything happens to me then the mechanics are in place for a lot more people to know.'

Churton sneered. 'That old ploy.'

'You had better tell Tranter that Round's dead. He used a shotgun on himself.'

Even that news failed to surprise Churton, who shrugged as if to say Round had confirmed his low opinion.

Churton handed Collard the attaché case. 'Cheap at the price. Now fuck off.'

He called his dog after him and walked away.

★ ★ ★

Collard went home for the last time. Tranter had assured Round that the police search had been called off. Collard wasn't so sure but he was past caring.

The door was padlocked again, meaning Sheehan hadn't done a Round and blasted his brains out. Collard presumed the shot Sheehan had fired was aimed at him. He thought it was the final proof of the man's insanity that he'd bothered to lock the door on the way out.

There were no new messages on the answerphone. Collard went through each room and said goodbye. He was not a sentimental man but Nick had lived most of his life there and was associated in Collard's mind with every room: where his toy boxes had been kept; the old location of his high chair; stair gates and all the other impedimenta of childhood. The memory of Nick as a small child was clearest in Collard's mind. He gave less thought to Charlotte, knowing he still had to confront the pain of that separation.

He paused outside Nick's door. The room was empty. Nick's possessions still lay on the floor. Sheehan had shot the mirror over the basin. There was a neat hole in the middle of the glass. The starring broke up Collard's reflection, making him look like the one who had been shattered.

He went to the room at the front of the house and looked out at the Sunday-quiet street. He remembered the last time he was there — the noise of police sirens he thought were coming for him, and a flash of light from the window opposite.

He took only two souvenirs to remember his time there. He picked out a tiny piece of broken mirror from Nick's room. As he removed it the rest of the glass fell into the basin. The second was Nick's guidebook. Collard thought he might need it.

He walked out and didn't look back.

Lazarus

Collard drove, aware only of the bare bones: streets, rooms, weather and all the other distractions receded. He thought of old man Angleton, still lurking behind the mystery, and knew how Angleton must have felt stuck living in his head. He knew there was more, that it wasn't over yet.

If anyone could reveal all the facets behind the mystery, rather than partial edited highlights, Collard knew it would be the departed spymaster. Perhaps that was the same as saying death was the only solution.

He stopped at a twenty-four-hour garage, an oasis of neon and bright green, to refuel. He paid cash at the night-security grille. The lonely attendant reminded him of Khaled's family, with their university qualifications, running gas stations outside Detroit. He could hear Sheehan's rumbling laugh as he declared, 'At least they're in the oil business.'

Tomorrow he would be stateless too. He remembered Neuss and the cell's safe house in Frankfurt, and Schäfer's unit logging suspects' endless drives through Europe, from Sweden and Czechoslovakia, gathering a suitcase or meeting a contact in an anonymous pizzeria or bar. Collard's life was theirs now.

Caught between bone-weariness and epiphany, Collard stared out into the night at his voyage into metaphysical abstraction, into Angleton space. He understood the zealousness of fanatics, the irrelevance of the flesh, admitting for the first time that he had buried his denial of Nick's death alongside his other great fear — that they had both got on the plane at Heathrow after all. There had been no Angleton at Frankfurt, no warning, and everything since was the wild imagining of a desperate mind in the time it took to crash.

Collard asked the expensive dashboard clock if everything that had occurred since could be compressed into under a minute. Yes, the clock said: time was irrelevant in the face of eternity and 46.5 seconds a lifetime.

He saw police everywhere, to his nervous eye evidence of Tranter's treachery. He was just another car driving through the night but he knew Churton and Tranter would not be beaten lightly.

At Alconbury, two police cars watched him and one followed long enough to see him turn off the main road into the flat reaches of the Fens, where the road's course followed long, straight drainage ditches.

Another car joined him. Collard couldn't work out if it was following until it dropped back.

He turned onto the road where the airfield was, ten miles further down. The flat countryside increased his unease. His lights could be seen for miles. There were few turn-offs, no trees and no hiding place. Daylight would reveal a landscape as unadorned as a child's drawing, straight horizon bisected by sky and a few scattered

384

buildings visible from far off. He gripped the wheel too hard. His neck and shoulders hurt from driving.

The road ran straight on and on. The waters of the canal gleamed like oil. Off in the distance he saw the lights of another vehicle. Collard's attention wandered. He knew he was falling asleep but he dared not stop. The Jaguar seemed to drive itself. There was only him now. Round's head exploded in his mind's eye. Everything was converging, too fast and too slow at the same time, on the brink of hallucination.

Black and white chevrons raced at him. He stamped hard on the brake and slewed the car round the unexpected bend and shot across a narrow bridge, with an impression of a stationary truck blocking the road, waiting for him to smash into it and kill himself, as they intended. He braked and turned the wheel hard. The car failed to respond, steering straight ahead. Collard shut his eyes and waited for the impact. None of it mattered. He had nothing left. Escape was only another postponement of the inevitable. The car skidded and Collard heard tearing metal. His head slammed against the door pillar and as he lost consciousness he was vaguely aware of the car suspended in the air, about to be sucked down into the black water.

He came to in the dark, the unseen pressure all around, closing in. The hot engine protested noisily at its dousing, steaming in pockets the water hadn't reached. He could see nothing. The lights had fused. Cold water filled his shoes. He groped for the door handle and shoved. Nothing gave. An air pocket released a stream of bubbles. Soon the car would be a flooded coffin. He tried not to think what would happen when the air went, tried to welcome the catharsis that would take him away but saw only mindless, animal terror followed by the triumph of nothingness, the moment when time and memory impacted.

Freezing water clutched at his heart. He struggled to lower his window. The handle turned uselessly. His mind was starting to separate. The car filled too fast.

The handle of the passenger window was jammed too. He used up valuable air climbing in the back. The window handle behind the front passenger seat resisted, beyond the point of despair, then turned. Water poured through the open window. He gasped. The cold alone would kill him.

The door refused to budge. He tried to haul himself out of the window. It took too long. He was forced back inside for more air but found only water. He turned and blindly wrestled his way back through the opening, giving in to panic. Counting. Each number exploded in his head. His lungs burned. He stopped counting.

★　★　★

Collard woke and thought he was dead. Naked, in blackness, unable to see, on a concrete floor, overwhelmed by all his childhood fears — darkness as isolation, darkness as cruelty, darkness as unknown — combined with the frightening adult knowledge that he had been saved only to be cast into perpetual darkness. The profound silence asked him what if no one came, a prospect more terrifying than his ordeal by water.

He felt his way round the room. There was a door with no handle, a light switch that didn't work. Under a narrow metal-framed bed was a tin chamber pot. There was no basin or tap. The window had been boarded over; through the tiniest crack came an impression of light.

He lay down on his front with his head in his arms, hoping to find he had been dreaming.

Harsh light dragged him back. It came from a bulkhead light in the ceiling, protected by a wire cage. The light went on and off, sometimes for minutes or hours until Collard could no longer tell. He knew he was being subjected to sensory deprivation and that his captors understood the damage done by waiting.

The silver in the boarded window told him nothing except whether it was light outside. He punched the board until his knuckle split. He tasted salty blood that increased his thirst. In the next spell of darkness he worked at the crack with a loosened bedspring. He dug away until a pinhole of grey appeared less dark than the surround.

He jammed his eye to the hole and saw a moonlit terrain and several strange, squat buildings, bulky and industrial. The streetlamps were broken. His impression was of nothing beyond, only empty landscape.

He had seen enough pictures to know he was in East Europe. He was behind the Iron Curtain.

He had no idea how he had got there. He had

been hijacked from death. He was still without any memory of the circumstances of his rescue — other than freezing cold and the surprise of lights — or the identity of his rescuers, unless Churton and Tranter's vindictiveness extended to pretending to kill him, then passing him on to Nazir's people with the information he was Nazir's assassin.

Once, his chamber pot was emptied while he lay passed out. Sometimes he was woken by the sound of his own howling.

Two men came for him in the dark. He smelt garlic and cigarettes and panicked at the prospect of sexual humiliation. They man-handled him to his feet, forced a hood over his head and spread him against the wall, with his toes and fingertips taking his weight. At first the position seemed supportable but he soon shook and cramped so much he fell on the floor and thrashed in agony. The men didn't hit him. They didn't need to. Collard's body did their work for them.

They spoke accented English. When the cramp passed they repositioned him and went on questioning: always the same, asking who he worked for and if he was a spy. He clung to the insistence he was nobody's spy. Each time he fell was like losing a layer. Soon he would be nothing.

Then it stopped. He was given a bowl of soggy rice, brought by one man who put the plate on the floor while the second guarded the door. They wore fatigues. They weren't masked and were Middle Eastern. Collard thought he recognized one. He went through everything since the crash, looking for a connection and found none until the man's prominent Adam's apple reminded him of the decorator in the Frankfurt house where he and Stack were to have met Nazir. Collard supposed it didn't matter if they showed their faces because they would shoot him soon, or worse.

His suspicions weren't allayed when his clothes and watch were returned and he was allowed to use a proper toilet and basin. They would build his hope only to dash it.

From the growth of beard on the deranged man staring out of the mirror, he judged he had been held three or four days, and tested beyond endurance.

He was given what tasted like regular supermarket bread and cheap soap that he recognized as Camay. His confusion increased when he read the name of the basin and toilet manufacturer: Armitage Shanks.

He was still in England.

The Old Fundamentalists

'I am, believe it or not, an ally. You would be well within your rights to say I have a strange way of showing it.'

The man sitting in front of Collard was American, but not quite. There were the remains of a foreign accent. He was elderly but still carried traces of the hard man he once must have been. He reminded Collard of a retired steel worker or a rigger. Delicate half-moon reading glasses sat oddly on a rough face that belonged outdoors. Weariness of expression suggested it had witnessed more than most, little of it good. He had the tough, punished look of a heavy drinker though only a bottle of mineral water stood on the old desk between them. The upholstered chair with wooden arms he sat on looked like it had been found on a skip. A transistor on the table was tuned to a Brahms violin concerto.

'Where am I?'

'Near the Thames. In East Tilbury.'

'I thought I was in East Europe.'

'You are, in a way. The place was built by a Czech shoe entrepreneur nostalgic for the old country. It was meant as workers' utopia in the days of benevolent capitalism.'

He held up a Thermos. Collard nodded.

'I'm going to put plenty of milk in.'

Collard warmed his hands on the mug.

390

'Kim Philby came in this way by Russian cargo boat in March 1986. I was the only witness to the man's first steps on English soil in more than twenty years.'

Collard remembered Valerie Traherne's description of the man opposite him: someone who had lived many years in the United States but came from Belgium and never quite lost his accent: Angleton's mysterious visitor arriving late at night, demanding a room, last heard of in Frankfurt removing the security tapes from the hotel.

'I recognized him from the stammer. The clothes were cheap and Russian and so were his cigarettes but the voice was very British — the thick glasses and beard did little to disguise him once I knew who I was looking at. He looked brand new in the English clothes I had brought him. 'Dear old Marks and Sparks,' he said.

'I expect you're asking what you're doing here and who I am.'

'You're Hoover.'

'I'm your fairy godmother. You were dead in the water.'

'And afterwards?'

'I'm sorry about that. I had to be sure. A man like you, who is what he says he is, is hard to read. Straightforward confuses in our business. But it can get you a long way. I've been watching you since you were in Wales. Valerie told me you'd figured out Philby, which was smart. I also understand you've been communing with the dead, which I would normally regard as superstitious nonsense, but in the case of Jim

Angleton I am prepared to make an exception. It's the damnedest thing.'

He smiled, sceptically.

'I've seen one of your men before. In Nazir's house.'

'He was there for me.'

'How do I know you don't work for Nazir?'

'I'm probably one of the few in all this who didn't work with Nazir. The man you know as Sheehan. Quinn. Churton. Tranter. Even Kim Philby worked with Nazir.'

'Philby?'

'Philby chaired the Soviet committee that advocated the production of a regulated, government-controlled poppy crop in the Bekaa Valley, as a way of Syria paying off its Soviet loans. Philby was the author of the Frankfurt Connection, in spirit if not in practice.'

Collard shook his head.

'Does it really all tie up?'

'There are always bits missing. You were unlucky enough to find yourself in a huge, three-dimensional puzzle and managed to put enough pieces in place to see some of it, but not the rest. You didn't know if it was one puzzle or several.

'You need to understand that Angleton was a fundamentalist, a Cold Warrior, undeviating and endlessly devious in his commitment to the cause. Angleton is also the metaphor for understanding that world.'

'Is Angleton the answer to what happened to that plane?'

'In surrogate terms, if not its execution.'

'Like Philby with the Frankfurt Connection.'

Hoover gave a wry smile. 'You're getting the hang of it. One might ask whether the bomb was a straightforward act of terror, or a diversion. Angleton would ask whether it was both, and other things besides. I can hear him say, in that circumlocutory way of his, 'What are the repercussions? Is it a straightforward act of terror or is it a diversion, gentlemen, calculated to take the eye off something else, in which case, what is that something, *and what is the something behind that?*' '

There was no doubt Churton and Tranter had taken advantage of the crash to do some tidying.

'Angleton taught the Israelis to run an operation from both sides, but we know that in this case the thing got jumped by someone else. That was the risk with Angleton — you had to watch the whole thing didn't blow up in your face.'

'Is my sitting here to do with Angleton?'

'Ask yourself what *hasn't* got to do with Angleton. He runs through this whole thing like a name in a stick of rock.'

'Why am I here? I thought I was dead.'

'You were pretty easy to follow. You left a credit-card trail, amongst other things. We lost you for a while after Sheehan came by and sent your graph right up, but picked you up again when you came back to the house on Sunday.'

'Was I that important?'

'You worked out Wales, which nobody else had, and you led Sheehan to it. I was interested to know where else you might lead. So we tucked in behind. When you resurfaced on Sunday in that fancy Jaguar we were curious and nosy enough to follow. I was keen to meet a man who believed he had seen Jim Angleton seventeen months after he officially died. It even crossed my mind that the old snake had faked his death for the sake of some last crazy hip-pocket operation.'

Hoover removed an envelope from the desk drawer and tipped out several photographs which he arranged on the desk facing Collard, who recognized the first three as the ones he had been carrying, distressed but still intact after their recent drowning.

There was Angleton standing on the banks of the Usk with Greene and Philby; the desert photograph of Sandy Beech; and the Polaroid of Sheehan's daughter.

To these Hoover added four more.

A blurry black-and-white snapshot of a man in the jungle, dressed like a native in a sarong, and a full head of wild hair that made him nearly unrecognizable.

'Taken in Laos in 1968. The man you know as Sheehan.'

Next was a young man in American uniform sitting in a Jeep, taken in Rome soon after the Second World War.

'Angleton methodology is: always ask, however big something is, what else happened? In this case, who else was on the plane?'

Collard saw an unsympathetic, sharp-featured man with a pointed nose, unaware the photograph was being taken.

'His name was Abe Stavinsky. Stavinsky was what Angleton called the shadow — not the main reason the plane got blown up, but his presence on the flight was no more coincidence than Barry's.'

'What did he do?'

'He was an old hunter of war criminals.'

Next was a portrait of a mild man of around fifty, wearing glasses that made him appear academic. Unruly hair gave him a boyish look.

'Brennan Jarrald.'

Jarrald looked dull. Collard couldn't see where he belonged and was about to move on when Hoover said, 'I grant you, he doesn't look the sort to authorize the destruction of an airliner.'

Collard looked up at Hoover, who held his gaze.

'Jarrald was responsible for the deaths of Barry and Stavinsky, and the incidental destruction of all those other lives.'

They were all shadows, Collard thought. Until that moment he had been dealing only with shadows — Churton, Round, Beech, Quinn, Sheehan, Tranter, Nazir and all the rest. Phantom narratives that disguised and distracted from the tight nugget at the centre. Collard was sure these separate stories all revolved around the centrifugal force of the plot but were incidental cover-ups of the kind Churton and Tranter were desperate to put in place.

'What does Jarrald do?'

'He makes Presidents,' Hoover said quietly and gestured at the last photograph, of former President of the United States, Ronald Reagan,

395

and his successor, former Vice-President George H. W. Bush.

The occasion was an informal outdoors party. Reagan grinned amiably. Bush gave the impression of a man failing to relax. They were talking to a third man, elderly and wearing huge spectacles. Compared to the photogenic Reagan and Bush, he looked unfit, clumsy and grey.

'The man who looks like Mr Magoo, that's Bill Casey, Head of CIA for most of Reagan's administration, from 1981 to 1987.'

Collard looked at the lined-up photographs and Hoover said, 'Every picture tells a story.'

Snapshots

The first photograph was a surprise to Angleton (and Hoover, going through Collard's belongings): of him standing by the Usk. Not out of the question that Greene and Philby played an unwitting role in the fate of the crashed airplane. Not impossible. Taker of the photograph: Hoover; not admitted to Collard, perhaps from embarrassment. It was a terrible picture.

★ ★ ★

The photograph of Sandy Beech; date and occasion: December 1979, the Raising of the Siege of Mecca after the seizing of the Grand Mosque by fundamentalists. Stun guns and chemical weapons. Firing squads to dispatch militant survivors.

The other man in the picture: CIA agent named Al Haines; prior to Mecca, he and Beech were undercover on deniable ops in Angola, with Quinn. Casey called them his Three Musketeers.

Taker of the Mecca photograph: Quinn. Quinn's refusal to have his taken in return was wise, as Haines's careless souvenir became his death warrant, removed from his Beirut apartment on the day of his kidnap by terrorists in March 1984. Haines was as good as dead once the photo was out of the bag. While the Iranians used his kidnap as leverage for arms, his captors strung out their negotiations and tortured him because too many relatives of those he had shot in Mecca knew.

Haines got killed in one of the nastiest and cheapest ways Angleton had ever heard of. They shoved a balloon down his throat and inflated it with an oxygen cylinder.

The Iranians got their arms. Casey's sweated deal was Haines's confession stayed off the table (all four hundred fucking pages of his history in deniable black operations) *in exchange for the sacrifice of the only penetrative ring of local agents the Americans had,* a team that had been patiently built up by one Colonel Charles 'Chuck' Barry. The betrayal of his agents earned Bill Casey the sworn enmity of Barry, who as a result was a recruit to Angleton's cause.

★ ★ ★

The Polaroid. Angleton was annoyed for not working out the girl. He had ignored an important lesson of his method — look for the personal. That was how these big things worked.

★ ★ ★

As for the girl's Daddy: how many passports; how many histories? A man rarely surprised. A notable exception, his first confrontation with Collard: Sheehan thought him a spy snooping for the Brits. Certainly not a civilian who should have been on the plane, dead, and the father of the boy.

Taker of the Laos photo: Hoover, again not admitted to Collard. Sheehan performed cross-border assassinations for Hoover and worked among the Hmong hill tribes, protecting their opium crop in exchange for their anti-communism. In the 1970s, Sheehan did Angola for George Bush, then CIA chief, and ran Quinn, Beech and Haines. After that, Australia, deep into a money-laundry operation that was a legacy of Vietnam, rinsing in Hong Kong.

★　★　★

As for Abe Stavinsky, the less said the better. Angleton didn't want to be reminded.

Jarrald.

Casey.

In the end they were the only two names that counted. And Angleton's.

The Last Cold Warriors

Collard neither trusted nor mistrusted Hoover. He now assessed people only on the information they had and Hoover knew more or less everything. He went back to the beginning, to Angleton in Rome at the end of the war. He was with Angleton in Wales in 1986. He worked with Sheehan. He worked with Barry. He worked with Beech. He understood the tight intricacy of intrigue and counter-intrigue surrounding events in the Lebanon in March 1984 and March 1986, which led to Angleton setting up a secret operation called Ghost whose botched outcome resulted in Barry's death and the destruction of all those innocent lives. He understood how that tragedy came down to a rift in ideology between an old order and a new one, between Angleton and Casey, though both Angleton and Bill Casey were dead by the time of the bomb. He understood that Angleton would have blamed Casey, and Angleton was to blame for Casey's methods. He understood the connections that linked fascist activity in wartime Zagreb to the highest echelons of the American Republican Party and why Abe Stavinsky had to die. He understood why Angleton used Mafia muscle to control the Italian docks after the war. He understood how intelligence and criminal activity were synonymous, both operating beyond the laws that governed societies. He understood how men like Nazir ended up with immunity at the same time as being in everyday danger of their lives. He understood how the Israeli sting operation worked. He understood how the bomb plot crystallized around the activities of a sanctioned black economy, specifically the sale of arms to embargoed countries; the temptation of the enormous sums of money to be made from selling drugs; the overlaps between the operating worlds of men like Nazir and Sheehan and Churton. He understood the mechanisms of those worlds, and how Casey's (Angleton-inspired) unofficial policy depended on friendly satellite countries with the most experience in secret activities and with less stringent arms-export laws. Casey's need was satisfied by Margaret Thatcher, who repaid the United States for its covert assistance in the Falklands War in her special relationship with Ronald Reagan, the rewards of which filtered down to those old friends and partners in crime, Sandy Beech and Nazir, who worked either end of the London-Tehran arms channel, organized by Nigel Churton of the Foreign Office and MI6, for Bill Casey of the CIA who ran the secret operation through the Vice-President's office in the White House.

Collard came to see that the world Hoover showed him had nothing and everything to do with his son.

Hoover understood how betrayal lay at the centre of everything. He understood that there never was such a thing as full understanding; it was always relative. He said he hadn't a clue what Philby was doing in Wales or what the outcome of that was. Hoover understood Angleton's belief in the metaphysical dimension.

★   ★   ★

Hoover initiated Collard into the wilderness of mirrors.

★   ★   ★

Hoover said, 'I was in Budapest in 1944 for Allen Dulles, who ran the American intelligence desk in Switzerland. Dulles was in secret negotiations with the SS about ending the war and turning round to fight the Soviets. Dulles and the SS used Jewish couriers who became fashionable in elite circles, the better to save German necks as the war drew to a close. Dulles and Angleton worked a plot with the SS to smuggle huge quantities of the Third Reich's assets — what later came under the generic title of Nazi gold — out of Germany, through Austria, down to Rome where the equally anti-communist Vatican bank dispersed it to places like Argentina. The same route was used to smuggle out Nazis and Fascists. As these activities were treasonable, the Jews could dictate their own terms and targeted Angleton, who ran the sharp end of the operation in Rome.'

Hoover retained a very clear memory of Angleton's introduction to Dulles's couriers on a clear late-winter day in Trieste when it had been unexpectedly warm enough to eat outside, on a restaurant terrace overlooking a partly destroyed old rice factory, near the sports stadium. Their contact had gone on to become senior Israeli intelligence. His credentials at that initial meeting included a firstclass meal of black-market goods. Angleton the trencherman ate greedily, hands circling between his plate, glass topped up and his cigarette smouldering in an ashtray. On being taken over the road afterwards to the rice factory and told it had been a German extermination centre for the Resistance and Jews, and shown the blood on the walls, Angleton spewed his lunch and brazenly asserted the lobster had disagreed with him.

Jewish terms were straightforward. In exchange for their silence, they would take a percentage of German assets smuggled by Angleton, which they called their reparation fee for the Zionist settlement, and access to the Vatican escape line, which from then on, as well as sending Nazis to Argentina, would smuggle Jews to Palestine, in anticipation of the founding of the homeland.

Seen one way, what Hoover told Collard was irrelevant. Seen another, it was crucial. It marked the start of an uneasy relationship between Angleton and the Israelis, which explained why, years later, an agent of the Jordanian secret service, heavily under American influence, was loaned to an Israeli sting operation to pose as a Palestinian bomb-maker.

On the night of that first meeting with the Jews, Hoover and Angleton (his appetite restored) sat down for another feast, this time for

Croatian fascists and their priests, a dubious bunch also inherited from Dulles. Angleton learned fast and proved as promiscuous as his mentor in the cultivation of strange bedfellows.

As a direct result of this meeting, some weeks later a five-year-old boy had walked out of Croatia in the company of a Franciscan priest, two among the millions of displaced people making their way west ahead of the Soviets. They ended up in a refugee camp in Italy and from there transferred to the diplomatic immunity of the Croatian delegation for the Vatican. Hoover knew of this first hand because he had driven the priest and the boy from the refugee camp to San Girolamo.

Hoover said, 'That boy became Brennan Jarrald.'

By 1947 the Vatican 'Ratline', as it became known, was the single largest smuggling route for Nazi war criminals, including Adolf Eichmann, and Angleton had his work cut out keeping it from being discovered by the rival US Army's Counterintelligence Corps, which worked in the same building in Rome as Angleton and Hoover.

'Stavinsky was a pushy CIC officer. It turned out he had uncovered the whole operation, except for identifying the Americans involved. He didn't know Angleton was running it and because Angleton was counter-intelligence Stavinsky went to him for help.'

'How did you feel about sheltering war criminals?'

'That's not how we saw it. It's the old saying: my enemy's enemy is my friend. The whole order was changing. We were fighting the next war.'

'What happened to Stavinsky?'

'Angleton framed him as one of the Americans assisting the fascists. It was pure Jim. After the war Stavinsky became obsessed with Angleton, trying to prove his fascist connections. He ran a small research foundation investigating war crimes but most of his time was taken up with fund-raising and budget problems. He never realized it was Jim financing him all along, the better to keep an eye on him.'

'What did Stavinsky have on Jarrald that was so dangerous?'

'Nothing on Jarrald. It was the priest he had the dirt on.'

'The priest?'

'Yes. Angleton got him out of Rome to the United States where he and a junior intelligence officer called Bill Casey became lifelong friends. The priest abandoned his vows, changed his name to Jarrald, officially adopted the boy and reinvented himself as a secular man. He was successful in business thanks to contacts old and new, became rich through investment and wealthier still by marriage, a staunch Republican, a major fund-raiser for the party and, like Bill Casey, a pillar of the Roman Catholic Church. Jarrald Sr. is as respectable as it is possible to get, a fine example of the great American success story.'

'And Stavinsky threatened to undo all that?'

'Yes. He became as embittered and resentful as the man who had destroyed him. Angleton's life also turned on a single betrayal by Kim

405

Philby — like Stavinsky, he spent the rest of his life trying to get even. They led lives that stank of loneliness and solitary endeavour. My guess is that's what Wales was about, and Angleton failed, as Stavinsky did. In Stavinsky's case we might still be able to redress the balance.'

Collard saw then what Hoover wanted from him.

'Plenty of blood was shed in Croatia during the war and plenty of heads rolled. Croatian genocide preceded the Nazis and even they blanched at its barbarities. The Roman Catholic Church saw itself in the front line of the struggle against evil. The priest not only incited his congregation to savagery, but Stavinsky found eyewitness accounts that he led by example in massacres of Orthodox Serbs, cutting throats, smashing skulls and gouging eyeballs.'

There was more. Stavinsky found evidence of a mistress in Zagreb who in 1940 gave birth to the priest's son, the man now known as Brennan Jarrald.

★ ★ ★

Hoover looked at Collard and asked, 'Are you with me on this?'

'What was your role in all of that?'

'Liaison. Go-between. Gofer. Driver. Dogs-body. Punchbag.'

'Spy?'

Hoover grunted. 'Spy is too simple a word.'

Cargo

Angleton followed Collard's disappearance with intense interest. Watching Hoover school him hard, he grew optimistic. A frequent problem when creating a lure was how messy to make it. The perfect, most believable fly often caught nothing, while the ones in which he had no faith — the clumsy, beaten-up ones like Collard — got the fish.

Collard looked different, thinner and starting to grey. He found it hard to remember the man he used to be. Angleton's voice grew louder in his head. Angleton, had he been Collard, would have asked Hoover if he had exploited Nick's relationship with Sheehan's daughter — maybe instigating it — and ushered her on the plane, knowing it would destroy Sheehan. Play that fast and loose, someone was going to get hurt.

Collard left the country as cargo on a freight plane in an empty horse palette, the route and loopholes of his vanishing readily available to a man like Hoover. Collard remained unable to decide whether this was the end or the beginning.

His first destination was a summer chalet on an estate of garden allotments somewhere in Europe; under a flight path near an airport was all he knew.

Hoover followed, his impassive presence a reminder it wasn't over. He gave Collard a list of apartments and sets of numbers to memorize, including a telephone number for a Swiss bank account, with passwords. Collard asked where the money came from and was told leaky pipelines. He thought about it and said OK. He asked Hoover if he was on his own and was told up to a point.

Collard became another man. With access to a large slush fund — a drop compared to the huge ocean of Bill Casey's black economy — he travelled on a South African passport provided by Hoover, bearer in the name of James Troughton. Har-dee-har! thought Angleton. Perhaps Hoover had a sense of humour after all.

★ ★ ★

Collard, watched by his black guardian angel, Angleton, gravitated towards a world where deals were done on the edge, where the geopolitical equivalent to future investments were made: Syria up; Iraq down; a world of limitless air miles, identical luxury hotels, slow drinks on terraces overlooking tennis courts where good-looking young men stood joined to attractive women, demonstrating the correct forehand, the first stage of a formal foreplay (memories of Stack); where arrivals and departure boards had more meaning than their destinations; of advisers in cities where you wouldn't expect to find them (Tranter, last in Malaysia); an insulated world. Black lines at the bottom of swimming pools, wriggling from the optical effect, became symbolic of the larger ripple of

408

clandestine movement, equally hypnotic and hard on the eye. All the while, tracking from a distance. It was not a straightforward trajectory.

An ex-*Rolling Stone* reporter named Burgh, whose counter-culture credentials Angleton thought otherwise impeccable, researched Jarrald for Collard, on a weekly retainer of more than he usually earned a month. Burgh was impressed an Englishman had even heard of Jarrald.

(Angleton knew it could only end badly.)

Jarrald was in armaments, officially electronics, and held lucrative government contracts almost exclusively for the defence industry. Jarrald sponsored think tanks with bland quasi-academic names that had problems with racial integration.

Collard's problem was that Jarrald lived an insulated life, protected by a quilt of money beyond the average dolt's comprehension, inhabiting an exclusive territory of armed response and privilege that yielded to no one and came dressed up in politeness and good manners, with shirts and ties imported from Jermyn Street in London (Angleton's old stamping ground). Brennan Jarrald, cushioned by deep conservatism, never met people outside his circle, conducting all alien business by telephone, ring-fenced by lawyers, investors and businessmen. To keep the shit at a distance there existed an informal network of local and national law enforcement, reporters and private security men that maintained a discreet presence in the man's everyday life; and below them dependable thugs to dispose of any nuisance, and rearrange the furniture, while teams of accountants, brokers and investors devoted their ingenuity to the real business of tax avoidance, off-shore investment and insider dealing. Money made money, effortlessly, because of the quality of the expensively maintained machine.

Burgh made waves. Cracks started to appear, filling Angleton with hope and dread. Fuckers get their comeuppance, always a cause for celebration, but what of his role in the affair: posthumous disgrace? Angleton recoiled like Nosferatu greeting the dawn (a memory of Rome rooftops all those years ago).

★ ★ ★

Collard's break came when he learned that rare and antiquarian books were Brennan Jarrald's indulgence, the one reason he ever met strangers. His passion was twentieth-century first editions, specializing in Wyndham Lewis, Ezra Pound, D. H. Lawrence, P. G. Wodehouse, Louis-Ferdinand Céline, and the Irish writers W. B. Yeats and Francis Stuart. The library had long been assembled but Jarrald still hunted duplicates, dedicated signed copies, associated works, correspondence and ephemera. Collard thought it odd such a reactionary man should, with the exception of Wodehouse, opt for visionaries and modernists.

Collard moved deeper into the limbo of men like Hoover and Angleton, jettisoning the usual reassurances of human contact. Yet he was rarely lonely. He felt called. His life became vocational.

410

He learned to appreciate the knowledge of books. He took time to read. He bought second-hand copies of the books Angleton had in Wales and read them, thinking of Angleton.

He became familiar with the exclusive end of the rare-book trade, where dealers sat in palatial surroundings that looked like minor embassies. After the same small display advertisement appeared in several collectors' magazines wanting the authors Jarrald collected, Collard called the New York State number to offer Francis Stuart's first slim volume of poetry, *We Have Kept the Faith*, published in 1922. He expected to talk to a machine, but when a man answered without identifying himself, Collard felt that it must be Jarrald. When Collard told him what he had he said, 'I might be interested,' but arranged for an antiquarian bookseller in New York to handle the sale. Collard was nowhere near sitting down with the man.

He attended a New York auction, hoping his adversary would be lured by a copy of Ezra Pound's *A Lume Spento*, one of 150 published in 1908 in Venice, its rarity greatly increased by the signed dedication to Hilda Doolittle, to whom Pound had been engaged.

Jarrald entered the crowded auction room alone, looking comfortable and anything but rich in a shabby brown corduroy jacket. Collard experienced none of the expected bristle of hostility, only disappointment at finally seeing this mild, innocuous man who sat down at the end of his row.

Collard drove up the bidding until Jarrald was

forced to turn and assess him. The price spiralled until even the impassive auctioneer looked embarrassed on Jarrald's behalf.

Jarrald stopped suddenly, got up and walked out. In their brief eye contact, Collard noted a flicker of cold amusement.

Furioso

As Angleton could have predicted, Jarrald's opening gambit took the form of a dead journalist in a motel. He added Burgh's name to a long list, a loose affiliation of mysterious deaths, a maze of the dead, and the deaths never just came in ones, all strange overdoses or apparent heart attacks: lonely room deaths. The death made a couple of papers as a dozen lines at the foot of a page, listed as suicide, the result of depression.

In Burgh's unquestioned death Collard foresaw his in another motel suicide; the heartbroken father unable to face the loss of his son. He ceased to be amazed by the ease with which these things were arranged. He doubted if news of his demise would even reach the ear of the charitable man with the soft, frayed collar of his imported shirt and his deeply held Christianity.

★ ★ ★

Angleton welcomed Collard's return to the nightmare. Everything was starting to shift. Now Collard knew how Lee Harvey Oswald had felt, and Khaled, strung out as history made its moves around them, the low whirr of conspiracy humming, which anyone else would have said was just the air-conditioning.

413

Collard haunted bookshops, searching. Angleton wanted to tell him he was wasting time, but even he was impressed by Collard's next calling card, found in a suburban bookshop in Washington DC — Angleton's personal copy of *Furioso* magazine, edited by him at Yale, with a contribution from Pound, signed, and a letter tipped in, from Pound declaring Angleton 'One of the most important hopes of literary magazines, in the US.'

Collard drove away down streets Angleton recognized, a journey into an irretrievable past that ended outside a suburban house at 4814 North 33rd Road, Arlington.

Angleton thought: How modest a home for a man who had called himself chief of counter-intelligence (and held destinies in his hand). He saw his old silver Mercedes parked in the drive. He saw his wife leave the house and take the car to go shopping.

He listened to Collard weep for his lost life.

★ ★ ★

Collard thought *Furioso* was worth as much as four figures to Jarrald, perhaps more with the Angleton association. He called the books-wanted number and got a machine. He left messages, naming for sale *A Lume Spento* and the *Furioso* with Pound's letter. The third time, his call was answered by the same man who named a diner in Hastings-on-Hudson, a small town on the river above New York. Collard took a suburban train.

414

Angleton thought the cars on the highway looked like something from a lost civilization as old as Ancient Egypt.

Collard got to the diner first, a regular old-fashioned eatery on the main street, with elderly waitresses in white socks.

Jarrald crossed the street at an angle, alone and looking nervously both ways for non-existent traffic. He seemed exposed by such ordinary surroundings. Collard noted the man's air of furtive excitement. He supposed book collecting was Jarrald's secret life in the way sexual affairs might be another man's. Jarrald hesitated when he saw Collard then gave a slight incline of recognition as he sat down in the booth opposite him.

He asked the waitress for a milkshake and inspected Collard with guileless eyes. Wanting to find meanness and gracelessness, Collard saw only the engagement of the collector. *Furioso* was the lure he hoped it would be.

Jarrald knew Angleton and Pound had met in Rapallo in 1938 after Angleton's freshman year at Yale, and that Angleton had persuaded Pound to contribute to his magazine and even travel to Yale to read.

'He had his father's salesmanship.'

'Did you know Angleton personally?'

'Now why do you ask that?' Jarrald asked. His glasses caught the light, making him hard to read.

'He went to the same school as I did, in England.'

'As a matter of fact, I did know him, slightly.

He was a friend of my father's rather in the way Pound was a friend of Angleton's father.'

Jarrald returned his attention to the magazine. In Hoover's safe rooms in different cities, firearms rested neatly in bedside drawers, alternatives to the Gideon Bible, tempting; Angleton doubted they were Collard's answer. Collard could have brought a gun and shot the man where he sat and walked out, but it was about more than that. It was about making plain what was at stake, confronting him with what he had done. Vengeance.

'Do you have children?' Collard asked.

Jarrald gave him a puzzled look. 'Whatever for?'

Collard knew in that moment of casual indifference lay what he couldn't prove: Jarrald had done it.

★ ★ ★

Jarrald was what Angleton called one of Casey's cowboys: civilian entrepreneurs in whom Casey confided. Jarrald appreciated how much the vested interest needed to be protected and that the state was not necessarily the best provider.

Jarrald understood how a world of billions was run by a handful of people. Presidents or prime ministers and politicians were just window dressing.

Jarrald inherited Casey's hip-pocket operations after Casey's death, fulfilling the initial stage of a vision of privatized, invisible security, indistinguishable from the real thing, beyond the interference of government: the ultimate hip-pocket operation on a global scale. Jarrald understood the real power of the black economy.

But Colonel Charles 'Chuck' Barry didn't see it that way, especially after Casey's botch of Al Haines's kidnap. Barry had tracked Haines down, but was blocked by Casey, hamstrung by Haines's confession, and the risk that all Casey's secrets would be put on the table.

Given Casey's incompetence in the case of Al Haines's kidnap, Angleton had believed he had no choice except to mount his own operation to rescue Quinn, funded with slush funds put aside for a rainy day. Operation Ghost was assembled in under twenty-four hours, utilizing Hoover, Beech and Barry, who was recommended as the best man on the ground. It was a good-guys' mission. Barry's team was back in the Lebanon, scoping the hostage situation.

Then Quinn was released without explanation and Angleton had never found out why.

After that Ghost mutated into an anti-Casey operation. The plain fact was Angleton didn't like Casey. Casey offended his dandy's sensibility. Angleton could dress it up all he liked but Operation Ghost turned into a vanity project *until he realized the quality of what he was getting.* Barry was too good: joining up dots the White House didn't know about or deliberately hadn't been told about (drug connections all the way down the line). Once he had seen the consequences, Angleton tried to make amends for his own flawed career and resolved to expose the dirty tricks he had once practised, which had got looser and dirtier with Casey. Barry was his white knight. Who betrayed Barry, he didn't know.

Ghost survived Angleton's and Casey's deaths. Operations that were barely under control in Casey's time span into chaos. Barry learned that US agents were using Nazir's connection — protected for years by Casey and Churton — for rogue operations, using confiscated drugs to pay for arms deals. Once it was realized how much Barry had exposed, and would reveal, he was a marked man.

As the endgame played out, the only remaining arrangements were the last personal ones: for Stavinsky to be routed via Frankfurt, which would have been easy to arrange by dangling another link in his case; and for Sheehan to fix Nick.

The more Collard thought about it, he was convinced Sheehan wanted Nick killed on that plane. Had Jarrald celebrated the news with a special book purchase and a milkshake? Collard wondered, as the man slurped up the last of the froth through his straw.

Collard carefully placed Angleton's magazine back in its cellophane, mimicking Jarrald's reverence.

A brief shiver passed through him.

Jarrald said dreamily, 'Someone just walked over your grave.'

'What led you to collect writers like Pound?'

'They had interesting minds.'

Jarrald sounded vague. Collard understood. Their appeal lay in their fascist, anti-Semitic associations, including Wodehouse.

'Bring what you have to the house, tomorrow evening about seven. We can continue our conversation there. I look forward to that.'

★　★　★

Jarrald lived further upriver, in a mansion on an estate, with the finest views, servants and an old colonial atmosphere. Collard took a car and drove out in plenty of time, booking into an empty motel not far from the house. He put the gun from his safe room in the glove compartment but didn't take it into the house in case he was searched.

Collard walked across a gravelled drive and was admitted by a manservant. He noted the inlay on the expensive parquet floor as he was escorted across the hall and shown into Jarrald's study, a large mahogany room lined with priceless books. Jarrald was not alone. A fire had been lit and Jarrald's companion stood with his back to Collard, facing the flames.

Jarrald looked fussy and awkward as he said, 'I took the liberty of inviting another collector. This is Mr Remington.'

Sheehan turned and stared at Collard like they had never met.

The Greater Scheme

For Sheehan, nothing matched reading the passenger list of 103, seeing how those several different people had been sucked into the conduit, unaware of the orchestration, believing they had taken that flight on that day at that time through choice rather than his organization of their fate. In his largesse, he had arranged for Barry to be moved up to first class and wondered at what moment, exactly, the smugness of upgrade had evaporated and Barry realized Sheehan was disaster's architect.

Conspiracy had no palaces. It belonged in transit areas, lonely hotel rooms, temporary accommodations, in the interstices, in cargo sheds in remote airfields, in departure lounges, in travel schedules, in the hidden exchange of money, in venal practice, sexual peccadillo, false passports, faked photographs, anonymous bank accounts, deep-cover fictions, false biographies. There was nothing grand about conspiracies. Their application dealt in first symptoms, after which viral infections travelled on the wind, multiplying out of all proportion to the events they had caused. They were clichés, close to predictable, at best an act of hope. Many conspiracies were stillborn. Conspiracy was heretical and voluptuous, denied while rampant. Those he enjoyed most were the ones where there was no conspiracy beyond the invention of overactive imaginations.

It would take one move to get from the end of the era of the Cold War to the new age of terror, via the destruction of 103, and Orwell's prophecy of permanent wars, but always somewhere else, never where you were, a TV event, although one day he believed the pigeons would come home to roost.

It was necessary to create from what had been destroyed. Through transgression came love and understanding. He was in the embrace of God's endless forgiveness.

He was not a Pharisee. He was a consorter of thieves and whores; his progress through the world was biblical. He maintained a dialogue with his maker. He was intimate with the parables. He stared for hours at the word *prodigal* on a translucent page of the Bible. In his heart he was humble and submissive. He wished only to serve. His meddling with the greater scheme had been undertaken as the most reluctant of duties. There was no hubris. He feared judgement and apocalypse.

Sheehan subscribed to the belief that no one was innocent.

The boy was not innocent.

Sheehan, grand juggler, paranoia fizzing in his digestive tract, flaring his irritated bowel, nerves humming like an electrical charge, sketched the boy into the plot, and saw the blackness of his conspirator's heart.

He had deceived with false approval, for the idle thrill of wrecking lives, as the boy had ruined his daughter's; from his fornications the bastard pregnancy.

Sheehan, as superstitious as Macbeth, regarded murder of the unborn the unpardonable sin, yet better his daughter mourn than ruin her life so young. Behind her back he arranged a date for termination; with the boy gone she would be persuaded. In Sheehan's own damnation, her future; what greater sacrifice?

While governments hung in the balance, he slipped the boy into his plans, feigning reconciliation while telling his daughter, 'I am happy for you.'

As a refinement and a precaution, as part of the deeper game, he cast the boy as history's understudy, the second patsy, the substitute suspect, the card in reserve to be played if necessary, were the Khaled scenario to come unstuck, the boy's body to be removed from the crash and held on ice, in the coffin brought up for the occasion.

Part of him was desperate for his daughter to know, so he could say, 'See what I was willing to do to protect your future happiness, twist the world on its axis and alter its boundaries.'

It hadn't been so hard to arrange. Few thought to try.

In Frankfurt came the terrible realization that he might be sending everything he most cherished to her death. He had tried in desperation to cancel the operation.

Word came back the decision was irreversible.

His search was fruitless. It was God's punishment for him that she was on the plane.

★ ★ ★

The boy's father had been a surprise, a ghost of a surprise, saved by premonition. They had something in common, he and the unsuspecting father. It was the start of his daring to hope in her survival.

He pitied the man, yanked from his dull, ordinary life and thrown into the pit by not staying on the plane but surviving instead to watch it all unravel. He turned the father into a specimen of curiosity. He sensed untapped compassion, a reserve of emotion. He wanted to know how Collard would respond to his life turned upside down; fall apart or become resolved. In one of those moments of neat inspiration that came along too rarely, he understood how much he needed the father to find his son, who would be with his daughter.

His great underlying fear was that the father had been sent. He could hear Nigel Churton's prissy Oxford tones, feigning indifference. 'Find out about our American friend. It sounds like the sort of mad thing he gets up to. Didn't he shoot a policewoman once and blame the Libyans?'

Worse, what if Churton had somehow manipulated the boy on to his daughter? He rejected the idea as unthinkable. Churton was not smart enough to come up with the equation that the way to fuck with him was to fuck with his daughter. Only Sheehan could have done that. On whisky-bottle nights he wondered if he wasn't running operations against himself, wanting, in the end, to be the target of his own destruction.

The Last Supper

Collard was forced to persevere with his charade, to show his wares to an appreciative Brennan Jarrald while Sheehan played Remington, toying with Collard's assumed name, Troughton, placing it in the lightest quotation marks. Jarrald asked him if he was related to the actor who had played Dr Who in the British TV show, which was a favourite.

They ate in the kitchen, a salad prepared earlier by the cook, whose night off it was. Jarrald apologized for the ad-hoc arrangement. The meal consisted of cheap, sweating supermarket ham, iceberg lettuce and tomato, with mayonnaise from a bottle. They drank Pepsi Cola. Collard chewed slowly and failed to detect any exchange of looks.

'Where are you staying?' Jarrald asked, making it sound like standard politeness.

'In a motel.'

Sheehan named the motel. Collard said nothing.

Sheehan carried on, sounding equable. 'That's where I am. I saw your car.'

Jarrald asked, 'Did you see a lot of police on the road on the way here?'

Collard said he hadn't.

'They're hunting a man who murdered his own child.'

'As opposed to killing a lot of innocent

people,' Collard said, watching Jarrald's face. There was a splash of mayonnaise on his chin.

Jarrald asked Collard if he played golf.

'Not often.'

'Join me next time. I just knock it around.'

'Where do you play?'

Jarrald named the country club where he went every Tuesday and asked if Collard was familiar with it. Collard knew it was Jarrald's way of saying he had no intention of him being alive come Tuesday.

'Perhaps Mr Remington would care to join us.'

Sheehan inclined his head and Collard asked what he did, curious to know how he would answer.

'I work as a consultant.'

'Consulting in what?'

'Problem-solving, mainly.'

'Come now,' Jarrald said. 'That's a tad disingenuous. Mr Remington is in the extermination business. Pests and rodents, isn't that right?' He looked at Collard. 'Do you have much cause to get rid of pests?'

'Not until recently.'

'I recommend the old Roach Motel.'

Jarrald tittered and wiped the mayonnaise off his face with a paper napkin while Collard wondered if this was what lay at the centre of the labyrinth: a mean last supper and heavy-handed metaphor at a rich man's table.

'You blew up that airliner,' Collard said.

'That sounds like a false accusation if ever I heard one. Wouldn't you say, Mr Remington?'

Casting pretence aside, Sheehan said, 'Mr

425

Collard should have been on that flight, so he takes the matter personally.'

'And is prone to jump to the wildest conclusions.'

'I know about Stavinsky.'

'Is that why you are here?' Sarcasm, previously held in check, gave Collard his first glimpse of the real man. 'We all know about Stavinsky! He was a pest and a fantasist. He was a stalker, as I suspect you are, and we had to put a restraining order on him. The rubbish he peddled about my father! My father lived here in the United States *before* the war, which makes a mockery of his lunatic ravings. He was a twisted failure who hunted the more fortunate to make their lives miserable.'

Collard knew Jarrald's family would be able to produce doctored immigration papers. It made Stavinsky's death all the more pointless.

Jarrald turned to Sheehan. 'What does he believe, that we orchestrated events to get rid of a man who amounted to nothing and because that other man, what was his name . . . ?'

'Barry.'

'That's the problem with you people. You're incapable of accepting the truth. You need to fantasize something bigger, something even more cold-hearted, because everything else disappoints.'

Collard pointed at Sheehan. 'He put my boy on that plane knowing it would crash.'

Jarrald said, 'You are obviously distressed. Grief does the strangest things.'

'My son was with his daughter.' He pointed at Sheehan.

'Is this true?' Jarrald asked, surprised for the first time. 'Your daughter, the apple of your eye? Do you owe the man an explanation?'

'I don't owe him anything,' Sheehan said.

Jarrald said, 'It sounds like you have plenty to talk about but not in my hearing. You should team up. I'm tired and it has been a long day. In the meantime, I look forward to our game of golf. Do you play to a handicap?'

Jarrald sounded almost merry as he thanked Collard for coming. He offered his hand to shake, which Collard refused. Jarrald looked more amused than insulted.

'I forgot Brits don't.'

He followed them out and stood watching Collard's hire car refuse to start. Jarrald looked apologetic.

'Everyone has the night off, otherwise I'm sure we could have fixed it.'

Collard checked the glove compartment. The gun was gone.

Jarrald and Sheehan played along with the accidental nature of events. Jarrald suggested Sheehan offer to drive Collard back to the motel.

'Unless of course his car doesn't start either.' He looked on the point of giggling. 'Unfortunately I don't have any beds made up. Goodbye, Mr Collard.'

It was the first time Jarrald had called Collard by his real name. He stood and waved them away, watching until the car was gone before turning back into the house, permitting himself a little shuffle of triumph.

Damnation

As he started to unravel with the pressure, Angleton's fishing trips became anything but — events that were just another metaphor. By then he was only pretending to fish. He drove drunk around Maryland and got drunker in bars, listening to music and talking to strangers, pretending he was regular by saying he worked for the post office, which was what he told his son. Whether anyone believed that was another matter. Angleton talked politics, took straw polls on what people thought and was shocked that no one gave a fuck. He was close to losing his grip. When was this? Sixty-four or sixty-five.

Angleton's formula had proved insufficient — elegance and lucidity turned to alcoholism, cancer and madness. In his late paranoia, he wanted to relate his own deeply compromised methods to someone. He needed to unburden. What he had once believed was a fight against an evil enemy wasn't anything of the sort. It was another form of useless control.

By the end of the 1960s, Angleton saw himself as a damned man and others saw him as mad. He was going to end up in hell next to a man who ate babies, that was how damned he was.

In the Land of the Blind

'Mint?' Sheehan asked, as they drove away from Brennan Jarrald, sounding like their company was the most inevitable thing in the world.

Collard refused.

'You know, Jarrald's right. We should team up. I change my mind every day about whether they are alive. What did you think of Jarrald?'

'What I think doesn't matter.'

'He's very integrated. Don't be a sore loser.' Sheehan gave a big laugh and added, 'In your case the standard threat no longer applies, which is we take care of the family first.'

He laughed again. Collard knew he was being toyed with. The tight space of the car emphasized Sheehan's physical presence. Sheehan was the sort of man who regarded possession as his right and had no doubt forced his bull-like way into numerous orifices on the grounds of superiority, physical and mental. Collard sensed the man sniffing at him. For someone with so little to lose, he was still afraid.

Sheehan said, 'Be careful when you play golf with Jarrald. He's prone to fairway tantrums.'

Collard almost believed Sheehan, saying he would play.

Collard saw the lights of the motel ahead. He supposed he would wait up and make sure Sheehan didn't kill him in his sleep. Sheehan drove him to his door.

'Maybe I do owe you an explanation.'

Collard wondered if Sheehan would invite himself in. Once inside, their unspoken bargain would be struck: Sheehan would reveal what he knew and Collard would never walk out alive. The question was: was his life worth the price of knowledge? He was living on borrowed time anyway.

'One of these days, we'll sit down and chew the fat,' Sheehan said. 'Goodnight now.'

It was the loneliest goodnight Collard had ever heard.

★ ★ ★

He remained up with the television on. The phone in the room had stopped working. He left the door unlocked. He saw no point in trying to barricade the room. Sheehan would only pick the lock or kick the door down.

The door handle started to turn. He heard Sheehan's soft sigh at finding it open. Sheehan's silhouette filled the doorway. Canned laughter washed round the room. Sheehan grunted. His face was blue in the light of the screen.

Sheehan went into a martial-arts crouch, taunting Collard to come for him. He snaked out a playful arm a couple of times then grabbed so fast Collard didn't see the move. His hand was pinned back and Sheehan was close enough to smell his breath. Sheehan applied pressure to the wrist and forced Collard to his knees. He succumbed in ambiguity and shame. Sheehan's life could be measured by physical confrontation

430

and his could not. Sheehan's lack of preamble and the way he had come at him without explanation left Collard feeling cheated.

He saw Sheehan's punch too late. The arm he raised to defend himself was swiped aside.

He came to on the bed, unable to breathe. Sheehan's weight pressed down on him. Collard was dimly aware of TV laughter and Sheehan's low grunts of satisfaction. Pressure eased then tightened on his throat, cutting off his air, as Sheehan continued to play with him. Sheehan's face filled the room.

Collard had tried to anticipate Sheehan's moves and got them wrong, except for ending up on the bed because he had guessed there would be an animal quality to his violence.

His arms were pinned by Sheehan's knees. As the pressure eased again, he tried to buck him off. Sheehan laughed at his pathetic effort.

The distraction was enough. Collard shook his right arm free and reached between the mattress and the base. The fork was his only weapon. He swung his arm and stabbed hard at Sheehan's eye, to the accompaniment of tinny laughter and applause from the TV. He felt the jelly resist then the fork slipped under the eyeball, through the socket into Sheehan's head.

Sheehan gave a silent howl and clamped his hand to his damaged eye. He fell back off the bed and crashed to the floor, the eye spraying blood, fork protruding between bloody fingers. Collard registered the rage in the undamaged eye as Sheehan realized he wouldn't be walking out of the room hefting his balls with the

431

satisfaction of another job done. He kicked Sheehan hard in the head. The throat rattle sounded like someone having the plug pulled on him. Instead of witnessing the man's final moments, Collard walked out, leaving Sheehan to die alone.

The Natty Dreamer

Angleton saw himself once more the natty dreamer (1943-1947), that formal dandy wreathed in cigarette smoke, soft Midwestern inflections, schooled in the confinement of a British boarding school in the defensive art of irony, an honorary Brit, always a little in thrall to the offhand mannerisms of the upper classes and their tyranny of charm, that peculiar form of double offensive: a languid attack, particularly with regard to women, and often a prelude to rudeness. He had shared their smut and secrecy, the giggles and filthy jokes, and those initiations of which upper-class Yanks managed only pale imitations. He enjoyed British clubbability.

The closer Collard got to his goal, the less Angleton wanted to know, dreading the worst (being told something he didn't know). He was fearful of Collard's cold rage. In Angleton's estimation, rage was the significant emotion of an historical span that began in the 1970s. The most extreme form of that rage was found in terrorism: how to convey outrage at that terror while at the same time understanding it? It was why Angleton never slept: because of the terror he found lurking there, the night-sweats, his dreams, and what of Philby's and Greene's? Three men who didn't sleep easy.

The fact was, if you wanted to go into the subversion business, collect intelligence and

433

move arms, you dealt with drug-movers.

He was back in Rome. The new boy in town. His operation was small and under-funded. It was sound counter-intelligence to expose sloppy security and he made a splash. Bright boy. Like the detective who knows who the murderer is because he had arranged for the murder in the first place. He knew he was good at conveying the impression of deep thinking: plucking the answer out of thin air. There was nothing to work out when you were running the agent selling secrets to US intelligence, which was naive and leaky. Scattolini worked for a Vatican newspaper as a movie critic but lost his job when they found out he had once written dirty books. Scattolini, resentful, specialized in selling Vatican secrets, all made up. The Israelis picked up the same trick from Angleton after the war. He ran the CIA Israeli desk for years (and the Vatican), along with counter-intelligence, which annoyed a lot of people because a man whose job was internal security shouldn't be running ops too. But the Israelis made it clear they would work with no one else. One of the old Agency faces who drank a lot of Scotch and rated Angleton a snob accused him to his face of being Mossad's man. What no one knew was Angleton had been forced to repeat the Scattolini trick to get in with the Israelis or they were going to blow what they knew about the Ratline: conspiracy, treason, consorting with gangsters. Angleton had copied Scattolini's (and Garbo's) method of embroidering information taken from newspaper articles to cobble together a Middle East spy ring that he sold to his superiors as the real thing. An operating budget was approved before Angleton revealed he had made the whole thing up 'as a joke', resulting in the removal of a rival superior from nervous collapse and the consolidation of Angleton's position as the acknowledged expert on Middle East affairs.

Now the span of the Cold War was pretty much over. The lateral question was, did it represent the end of something or the start of a whole new perspective. That was his method, to look for clues from the past to explain the present as once he had pored endlessly over pre-war Soviet operations to discern later patterns. It was too much like hard work. One of his favourite records was 'Cut-across Shorty'.

In the end, Angleton came to the conclusion that Flight 103 came down to what could not be admitted. Her name was Afghanistan.

Syria, Iran and Iraq were casual dates. Afghanistan was what had to be kept off the table, the geopolitical equivalent to Al Haines's confession if it were revealed. Afghanistan was planned as payback time for Vietnam, a chance to tie up the Soviets in a costly and morale-sapping war. Casey's problem was covert sponsorship without accountability, no audits or bookkeeping, a bottomless pit into which money was thrown, with kickbacks and bribes all the way down, and skimming off the top. It was a short, logical step to exploit the region's most valuable crop — the poppy — to feed the pipeline. The Frankfurt Connection became expendable. More money than anyone would admit: huge, leaping subterranean rivers of the stuff — profits of between one and two hundred billion, give or take a billion, *after* everyone had taken their cut, and that was a lot of cut, from the Afghan Connection alone.

All this Barry had uncovered with evidence against those Jarrald and Sheehan were prepared to protect by blowing up a civil airliner.

Barry's betrayer, the last mystery.

Force of Impact

Collard rented a house overlooking the country-club course where Jarrald played golf. There was no sign of him, week in week out. There was no report of any untoward incident at the motel, which meant the number Hoover had given him for a house cleaner had done its job.

Collard overlooked the fairway of the second hole and kept a telescope trained on the course.

Then on a still morning, just after nine, he saw Jarrald with three other men playing off the second tee. They had a cart but no caddies. Jarrald ended off the fairway with his drive. For his second shot he dug his iron in short, sending the ball a few feet. Collard watched him look around to make sure no one had seen then take a free stroke.

For five holes Jarrald played to the fairway. On the par five eighth he mishit his drive. Jarrald's tendency to slice had decided which side of the fairway Collard waited and he was rewarded by the sound of the man's ball clattering into the trees not far from where he hid.

He had no silencer for the gun. He had wrapped the barrel in a couple of shirts and a jersey, meaning to get close enough not to miss and for the wadding to deaden the report.

Jarrald began searching in the wrong place. Collard was about to move when a quiet voice behind him said, 'Drop it.'

A gun pressed against his head. He did as he was told. Jarrald moved further down the hill searching for his lost ball.

'Call Jarrald. Tell him his ball's over here.'

Again Collard did as he was told.

Jarrald looked up angrily. Collard shouted again, pointing, berating himself for believing he ever could have succeeded. Jarrald's like always got away with it. Such men were never accountable.

Jarrald demanded to know who they were. He turned livid at the sight of Collard.

'What are you doing here? This is private ground. You are a dangerous animal. You also have no right to be here. Do what you have to do, Mr Quinn. I have a game of golf to continue.'

Collard thought: So the man behind me is Quinn, the most elusive of them all, and now I will die without ever seeing him.

'How is your father, the old priest?' Collard asked. 'Is that the dirty secret you didn't want to come out?'

He experienced the brief satisfaction of seeing Jarrald riled. Jarrald swung his club, clipping the side of Collard's head, dazing him and leaving him on the ground.

He waited for Quinn to shoot him. Instead Jarrald fell down beside him, his face contorted. Quinn straddled him and stuffed his mouth with one of the shirts Collard had used to wrap around his gun. A soft percussive tap was followed by a wet, shattering noise. Jarrald bellowed into the gag, eyes wide with shock.

Quinn ordered Collard to get up.

Quinn had shot away Jarrald's knee. The force of impact had sent fragments of splintered bone through the material of his checked golf pants. The knee was shredded, a soft mess of pulp soaked in blood. Jarrald's gagged screams turned to sobs as he inspected the damage. Quinn aimed at the other one. Jarrald scrabbled with his good foot in a futile effort to get away.

'That was for Barry,' Quinn said.

Jarrald was like a frightened little boy. Tears ran down his face. Snot bubbled from his nose. Collard felt almost sorry for him.

Quinn asked, 'You killed Barry, didn't you, because of what he knew?'

Jarrald nodded furiously, transparent in his hope that anything agreed to would save his life.

Quinn handed his pistol to Collard. 'He's yours.'

Collard thought about it, took the gun, pressed the muzzle against the head of the whimpering Jarrald, looked away at the trees and pulled the trigger, sensing rather than seeing the life leave the man.

The eyes were gone. The legs scrabbled at the bed of pine needles, still trying to escape.

Collard followed Quinn up the hill away from the course where Jarrald's companions were calling out. They reached the end of the tree line.

Quinn turned and said, 'You should have made sure Sheehan was dead.'

'Sheehan's alive? He can't be.'

'He is.'

Quinn's economy of movement spoke of precise and dangerous skills. The eyes indicated

439

profound indifference.

'Sheehan sent you?'

'That's why I am here.'

It didn't matter now, Collard thought. He had done his job. Jarrald was gone. He supposed it didn't make any difference to Quinn who he killed. It was a cruel piece of logic that the man who had inveigled Nick into the plot was now the one sent to finish him.

'Tell me one thing before I go. What did Barry know?'

'Enough to ruin the house of cards men like Jarrald build. They're the playmakers. If their puppets are exposed they feel threatened. What's an airliner in their scheme of things? Newspaper headlines for a month or two.'

Quinn was not a man of words and that probably constituted a major speech.

Collard realized Quinn wasn't going to shoot him after all.

'What will you tell Sheehan?'

'That you were gone. You'd got Jarrald and moved on. Make sure we don't meet again, because next time I do the job I'm paid for. A contract is a contract.'

The Catacombs

Collard spent Hoover's funds, cushioned and corrupted, a tourist of the world of black economy, a strange and restless traveller. The more he journeyed, the more he had the sense of being nowhere, a life stitched together by air miles, in futile search of a son he believed against all evidence was still alive. He hardened. He contemplated the murder of the sons of the President of the United States and the Prime Minister of Great Britain, so they as parents could experience his grief.

Both countries had colluded in looking away from the truth, building a case around lies and false evidence, involving that old pariah and whipping dog, Libya, so on a limb and unwanted she could be blamed for anything.

Any big event was about what preceded it and Angleton argued that always went further back than anyone allowed. Angleton had in fact been instructing Casey *before* Reagan's election. Casey went to Angleton because Reagan's people were worried Jimmy Carter would win re-election if he secured the release of the hostages held by the Ayatollah's people in the US Embassy in Tehran. Angleton showed Casey how to open up a back channel and do a deal that fucked Jimmy Carter. Reagan announced their release on his inauguration day. Hallelujah! If Angleton had been British he would

441

have been made a lord.

When it was Vice-President Bush's turn to run for President, eight years later, he demanded a repeat of Reagan's triumph and got turned down. The Syrians called the shots and blackmailed Bush into reversing US hard-line policy. Syria was broke. The Soviet economy was in a shambles. America had money to burn. Al Haines's confession and what Syria knew about Iran-Contra — far more than was allowed to come out — culminated in any connection to the bomb plot being forgotten and Bush's statement, which signalled the change of direction in the investigation, that Syria had taken a bum rap on terrorism. So would Libya, thought Angleton.

Collard came to understand Angleton's world was one turned inside out, held together by secret deals and illegal money. And behind that world still lurked the Vatican as it had in 1946. In Rome, Collard talked to an old connection of Angleton's, Cardinal Xavier Mallory, an Englishman who had fallen under Angleton's spell while in British intelligence during the war, before taking holy orders and becoming a Vatican expert in foreign affairs. Mallory, with his patrician looks, had the demeanour to which Churton could only aspire. He admitted hiring Hoover to watch Angleton in Wales because a whisper had reached him that Philby and Angleton were about to meet. Mallory professed a personal curiosity because he had never worked out which was the real double agent. Whatever happened in Wales, no one was saying.

Collard suspected Mallory had played a

deciding role in the events of 1986 because he was consulted by the two principal players, Angleton and Casey.

Collard asked if Mallory had passed on Angleton's confidences to Casey. Mallory said it was his belief that Casey had never found out about Barry. He held Collard's gaze with the eyes of a born dissembler.

'Did you know about Flight 103?'

'My soul will rot in hell for many reasons but not for that.'

They remained on vaguely cordial terms. Collard never trapped him into any admission but he managed to use him to effect an introduction to Graham Greene in the South of France.

Greene, another Roman Catholic, and Mallory were the last ones left.

*   *   *

Greene was very tall, with a limp handshake, an insolent gaze and a schoolboy laugh that occasionally lit up his sour face. They met in one of Greene's regular bars. Greene was on doctor's orders to take no more than one drink a day, which made him a poor companion. He appeared bored and evasive, trapped by his own sense of superiority. Collard read his books with difficulty. He preferred Patricia Highsmith, admired by Greene. The anxiety in Highsmith's writing, caught in the everyday fears, corresponded to Collard's.

'She's a lesbian, of course,' Greene said,

offering only small talk.

At Collard's account of Wales, he shrugged and said, 'It sounds like the kind of thing I might have written about.'

Greene remained supremely unconcerned, revealing not even a flicker of surprise. Collard found him like the riddle in one of the Borges short stories Angleton read; enigma replaced answer. Faced at last by one of the men he had been shadowing for so long, Collard got nothing. Greene seemed mildly inconvenienced by his presence and showed more interest in his drink and the pretty young waitress. His attitude and body language told Collard whatever secrets he held weren't going to be shared. Greene's lofty indifference reminded him of Churton. They shared the same languid assumption that someone like Collard, lower down the pecking order, wasn't there to be confided to.

He ran into Greene again, shopping alone in the fish market by the harbour. In a short-sleeved blue shirt and tan trousers and wearing large sunglasses, he looked very English. He professed at first not to remember Collard and thought he was a fan. Greene seemed at home among the dead fish.

'I'll tell you about Wales,' he said, inspecting a large octopus. 'If it'll make you go away.'

The stalls smelled of ammonia. The angler fish and the big squid pulled from the deep looked otherworldly. Collard wondered why Greene had changed his mind and decided it was because Greene enjoyed showing off his superiority.

Valerie Traherne had noted his trivial, contrary behaviour, complaining about ice in his drink one night and its lack the next.

Greene asked with false modesty if Collard remembered *The Third Man*. The film had been due to be set in Rome because the producer Alexander Korda had lire there from before the war. Greene had been considering the catacombs as a location and sketched an idea based around the black market.

'Kim's pet, Angleton, was in Rome. I had heard he was consorting with all kinds of strange people, from local Mafia to Lucky Luciano. My plan was he would introduce me to his connections. Angleton had always been willing and obsequious in the past, but Rome had turned him paranoid, and rather above his station. He was convinced Philby had sent me to spy on him.'

Certain things had happened in Rome, for which Greene blamed Angleton, though he had him to thank for a diversion to Vienna, with which the film became inseparable.

'As for Kim, I stayed in touch after he did his flit in sixty-three and we met up from time to time in Budapest or Bucharest or one of the Soviet resorts. The Catholic Church was softening its line on communism and sometimes Kim and I were allowed to get together to chat about it.'

'Were you acting for the Vatican?'

'Nothing so grand,' said Greene airily.

'What was Wales about?'

Greene sniggered. 'Angleton's comeuppance.'

445

Philby had never forgiven Angleton for going after him in 1963 before his defection. In 1985, he made contact with Angleton, suggested a reunion using Greene as go-between. Angleton was led to believe it was about Philby wanting to come home and repent and Angleton was his choice for debriefing.

Angleton had gone to Wales thinking he was about to pull off his greatest coup, only to find the whole thing was a practical joke at his expense and Greene's revenge for a minor episode in Rome that Angleton had quite forgotten. He had once fixed Greene up with a woman, knowing she would give him a dose of the clap.

Greene said the last laugh was on Angleton because the episode had given him his penicillin plot for *The Third Man*. 'Harry Lime was based on Kim, of course.'

Angleton was the model for the naive American writer of cowboy stories, played by Joseph Cotten, in a swipe at Angleton's intellectual pretensions.

'He didn't read half as much as he pretended. He was a terrible cheat and those dime-store cowboy stories were a proper indication of his real level. Without his father's contacts he would have been nothing.'

Greene turned away without saying goodbye and soon was another head in the crowd, taller than the rest.

★ ★ ★

Greene was being disingenuous. Philby had played his trump in Wales, Angleton's final humiliation. Quinn's confession. It was Philby who had arranged Quinn's kidnap, flown to Beirut and struck a deal with Quinn in exchange for release. Twelve hours of tape followed. Stenographers worked around the clock transcribing them in time for Philby to return to Russia and take his cargo boat to Tilbury, with a bound copy of Quinn's confession, naming Angleton's involvement in deniable operations, his black Valentine to Angleton who shook with humiliation when presented with it. Greene smirked. Philby was more gracious. 'Just between the three of us, Jimbo.' A demonstration of his final superiority. A time bomb.

Angleton thought about the hollow wunderkind he had been, with his affected cough, way out of his depth, kept afloat by Daddy's fascist contacts, whose castles and palaces had hidden the procession of migrating German assets. He thought of the plans others had for him (Allen Dulles, the Holy See of Rome, the Jews, the Jewish gangster Meyer Lansky, and Luciano in Rome, taking meetings, with scarcely an arch of the eyebrow, to discuss the threat of communism to free enterprise). Angleton was an existential cipher with an ulcer, the complexity of his nervous system matched by the enormous mental labyrinth created over the years. Angleton, cackling master of the hip-pocket operation, had found himself so deep in the pockets of others there was no way out. He had a family he didn't want to go home to, a son whose existence he denied. He had been cast in the shadow of his father. He was desperate to get out, wanted a civilian life. Yet when the time came, and his father told him of the fortunes to be made in the post-war rebuilding, he said no. The truth was too many people wanted him in. The Jewish gangster Lansky said to him: 'You can make it work for you too.' So many connections. Lansky did big laundry in the new state of Israel whose founding he had helped underwrite.

He remembered Lansky in later years, wry, on a pool lounger with a little yapper of a dog, the only thing to spoil the party. Angleton, hot in a suit, played the stuffed shirt for the benefit of the bathing beauties, bikinied goddesses. Angleton watched the drift of an inflatable mat across the surface of the water wiggling hypnotically, inviting him to throw off his clothes and jump in. It hadn't turned out so bad after all, the American dream.

'This is heaven,' said one of the bikinied goddesses.

Some mornings Angleton looked in the mirror, after scraping away the surface residue that had accumulated on his tongue, a thick fur from excesses of alcohol and nicotine (spiny fingers elegantly opening yet another packet of Virginia Slims, as delicately as though it were a lover he was unclothing), and imitated Lansky: 'Jimmy, we've got you fucked all the way up your back channel.'

★ ★ ★

In Sheehan's final destination, Angleton read his own legacy, a central African rat-hole, a collapsed state, caught up in meaningless civil war and undermined by epidemic, where the long game was played out, with rebel and government forces armed by Nazir's people. Angleton thought he saw Nazir once in the lobby of a firstclass hotel; technically as impossible as Collard's sighting of Angleton in Frankfurt.

Sheehan, wearing his eyepatch, drifting though a city Angleton had never heard of, in a country which failed to register as a cause for humanitarian concern, on a journey into the surreal darkness of the stinking jungle of the old colonial continent, beyond television crews and the reports of correspondents, into a realm of fiction and bad imagination. The inside-out world in its extreme.

In a gutted town, full of destroyed prefab concrete, Angleton saw the future: the one hotel still open, lit by 40-watt bulbs, and in dingy corridors the swamp smell of toilets and sex offered by preteenage girls for next to nothing while downstairs the band played on, a strange phonetic rendering of 1960s' British pop 'He's Not Heavy (He's My Brother)', in a country where the official language remained French. The promise, the futile hope, was that the Americans were coming. Nothing made sense except the mortar fire that occasionally fell on the town. No one knew why or what they were fighting. Sheehan moved up country, ahead, as always. His body had turned into a temple to disease, scabbed, bloated and oozing running sores. The molecular conflict battling for its possession had been as savage as the war going on around him.

Next would come famine, said the local doctor who showed Angleton Sheehan's corpse, freshly dead, naked on a dirty mattress in a concrete room with a single high window. His heart had been cut out, with his liver, penis and testicles, taken as delicacies by those who had killed him. The doctor said Sheehan had been a willing donor.

Extras

Collard found them in the seaside town of Essouira in Morocco where hundreds had gathered to play extras in a multimillion-dollar American film. Collard got hired for a big battle scene. Most of the day was spent sitting around in the heat, waiting for the shots to be prepared. Collard was given a uniform. The extras covered a couple of acres. It looked more like a music festival than a film set. They did their take twice and had to do it again because wristwatches were spotted. The scene seemed chaotic to Collard, with none of the extras much interested or motivated. An assistant director addressed the crowd through a megaphone in English and French, asking for more energy. The next time, as he faced the charging crowd, Collard believed he had been transported back to the actual battle. Skirmishes became real. Two hooded figures threw themselves on him. He brushed them aside, moving deeper into the battle, with his fake rifle and bayonet, his blood up. He made to stab a figure crouched over a fallen soldier but his shadow gave him away. The figure turned to find him poised, bayonet ready. They made eye contact. They were both the same, but changed. It was like looking at Nick but Nick as someone else. About himself, he couldn't say. They were just a couple of extras, as they had been when it had all started in Frankfurt.

Nick moved quickly, feinting and running off in the other direction. Collard let him go.

* * *

That night he saw them sitting at an outside table in a crowded café. Nick's hair was very short, making him almost unrecognizable. Collard asked if he could sit at their table because there was nowhere else. Nick made no show of recognizing Collard, who was in his own state of shock, less from seeing Nick with the girl in the Polaroid than from the infant in her arms.

Collard sat down as a stranger. He asked Nick his name. Finn, said Nick. They talked about the filming.

Nick was gone for ever.

The girl asked Collard if he had children.

'I have a boy named Nick. He's a good son. I love him very, very much.'

He asked the name of the child. It was the same as his.

Collard paid for the two beers and a bottle of water, leaving the money and the bill on the table, with Nick's Polaroid of the girl slipped underneath.

'Maybe we'll meet again.'

'We're here for a while,' the young man answered. They were two strangers exchanging pleasantries. 'We could eat together one night.'

'I would like that,' Collard said.

Nick smiled and looked him in the eye and in

that look Collard recognized the dream he was in and his 46.5 seconds were about to begin — he had been the one, not Nick, on that flight all along.

The Nervous Passenger

December 21 1988

Angleton was back in the Frankfurt terminal, on the day, and forewarned but lost in a fog of his own making. He recognized Barry only in terms of trying to remember where he had seen him before. A spy to the last, Angleton censored his betrayal. Nobody had learned his secret.

Angleton could see the boy was the future, with his girl waiting at Heathrow. Whenever he pursued the line of their story he saw flailing limbs as they were ejected side by side into the night, the tiny embryo in her womb condemned with them.

He was not a sentimental man but he decided he would take their place on the doomed flight, the last gallant gesture of an incurable romantic, which would also perform the task of getting him out: a piggyback into oblivion. He feared the end: one of the finest minds of its generation snuffed out (but so wrong so often). The Cold War stood as an empty joke. The future would be terrifyingly different, determined by the disenfranchised mass, poverty and repression the breeding ground for terror motivated by a hatred its victims would fail to comprehend. All the useless baubles of the marketplace, the great slide of consumerism, predicated on the understanding that everything

454

was replaceable and you could never want or get too much, as Evelyn had worked out. It made sense only as a gigantic devouring conspiracy.

★   ★   ★

Angleton tried to reach the boy, to tell him to flee for valid reasons; he wanted to warn of the girl's father. Angleton was jealous of their youthful physical passion, something always missing in his life, with its higher, misplaced calling. As for the unrequited Valerie Traherne, her affair with Hoover had affected him as badly as Evelyn had been by Collard's brief encounter with Stack. Had he ever been young?

The boy's worship of the girl and their future made everything else superfluous. Angleton would explain the terms of their contract: if it were broken everything would be undone. The boy would find he was back on the plane, his future nothing.

Whatever Angleton said to him, he fucked up and the boy looked at him like he was crazy and (worse) a bore. He had failed, as always.

In transit at Heathrow, Angleton saw the boy again, in urgent discussion with his father, saying something had come up and he needed to delay his onward flight.

The father sounded concerned and understanding. He offered to stay too if needed but the boy said he could take care of matters. He would bring the girl with him to New York, if that was all right. The father said yes, and they agreed he would fly on in order not to disappoint Charlotte.

A detail of coincidence: Angleton recognized the father's tie; the same as one of his.

★ ★ ★

Angleton sat in departures next to a very drunk American Indian who was way too gone to fly. He saw Sheehan make a couple of passes through the lounge, frantic, searching in vain. He listened to the Indian snore and contemplated the boarding card clasped in the man's hand. He felt so tired. Angleton's hair was long now, like an Apache, tucked up inside his homburg. The presence of the slumbering Indian encouraged him to let it down. He rocked rhythmically as he recited the Apache death chant under his breath before removing the Indian's boarding card and joining the passengers as they crowded in an impatient shuffle through the umbilical tube that connected the terminal to the fuselage. Welcome aboard, said the stewardess.

'You bet,' Angleton said, frisky for the first time in years.

He turned right where he once would have gone left into business and first class, glimpsing Barry who had got an upgrade.

It took a long time to get to the back of the cabin, past the settling passengers who blocked the aisle. The pressurized air reminded him of old soda siphons, with torpedo-like tubes to inject fizz.

There was a muddle over his seat. The boy's

father was sitting in it. They examined boarding cards. Through an administrative oversight they seemed to have been issued with the same seat. They shared a joke about airline inefficiency and introduced themselves.

There was plenty of room and Angleton sat down next to Collard, leaving a space between them out of politeness. He said he recognized Collard's tie. On such small coincidences life turned.

'*Sapiens qui prospicit.*'

Collard looked surprised to be reminded. They talked about their days at school. Angleton thought: Perhaps it would not be such a bad flight after all.

The captain sounded reassuring on the intercom, in the way airline captains always did. Angleton had never met anyone off an airplane with the same tone, combining boredom, reassurance and an absolute faith in the ability to defy the laws of gravity. The captain announced a delay while they awaited clearance for take-off.

The cabin staff went through their safety exercises (for the very last time), 'in the unlikely event of an emergency'. *In the unlikely event of a fucking emergency!* He wanted to stand and shout, make a public exhibition, demand to be let off; always a second from panic, always a nervous passenger. So much he had flown from.

Most passengers ignored the cabin crew's rigmarole. There was no sense of forewarning in anyone's voice or action. Angleton was reassured by the banality of it all and decided his fears were groundless. So much humanity going about its humdrum business would prevail: the folded coat on the empty seat would be there in seven hours' time, undisturbed. His eyes misted at the thought of all the mistakes he had made, a fine catalogue of errors. Lee Harvey Oswald. That was one secret he would take with him.

Angleton asked if Collard was a nervous flier.

'Not particularly.'

'You're a lucky man', Angleton said. 'Was that your son I saw you with earlier?'

They talked of Nick, who had been unable to join Collard at the last minute.

'He's having some trouble with a girl. Not trouble, exactly. He seems very devoted to her. They have to sort some things out then they'll fly out and join us tomorrow.'

Angleton sighed and thought it would be nice to be young enough again to have girl trouble.

At last the big jet swung on to the runway.

Here we go now, Angleton thought, listening to the captain's voice smooth away the last of their delay, preparing for take-off.

★ ★ ★

KISS, Angleton thought: keep it simple, stupid. Well, quite simple. Sheehan fed a bomb into the Frankfurt system for Barry to discover. Barry defused it and added it to his evidence, contained in the several bags he personally loaded onto the plane, believing his mission accomplished.

But Sheehan wasn't done.

Glorious, inefficient Heathrow, where baggage

handlers wandered off for official forty-five-minute tea breaks, leaving containers on the tarmac prior to loading, where conditions were so chaotic and insecure that for a man like Sheehan, dressed in a Day-Glo coat, it was a piece of cake to walk the case across the tarmac and load it on the abandoned container, positioning it where it would achieve maximum damage. Maybe he thought twice, given his daughter. Exquisite dilemma: family or country. Fuck family; Angleton would have. Not even a complicated device, like they would try to claim in the evidence, just a regular 'ice-cube timer', favoured by terrorists from the Middle East, a device not that reliable but usually up to the job, primed on the ground and activated seven or eight minutes after take-off by the drop in air-pressure and set to detonate half an hour after that. Two bombs on board below them, then; one inactive, one not.

A basic lesson of counter-intelligence was that any given event was open to every possible interpretation. Few thought to consider the obvious.

Angleton remembered his last great personal and spiritual crisis, prompted by the man sitting down the front of the plane, upgraded to first class. He had encouraged Barry with the best of intentions but with the diagnosis of his final illness he realized what untold damage Barry could do to the country and institutions Angleton held most dear. He was dying and Casey was dying too. He confessed his plot to Casey and returned to the fold. He was Barry's betrayer. After that Sheehan ran Barry and knew his moves. *Mea culpa.*

They hurtled down the runway and then they were up in the air. Angleton watched the last of the dark ground rush away. It had all gone so fast.

Officially he had been dead nearly seventeen months. He would sit and watch it all fall apart and Cocteau's outriders would bring his coffin with them (that single coffin!) and he would dine that night with Marie Cesares, star of *Orphée*.

The plane climbed steeply into the night skies.

Collard listened to the old man humming. One for the money. Two for the show.

Half an hour later he looked at his watch. It was coming up to seven o'clock on the evening of December 21, 1988.

'What's the movie?' Angleton asked a passing stewardess.

Collard settled back and dreamed vividly of a strange encounter with Nick in which they seemed not quite to recognize each other. There was a baby and the young mother he knew only from a Polaroid. Collard surfaced from the dream, aware he had barely dozed, struck by the clarity of it.

He opened his eyes and thought: Without hope there is nothing.

Acknowledgements

Of the many books consulted and trawled through, the following, along with Google, were referred to most. *Cold Warrior* (Simon & Schuster, 1991) Tom Mangold's biography of Angleton contains many details used in this book, including a copy of the photograph of Angleton as a prefect at Malvern College. Ron Rosenbaum's *Travels with Dr Death* (Penguin, 1991) contains essays on Angleton and on Mary Meyer, briefly mentioned. Books consulted on Philby include Anthony Cave Brown's *Treason in the Blood* (Robert Hale, 1994), on Philby father and son; *Philby: The Spy Who Betrayed a Generation* (Andre Deutsch, 1968) by Bruce Page, David Leitch and Phillip Knightley; and *Philby: The Long Road to Moscow* (Hamish Hamilton, 1973) by Patrick Seale and Maureen McConville, which most resembles Evelyn's fictional effort. *Bob Woodward's Veil: The Secret Wars of the CIA 1981–1987* (Simon & Schuster, 1987) is self-explanatory. Useful background works include Alan Friedman's *Spider's Web: Bush, Saddam, Thatcher and the Decade of Deceit* (faber and faber, 1993) and *Gideon's Spies* (Pan, 1999) by Gordon Thomas. The most extreme interpretation of events covered by this book is offered by *Trail of the Octopus: From Beirut to Lockerbie — Inside the DIA* (Bloomsbury, 1993) by Donald Goddard with Lester K. Coleman. Other works on the subject include *On the Trail of Terror* (Jonathan Cape, 1991) by David Leppard; Paul Foot's special report, *Lockerbie: The Flight from Justice (Private Eye*, 2001); and Ashton and Ian Ferguson's *Cover-up of Convenience* (Mainstream, 2001). This book owes a debt to all the above but could not have been written without the following three works. John Loftus and Mark Aarons' *The Secret War Against the Jews* (St Martin's Griffin, 1997), remains indispensable; it was Loftus who suggested to me that Angleton's father was probably the key to the man. *In the Public Interest* (Little, Brown and Co, 1995) by Gerald James is a sobering and frightening account of a man who went into covert arms dealing, at the bidding of the Conservative government, and was sacrificed in the cover-up. The most lucid contemporary account of how money really works is Loretta Napoleoni's *Modern Jihad: Tracing the Dollars Behind the Terror Networks* (Pluto, 2003).

★ ★ ★

Thanks are owed to Gerald James, John Loftus, Loretta Napoleoni, David Pirie, Emma Matthews, Richard Williams, Vikram Jayanti, Jennifer Potter, my agent Gillon Aitken, and particularly to my editor Ben Ball for his persistence beyond the call of duty, and his insistence on clarity.

We do hope that you have enjoyed reading this large print book.

Did you know that all of our titles are available for purchase?

We publish a wide range of high quality large print books including:
Romances, Mysteries, Classics
General Fiction
Non Fiction and Westerns

Special interest titles available in large print are:
The Little Oxford Dictionary
Music Book
Song Book
Hymn Book
Service Book

Also available from us courtesy of Oxford University Press:
Young Readers' Dictionary
(large print edition)
Young Readers' Thesaurus
(large print edition)

For further information or a free brochure, please contact us at:
Ulverscroft Large Print Books Ltd.,
The Green, Bradgate Road, Anstey,
Leicester, LE7 7FU, England.
Tel: (00 44) 0116 236 4325
Fax: (00 44) 0116 234 0205

Other titles published by
The House of Ulverscroft:

THE OPERATIVE

Duncan Falconer

In war-torn Iraq, SBS operative John Stratton's closest friend is killed, leaving behind a grieving wife and child — Stratton's godson. When the widow moves to Los Angeles she is murdered and her child is placed in state custody. Stratton, rocked to the core by the killing, uncovers an FBI plot to hide the crime and sets off on a private operation of revenge against one of the most powerful Eastern European crime syndicates in America. Hunted by the CIA, the FBI, and Albanian mobsters, using only his wits and his skill with explosives, Stratton pursues his private war — a fight he suspects could be his last . . .